THE TAKEN

INGER ASH WOLFE

OTHER HAZEL MICALLEF MYSTERIES
BY INGER ASH WOLFE

The Calling

THE TAKEN

 McClelland & Stewart

LIBRARY AND ARCHIVES CANADA CATALOGUING IN PUBLICATION

Wolfe, Inger Ash
The taken / Inger Ash Wolfe.

(A Hazel Micallef mystery)
ISBN 978-0-7710-8898-8

I. Title. II. Series.
PS8645.O442T34 2009   C813'.6   C2009-901638-9

We acknowledge the financial support of the Government of Canada through the Book Publishing Industry Development Program and that of the Government of Ontario through the Ontario Media Development Corporation's Ontario Book Initiative. We further acknowledge the support of the Canada Council for the Arts and the Ontario Arts Council for our publishing program.

Typeset in Van Dijck by M&S, Toronto
Printed and bound in Canada

ANCIENT FOREST
FRIENDLY

McClelland & Stewart Ltd.
75 Sherbourne Street
Toronto, Ontario
M5A 2P9
www.mcclelland.com

1 2 3 4 5   13 12 11 10 09

To the Eclipse Café,
with thanks for the corner

Love never dies a natural death.

— Anaïs Nin

Prologue

What always broke his heart was the way they dressed themselves. Divorcées in wedding gowns slumped behind the wheel
in their garages; stockbrokers in Armani hanging from basement joists; the jilted plunging from rooftops drenched in
cologne or perfume, as if to say their wrecked bodies still had
more to offer in death than anyone had ever known in life.

This one wore a pair of black jeans over Blundstone boots, a
faded green T-shirt, and a black wool sweater. A thin leather
cord served as a necklace from which a silver lamb hung, her
only piece of jewellery apart from a gold hoop edged with a
curlicue design, like a Sufi sun, dangling from one ear. He pictured someone giving her that lamb and wondered what had
been meant by it. That she was innocent? That she needed protection? Obviously, it hadn't been enough.

They'd pulled her up onto the grass, and the discoloured
lakewater drained from inside her pantlegs, a thin, greyish

trickle that ran down between the green stalks. He couldn't help thinking that the roots of the grass would gratefully take in this water, insensate to its origin, because it had been a dry summer and grass was oblivious to what came from it or what returned to it.

The photographer was taking pictures. The girl would never know. Her story was only just beginning to be told. You lived your life, making choices that you thought would become the plot of your life as you wanted to live it, but the fact was, someone else always wrote the end. It was no mystery people hated movies where the protagonist died: who needs that kind of realism?

He didn't want to imagine what she'd been through, but he was like a receptor that has no choice what signal enters it. He imagined the cold, pressing lake, the way water holds you, its molecules tight against your body. She'd probably heard it was a peaceful way to go: it wasn't. Even if you want to die, your body resists. You know breathing is the only way to make it work, but you don't want to, you can't. And then you begin to change your mind, you want to live because you've never felt pain like this, but it's too late, the screaming in the blood has started, the brain starving for oxygen, and you fight, using up all your reserves, the urgent craving for air gets worse. You're just an animal now, one in the wrong element, you flail for the surface, the sun fractured into diamonds above you, but finally you breathe and for the thirty seconds, before the water adulterates your blood and makes your heart a double ruin, the agony is unnameable, your mind is a fiery mass, you really *die*, you feel every moment of it. He kneeled down beside her. All that terror was over now, but she still wore the surprised expression he'd seen too many times on floaters. She was no older than thirty.

For the rest of his life, she would be dead. She would miss all the changes that would have come to make her think twice about what she'd done. He, himself, would go through depression and contentment, joy and agony. He would fail, he would thrive, and still this girl, like all the others who couldn't give life one more day, would be gone. What he tried to do for them in death always felt like an empty triumph, but at least he would try to do it. *Tell me everything,* he said to her in his mind. *Tell me the truth and I'll let it be known.*

Thursday, May 19

Glynnis Pedersen's house was full of clocks. There were silver mantel clocks with lunar white faces, wall clocks made from antique car parts, clocks created from the refuse of old metal advertisements, a couple of small digital clocks, one grandfather clock in the front hall that no longer worked, and, beside the bed in the basement apartment, an LED motion clock that displayed a message in mid-air between two prongs. This one Glynnis had programmed to read "Rise and Shine!!" which message it displayed no matter one's state of wakefulness. For Detective Inspector Hazel Micallef, once a Mrs. Pedersen herself, it only served as a reminder of whom, exactly, Glynnis Pedersen was rising and shining with.

To have to take charity from a hated person was bad enough, but to do it out of necessity entailed a diminishment of one's sense of self that Hazel found hard to accept. She knew loss of pride was an occupational hazard for those who were proud, but did it have to mean being vanquished as well? Sometimes it seemed to Hazel that the situation she found herself in was one concocted for her by the Greek gods. To punish what, she couldn't be sure. But she had a feeling she was going to find out.

She was now a tenant in her ex-husband's house. The roots of this strange situation were in an evening she'd spent the previous fall with him at The Laughing Crow. It was there, over drinks, that she'd hinted she might need some extra-marital nursing if her damaged back finally gave in. She'd asked him to imagine her eighty-seven-year-old mother carrying her to the bathroom. He'd fairly blanched at what she was asking him, and Glynnis, hearing of it, laughed at it as if it were a hare-brained scam cooked up by one of her drug-addled clients. But then December had happened. A serial killer had drifted through their town like a deadly gas. A murder under her own roof. And a night in the bone-chilling cold and dark that left her back shattered and her mother nearly dead. Remembering, the events lined up in her mind with a kind of dreadful inevitability, but that didn't make them any more believable. She'd had emergency surgery, but by the end of March it became clear that, in the words of her specialist, her back had "failed." *Your first surgery is your best chance, your second is your last*, was something Dr. Pass had been fond of saying, but he'd stopped saying it in March. By that point, last chances were all Hazel had.

She and her mother had lived together not unpleasantly in the house in Pember Lake for over three years, since her divorce from Andrew. But the pain was keeping her from work, and more than once after the new year her mother had supported her on frail shoulders and taken Hazel to the bathroom: the hyperbolic scenario she'd described to Andrew boiled down to something real. Emily had finally gone to Andrew and Glynnis and laid it out. She characterized the discussion as "brief."

"I used legal language so they'd understand it," she explained to Hazel. "I said the statute of limitations on marital duties was five years and that it covered all pre-existing conditions."

"How did Glynnis like that?"

"She was smiling so tightly I thought her lipstick would squirt off her little lips." Emily smiled herself, that wicked smile that said she'd been in charge her whole life. "That woman has a mouth like a cat's anus," she said. "Andrew understood though."

"And?"

"They've given their tenants a month's notice. Family, they said."

"Well that's nice," said Hazel. "At least we're still family."

She lay in bed, staring at the small, high window in the wall opposite. The suggestion of late May sunlight was faint, but her mother had assured her it was there. She popped the lid of the little orange vial she was gripping in her fist and put the edge of it against her bottom lip. The thick, white pill tumbled onto her tongue. Sometimes she chewed it, this salty, bitter capsule. It worked faster this way, and the truth was, it had a little kick on it if it went down pulverized. It was now ten days after her second operation. She was taking three of them a day and there were two more refills on the label of the little orange vial. Sometimes the pain came back before it was time for the next pill and she'd take it early, send it like a fireman down a pole, the alarms shrieking everywhere. The one she'd just taken was already working: its promised six to eight hours of relief had begun with the May light outside the tiny window suddenly thickening. Glynnis might have had her clocks, but she had her pills, and they told the time with utter accuracy.

In her current state, she had more in common now with her younger daughter, Martha, that beloved and feckless child who kept Hazel more or less in a state of constant worry. Jobless, loveless, dogged by depression and incapable of making a constructive choice, Hazel sometimes wondered if Martha's problems were selfmade, or if they were genetics. Looking at either side of the family (Andrew? Emily?) it was hard to credit heredity, but shipwrecked and miserable as Hazel was, she had to wonder if there wasn't some kind of tendency in the blood to fall apart. Maybe only on the Micallef side. She hadn't seen Martha in a couple of months, and she'd been careful to keep upbeat on the phone with her: no point in getting the girl more worked up than she normally was. Hazel knew that Martha teetered on a thin line when it came to her mother: on one side was resentment for everything Hazel did and had to do for her, on the other was a savage terror of loss. It meant shielding her, softening reality for her. And with her elder daughter, Emilia, living out west, it meant that Hazel felt even more alone than she needed to. But such were the facts of her motherhood.

Her own mother came down the stairs bearing a tray. Andrew's beef stew, one of three things he cooked, all in the key of cow. Emily put the tray down beside the bed and arranged the pillows behind her daughter's back so she could sit up straight enough to eat. It was this routine three times a day: the prisoner brought her meals. "Glynnis too tired to cook?"

"She's got a late night," her mother said.

"He should keep tabs on her." She accepted the bowl of steaming stew and the end of a crusty loaf. "She's got a wandering eye."

"That's wishful thinking."

Hazel tucked into the meal. Everyone had a beef-stew "secret"; Andrew's was Guinness. The only real secret was time. Given a pound of stringy, nigh-inedible beef, a few cups of water, two mealy potatoes, and maybe an onion, anyone with six hours could make a perfectly edible stew. She leaned forward to put the fork in her mouth and her scarred lower back resisted her. The pain was different than it had been before either surgery: it wasn't sharp, like there was broken glass rattling around in her; it was deep and resonant. Seated in her marrow. She had to breathe through it. "You eat?" she asked her mother.

"I kept Andrew company."

"Are you working both ends against the middle?"

"What's the other end, Hazel?"

"Glynnis."

"I gather that makes you the middle."

"I'm always the middle, Mother."

"May 26 you get to be the middle, Hazel. Birthdays and anniversaries only. All the other days you're on the outside looking in, like the rest of us."

"You had to remind me, huh?"

"Sixty-two," said Emily. "My little girl is finally going to be a woman."

Emily continued to leaf through the growing pile of magazines beside the bed. Celebrity rags, local newspapers, travel magazines with colourful full-page pictures that teased Hazel with hints of a future out of bed. She ate in silence as her mother idly flipped the pages of one of the celebrity magazines. She held up a picture of a woman no older than twenty, one of the new crop of pop stars whose names neither of them could ever remember. She was parading down a street in Hollywood in a dress big enough to cover a volleyball, almost, with a grease-soaked paper bag in one hand and her purse slung over her shoulder. A tiny dog with a pointy face poked out of the top of the purse. "In a just society," said Emily, "almost everything this child is doing would be illegal. She should be arrested, stuck in a housecoat, and made to listen to Guy Lombardo records until she smartens up." She held the page up to her daughter. At that age, the worst either of Hazel's daughters had ever done was wear torn jeans, listen to Madonna, and occasionally puke hard lemonade all over the bathroom. How did girls like this one get so lost? Did people get lost quickly, or did it happen over time?

Emily collected the tray off the bed. "You want dessert?"

"No."

She held up a newspaper. Thursday's *Westmuir Record*. "You read this yet?"

"It's probably the same as last Thursday's. Not to mention Monday's. But leave it."

"You're falling behind on your papers. You don't want your news getting stale, do you?" Hazel laughed at the thought of events passing so quickly in Westmuir that you'd have to make an effort to keep up. "At least it'll pass the time without your having to resort to staring at pictures of nearly naked girls eating hamburgers." Apart from the biweekly visits from

Detective Constable James Wingate, the *Record* was her only window on the world she lived in. The paper that had been a thorn in her side for all of the previous fall was now necessary to her sanity. She held her hand out for it.

"What are you going to do now?" Hazel asked.

"I told Andrew I'd do the crossword with him."

"I should have seen Andrew's facility with those things as a sign."

"Of what?"

"That he knew how to disguise himself."

Emily Micallef patted her daughter's hand. "If he didn't, he'd be the only man on earth who lacked the talent." She put Hazel's fork and napkin in the bowl and moved the bowl into the middle of the tray. When she got to the door that led to the upstairs hall, Hazel called to her.

"Mum?"

"What is it?"

"Ask him to come see me. Please?"

"Read the paper," Emily said. "They've already started the summer short story. *The Record*'s gift to us all for putting on our best May-long-weekend faces."

Hazel glanced at the headline – "Welcome Cottagers!" – and immediately put the paper down.

2

Friday, May 20

Detective Constable James Wingate did not like being in charge of anything. His whole life, he'd been a brilliant follower of instructions: he'd been born to carry out the orders of others. He'd sometimes wondered if this made him some kind of perfect soldier, if, in another time and place, he'd have been the tool of a lesser regime. He knew he had it in him to cross the line; he'd been inspired at times by anger. But a righteous anger, he told himself, usually carried out a just vengeance.

Following orders had landed him in temporary charge of the Port Dundas OPS detachment, much to the mostly silent discomfort of many men and women his senior. He'd been the new guy when he arrived from Toronto only six months earlier and his nature had permitted him to navigate the many twists of fitting in to a new place. But with her deputy, Ray Greene, gone, he was the one OPS Central had turned to to hold the fort while DI Micallef got back on her feet.

He played messenger as best he could, but he knew even his biweekly visits to the house on Chamber Street did not disguise the fact that he was actually in charge. He came back bearing her instructions, but the other officers knew he had her blessing in most things to do as he saw fit. He wrote out the weekly schedule, heard out differences of opinion, assigned the beats, and approved time off. The only thing he didn't do was sit in Hazel's office. His co-workers accepted his strange ascent only because failing to do so would add to their CO's suffering. But Wingate could feel their resentment simmering.

Luckily, the late winter and early spring had been quiet in Port Dundas. Life had returned to the normal Hazel had described to him when he first arrived. The weekly B & E, the biweekly domestic, the monthly car theft. It was so regular here that the older cops joked they should have sign-up sheets for perps to fill in *before* they committed the quota of small-time offences they dealt with in the county. Once in a while something would crop up that would knock them out of their rituals, and the meeting room would fill for an hour while they discussed what to do. They'd get Hazel on conference call and try not to picture her bedbound as she listened and responded to the case. In early April, there'd been a rape in Silltoe, halfway to Humber Cottage on the 121. A sixteen-year-old girl had been thrown from a car, naked and unconscious. She'd had no memory of what had happened to her. They listened to Hazel's silence from both sides of the table, her breathing audible in the little black console. "Jesus," she finally said. "Are we sure she's not protecting someone?"

"Who would she want to protect?" PC Ashton had said.

"The assholes who presumed she'd be found dead by the side of the road?"

"Do you have daughters, Adrian?"

"No."

"Girls this age think whatever happens to them is their fault. In my day, it was unthinkable to report a rape. If you got into trouble with a guy, it was your own damn fault. Things haven't changed as much as we like to think."

Wingate leaned forward over the speakers. "I really think this girl doesn't remember a thing."

"Get one of her girlfriends into the room. Have her tell the victim that no one thinks what happened to her is her fault. Tell her the whole school is sick about it and everyone wants these monsters to pay. See what she says."

The girl was a student at St. Pius X in Rowanville. They brought two of the most popular girls down to the hospital and they sat by the victim's bed weeping and holding her hand. At the end of the visit, the girls left and one of them leaned over to PC Peter MacTier, who was waiting for them in the hallway, and gave him a name. They made the arrest that same afternoon.

Wingate, sitting in a chair in the Chamber Street basement, passed Hazel the file. "They want to go to trial," he said.

Hazel sat opposite him, the small coffee table between them doing double duty as a desk. She was listing to one side, but he ignored it. He'd told her a number of times that she should stay in bed when he visited, but she wouldn't have it. It was bad enough she had to greet him in a housecoat; she would not play invalid to the hilt. But he could see how difficult it was for her to sit in a chair.

"Idiots," she said. "They want the whole thing on record?"

"It's her story too. This one" – he reached across and pointed to a name in the file – "he's got no way out and he knows it. He just wants to shame her. And his lawyer is telling him the girl's amnesia is going to make her unreliable on the stand."

"She gave a name."

"They're going to argue her friends suggested it to her. Although when we ran the kid through CPIC, he had two priors, one violent."

Hazel sighed.

"You know she's changed schools," Wingate said. "She wouldn't go back to St. Pius."

"Is she getting the help she needs?"

"Our job ends with the collar, Skip. You know that. We gave her mother all the phone numbers."

She closed the file. "Justice 'done' and another life ruined," she said. "We give the mother a list of phone numbers and hope for the best, right?" He shrugged sadly. "It's a wonder we don't have more heartbroken mothers on the trigger end of revenge killings, James. Honestly. If someone had done this to one of my daughters and then basically walked, I don't know what I'd do. But you'd have to take away my sidearm for a year, I can tell you." There was no role for the law in prevention, she thought, no role in giving solace. They said the law was an ass, but those who enforced it knew it was blind, deaf, and mute as well.

She tossed the file onto the table. "Anything else?"

"Well, there's one thing," he said, and he fished in an inside pocket, removing an envelope that had been folded in half. "This came addressed to the station house, no stamp, just a drop-off. No one has any idea what it is." He handed it to her, and she unfolded it, noting that the address had been typed out on a label and glued to the envelope. It read "Hazel Micallef, Port Dundas OPS/Port Dundas, ON – PERSONAL AND CONFIDENTIAL" and there was no postal code. She tipped the contents of the envelope out into her hand: a small pile of dark photographs.

She spread the pictures out on the table in front of them. There were twelve of them. To call them *photographs* was generous, they were nearly black images on glossy photographic paper, but there was nothing identifiable in them. In some of them, differentiation between shades of black suggested shapes, but in none of them could a concrete image be made out.

"What do you think?"

"Maybe someone wants to file a complaint against a local photo lab?" she said.

"Forbes said he thought they were pretty menacing. Like someone had sent us pictures of people with their faces X'ed out."

"Well, if he can find any faces in these pictures, then we'll talk. But otherwise, I've got no idea what it is."

"Okay." Wingate swept the photos off the table and put them back into the envelope.

"There was no note or anything?"

"Nothing," he said.

She shrugged. There were crackpots everywhere, even in Westmuir County. "How are things with you? People treating you right?"

"You know. They resent me with a smile." He cast a look around the dim room. The bed was made, the pillows squared. "And you?"

"I'm in hell. I keep hoping you'll show up with a saw and a change of clothes."

"How much longer?"

"I don't know. I saw Gary – Dr. Pass – yesterday. He seems to think I'm coming along."

He shook his head. "We all hate knowing you're trapped down here. I wish we could make up one of the cells for you and keep you safe from all this."

"Anything that would get me back into work would be fine with me. I'm going crazy down here." She saw him mask the look of pity that crossed his face. There was no way to reassure her that the situation didn't look as strange as it did.

He got up and put his cap back on. "Is there anything you need? I don't mind being in charge of contraband if it would help any."

She fished her pills out of the terrycloth robe's pocket and held them up to him. "I'm covered," she said.

"You want to go back to the bed?"

She shook her head. "Glynnis is coming home for lunch in an hour. She'll get me."

He didn't know what to say. He returned the few files he had with him to his bag. "I'll see you again on Monday," he said.

"I'll be counting the hours. Literally."

"How is she?"

Wingate took the day's mail out of Melanie Cartwright's hand and shuffled through it slowly. There was nothing else like the envelope he had in his pocket. "She's like a tiger in a cage. It's awful."

"You could always put her up in your apartment."

"I'm three floors up," he said. "And anyway, no thanks. This is strange enough as it is. Anything happen while I was gone?"

"You mean like a palace coup?"

"Sure, anything like that?"

"Not so far." He handed her back the entire pile of mail. She was the one who had to deal with it anyway. "They *are* stockpiling arms in the cells, though. I'd watch my back if I were you." He could only manage a half-smile.

"Is that everything?"

"That's everything," she said.

He went into the squad room, what they all called "the pen" here, a charming touch, he thought. For a small-town shop, the Port Dundas detachment always seemed busy to him. At Twenty-one Division in Toronto, on an afternoon like this, his old squad room would be buzzing with activity of a similar-seeming sort. Desk-phones ringing; cellphones playing snatches of music; people shouting over their desks for one thing or another. And the doors to the interview rooms busy, officers marching men and women (about equally at Twenty-one) in and out of these rooms to take statements, ask questions, cops plying their peculiar forms of conversation. It was hard, after spending a day in and out of those rooms, to engage in normal conversation with normal people – the leading question was an occupational hazard. James frequently had to remind himself to ask David if anything "interesting" had happened at work rather than something "unusual." His colleagues with families found it even harder: children and criminals often hid the truth, but for different reasons. At home, you wanted to make it safe for your kids to tell you everything; at work, you knew you had to catch a mutt in a lie. There were ways to make it safe to tell the truth, and ways to make it hard to hide it, and the tactics were different. He knew a lot of detective-mums and detective-dads who didn't leave enough of the investigative mind at work. There was no room for love in an interview, but you had to find it in yourself again when you went home.

He wondered how well that skillset was developed here. With these people, who rarely brought in a person they didn't know, it had to be hard to create and maintain the atmosphere you needed to fish out something hidden. The interview room was a place where the law traded safety for the truth. But there was no motivation to trade the truth if you didn't feel you could be endangered, and Wingate had to admit, this place felt like everything was between friends.

Still, he marvelled at the amount of activity here. The jail cells seemed permanently empty, and yet the phones rang off the hook. The waiting area in front of Staff Sergeant Wilton's desk was always busy. There were desks in the pen, rather than cubicles, and it created the aura of a squad room chock-a-block with humanity. Even the unoccupied desks, piled with papers, coffee cups, family photos, desk calendars, Rolodexes, and pens, seemed poised to burst into action. All this with a staff of sixteen, only eight or nine of whom were in during daytime hours. The station house was a tenth the size of Twenty-one, but it was its own thing, in its own scale, and it was alive.

He'd been through difficult adjustments before. His life had felt like a chain of difficult adjustments – this one didn't really rate – but he was hoping the day would come when he wouldn't have to question anymore where he fit in. He'd just *be*. Back at Twenty-one, he'd been respected, but he wasn't sure he'd actually been liked. Naturally, a gay cop wasn't going to end up being "one of the guys," but he wondered if his sexual orientation actually had anything to do with it. He suspected they'd looked on him as the one who'd report an internal irregularity, the narc in their midst. They'd never had a reason to suspect him on this level, and in fact he'd turned a blind eye as often as the next guy. But there was a wall between him and his fellows and he would never know now what it had been made of. Or how to avoid the same thing here. Certainly being who he was in a small town wasn't going to be any easier than it had been in Toronto. He'd already decided no one would know that side of him here. There was no reason to think he'd have cause to advertise it; he wasn't interested in meeting anyone and even if he were, he doubted there'd be an opportunity. After David's death, that part of him had gone to sleep, and he didn't care if it ever came back.

He'd kept busy for part of the afternoon, and then gone home for a two-hour nap. Three days a week now, with Hazel gone, he was working doubles. In at six, break from three to five, and then back in until eleven. When he returned to the station house, the evening shift change was starting. Half the cars were out on the roads already, dealing with the developing mess that was long-weekend traffic. He went to his desk to check his messages and get ready to go through the day's reports. That was part of his job now, too. Cartwright appeared behind him. "There you are," she said.

"Where am I supposed to be?"

"You missed all the excitement. We got a call from a hysterical lady up in Caplin. We sent three cars up there."

"What's going on?"

"Says she found a body."

He immediately stood and put on his cap. "A body? Where?"

"She said she found it in Gannon Lake. The body of a woman."

3

She was still sitting on the couch, lost in thought, when Glynnis unlocked the basement door and came in. She hated it when Glynnis used her key; she felt she deserved at the very least a courteous knock. Glynnis looked to the bed and then her eyes tacked across the room and found Hazel. "There you are," she said.

"World explorer."

"You want to eat lunch there or will you be more comfortable at home base?"

"I'll lie down."

Glynnis put a paper bag on the bedspread and came over to offer an arm. Glynnis was the one who lifted her, who carried her. Twice a week, she bathed her and that was the *sine qua non* of Hazel's humiliation, an unthinkable abasement, to be bathed by the woman for whom her husband had left her. But she had come to accept that there was no other way. She wrapped an arm around Glynnis's shoulders and the two of them hobbled to the bed. "You need a pill?" Glynnis asked.

"I'm fine for now."

"I brought us tuna today. Okay if I eat with you?" She asked this even as she dragged one of the chairs to the side of the bed. "I know I'm not your preferred company, but it's silly for me to eat alone upstairs and you alone down here."

"Is it?"

"Yes."

"You should be careful," said Hazel. "People might start to think you really care."

"Well, if they do, I can just smack you around a little and clear up any confusion."

Hazel took a long slug of her coffee. "Do you want to smack me around, Glynnis?"

"I can wait until you're done your lunch."

"See, I knew you cared."

Glynnis smiled. "Keep up that positive thinking, Hazel."

After lunch, Hazel reset the bed into afternoon sleep-mode, but when she lay down, she wasn't as tired as she thought she'd be. Visits from Glynnis always rattled her. The woman's kindness was the hardest thing: it would have been for anyone. Surely Glynnis deserved to be punished for her kindness? Everything else, Hazel had earned: Andrew's cheating on her, the divorce, her life alone with her smart-mouthed mother. But did she merit this? This awful tenderness?

She reached across to the bedside table to choose something to read. The gardening magazines were too much for a shut-in, and she chose instead Monday's *Westmuir Record*. Her mother had mentioned it was publishing the summer story. She silently prayed it wouldn't be a romance this year. She opened to the story. It was a little mystery called "The Secret of Bass Lake." A man and his son fishing. A cooler full of beer. The sun peeking up over the horizon. Christ, she thought, it *is* a romance. The writer's photograph was printed beside his name, a cheesy image of the man standing with his legs set widely apart and his hands in his pockets in a parking lot somewhere. She closed the paper and tossed it onto the floor.

An hour passed. Slowly. She sat up and put her legs over the side of the bed. Dr. Pass hadn't actually told her she was "coming along." He'd gone down her left leg with a pin he'd taken out of his bulletin board – a nod to country doctoring – pricking her leg with it every few inches. She knew about these nerve paths because they'd gone dead on her so many times. He wasn't dissatisfied with the neurological signs, but he told her off for the atrophy he found in the muscle. "You know what this tells me?" he said. She waited him out and he lowered her legs. "This is the sign of a woman feeling sorry for herself."

"Don't you have to feel my head for that?"

"These are legs shrivelling from bedrest, Hazel. You can't heal in bed. You have to move."

"It hurts to move, Gary."

"It should. Your back is a mess. But movement and pain are the only way through to as full a healing as you're going to get."

Now, after Wingate's visit and lunch with Glynnis, she was so bored even exercise seemed an escape. She decided to try the stairs. She crossed the basement to the door that led to upstairs and opened it. The stairs looked like a job for a professional climber. She grabbed the banister and started up. She felt like she was emerging from a cave.

The upper part of the house was full of light. The upstairs clocks her mother had told her about she now saw for the first time; their incessant ticking gave the house a fugitive presence, like there were people whispering in its rooms. What kind of person needed to know the time wherever they stood? Perhaps a woman who was counting her luck, and had to mark every blessed second of it.

She strolled slowly through the living room, with its leather couch and chairs, the widescreen television sentinel in a corner, the fireplace with its pristine unburnt logs waiting for another winter to lend their hearthy romantic glow to the house. She saw Glynnis and Andrew cuddling on the couch, murmuring things to each other, indulging whatever conversational short-hand they'd developed with each other, only a word of which would be enough to make her crazy. She touched nothing, but looked closely. A line of old, heavy books lined the mantel-piece on either side of a rococo silver clock. Decorator books, never read. Probably cost them a pretty penny, too. There was another set of stairs off the living room that led to the bed-rooms, although she knew her mother slept on the main floor, in what was Andrew's office. She went there next, passing the dining room. She glanced in and saw the exact centrepiece she imagined would be there: a tangle of twigs with dried berries and little silver objects in it, stars and planets, and a big, thick red candle sticking up out of the middle of it. The wick was white; Glynnis had never lit it. Perhaps they argued about it. *Why did I buy you this nice thing if you never use it?* But then Glynnis's answer presented itself right away: *Because if I use it, it won't be the lovely, thoughtful thing you bought me one day for no reason but that you loved me.* Goddamnit.

Emily's bed was tightly made and covered with a thick hand-sewn quilt. She didn't recognize it. Did Glynnis quilt, too? There was a pile of books by the bed. A couple of puzzle books with a pen clipped into one of them, and a novel or two. But the book on top was one of Glynnis's for sure: *Talking to Yourself: A Dreamer's Guide*. Hazel hoped it was evidence of her mother ingratiating herself; it frightened her to think of Glynnis trying to inculcate her mother. But she couldn't imagine it; Emily was the original skeptic. She opened the book at random:

SHRUBS, SMALL FLOWERING PLANTS: Red or yellow flowers signify financial windfall; white flowers are unexpected visitors. Flowerless shrubs can mean respiratory problems or digestive issues. A dream of potted flowers is a warning of a suffocating relationship, especially if the petals have begun to fall.

She closed the book and put it back exactly where she found it. The phone began to ring in the kitchen and she hobbled down the hall to it. When she picked it up, she was out of breath.

"You okay?" came Wingate's voice.

"Fine, I'm fine."

"Were you sleeping?"

"No, James. What's wrong?"

"I think you better come in. Can I send a car around?"

"What's going on? What happened?"

"I'm sending a car."

Hazel knew the name Barlow. A George Barlow had once owned one of the largest apple orchards in Westmuir County. He'd sold it fifteen years ago and now it was a pick-your-own operation that was gradually transforming into a county fair/family amusement park that did most of its business during pumpkin season. Hazel remembered going there with her father in the fifties and coming home with bushels of tart, mottled apples. Not supermarket fruits designed for long journeys, but misshapen, delicious real apples.

The woman sitting in front of them – Pat Barlow – might have been a relation. She looked about as pale and shiny as a supermarket apple right now. She was on the other side of the slightly warped table that sat in the middle of the room, in her worn quilted coat, her black hair done up messily on top of her head. She had a smoker's complexion: watery eyes, greying, pellucid skin. One hand curled loosely around a Styrofoam cup of coffee, her gaze lost in the dark liquid it held. Hazel sat down across the table from her, lowering herself slowly into the chair and hooking the cane over its arm. All eyes had settled on her when she walked into the station house and a couple of her people had come forward almost reverently to shake her hand. No one commented on her being half in uniform, for which she was grateful, but Barlow had cast her a strange look when she came into the room. Wingate brought another chair to the table and sat beside her. "Can you tell DI Micallef what you told me, Miss Barlow?" The woman nodded. "Take your time."

Hazel already knew what this woman had told Wingate, but when there was suspicion about a witness, a twice-told story usually shook loose its inconsistencies. Barlow brought the coffee to her mouth, sipped it, and grimaced. "I took a couple out this afternoon. They wanted to go for pike."

"You and –" Hazel checked Wingate's notes, which were open

on the table between them. "– Calvin Jellinek own Charter Anglers, is that correct?"

"Yes."

"And what were the names of your clients yesterday?"

"Dean Bellocque and Jill Perry-something."

The second name was Paritas. The woman spelled her name "Gil." The other name checked out in Wingate's notes. "Okay, go on."

"We were about two kilometres out, on a shelf in like ten metres of water. I saw a school of something in the finder, probably bass, hugging the edge of the shelf, four or five metres down. We'd fished two beds and got nothing, so I told them this was their best chance to catch today."

"You knew these people?"

"Never seen 'em before."

"So you fished the shelf."

"Yeah. And we caught a couple little ones. We threw them back." She swirled her cup and looked into it like she was expecting to see a tiny school of something to go by in its surface. "I had an eight o'clock and I told them we had to go back, but they wanted ten more minutes. That's when they hooked it."

"Hooked what?" said Hazel.

Barlow sent a worried look across the table to Wingate, and he gave her a faint nod. "A body," said Barlow, her voice almost inaudible.

"Keep going."

"One of them – Gil – says, *Jesus Christ*, and I look at her rod, and it's bent double, you know, like she's hooked a monster. But there's no action on the line – it's a dead weight. I take the rod from her and let the line out because I figure she's caught on a log, but it's hooked hard. I whip the line a little to unsnag it, 'cuz it's in there good, but then, when I try to reel in, I feel the log come off the bottom and I start drawing it in. And then I can see the log there under the water, the shape of it, and it's coming up. I figure I can save my rig and not have to redo it for the four o'clock. Then Gil starts screaming. And we see it."

Hazel was writing in her own pad now. "You see what, exactly?"

"A body. Tangled in some kind of net and completely naked. I'm surprised it didn't snap the line. I dropped the whole rod and it went over the edge and the whole thing went back down. I about almost puked."

"How did you know it was a body if you dropped the rod right away?"

"I saw it."

"Tell me what you saw," Hazel said.

Barlow looked to Wingate again, and received his silent reassurance to go on. "I seen a person's rear, okay? She was bent double, like she was touching her toes, and her . . . ass was coming up out of the water."

"How did you know it was a woman?"

"Geez," said Barlow, shaking her head. "I know what a woman looks like."

"What happened to your customers?"

"They got in their cars and left."

"You have contact information for them?"

"We've got the numbers in our log at the shack."

"Okay," said Hazel. "So you called us, but when the cops showed up, you were back on the lake."

"Season's just opened," said Barlow unhappily. "I got bills piled up from winter. Gannon doesn't freeze anymore, you know, I lose all my ice-fishing gigs and I'm drydocked for five months. I can't turn down customers when I get them."

"You've got quite a constitution. You find a body in the lake, you're almost sick to your stomach, but ninety minutes later, you're back on the water."

"I didn't go anywhere near that place, trust me," said Barlow, splaying her hands as if to fend something off. "I just left that thing where it was. I don't want anything to do with it. The whole thing is way too eerie."

"Eerie," said Wingate, "why is it eerie?"

Barlow tilted her head at them. "Don't you read the paper?"

"Oh, *Jesus*," said Hazel.

She told Wingate to go get Monday's and Thursday's *Record*s. He brought them in, and they opened them to the two story instalments, spreading the papers out over the table in an empty interview room. Hazel hadn't read past the first paragraph of the first chapter. Now the two of them leaned over the papers, Hazel supported on her cane, and hurriedly read through both.

"The Mystery of Bass Lake," by Colin Eldwin, began:

The biggest muskie ever landed on Bass Lake was a forty-pounder with a face like an old lady's. Dale Jorgenson and his son Gus headed out early on that Sunday morning with a mind to breaking the record, but when they tossed their lines into those murky waters, with the two flies they'd tied themselves that morning beside their campfire, they had no idea what strange catch waited for them at the bottom of that lake.

Dale stood at the stern, smoking a thick hand-rolled, and smiling at his son. What a big kid that one's turning into, he thought. Dale owned the town's best landscaping company, but he was going to retire one day, and then it would all belong to Gus. If Gus would take it. Dale had to be careful when talking to his kid about the future. The siren call of the big city could be audible even out here.

Dale threw open the lid of the cooler. "Time for a beer, I'd say."

"A bit early for a brew, isn't it?" Gus said, laughing.

Dale cracked two big cold ones and tossed one of them to his son. "The fish'll know if you're not drinking, kid."

The two men tipped their cans back into their throats and drank thirstily. Gus finished his in one long gulp. If Dale ever wanted proof that he really was Gus's dad, he'd need no more than the sudsy smile on that kid's face to have it.

"Well, if it's the writer's body down there, there might be just cause," said Wingate. "So this is him?" he said, indicating the picture of the man in the parking lot. "He looks like a piece of work."

"Who the hell fishes muskie with a fly? Who is this idiot?" said Hazel. They read on. At the end of the first section, which had been printed in Monday's paper, Gus'd had a heavy bite, but when he tried to reel the fish in, his line snapped. The chapter ended with father and son staring at each other in wonderment, and Dale saying: "The fish of our lives is down there, Gus, waiting for us to catch it!"

In the second instalment, the two determined fishermen had rerigged with heavier line and this time, when Gus felt his rod bend against the force of something big, he and his father reeled it in together. The story ended with a shocker.

The big fish – and goddamn if it wasn't going to be at least a fifty-pounder – had given up the fight. Dale held the net at the ready and said to Gus, "Easy, there, easy, he'll wake up when he realizes what's happening."

It was murky in the water, and father and son looked over into it, anticipating the lunker of all time. But then they saw it, and what they saw stopped them cold.

"Oh god –" said Gus.

The hook was in a torso. A human body. Dale was speechless.

The terrifying vision hung in the water like it was floating in mid-air. Gus saw the body had no head.

"Great," said Wingate. "I guess we better call the Marine Unit?"

She looked at her watch. It was already seven-thirty. "It's going to be too dark to look tonight. Get someone up here for first thing and send Barlow home. Tell her we'll see her in the morning. And hope to hell this thing doesn't wash up some-where before we find it."

4

Saturday, May 21

Charter Anglers operated out of a shack on the shore of Gannon Lake. A couple of white wooden hulls with peeling paint lay on their sides in front of the shop, and below it, at the bottom of a short slope, was the Charter Angler dock with its sign on a post at the end of it. They had a single pontoon boat tied up, big enough for five adults. It was rigged for a trip, with three rods leaning against the back railing. "I thought they were expecting us," said Hazel.

"I'll go see what's happening," said Wingate. They parked the car on the grass halfway between the dock and the shack. Wingate knocked on the door and went in. A moment later, he was leading a man toward the car.

"This is Calvin Jellinek," Wingate said, leaning in the driver's side window. "He says Ms. Barlow called about an hour ago and is feeling too nauseous to come in."

"You're going to fuck up my ten a.m., aren't you?" Jellinek said. The muscles on his arms stood out like cables. He was a strong-looking, squat man with a face ravaged by acne scars.

"Your partner was supposed to take us out."

"She was, eh? Why do I think that honour's going to fall to me?"

"Do you know where Ms. Barlow found the . . . um?"

"I know this lake," he said. "I can take you anywhere. But why don't you folks come back at noon? It's the Saturday of the long weekend. I have customers. Look —" He waved behind Wingate, and Wingate turned to see a woman and two little boys coming down toward them. The boys were wearing one-piece, full-body swimsuits that looked like diving costumes. Overtop of these suits they wore enormous, blocky red life-jackets. "They drove up from Mayfair. It wouldn't be right —"

"What we're here for is a little more urgent than catching bass, I think."

The woman and her kids were standing slightly behind him. The boys were excited. One of them said, "Can I kill them?"

"Be quiet, Tom. You can see Mr. Jellinek is busy."

Jellinek leaned forward with a pleading look on his face. It was a mean look. "Come on, Officer. Three hours. It means a hundred and fifty in my pocket, and whatever it is you're looking for, it'll be there at lunchtime." He turned to his customers. "You folks just head on down to the dock. I'll be two minutes."

"You're going to have to cancel this expedition, Mr. Jellinek," said Wingate. "I'm sorry. We've got a marine unit coming up from Mayfair — they're going to be here in about an hour."

"You going to reimburse me for my lost income?"

"I'm sure these folks'll make it up to you. Those boys aren't going to let their mother off the hook." He immediately regretted his choice of words, thinking of what was lying out there in ten metres of water. "This is more important."

"Jesus," he said, shaking his head. He turned angrily and went down to join his customers. Wingate watched the boys' faces fall in unison. The littler one started to cry and the mother looked up toward him where he stood on the gravel, her face set in an expression of profound disappointment. He hoped Jellinek wasn't telling them why the police needed to go fishing. The family walked back up the slope, the boys both with slumped shoulders. The elder murmured "Thanks for *nothing*," as he passed.

"I'll be waiting in my shop," said Jellinek. "I have another group at two. I hope to hell you're not going to need more time than that."

Wingate found a couple of vending machines a few hundred metres down the shore, standing outside a kind of corner store that was closed. He brought back two bags of tortilla chips and two bottles of water, and they sat in the car waiting for the Marine Unit. "My mother's going to kill you for this," Hazel said, crunching the chips. It hurt to lean back against the seat, so she was bending forward a little, as if she was expecting Wingate to put a pillow behind her. He had the radio dialled to a local classical music station and inoffensive orchestral music played quietly.

"She's gotta catch me first," he said.

"Oh, she'll catch you," said Hazel.

Wingate wagged a finger at the radio. "I played sax, you know. I played seriously. I was in my corps' marching band."

"I admire that. I don't have any talents at all."

"You don't have musical talent, but that's probably because you just don't have room for it given your other talents."

She looked over her shoulder at him, raising one eyebrow. "You don't have to butter me up, James. You already have my job."

"You can have it back, Skip," he muttered. "Just tell me when."

The Mayfair cops arrived at ten-fifteen. Jellinek was staring at his watch. One of the cops was wearing a wetsuit under his uniform and as he stripped down to it in the van, his partner, PC Tate, leaned over into Hazel's window and got caught up. "Buddy's going to take us out then?" he said.

"Not willingly from the sounds of it. But you take whatever time you need out there."

"Water's going to be cold."

She looked out toward the van where the other cop was transforming himself into a diver. He looked like a larger version of one of the kids who'd come down with their mother. "You guys get much call?"

"Not this time of year," said Tate. "Mostly it's going down to hook up a Sea-Doo or a smashed-up motorboat, but that's in June or July. Over-exuberance, you know, summer arrives and every idiot's out there gunning it. Once in a while, it's sad, you know, there's a real accident, and we get called out to recuperate. But rarely in May." He lowered himself to see Wingate. "I got a handtruck in the van, but I'm going to need some help getting the winch on it."

"Sure," said Wingate. He got out of the car and the two men walked to the white OPS van parked down by the dock. Jellinek was watching from the front door of his shack, and when he saw the big equipment come out, he came down and helped them get it onto the boat. Hazel watched them from the car. The one called Calberson hauled his tank and flippers out of the van, and then Jellinek tied off. Wingate dashed back to the car. "You going to be okay?"

"I hate the water, James."

"You picked a good place to be born then."

"I can get seasick looking at the back of a dime."

He laughed. "What's your best guess about what's out there?"

"Guess or hope?" she said.

"Yeah." He pushed off the side of the car. "We'll know soon enough."

"Too bad you guys aren't paying customers," Jellinek said from the wheel. "I'm drifting over keepers here."

Wingate looked over the side of the boat, but the water was black and he couldn't see anything. "How do you know that?"

Jellinek indicated what looked like a miniature computer monitor attached to the boat's dash. "I can see them here."

Wingate looked at the screen. It was a console with a black and green display and it showed cartoony images of fish drifting past with numbers attached to them. Jellinek explained the size of the images correlated to the size of the fish, and the numbers told how far down they were. "Fish-finder's the best cheat there is," he said. "When you got three hours and you've made your clients a promise, you can't dick around casting into the dark."

Tate was looking over their shoulders. "Obviously you've never been on an OPS investigation. Can you get that thing to scan the bottom for us?"

"It won't be much use. It can't pick out something lying against the lakebed."

"What if it's floating slightly off the bottom?"

"Maybe," said Jellinek. "But it can tell a fish from a log and it's not going to find you a log, you know. It's not a log-finder."

"Do it anyway," said Tate, tilting a black handheld device back and forth in his palm. "Start over there" – he pointed at a spot five hundred metres to the right from where they were – "and crisscross back and forth."

"You're the boss," he said.

"No, *he's* the boss," said Tate, gesturing at Wingate. "Right, Boss?"

"I'm *acting* boss," he said. "The real boss is in the car."

"You're the acting CO for an acting CO, right? You guys have commitment issues?"

"Funding issues, Officer."

"Ah. Not *your* commitment issues then, eh?" He squinted into the thing he was holding. "Okay, here we go. Can you write this down, Detective?"

"What is that?"

"GPS. Write this down: latitude 44.9483, longitude 79.4380."

Wingate wrote down the coordinates, and Jellinek reversed the boat to the point Tate had told him to start. Calberson had sat the whole time at the back of the boat staring off at one of the islands. Wingate imagined he wasn't a guy whose little tasks had a lot of happy endings. His thick goggles hung against his chest.

The boat moved slowly across the surface of the water. They kept their eyes on the fish-finder. "Goddamn waste," said Jellinek as what appeared to be a school of ten or more fish drifted across the screen. "Bass. Four-pounders."

"They'll be bigger tomorrow," said Tate.

"They'll be gone tomorrow."

They made three crossings and saw nothing the finder didn't image as a something you'd roll in breadcrumbs and fry in butter. Behind the boat, some of the fish were hitting the surface, making rings in the water.

"Stop there," said Tate. Jellinek cut the motor. There was something in the finder at nine metres. It was massive compared to the bass they'd been watching get off scot-free. Wingate's stomach flipped. He'd been hoping all along it would turn out to be a goose chase.

"Well," said Jellinek, "either this lake is sprouting tuna, or there's your man."

"Let's get down there then." Calberson was up at Tate's signal, shrugging the tank onto his back and shoving the mouthpiece between his teeth. He pulled the goggles down over his eyes. He hadn't said a word yet. "You good to go?" asked Tate.

Calberson gave him a thumbs-up and sat on the edge of the boat with his back to the water. Tate smacked his tank hard, some kind of superstition between the two men. "Go," he said.

Calberson pushed himself backwards off the boat and hit the water with a heavy splash. Wingate saw Jellinek shake his head ruefully. Then Calberson was gone and the surface was still again. They returned their attention to the finder, which showed Calberson as a kind of shark under the boat. It gave him a sleek missile-like form and translated his flippers as a long, forked tail. The number on his body grew as he descended. Five, seven, nine metres. His sharkform tracked slowly toward the tunaform, and finally obscured it. "Let's get the claw over the side," said Tate, and he handed a hook attached to a thick cable to Wingate, who dropped it into the water as Tate turned the winch on. The hook vanished into the black. On the finder, Calberson's body and the object in the water appeared to be dancing around each other. And then, suddenly, Calberson's form vanished. They stared at the screen in silence. Tate said, "What just happened?"

"I don't know." Jellinek fiddled with the controls, but only the smaller, unmoving object at ten metres registered.

Tate looked over the side, then quickly crabstepped a circuit of the railing, scanning the water. "Go aft, Detective! Forward!" he shouted from the rear of the boat. "Look for his air!"

Wingate went to the front of the boat and looked down, but the surface was undisturbed. "You see him?" he shouted over his shoulder to Jellinek.

"Nothing!" Tate was in a full-fledged panic and ran to the console, his eyes wild. He smacked the finder once with the flat of his palm. "Hey!" shouted Jellinek.

"Where the hell is he? Move this fucking barge! Find him!" The tone of Tate's voice seemed to wake Jellinek up to the seriousness of the situation and he put the boat in reverse, but as he did, the thing on the finder began to rise. "Is that him?" Tate said, pressing his finger to the screen.

"Not unless he lost half his body weight down there."

"Jesus Christ," said Tate. The depth measurements on the object were declining. It was coming up slowly. Nine metres, seven metres. "Where the fuck is he?" The object was at four metres. Jellinek said it was surfacing starboard.

"English," said Wingate.

"To your *right*," said Tate. He unhooked his walkie from his belt and called his dispatch. "Come in Eighty-one, Eighty-one come in."

"Eighty-one," said the walkie, "go ahead."

"10-78 Marine Unit 1, silent diver, repeat, I have a 10-78 —"

Wingate stood over the railing, his heart hammering against the steel bar. He could see something rising through the dark water. It looked like a body, but why was it rising on its own? He unsnapped the clasp on his holster. "Two metres," said Jellinek. Dispatch was getting the boat's coordinates off Tate's GPS. The thing was almost at the surface. Wingate saw it was human. Somehow greeny-beige. Then he saw the green was a small-gauge nylon netting wrapping the body, two or three layers of it, and the fishing rod Barlow had said she'd let go of was still hooked to it. It reeked of mud and rot, and Wingate felt the back of his throat opening. Tate was staring at his walkie as if his vanished partner's voice might issue from it. And then it seemed to.

"Motherfucker was weighted to the lakebed," came Calberson's voice from the back of the boat. "I had to swim along the bottom and cut it loose." He was treading water behind them. "Someone want to give me a hand?"

Tate leapt to the rear of the boat, shouting "10-22! 10-22!" into his walkie, the code for *disregard*. Jellinek handed Wingate a short grappling hook, and he latched the netting with the end of it and pulled it in. What he drew over the side of the boat weighed no more than fifty pounds. But how could it?

Calberson was tumbling back over the rear, and Tate was slapping him repeatedly on his upper arm as if to assure himself his partner was really alive. "You okay, Calberson? You okay?"

The man had his forearms up to deflect the blows. "Jesus, Vic, I'm fine, stop pounding me."

"Holy frig, I thought you were dead, I thought you were a fucking dead man."

"I'm not! Okay? Now what is that thing?"

Wingate was kneeling over it, disentangling the end of the grappling hook from the netting. The three other men gathered behind.

It was a mannequin.

5

They took over one of the cells in the holding-pen hall, cells that were almost always empty, and this sometimes struck Hazel as a pity because they were nice cells, as far as cells went, with barred windows looking across Porter Street to the little picnic park, and they had passably comfortable chairs and cots. Only one of the cells had a sink and a toilet, as even the most pessimistic predictions of the men who had built this station house in 1923 did not foresee a time when more than one man too dangerous to be permitted access to the public washrooms would ever be kept in these cells at the same time. And indeed, they had been right. The cots had been added in the fifties, when the most common inmate was a drunk needing an airing out before being sent home to his wife. The predictable roster of overindulgers were still the most frequent guests in these cells. That is, when it wasn't the officers themselves, catching fifteen minutes in the midst of a quiet shift.

For their purposes, they dragged an unused desk into the cell and covered it with a tarp. The mannequin was in a body bag, and had attracted its share of attention as it was brought from Tate and Calberson's van into the station house. "It's not what you think," Hazel had said repeatedly, until everyone went back to their work. She hobbled into the cell on her cane. "Do you think we need Spere?"

"Do you?" asked Wingate.

"No," she said, lowering herself carefully onto one of the cots. "Go get Cassie's camera and you can take some snaps of this thing. And give her this." She handed him her notebook. "Tell her to call the numbers Jellinek gave us for Bellocque and Paritas and get those two in. I want to know how a pair of Sunday fishermen managed to hook a mannequin weighted to the lakebed."

"Maybe they used flies," said Wingate. "Should I get Pat Barlow back in?"

"I want to see how their story jibes with hers before we talk to her again. Go on, get started."

Wingate left as Calberson and Tate put the bag on the desk and unzipped it. The opened bag emitted a stench of rotting vegetation and when they tipped the putty-coloured form out, runnels of grey lakewater ran over the side of the table and onto the floor. It was a female model, tinged in places with light blooms of new algae. It was headless and without hands or feet, her sex vaguely hinted at in the rise of two small, nipple-less breasts, and a smooth pubis. Hazel could imagine the staring, painted blue eyes, the blush on the cheeks, the dark black eyelashes. After they'd freed the mannequin from the bag, Calberson fished out the five two-pound weights that had held the hollow form to the lake bottom. "Someone wanted to make sure this thing stayed down there," he said.

"Or that it was easy to find," said Hazel. Wingate returned with PC Jenner's digital camera. "Get some close-ups of the extremities," she said. "What there is of them."

Wingate started shooting. Whoever had put this thing into the lake had gone to the trouble of sawing off the missing parts rather than detaching them at the joints that were designed for easy mixing and matching. In fact, all five joints were still intact: the cuts had been made below them. There was a sixth joint at the waist, to pose the figure in some fetching position. That was why Barlow had seen the rear end rising out of the water. Tate and Calberson stood against the wall, watching Wingate make his pictures. He flipped it over onto its belly and photographed the smooth, featureless back.

"What's that?" asked Hazel. There was something printed right over the spot where her own back had broken down.

Wingate leaned in. "The manufacturer's name. Verity Forms, it says. And a serial number."

"Well, it's something."

"I'll look them up after I'm done making pictures," said Wingate.

"You going to ask them if they're missing a mannequin?" Tate asked. "This is just someone's idea of a prank. It's a waste of time, and what's more, it almost cost my partner his life."

"The boat drifted," said Calberson. "Calm down already."

"This is bullshit," said Tate, and he went out of the cell, slamming the door.

"It's stressful," said Calberson. "Diving. Do you need us anymore?"

"No," said Hazel. "Thanks for everything." When the door

was shut behind them, she said, "Now we're down to one dummy."

"I hope you're not talking about me," said Wingate.

Hazel raised a sarcastic eyebrow at him.

"You didn't think they needed to know about the story in the newspaper?"

"They're scuba-heads, James. They don't do well on land. What I want to do is talk to the couple on Barlow's boat and see what they were really up to."

"What about this Colin Eldwin?"

"Who?"

"The writer standing in the parking lot?"

"Right. Him," said Hazel. "Fine. Get all of them in. If it's a publicity stunt, it cost the county at least three grand; get each of them for dumping, maybe we'll get half of it back." She levered herself up to standing with difficulty. "But if you can get anyone in today, you're going to have to do the interviews yourself. I'm in no shape to do anything but drink a Scotch and go to bed."

"I'll start on the manufacturer."

"Your first dead end. Good luck."

Wingate had PC Forbes take her home and then, after his lunch, he tried to raise all three people Hazel wanted him to call, with no luck. Bellocque's number seemed disconnected, Paritas's went to voicemail, and when he called the Eldwin number, his wife answered and told him her husband was in Toronto for the long weekend. It was a bad weekend to try to raise anyone, and with the weather the way it was (bright and warm) the likelihood of someone actually being near their phone was pretty low. Just in case any of them were known quantities, he ran the names through the Canadian Police Information Centre database, but CPIC came up empty on all three of them.

After striking out on the phone, he spent some more time alone in the cell with the plastic corpse. Its silent, ruined form was eerie; it made his stomach flip to look at it. With the head and extremities missing, it had no identifying characteristics but the tiny letters on its lower back. He wrote the name and serial number down and went out to his desk.

He wasn't sure what the manufacturer would be able to tell him about a drowned mannequin, but maybe with some luck he'd be able to find out where a person might buy a Verity product. Was it local enough to suggest someone near Caplin had done this on purpose? Or was this just a dumb boondoggle: a discarded mannequin tangled in fishing net?

He looked up Verity Forms on the web but found nothing. He tried "Verity Mannequins," and came up empty again. A wholesale mannequin site had an ordering number in Fresno, so he called it and the lady on the other end told him, as far as she knew, there was no "Verity Forms" manufacturing man-nequins. She gave him the name of a Canadian wholesaler who told him the same thing. Wingate put down the phone and squinted at his handwritten notes. Maybe he'd transcribed the name incorrectly? Maybe it had said *Vanity* forms?

He went back into the holding pen and looked closely at the name. He'd not made a mistake. Maybe the serial number was actually a phone number . . . but it looked strange for a phone number: 419-20-028-04. He checked online and found that the 419 area code was for the northwest part of Ohio. Toledo, specifically. He dialled 419-200-2804, and a woman answered, saying "Yeah?"

"Hello?" said Wingate.

"Um, *Hi*."

"Is this Verity Forms?"

"No, it's Cynthia Kronrod. You're looking for Verity?"

"I . . . yes, I am."

"Do you know if she's on this floor?"

"I beg your pardon?" said Wingate.

"If you think I'm knocking on every door in the res, you're wrong, pal. Maybe you have the wrong floor."

"Maybe I do."

"Hold on," the girl said, and he heard her cup the receiver. Her muffled voice reverberated through her hand. "HELLO? IS THERE ANYONE NAMED VERITY ON FOUR?" There was a long pause, and then the girl came back. "People *live* for phone calls here, so if no one answered, I think there's no one by that name here. Sorry."

"Okay," he said, "thanks."

"Are you in Carter Hall, too?"

"Um, no."

"Too bad."

"Okay, thank you," he said, but she wasn't ready to let him go.

"If your feet point you Carter-way, I'm in the west tower. Fourth floor. I have to buzz you in, but it's no problem. You have a nice voice, you know."

"Well, thank you —"

"Cynthia Kronrod," she said, and she spelled her last name. "If you can get here for seven tonight, we're having a hall party.

Two bottles of Everclear, six gallons of orange Gatorade, and one garbage can, and you know what that means, right? We're getting perfectly hooped. Come if you can, okay? What's your name, by the way?"

"Um, Jimmy."

"Awesome," she said, and he hung up before she could get another word in.

"Good grief," he muttered.

He walked over to Cassie Jenner's desk. "I don't suppose you feel like going to a totally rad party at Carter Hall tonight, do you?"

She looked at him strangely. "I've got plans."

"Too bad," he said. He put the paper with his notes down in front of her. "What do you make of this, then?"

She studied his scrawl. He noticed her checking out his clean fingernails and wondered if she could tell he wore a light gloss to protect them. "You dialled it?"

"I did."

"I see," she said. "I gather it was a dead end. Maybe it's a serial number? A thing like that would need a serial number anyway, wouldn't it?"

"I was thinking that, but the serial number's for the model, isn't it? It's not going to get us anywhere," he said.

"It's all you got, Detective. Run with it."

He bent over her and typed the number into Google, but the search brought up nothing. He stood staring at Jenner's screen. Then he turned and went back into the evidence room and leaned down close to the letters on the mannequin's back. This close up, it stank of sulphurous rot, but his instinct had been right: close up, the letters of the name and the numbers weren't straight and they showed a faint crackling around the edges. Without taking his eyes off them, he reached into his pocket and removed his penknife. Jenner was standing in the doorway.

"You want to borrow my microscope?" she said.

He pried open the knife and used the very tip of it along the top edge of the capital "F" in *Forms*. It peeled away cleanly and he lifted it off the plastic and held it out on the point of the blade to her. "Look at that," he said.

She took the knife. "It's an 'F.'"

"It's Letraset," he said. "Someone rubbed these letters onto the mannequin. The numbers too. They've been put here."

"*Get* out," she said.

"Someone's playing a game." He went past her in the doorway, returning to her desk. He sat and looked at the numbers again. Then he remembered the GPS coordinates Constable Tate had made him write down. "How do we find out a location from its latitude and longitude?" he asked her.

Jenner had pulled up a second chair from the desk beside hers. "There have to be convertors online." She reached over him and tapped another search into Google. It brought them to a page that mapped coordinates.

"The numbers Tate gave me were six figures each."

"Just try some combinations," she suggested.

He typed in 41.920 and -02.804 and they found themselves somewhere in the north of Spain. 4.19200 and 2.804 got them into the ocean off the coast of Nigeria. 41 92.0 and 02 8.04 moved them above the border between Spain and France. He entered 4 19.200 and -28 0.4 and plunged back into the ocean near Accra. "I don't think this is going to work," he said, sitting back heavily. "But someone put those numbers and that name there deliberately."

"It was a good idea," she said.

Then he had a flash. "Wait a second. Webpages have names so we can remember them, right? But don't they all have numerical addresses too?"

"Try it," she said. He typed HTTP:// 419.20.028.04 into her browser and after a couple of seconds, something began to happen. A page was loading.

"That's it," he murmured. "Come on . . ."

There was a box in the middle of the screen, like an abstract painting. The browser rendered it slowly, finally revealing a dirty whitish image. They stared at it, disappointed again, but then the image began to drift. "Whoa," said Jenner. "It's a webcam, I think."

She was right. They were looking at a moving image. A camera was scanning slowly to the right, tracking along a wall, a painted concrete wall, it seemed, stained by water. There was a shag carpet and some litter scattered around the bottom of the wall. It was a basement. The camera moved slowly, in total silence, picking up faint pools of light and leaving them behind. There was nothing of interest in the room, and the pan took a full minute to reach its farthest righthand extremity and then the image flickered, went black, and renewed itself where it started: an image of the empty room and the camera beginning its pan to the right again. They watched the entire sequence a second time.

"I can't believe this," said Wingate.

Jenner stabbed the screen with her finger. "Wait – did you see that?"

"I saw someone's dirty basement."

"No," she said. "At the end. Watch again."

He leaned in closer to the screen and followed the camera's gaze. As it got closer to the end of its movement, he noted again a shadow on the wall: it stretched to the left. But something was moving within it.

"There," said Jenner, and she held her forefinger against the right-side edge of the screen. "It's a person."

He hadn't seen it, and he watched again. And on the fourth pass, he saw it. Just a flash, onscreen for less than a second, but unmistakable: the right leg and arm of a person, someone seated in a chair. Visible for an instant against the gloom of the wall behind and then gone, and it was moving: a jittery motion caught on its downbeat. On the fifth viewing one more detail popped out, and Jenner clamped her hand to her mouth. In the upper third of the image, glinting for a millisecond, there was an eye, floating in the dark in an unseen head, an eye wide open in terror. Someone was looking at them, someone knew they saw. A fraction of a second was all they needed to read the message in that eye. It said HELP ME.

"Good Jesus," said Wingate. "I better get hold of the skip."

] 6 [

She'd told Wingate she'd meet him upstairs: there was no computer in the basement, but when he got to the house, she was still downstairs putting on a housecoat and getting ready to negotiate the stairs. Glynnis offered him something to drink, but he declined and waited in the front hallway, uncomfortable and nervous. There was something roasting in the oven – a rich, meaty fragrance filled the main floor of the house. "Sit at least," said Glynnis. "Or has she told you to refuse all hospitality?"

"No, no, not at all," he said hastily, and sat in the chair in the living room closest to the hall. It felt like he was taking Hazel out on a date.

Glynnis vanished into the kitchen and then reappeared with what looked like a glass of beer. "You like apple juice?"

"Uh, yeah, I like it."

"Fresh-pressed," she said. "No preservatives."

He thanked her and sipped it in her presence and then nodded to show how much he liked it. He could hear Hazel coming up the stairs, and Glynnis opened the door for her.

"Orpheus arrives from the underworld," she said, and Hazel waved her off.

"What was so urgent?" she asked Wingate.

He stood and put his drink aside. "Can you take me to the computer you said was connected to the internet?"

She took him down the hallway, ignoring both Glynnis and the smell of supper. As they went into what he presumed was Glynnis's office, the front door opened and they heard Andrew greeting his wife.

"Is your mother still living here?"

"She's having her pre-dinner nap," said Hazel. "Now show me what you were talking about."

Wingate waited for the computer to boot up and connect. They were still using dialup in this house, and it took a few minutes. He typed in the url and waited for the image to load. On a slower connection, the pan wasn't as smooth as it had been at the detachment, and the irregular movement across the room made the short clip seem even more menacing. She sat down in front of the screen and he showed her where to look at the end of the sequence, and when she saw the flicker of the two body parts, she started. He pointed out the eye to her and she was silent, taking in its significance, as he and Jenner had. He was surprised to see that the pan ended a half-inch or so past where it had terminated an hour earlier. "There's more now," he said.

"It's longer?"

"It shows more," he said. "At the station house we could only see the very edge of the knee and arm. And that eye. Now there's a bit of bicep and more pantleg." The leg was still juddering nervously and the floating traumatized eye stared out ceaselessly. An extra second or so had been made visible at the end owing to the extension of the pan. Hazel was shaking her head slowly.

"Well, that's creepy as all hell. Is it happening right now? Is it live?"

"I can't tell."

"And an hour ago, there was less?"

"Just a bit."

She studied the sequence a couple more times. "So someone sinks a mannequin expecting it to be pulled up in order for us to decode a set of numbers and tune in on time to see *this*?" She swivelled in the chair. "Where are we with our fishing couple?"

"We have two numbers and one seems to be disconnected. It rings a couple of times and then there's a busy signal. The other just rings. I don't know if one's a cell or what, or if these people live together even."

"How many times have you called?"

"A few. But it's the long weekend and until I saw this, I wasn't sure how urgent –"

"Did you run the names?"

"CPIC has nothing. I can do a reverse trace on the numbers and get some addresses."

"Good. And in the meantime, get Howard Spere's eggheads on this site and see if they can figure out who's uploading it."

"I also tried Eldwin's number, but his wife said he was out of town for the long weekend."

"I bet he is. Who is this guy, anyway?"

"Apparently, he's a writer."

"Well, either he has some strange fans, or he's working out writer's block in a very active fashion. Find out more about him, would you? And keep trying to reach him."

"I will."

She looked at the screen again. "Judging by the rate at which the camera is exposing our friend here, we might have the whole face by morning. It'd be nice to know who it is." She touched the screen with her finger. "What do you think the shadow behind the chair is?"

"I can't tell," said Wingate. "It tapers a bit as it approaches the ceiling. It could be a person. But it's pretty still for a live person."

"It's not hard to stay still for as long as we're seeing this." She turned off the browser and pushed the chair back. "So," she said, "someone sinks a mannequin in Gannon Lake so we can watch their mystery show. Is this an elaborate prank, or not?"

"I'm leaning toward not a prank."

"When you talk to Spere about this upload, give him those black pictures you showed me, too. I'm getting a bad feeling about all of this."

"Me too," he said.

"Catch me up in the morning."

A voice was waking her up. She thought maybe she was dreaming that she was trying to wake up and she attempted to open her eyes and see the room. She heard the voice again. It was saying *don't be late, don't be late*. She forced her eyes open and saw her ex-husband sitting on the edge of the bed. "Too late for what?" she said, but he seemed not to hear her. "Andrew?"

He was holding out a glass of water. "You awake?"

"What am I too late for?"

"What are you talking about?"

She took the glass of water and drank it down. She tried to sit up, and he reached out feebly, not sure how to help her. He wasn't the one who did the heavy lifting down here. She shook her head at him when he tried to pull her up by the wrist and she shimmed back painfully against the mattress to a half-seated position. "Who deputized you?"

"I deputized myself."

"What time is it?"

He looked at his wrist. "Almost nine."

"It was a rather exhausting day. Does Glynnis know you're down here?"

The friendly look on his face faded a little. "You've been pissing and moaning that I don't come down here enough. So here I am. I don't need anyone's permission."

"You don't?"

"I can go if you'd like."

"I like your bedside manner better," she said. "At least I used to." His position on the edge of the mattress unconsciously mimicked one of the common poses from their marriage. A fight would often lead to the two of them separating, her to the bedroom, him to wherever he went to lick his wounds. Afterwards, he'd show up in the bedroom to pretend going about his business, and she'd ignore him from the bed, reading work papers or a book, and eventually he'd come and sit on her side, stare at her until she laid the reading down. Then they'd talk and work it out or not. Sometimes it took a morning and an evening of bedside conversation to unknot whatever it was that had come between them. "I remember this," she said.

He was leaned over facing her, his chin in his hand. His fingers barred his mouth. "You remember what?"

"You sitting there."

He lowered his hand into his lap. "Do you want anything?"

"A bath."

"You should eat."

She swivelled her legs out from under the sheets. "Afraid I'm going to wither away?"

"No," he said nonchalantly. He stood and started for the stairs, his hands in his pockets, another familiar stance. This one meant irritation. "If you change your mind, you know where the food is."

"Well, *hold* on."

"What?"

"That's it? First time in the dungeon in four days and you offer me the menu but nothing else?"

"What were you expecting?"

"How about *how are you*? Or something about *you* maybe? Are *you* doing well."

"I'm doing fine, Hazel. How are *you*?"

She shook her head at him. "Never mind. Off you go to your throw-pillows and your tarot reading. Have fun."

"Never short of charm, are you, dear?"

He was through the door and up the stairs before she could reply. She heard his staccato footsteps tapping in the space above her. This time she could see through the joists and the pennynails in the floor panels and the linoleum directly to his face and she saw the dread expression there, the black, dead-eyed look of anger on his face, that hurt anger she'd been so good at drawing out of him for so many years.

She desperately needed that bath. She hadn't had a day this active since before the surgery and she was sure she smelled like bear. Glynnis had been helping her in and out of the tub, but if she could muddle through an afternoon half back in her official capacity, she could get herself into a bath. It took five minutes to cross the room again, to the washroom. She shed her clothes and kneeled on the floor to run the bathwater. She rose with difficulty and stood in front of the mirror as the tub filled. She'd lost weight. All that extra weight her mother had been fighting her to lose last fall was gone now. Her skin looked dense and sallow, like she'd been cured in bleach. She sagged in all the places she'd once feared she would sag, and where gravity had not done its cruel work, a kind of fleshly drift had taken place. Her navel was somehow not centred. It might have been her skewed posture, but she suspected something more sinister. Her twisted heart communicating its ways to the outside.

She had to hold on to the sink while the hot water rose up the sides of the tub. Five minutes gripping its cold edge. Then the bath was ready and she manoeuvred herself over the rim and into the hot water. It was always an instant relief to be in this heat and she shuddered as she lowered herself into it. She had to sit with crossed legs as it was too hard to sit flat with her legs out in front of her. The warmth spread in her limbs and climbed her trunk.

She leaned back and closed her eyes. Immediately, the room Wingate had shown her online appeared in her head. The stink of the lake-rotten mannequin and the vision of that dank room were immediately allied in her mind. These two presences, the black photos, and the story in the newspaper triangulated to something that demanded attention. Who were this couple, Bellocque and Paritas? Or should they be focussing on Barlow and Jellinek? And this Eldwin — it was as if his story had metastasized, and now he was "out of town." On the lam, or out of commission? She rotated the facts as she knew them in her mind and looked through their facets, but there was nothing in them but a bending of the light. It made her think she was standing on the outside looking in. Waiting was the worst part when it came to an investigation, but sometimes you had no choice. She was still weaving and reweaving the facts when she heard the door to the upstairs open. Andrew called her name.

"What is it now?" she said, and she cupped a handful of water to her face.

"I come bearing orders."

"Whose?"

He came and stood outside the door. "Your mother's. I believe she said *take my mulish daughter her dinner and tell her to eat it or I'm pouring every drop of whiskey in this house down the sink.*"

"She said that?"

"Doesn't sound like her?"

"Whatever." She heard something clinking. He'd laid a tray on the floor. "I'll leave it here. Glynnis can come down and help you out in a few minutes."

"I'll be fine on my own."

"Okay then."

She waited for the door to upstairs to close, but then she heard his clothes brush against the door. "Are you still there?"

"Yeah," he said almost inaudibly. "I just wanted to apologize. I didn't mean the charm thing. Well, I *meant* it, but it wasn't nice."

"Some apology." She ran the hot washcloth over her arms. "I'll accept it, though. I collect your apologies."

"How many you got?"

"I don't think I'll be completing the set any time soon."

"I'll send Glynn down in ten minutes."

"Hey, you know?" He didn't say anything, as if dreading participating in this conversation any further, with its strange intimacy. "You there?"

"Yeah."

"Let me ask you something." He waited. "Do you think the world would end if you came in here?"

"Absolutely. In a flash of light."

"Well, you have to agree, it's not much of a world." He laughed. Then there was another long, agonized pause. "Oh for god's sake, Andrew, bring me my supper before it gets cold, would you?"

She heard him retreating into the room, but then he returned and the door opened and he was holding a chair in one hand and the tray in the other. He put the chair down behind the tub and laid the tray down on the floor, pushing it with the tip of his slipper toward her.

"Andrew."

"I'm fine here."

"I can't reach it." She heard him sigh – the sound was directed toward the floor, and she turned as best she could and saw him sitting there with his head in his hands. "Just come here," she said. "You've already crossed the Rubicon. You might as well help me eat."

He got up and moved the chair over and sat down again, this time facing her at the side of the tub. He looked sad and amused all at once. He picked the plate off the tray and held it balanced against the rim of the tub as she plucked one of the ribs out of its sauce. The meat fell apart in her mouth. He said nothing as she ate, his eyes unfocussed on her, but she knew he saw her, although she had no idea what the sight of her meant to him now. Her once-beloved body. She finished the rib, put it on the plate, and rinsed her fingertips in the water.

"You're going to smell like barbecue sauce when you get out of there."

"Better than how I smelled before. You could get an onion and a handful of carrots and toss them into the water. Make enough soup for the weekend."

"What a vile image."

"Isn't it."

He held out another rib. There was rice and creamed spinach on the plate, but all she wanted was the meat. Maybe protein would cure her, she thought. He picked up a rib as well and started absently chewing on it. Finally they were sharing a meal. She had to smile.

"You're an impossible woman," he said. "You must know that."

"I'm sorry."

"You're going to end up chained to a bed with the nurses avoiding you."

"A fitting end to the mess I'm making of my life."

"Now, now," he said. "Self-pity doesn't suit you."

"But I'm good at it."

He put a bone down on the plate and leaned forward to dip his fingers into the bathwater. "Listen. You've raised two beautiful girls, you're a good daughter, and you're a beloved member of an important public institution. People count on you. They admire you and they care for you. No one but you thinks you've made a mess of your life."

"You do."

"You gave me thirty wonderful years."

"We were married for thirty-six, Andrew."

"I know."

"*God*," she muttered, and she shook her head. He laughed. "Stop eating my supper."

He passed her the last rib and she pushed herself forward in the bath and leaned down to expose her back to him. "You might as well make yourself useful."

"No," he said, and he stood, pushing the chair back toward the door. "I've done my duty."

"Just wash my back, Andrew. Then you can go."

"Feeding my naked ex-wife in the bathtub while my new wife and my ex-mother-in-law are upstairs watching *Wheel of Fortune* is about as much poor judgment as I'm prepared to exercise in one night. I'll send Emily down."

"It's fine," she said, and she dropped the stripped bone into the water. It floated on the surface. Seeing it there, she thought of what they'd pulled out of the lake. "Just sit down for another minute. Make sure I can get out." She heard him pull the chair back behind the bathtub. "So did you hear about my day?"

"I heard you went in to work. That's good news."

"It's the only good news from the day. We had a report of a body in Gannon Lake, you know."

"You're kidding me. Who was it?"

"Have you been reading the story in the *Record*?"

"I skimmed it."

She pushed the bone along the surface. The dark sauce bloomed off it and stained the water pink. "They find a headless body in the story."

"You found a headless body in the lake?"

"Not quite. A headless mannequin. She was missing her hands and feet, too."

"That's a bit of a strange coincidence," he said. She heard the washcloth dip into the water behind her.

"There's more."

"Are you supposed to be telling me this?"

"There was a web address on the mannequin, if you can believe that. We went to the site and there's some kind of feed, you know, like a video feed from somewhere. A room. Looks empty, but then you see a sliver of a person. Sitting in a chair. He seems to be staring at the camera."

"That's creepy."

"As fuck," she said. "What does it sound like to you?"

"Uhh," he said, "a riddle wrapped in an enigma?"

"You're a puzzle fan, Andrew. Does it make you think of anything?"

"It makes me think you should get some computer expert in and figure out where the upload is coming from."

"Thanks, Sherlock."

"Is there anyone in town missing a mannequin?" The cloth paused at her lower back. He'd seen the stitches below the waterline. "Goddamnit."

"You thought I was faking?"

"No . . . but. I'm not going to touch it."

"The skin doesn't hurt, Andrew. It hurts inside."

"Jesus," he said quietly. "They really opened you up." She felt the cloth move in a slow circle above her stitches. She pictured pulses of energy coming through the cloth from his hand and passing deep into her spine. Cleansing and healing her. She closed her eyes. His hand moved slowly along her lower back.

"Ah," said Glynnis from behind them. "I was wondering where you'd gone."

Andrew dropped the cloth into the water and reached for the towel on the rack to dry his hands. Hazel turned to look at Glynnis leaning against the doorframe.

"She got herself into the bath," he said. "We ended up talking."

"I can see that. You want me to take over?"

"I'm fine," he said.

"I'm not a wayward pet," said Hazel. "I can handle myself." She tried to lever herself out of the water and failed.

Andrew was unhurriedly arranging the dinner things back on the tray. He held it out to Glynnis. "I'll be back up in ten minutes."

Glynnis took the tray. Hazel couldn't tell if she was furious or uninterested in the scene she'd come upon. "Are we all going to have a fight now?" she asked.

"Is that what you want?" said Glynnis.

"I'm just asking."

"Why would I be upset to see that my husband has the capacity to care for another human being? Even one who broke his heart?"

Andrew had stood. "Just go on back up, love."

"There's tea," said Glynnis, and she turned with the tray and left.

Hazel had managed herself to a bent-over standing position. She was staring at the place where the spectre of Andrew's wife had appeared. "Jesus," she said. "She's either amazing or terrifying."

Andrew draped a large blue towel over her shoulders and put his hand under her elbow. She accepted his aid, putting her weight on him as she stepped out of the tub. The hot water had loosened things considerably, almost as well as the painkillers did. "She can be both," he said, leading her out of the bathroom. They slowly crossed the room and she sat on the bed. "Where are your night things?"

She pointed at the dresser that doubled as a sidetable. She watched him go through her things, his touch light, and she could feel his hand on her again. "Did I break your heart, Andrew?" He laid her warmest things on the bed. "I thought it was my heart that was broken. Maybe she's confusing us." He didn't say anything and she reached out and grabbed his wrist. "Did I?"

He looked down to where her fingers had encircled him. She saw him mark her naked wedding-ring finger. Had he never noticed the ring was gone? Why would she still be wearing it? "Yes," he said. "Of course you did." He loosed himself from her hand and ran his palm absently against his chest.

] 7 [

Victoria Day, Monday, May 23

The body hung in the water like a closed fist. Dale held on to the railing, his fingers cold on the metal, and listened to himself breathing. His son was sitting on the cooler behind him, his head in his hands. Gus had thrown up three times after they realized what they'd found in the water. Some bonding experience, Dale thought. This lake was poisoned forever for them now.

He'd secured the body to the side of the boat by tying a rope to the ankle. To do this, he'd had to dangle over the side of the boat with Gus gripping his own legs in trembling arms. Dale knew nothing about bodies, but he knew they decomposed after death, fell apart, and this body was still, despite its missing head, intact. But the water was cold, and maybe that had helped to preserve it. When his fingertips brushed up against the bottom of the corpse's foot, it had been as if a wave of electricity shot through him. He thought he'd light up like a fluorescent tube.

"Okay," he said, sitting against the gunwale and panting for breath as his son puked onto the deck beside him. He laid the hand that hadn't touched the body against Gus's back. He felt like the other hand would never be clean again. He had the urge to cut it off and throw it away so it could not reproach him with what it knew. "It's okay. We'll calm down and we'll call the police."

"Aw Jesus. Jesus Christ," sobbed Gus. He threw up again. "Who would do such a thing?"

"It's not our job to figure it out," said Dale, his hand moving in slow circles against his son's back. "I'm sorry you had to see that."

He helped Gus to his feet and sat him gingerly on the cooler. He took out his cell and saw he could still get a faint signal on it. He dialled a number and spoke to someone, keeping one eye on Gus to make sure the kid didn't faint. He folded the cell and put it back into his pocket. "Someone'll be here soon," he said. "We just have to keep it together until then."

Gus nodded, his eyes locked to the decking. Dale stood against the railing, looking out over the water and trying not to look down at what was secured against the hull, that sad, wrecked form.

A half-hour later, the two of them hadn't moved from their positions, both of them lost in their thoughts. The sun was pouring down its light from a sharp angle, and Dale had to pull his cap down over his forehead to keep his eyes from watering. He heard the boat first before he saw it, and then, coming around the point of one of the larger islands, it turned on a direct heading toward them. Gus stood up. "Jesus, that felt like it took two hours."

Dale dug in his jacket pocket and pulled out his car keys. "Listen to me, Gus. You can get the boat back to the dock, right?"

"What do you mean?"

"I'm going to go with this guy, okay? Answer some questions if they need me to. There's no reason for you to get mixed up in this."

"I'm not leaving you, Dad."

"And then you get in the car and go home and you tell your mother I went to the Super C to get lemons, okay? I'll be home after lunch."

The approaching boat had cut its motor and the driver was angling the wheel to pull up sideways against them. The boat moved in a slow, unnatural skid toward them. The man in the boat wasn't in uniform. "What's going on, Dad?"

Dale took his son by the shoulders. "I want you to trust me. Tell me you trust me."

"I do."

"Can you get the boat back and then get home?" Gus was looking over his shoulder at the man standing in the other boat. Dale put his hand under his son's chin and tenderly brought his attention back to him. "Gus?"

"Yeah."

"I know you wish you never saw this, but I have to do the right thing, and you've got no place in it, do you understand?"

"No. But I'll do what you tell me to if that's what you want."

"That's what I want." He released his boy and then stepped to the railing and put his foot on it. The man in the other boat held his hand out, and Dale gripped it and leapt the space between the two crafts. "Hand me the other end of that rope, Gus," he said, and his son untied the rope where they'd secured it to the railing. Dale caught it and began to draw it in, hand over hand. The body bobbed in the water and then sank a little under the weight of being dragged. The other man leaned over, bracing his knees against the gunwale of his boat, and gripped the arm furthest away from him, and the two men began to lift the inert form into the other boat. And as it came out of the water, resisting them, magnetized to its resting place, Gus saw the corpse turning and his heart seized in his chest. It was a woman.

"Go!" said Dale, and Gus started from his staring and turned the key in the ignition. He pushed the throttle and the boat curved away from the scene in a wide circle.

The body was almost in the boat. "Where's your truck?" Dale asked the other man.

"It's backed up against the dock."

"Anyone there?"

"We'll be sure before we tie up."

The other man put his boat in drive again, and headed back in the direction he'd come in. Dale sat in one of the leather seats, his eyes locked to the heartbreaking form, and for the first time, he wept. Even without her eyes to look emptily on him, it was as if her entire body could see him.

When they came around into the island's lee, the shore seemed quiet, and they went directly to the dock. The other man backed his truck down as far as it was safe, and the two of them wrapped the body in a tarp and hefted it together into the flatbed. They drove the short distance to town and down into its streets. "There," said Dale, pointing at one of the pretty gabled houses in the middle of the street. "Pull into that driveway."

They parked under the big willow. Its feathery flowers had gone to seed and a carpet of soft catkins lay on the asphalt. "He's done well for himself," said Dale. The garden was well kept, with rare trees and a small burbling fountain in the bend of a serpentine flagstone path that led to the door. They lifted the corpse out of the back of the truck and carried it down the path and laid it on the broad granite step in front of a heavy oak door. Dale took a note out of his breast pocket and, with a fishhook, attached it to the tarp. Then he rang the doorbell and the two men walked in a leisurely fashion back down the path.

"What the good goddamn?" said Hazel Micallef. Wingate was looking at his copy and held his finger up. He was a slower reader. He was sitting across from her in her office, the first time she'd tried to occupy that chair since the end of March. She realized, a little surprised by the thought, that she was finally on the uptick. After a minute, Wingate laid the newspaper against her desktop.

"I didn't see that coming," he said.

"Is this Eldwin character back yet? I want him in here, like now."

"I did try him again, this morning, but his wife doesn't expect him back up until this afternoon."

"Did she say where he went?"

"Toronto. He had meetings, she said."

"He writes three chapters of this thing, all hell breaks loose, and he's in meetings in the Big Smoke? Who is this guy? Call his wife back. Tell her we want to talk to him. Now."

"Okay —" He flipped open his PNB and found Eldwin's number. "You want me to do this here?"

"On speakerphone."

He dialled and a woman answered. "What is it?"

"Um, Mrs. Eldwin?"

"Speaking." She sounded mad as hell.

"This is Detective Constable James Wingate calling again."

"You called this morning."

He and Hazel traded a look. "That's right, Ma'am. I was hoping your husband was home. You said you were expecting him."

"'Expecting' is the wrong word to use in relation to my husband."

"So he isn't home?"

"Wow, you *are* a detective."

Hazel bent over the phone. "Mrs. Eldwin," she said firmly. "This is Inspector Detective Hazel Micallef. I'd advise you to drop your tone."

"Jesus Christ," Mrs. Eldwin muttered. "What did he do?"

"Why do you think he did something?"

"Well, you're bloody eager to get him on the phone."

"We just need to talk to him," said Wingate. "Clear a couple of things up."

The unmistakable sound of ice tinkling in a glass came over the speakers. "Let me ask you something, detectives. What do you know about PIs?"

"I'm sorry?" said Wingate.

"Do they even exist?"

"Private investigators?"

"Yes."

"Mrs. Eldwin —" he began in an effort to get her back on track, but Hazel interrupted.

"Are you considering hiring a PI? Do you think something's happened to your husband?"

Eldwin snorted derisively. "God no. At least I hope not. I wouldn't want anything to happen to him before I got my hands around his neck myself."

"What is going on here, Mrs. Eldwin?"

"He goes to town Friday, saying he's got meetings and research – who has meetings on the May long weekend, huh?"

"Well, some people –"

"– and then calls and says he's stuck in town until Monday. And then he stops answering his phone. What does that sound like to you?"

"I don't know," said Hazel. "What does it sound like to you?"

She swallowed something lustily. "It sounds like the same old story to me."

"Is he not the kind of person to have meetings?"

"He's the kind of person to penetrate other women."

"I see," said Hazel. "So you think he's having an affair. And you want to hire a PI to catch him in the act?"

"So how much?" Eldwin asked.

"How much what?"

"How much for a PI? And do I have to pay expenses too?"

Hazel was getting frustrated, but she could tell this Mrs. Eldwin wasn't going to turn out to be willing, so Hazel was going to have to be careful if she wanted to get anything useful out of the conversation. "I'd say a hundred a day is fair," she said. "But you could save that money."

"Oh yeah? You guys going to offer me a twofer?"

"We've got resources private eyes don't. We might be able to track him down for you. But we need somewhere to start. Do you know the names of any of his associates in Toronto? What about the number of the person he went down to meet?"

"Look in the gutters," she said. "Back alleys, whorehouses, dingy bars, that sort of thing. You'll find him sooner or later. Let me know when you do."

She took another big long drag on a cigarette and hung up. There was a pause and then a dial tone. "Wow," said Hazel, "did you run *her* through CPIC?"

"I will."

"Okay, so Eldwin's gone to ground for whatever reason, his wife is drinking before noon, and we still have two amateur anglers at large. Where are we with Bellocque and Paritas? Do we have addresses?"

"Nothing for this Paritas woman, so I assume she and Bellocque live together."

"How can there not be an address attached to her number?"

"Maybe it's a cell."

"Aren't cells registered?"

He looked at her, a little sadly, she thought. "Well, they can be but you can also walk into Loblaws, buy your groceries, a bunch of flowers, and a prepaid cell with nothing but a handful of cash."

"Fine. But you have an address for this Bellocque?"

He put his finger on it. "It's a Gilmore address. You know where that is?"

"Yes, James. I live here, remember?" She shook her head. "Jesus, it's been three days and we still don't have a single state-ment. What the hell ever happened to *the police called, call back* as a working notion?"

"I'm sorry. I should have been more active yesterday, but the truth is, with this thing not changing much" – he gestured at the laptop – "and most of our primaries out on long-weekend DUIs and fender-benders, I guess I just thought some of this could wait until today."

"There's a man *tied* to a chair somewhere, James. A man we were pointed to by a broken, drowned mannequin. What about that seems not urgent?"

He breathed slowly to get his heart to stop pounding. "I hear you, Skip. But the truth is, we don't know if that man is 'tied' to a chair, or if he's in any danger, or even if what we're seeing is real. And the truth is . . ."

"What? What is the truth?"

"The truth is, I'm not sure who's the lead on this now. Is it me? Because if it is, I think you need to trust me to run it my way."

She looked at him flatly, but he saw the fire behind her eyes. "Thirty-six hours have passed in idleness over a question of chain of command? Is that why you've been sitting on your ass?"

He stilled his face. She'd never spoken to him like this before. "I should go run Mrs. Eldwin through the database. Is there anything else you want me to do?"

"Go see Burt Levitt and show him a picture of the mannequin. See if it means anything to him. Ask where a person could buy one or find something like it."

"Fine," said Wingate, and he left without another word. The space he'd been standing in seemed to be buzzing. She had an instinct to call him back in and apologize right away, but she let him go. She'd been itching for weeks to come back to work, but now that she was here, she wasn't sure her head was right.

She'd spent much of Sunday in Glynnis's office with the door closed, reading the newspaper and keeping an eye on the site, but nothing had changed from the night before. Against their expectations, the camera's pan hadn't progressed anymore. It was as if someone had jarred it during that first hour after Wingate had discovered the page. It had been panning through the same visual field since then and it was making her more and more nervous. Maybe this was why she'd snapped at Wingate. She wanted them to *make* something happen.

She returned her attention to the screen. The camera was midway through its usual movement. In a minute, it would terminate on that mysterious, nervous leg. She watched it until it did. Was this the house? The house where a corpse with a note attached to it had just been dropped off, according to "The Mystery of Bass Lake"? She didn't want to make the wrong connections, but her mind was eager to find a link, any link, between these things.

She looked at her watch. It was just past noon. In three hours, the highways heading south were going to fill with sad revellers returning to the city, and she was going to have to have more cars on the road to deal with the inevitable mess. Like the first snowfall of the year, when it seemed as if people simply lost their minds, the end of the Victoria Day weekend always meant a massive traffic snafu. By 5 p.m. every tow truck in the county would be on call.

She popped the lid of her Percocets and gazed into the vial. There were still twenty or more left in the bottle. She put one of the white pills in her mouth and swallowed it dry. On Sunday, she'd taken only two, and at their correct intervals. And she'd had only one this morning, but foresaw it would take at least three to get through the day, and she knew the next one she took would be more out of want than need. If she could get down to only the ones she needed, then she'd come off them. It was probably a good idea to come off them. Soon.

She knew, and she'd been told, how addicting these pills were, but she'd been on them in one form or another for almost three years, and although she depended on them now, she still told herself she was not dependent on them. And if she was, wouldn't someone tell her? Wouldn't someone notice? In any case, if she *really wanted* to stop, she would and could. Of course she knew addicts always told themselves they could stop at any time, so her confidence was not evidence one way or the other.

But she knew herself. She knew her weaknesses were things she could exercise her will over when she wanted to. The things you told yourself tended to come true, and Hazel told herself she did not have a problem. If she did, she'd have to wait until she was out of the woods before she dealt with it.

She checked the screen on her desk again and watched the feed from the beginning of the pan. Now that she knew how it ended, just the sight of the waterstained back wall of the space was enough to get her heart pounding. She stared at it, willing it to show her something new, and her phone rang. She jumped.

"Jesus," she said into the receiver.

"No, Spere."

"Tell me you've got something for me, Howard."

"Nothing good," he said. "The DNS number resolves to gobbledegook. Not even a provider we can trace comes up. It's just out there, beaming in from outer space, for all we know."

"What about those pictures James sent you? What are they?"

"Just badly exposed snaps, I'm afraid. I've sent them to Allen Barry, our imaging guy, but he's in Toronto, so it might be a while before he weighs in."

"Thanks for nothing."

"A pleasure as usual," said Howard Spere.

] 8 [

Burt Levitt's store was still called Micallef's; it had been the town's largest clothing store since 1890, and no one was ever going to change its name. It had been sold to Levitt after Hazel's father died in 1988, and when people came in asking for Mr. Micallef, he presented himself without correcting them. In small towns like Port Dundas, the forces of multinational retail had been successfully held at bay for a long time, but now the tendrils of Walmart and Mark's Work Wearhouse and other bottom-liners were reaching further and further, and a cornfield to the south of town had been asphalted over and planted with big box stores. Levitt was feeling it, but not as badly as the mom-and-pop grocery stores, the few that had survived on the main drag. His time was coming, he knew it, but there were still enough of the older generation who were loyal to him that he could keep going.

James Wingate had never seen the store in its heyday. The ceiling was still wired with the capsule and pulley system that had once been used to shoot cash from various departments to

the cashier, who sat at the back of the store, receiving pay-
ments and making change, which would be ferried back across
the ceiling to the customer. Hazel could remember the sound
of the little compartments zipping over her head and the
squeak of a wooden cup being unscrewed to disgorge its contents. Micallef's was the only store in Ontario to still have its
original cash trolley.

Now the system was dusty and rusted in places and the
various departments had been collapsed to make a single room.
Levitt had cut employees back from the five who came with
the store in 1988 to three, including himself. James had never
been inside the store before now, and it had never occurred to
him, in his six months in Port Dundas, to go in. But crossing its
threshold, he was reminded of the Simpson's store at Yonge
and Queen streets in Toronto that his mother had taken him to
to shop for a suit when he was nine. It smelled the same way
and the fixtures looked the same. He had the instinct that
Levitt would know something about mannequins.

Levitt, now almost eighty, came around from the cash desk
and shook Wingate's hand. "I'd heard rumours about new
blood during that nastiness with poor Delia Chandler, but I
admit this is the first time I have proof of your existence, Sir."

"I guess it's a good sign that you rarely see a detective in
the shop."

"Not necessarily," said Levitt. "Even detectives have to buy
underwear."

Wingate smiled sadly and made a mental note to come to
Main Street next time he needed something. He unsnapped his
dossier case and pulled out three pictures of the Gannon Lake
mannequin. His walkie buzzed; it was Hazel. He said, "I'm

where you told me to go," and he turned it off. He held the pictures out to Levitt. "Hazel sent me over to show you these. It's of something we found. We're wondering what you make of it."

Levitt took the pictures from Wingate and retreated to his cash desk, where he spread the pictures out in a row and put his glasses on to look at them. "Rather beat up, isn't she?"

"Where would a person get something like this?"

Levitt took his glasses off. "Oh, there's all kinds of places you could buy a mannequin. Or steal one. You can even buy them online now. This girl is rather old, though – not quite as old as mine, but not exactly up to date."

"Would you know if you were missing one?"

"Oh, yes," he said. "But I've never had anything like this. I'd guess she was at least twenty years old. The new ones now are much more realistic, and you can get them Chinese, overweight, black, short, voluptuous, whatever you want. You'd think you were shopping for a mail-order bride from looking at the manufacturers' catalogues."

Wingate looked around the store. All of Levitt's mannequins were headless. He realized he preferred headless mannequins to the headed ones: mannequin faces sent a chill down his spine. He recalled a horror film he'd seen in his teens where store mannequins came to life. Had the person who'd sunk their mannequin seen the same film? "Is there a place where unloved mannequins go? Like some kind of mannequin dump?"

"Yeah," said Levitt. "It's called eBay."

"I was afraid you'd say that. So we have little or no chance of figuring out where this one came from."

"Even if your girl still had a mouth, I doubt she'd be able to tell you anything."

Wingate thanked Levitt and went back out onto the sidewalk and started back toward the station house. Then he stopped and took his PNB out of his pocket and wrote "Headless also = mouthless. Silenced."

It was coming up to three o'clock. She walked out into the pen and looked around at the only place that was really her domain anymore. She went in to the dispatch and put her hand on PC MacTier's shoulder. "Might be the time to get some rubber on the roads, don't you think?"

"At least one step ahead of you. I've got one car here in reserve and one more in Kehoe River; the rest are waiting on the grass at various exits across this great county of ours."

"Anything yet?"

"Not much happens at thirty kliks an hour, but something will come up, you know it will."

"I'm putting twenty on it involving a motorcycle."

"No one will take that action, Chief."

She went back out into the pen and sat at PC Julia Windemere's desk. She'd taken the long weekend to visit her mother in the Kawarthas and wasn't back until Wednesday morning. She switched on Windemere's computer and dialled up the site. Nothing had changed. She switched it off and opened her notebook to the two numbers they'd spent all weekend calling. Bellocque's number performed its strange ringing followed by the bleat of a busy tone. But to her surprise, Gil Paritas picked up after two rings.

"Hello?" said a surprised-sounding voice.

"Is this Gil Paritas?"

"Yes."

"Do you check your messages much, Ms. Paritas?"

"I'm sorry, who is this?"

"This is Detective Inspector Hazel Micallef of the Port Dundas OPS. We left you at least six messages over the weekend which you saw fit not to return. Is there a reason you're reluctant to talk to us?"

"Oh, god, I'm sorry – we had the cell off all weekend. It was so nice out – we never even checked."

"Who's *we*?"

"Me and Dean. This is about that thing in the lake, right?" The sounds of a car radio came in clearly over the line.

"What about your experience Friday afternoon felt like it could wait three days, Ms. Paritas?"

"It's not like that. It's just Pat Barlow said she'd handle it."

"That's what she said."

"Yeah. Did she not call?"

"She called. She came in. But I don't think it's up to Ms. Barlow to decide who's obligated to talk to the police and who gets to turn their phone off and drink gin-and-tonics with hubby all weekend."

"Dean's not my husband."

"*Okay*," said Hazel. "The point still stands. I find it hard to believe you thought you were free and clear."

"It was bad judgment on our part," Paritas said. "I'm sorry."

"I can hear you're in traffic. You're heading home?"

"I am."

"And where's home?"

"Toronto."

"Is that where hubby lives?"

There was a pause on the other end. "What are you suggesting?"

"I guess I don't know much about modern mores. Fill me in on one more thing: Do they leave crime scenes down there in Toronto?"

"Well, Detective, just a minute now. I explained what happened. I should have checked my messages, but I didn't have any reason to think I'd left a crime scene."

"You reeled up a body in Gannon. What's your definition of a crime scene, Ms. Paritas?"

"I never saw a body. That was Miss Barlow's story. I have no idea what it was."

Hazel waited to see if she'd say anything else. "How far south are you?" she asked.

"Oh for gosh sake," she muttered. "Are you serious? I'm on the other side of Mayfair. It's taken me *two hours* to get here."

"It should only take you half an hour to get to us. You know how to get to Port Dundas?"

"It *wasn't* a body, Detective, I'm telling you."

"I'll expect you here by four at the latest." She hung up without allowing Paritas another word and she smiled. She got Wingate on his walkie and told him she'd raised Paritas; he was welcome to sit in. He told her curtly he was already following orders and hung up on her. She realized she was going to have to apologize. She hated apologizing.

She'd had lunch, but the prospect of moving this case forward even an inch made her hungry again. She sent Melanie out for a club sandwich. While she waited, she watched the filmed sequence on the site a few more times, once writing down every detail she could see in it. There wasn't much beyond carpet, wall, waterstain, and leg. You couldn't count a shadow as a *thing*, could you? Although discounting shadows was an elementary mistake in her line of work.

She was midway through a viewing when the screen flickered too early in the camera movement and the image failed. Then it returned, but now it was totally different: a field of blurry black and white. She dropped the pen to her desktop and turned the computer screen face on to her. Someone was pulling something away from the lens to bring it into focus. It was the front page of a newspaper. It was the *Record*: today's. Her heart sped up and she felt paralyzed. How to record this? The newspaper dropped below the frame and ratcheting into focus behind it was the figure in the chair, the whole figure, a man, but unidentifiable because someone had tied a width of cloth around the upper half of his face. But it was a man. His mouth was moving, and he struggled in the chair, his arms secured behind it. He listened to a voice, his head tilted sideways toward it (the voice seemed to be coming from the right) and then he shook his head ferociously in the negative. Hazel leaned in toward the laptop and spoke into it – "Hello?" she said into the microphone in the lid. She wasn't sure her voice was being transmitted, but as soon as she spoke, the form in the chair became totally still.

"Hey!" she called. "I can see you! If you can hear me, nod your head –" But the trapped figure did not nod, rather, it shook its head from side to side in terror and the image was blotted out and went black. Hazel held her breath, wondering if now the sequence would repeat with the newspaper again, but she realized, seeing the play of shadow in the image, that she was looking at a person's back, a person who now approached the man in the chair. "I can see you!" she shouted. "Stop what you're doing! This is the police!"

But the figure moved slowly toward the chair and finally the masked face was visible again over its shoulder and it was shouting desperately and trying to push away. An arm flew out and struck the man on the side of the head and Hazel leapt up muttering *oh fuck*, and the man, still bound to the chair, was thrown sideways to the floor. Melanie was in the doorway.

"Skip? Did you say something?"

"Get Wingate back here. Call him in!"

"I have your sandwich."

"Just get him!"

The figure loomed over the man tied to the chair and then Hazel saw the knife.

Cartwright was standing outside her boss's door, as if to guard it. "What happened?" Wingate asked her.

"She only wants you."

"Fine, then let me past."

Cartwright opened the door, and Wingate saw Hazel behind her desk, staring intently into the laptop. She glanced at him only fleetingly and waved him over to her side of the desk. "This is unbelievable." He saw the screen as the newspaper was being drawn away from the lens. "You better brace yourself."

She gave him her seat and watched his face. His lips parted and then pursed. He sat completely still. "Holy god. What is he doing?"

"If you can figure it out, let me know."

They watched it again. The figure with its back to the camera had shown a knife in a flash of light and then fallen on the stricken man in the chair. But before any motion could define what was happening, the picture warped, went black, and then the blurry newspaper appeared again.

Wingate turned slightly in the chair. "Did Spere's people find any way to trace this?"

"Nothing," said Hazel. "It's just there, floating in space."

"Man," said Wingate under his breath. "We're nowhere."

"Not quite." She moved away from the desk, exhausted from monitoring the image. "I got Gil Paritas on the phone. She was in her car driving back to Toronto. City girl, I gathered."

"You question her?"

"Not yet. I told her to be here by four. That's" – she consulted her watch – "ten minutes ago."

"What are we going to do? Do you think the person who's uploading this knows we're watching?"

"Oh, I think so. I think someone is getting right off on this."

He looked at her carefully. "Why though?"

"I don't know. But we're not really being shown anything. If this person's in danger, you'd think, having our attention now, they'd want to prove it. This is all just . . . innuendo. Why bring us here and show us nothing except cheap tricks?"

His eyes flicked to the screen momentarily. "I guess if this gets updated and we see some guy twitching in a pool of blood, we'll know for sure."

"Or not. Keep your eye·on this, okay? Do you mind?"

"No," said Wingate. "Your interview is probably waiting for you. I'll holler if anything changes."

She thanked him and went back out into the hallway, told Melanie that Wingate wasn't to be disturbed for any reason. There was a woman waiting on the other side of intake. Hazel watched her carefully. She was a strong-looking woman of about fifty-five, in an expensive, light shearling coat. She wore a faded layer of lipstick. Hazel couldn't remember the last time she'd worn lipstick, or even had a reason to. Paritas was obviously put out, taking deep, frustrated breaths. Hazel felt like making her wait another ten minutes. She picked up the nearest extension and dialled Wilton at the front desk and told him to bring Paritas into interview one. She waited there for the desk sergeant to bring her in.

"Ms. Paritas?" she said.

"Detective Micallef?"

"Detective Inspector. Have a seat."

Paritas took her coat off and draped it over the chair before sitting down. She was wearing a grey silk shirt and a long beaded necklace. There was a second necklace tucked inside the shirt. She was a good-looking woman, not the type you'd expect to find on Gannon Lake holding a fishing rod. "Ms. Paritas, do you mind telling me where your boyfriend is this afternoon?"

"I told you –"

"Whatever you call him. Where is he?"

"He's at his house . . . why?"

"Describe him for me."

Paritas's brow creased. "What's going on here?"

"I'm asking the questions."

"He's big. People call him bearlike. But not fat, just a big man. He has a beard and –"

"Fine."

"Fine?"

"Yeah, that's all I need to know."

Paritas kept her gaze on Hazel, and then decided she wasn't going to press her luck. She crossed one leg over the other. "Are we allowed to smoke in here?"

"Not since 1998. Let's talk about your fishing expedition. You say you *didn't* see a body coming out of Gannon Lake, but it was on the end of your line. So what *did* you see?"

"I really have no idea," said Paritas. "By the time it was coming out of the water, Pat had taken over. It was too heavy for me to reel in. I just caught a flash of it. It was round and sort of orange and green. It had lines on it, I think."

"You know, you don't strike me as the kind of person who goes out for bass."

"I'm not. It's Dean's thing. He has about twenty stuffed fish on the wall of his house. He doesn't even eat them. I go out with him once a year and he goes to the craft show with me. It's a trade. It would be different if he *ate* them, but he says he's into the 'sport' of it."

"Did Dean see what was on your line?"

"Yeah. He said it was a buoy or something."

"Don't buoys float?"

Paritas sighed. "I'm honestly not an expect, Detective. Inspector, I mean. If you want to talk to Dean, I can give you his number." Hazel turned her notebook to Paritas and laid her finger on the number they had for Bellocque. "That's it," said Paritas.

"It's out of order."

"Oh. I'll mention it to him."

Hazel smiled at Paritas with a tilted head. "Handy, huh, the two of you go out fishing, find something that might have been a body on the lakebed, and then you're unreachable for the rest of the weekend."

"I'm not sure what you're getting at."

"Does Dean have internet access at his house?"

Gil Paritas laughed. "That's funny."

"Why?"

"You don't know Dean, obviously."

"No . . . no, I don't," said Hazel. "Tell me about him."

"He can fix anything with his hands, any mechanical little thing. He's got projects all over the house. It's how he makes a living. Fixes people's washing machines, wires houses, digs septic tanks. It's how we met."

"He dug your septic tank?"

"It was more romantic than it sounds."

"It would have to be." She poised her pen over the PNB. "What's the address?"

"Of what?"

"The house where Mr. Bellocque dug your septic tank?"

"Oh," said Paritas, waving her hands in front of her. "That place is long gone. It was just outside of Gilmore. But I sold it after my divorce."

"You're divorced, are you? When was that?"

"What's my divorce got to do with anything?"

Hazel thought about that. "Nothing, I guess. So you stay with Dean now if you come up to Gilmore."

"That's right."

"Fine, then. You were saying he's good with tools."

"Well, he's good with *real* things. But computers? The internet? Forget it. He thinks it's modern witchcraft."

"So your boyfriend wouldn't have a webcam or anything like —"

"Honestly, I told you, he's not my boyfriend. I'm *fifty-four*, for god's sake. I don't have a *boyfriend*. He's just a . . . a *friend*. He lends me a hand once in a while."

"I'm sure he does. So what is he then? What is the *nature* of your relationship?"

Paritas looked down at the tabletop, wiped away some invisible smudge with her finger. "Can I ask what my relationship with Dean has to do with anything?"

"Nothing," said Hazel, brightly. "Let's move on. Why were you fishing where you were fishing?"

"There was nothing biting. Pat said she knew a better spot."

"So it was Pat's idea to fish there."

"She's the one who knows the lake."

"Did she seem . . . *eager* for either of you to fish that spot? Did she tell you exactly where to fish?"

"No," said Paritas, "she just said there was fish there. She had a radar-type thing on the boat that could read the water. There were supposed to be fish."

"And were there?"

"Just that thing we caught. That I caught. Then we went back, as you know."

"To Dean's?"

"That's right."

Hazel turned back a couple of pages in her PNB and read her notes from the interview with Barlow. "You came in separate cars. You and Bellocque."

Paritas narrowed her eyes at Hazel. "So?"

"Just seems odd, if you're living together, that you came in separate cars."

"We're *not* living together, Detective Inspector. I live in Toronto. Remember? You interrupted my drive home. I *have* my own car."

"Okay, okay," Hazel said, trying to mollify the other woman.

She decided to try a curveball. "So it was Barlow who drove the two of you out to that shelf. But do you think you could find it again?"

"Me?" said Paritas. "You mean on my own?"

"Yeah. Could you direct us to that spot?"

"Why?"

"Well, we never found the thing you say isn't a body, and Barlow is too scared, so she says, to go out there again. So I thought –"

Paritas shifted in her chair, looking alarmed. "You're kidding me, right?"

"Could you find it?"

The woman, her mouth slightly open, stared at Hazel. "I probably could, but I don't think I want to."

"And why would that be?"

Paritas leaned forward over the table. "I didn't *see* it, okay? I told you. It was Pat who insisted it was a body. And if there's any chance it actually *was*, I don't want to have to look at it, do you understand? I was a *guest* on that boat, there against my will to appease my . . . my friend. I'm not going back out on that lake to help you find some half-decomposed body. You can't force me."

She was scared. But Hazel could see, not in a way that was useful to her. "And you're sure Dean didn't somehow direct Pat Barlow to that part of the lake?"

"And then somehow ensure I fished a body off the bottom of the lake? So . . . what? Dean's a killer and I'm his accomplice and he thought it'd be fun if we went out, with a witness, and just made sure one of his victims was right where we thought it was?"

"Well?"

"Am I charged with something, Detective Inspector? I've watched enough television to know that I'm here by choice, and that I can leave at any time, unless I'm to be charged with something."

Hazel looked at her watch. She'd got fifteen minutes of questioning in – pretty good. "If you don't mind, I'd like you to look at something before you leave."

"Do I have to?"

"No."

Paritas stood and seemed to be lost in thought. "What is it?"

She followed Hazel out of the room, and they crossed behind the pen. The evidence room, such as it was, was a small chamber with a single file of metal shelves fitted against a wall. There was so little call to store anything meaningful in this room that over the years it had become a catch-all for sundry crap belonging to both the station and its personnel. There was a stack of notebooks and other paper goods on one shelf, a miscellany of police caps in different sizes still wrapped in plastic, and on a lower shelf, a roll of green felt that unfurled over a desk and became a poker table. It had been confiscated six years ago when Sergeant MacDonald broke up an illegal rake-game in a private home. Now, sometimes, it was pressed into duty at fundraisers. Or the occasional backroom game that broke out in the station house.

Hazel held the door open for Paritas, who peered into the room uncomfortably before entering it. She snapped on the overhead and gestured to the back of the room. There, now dried out but still faintly stinking, lay the mannequin on its tarp. "Recognize that?" Hazel asked.

Paritas stood over it, looking at the mannequin with an expression of blank surprise on her face. "Is this it? This is what I caught?" She turned to look at Hazel and Hazel nodded. "I thought you said you hadn't found it?"

"We found it."

"So Pat *did* take you there."

"It was weighted down to the bottom of the lake."

"Why?"

"So it would stay down. Or so it could be easily found."

Paritas studied her face. "So you really *do* think I deliberately fished this stupid thing out of the lake? Do you have a theory *why* I'd want to?"

"Do you know Colin Eldwin?"

"Who?"

"Do you read the *Westmuir Record*?"

"The *what*?" Paritas was getting really exasperated now. Hazel felt the walls closing in. There was a man in a room somewhere either injured or dead and her only lead, so far, was a woman so desperate for companionship that she'd come to Westmuir County to find it. She'd even gone fishing for it. Hazel cast one more look at the strange, bereft form on the shelf and held her arm out to indicate to Paritas that she was free. She stepped out into the hallway.

"I can go?" Paritas asked.

"You can go."

"I've never been questioned before," she said. "It's really not very pleasant."

"It would have been worse if you'd actually done something."

"And you'd have been able to tell? By browbeating me into contradicting myself or something?"

"Something like that," said Hazel, leading her through the pen to the front of the station house.

"Nice to know the police have so much faith in the average citizen," said Paritas, "that they have to trick them into telling the truth."

"Would you trust the average citizen, Ms. Paritas?" Hazel asked her.

Paritas thought about it. "More than the police?" She smiled tightly and pushed the door open.

She was halfway to the sidewalk when Hazel asked, "What kind of name is Paritas?"

"Woman-stuck-in-traffic," said Gil Paritas, smiling.

Hazel went back into her office, and Wingate was still there, watching the screen and absently signing reports with one hand. Hazel sighed and ran her hand through her hair. "Anything?" she asked him.

"No. Well, nothing else. I've got a knot in my stomach watching this guy get attacked over and over again. Although I take your earlier point – why hint at things? What do they want us to think of this?"

"We should be careful what we wish for."

"What did you find out from Paritas?"

"She's a tourist. She's got no clue what it is she hooked on the lakebed. But I think she's afraid her boy-toy might. So I have to go up and see this Bellocque guy."

"You want company?"

"No. I'm going to go in the morning, when I have more energy. In the meantime, we have to have eyes on this screen twenty-four hours a day in case something changes."

"She's sure Bellocque is accounted for?"

"He's big and bearded, so he's not the man in the chair. Too bad we didn't see the face of the knife-bearer."

"That would have been accommodating of him."

She sat heavily in the chair. "Listen, James —"

"It's okay," he said. "Your first week back, you deserved something easier than this."

"It's still not an excuse. I'm sorry I blew up at you."

"It's okay," he said, and he seemed to mean it. "You should go home, Hazel."

"Yeah. I feel a little . . ." A night of sleep would be a good idea, especially if any of this blew up further. "I do need to lie down. But you'll call —"

"If anything even slightly interesting comes up."

"You ran Claire Eldwin?"

"Yeah. Nothing."

"Well, keep on her. If hubby's not back soon, I think we have a problem."

He agreed, and reassured her he'd keep on top of everything. She went back out into the pen. Almost all of her officers were out on calls, dealing with citybound traffic after the long weekend. You wouldn't know from the look of it that the station house was dealing with what seemed at least to be an abduction or perhaps a murder. She was hoping they wouldn't have to leap into high gear, but she was ready to bet against it.

She thought she might try to walk home, but she was well past anything like a walk. PC Kraut Fraser was playing Tetris on his computer when she went past. "I seem to lack certain spatial talents," he said.

"Can you keep a car on the road? I need a lift home."

He seemed relieved to switch off the computer. "We'll take the long way," he said. "Kill some time on this holiday Monday. Time-and-a-half isn't worth it, I'll tell you, Skipper, not when I could be with my kids."

"Then take the short route," she said.

"They're down in Toronto with their mother." He grimaced for her. "I got all the time in the world."

They got into his cruiser, and he backed out of the lot and started driving north along Porter Street. "You weren't kidding about the long way."

"Unless your back is really bad."

"No," she said, "it's a nice afternoon, and I could use a drive to clear my head."

"Any ideas on what's going on in this mannequin case?"

"Too many for any one to be useful. You?"

"Feels like the tail's wagging the dog a little."

"That's the life of the investigator, isn't it, Kraut? You only get the tail at first and then you hang on for dear life and try to crawl up to the head."

He took her up north of the town and then turned onto one of the smaller highways leading to one of the little lakes that fed into Gannon. This one was called Echo Lake. A banner promising fireworks dated the night before had fallen down onto one of the little beaches. Fraser turned down onto the verge and faced the water. In the distance, pleasureboaters zipped back and forth over the surface of the lake. He turned off the motor. "In a couple of hours it'll be peaceful out here again," he said.

"It's peaceful now."

"I can always handle a little more quiet." He powered down a window. It smelled of pine and wet earth outside. It had rained heavily overnight. "So listen, I know you got a lot to think about right now, but I felt I should give you a heads-up."

"Oh-oh. I *thought* this drive had an ulterior motive."

"The new guy at OPS Central, Commander Mason's replacement?"

"Chip Willan?"

"Yeah. Well, we all got questionnaires."

"Questionnaires."

He reached into an inside jacket-pocket and took out a folded sheaf of papers and handed them to her. She opened the papers up – it was a fairly detailed document with the title *Ontario Police Services Central Region Work Environment Survey.* The first page was mainly demographic stuff, followed by a couple of pages asking the respondent various questions about resources, clearance rates, prevalence of certain kinds of crime in their jurisdiction, job satisfaction, and so on. She said, "This is pretty standard. In fact, it's good to know he's sending these around. Maybe it means he's serious about making things better."

"Look closer. Page five."

She turned to that page and Fraser indicated question thirty-six with his index finger. It read, "If you were redeployed to another detachment within OPSC, which one would be your first choice?"

"Goddamnit," she said.

"It asks for our full names and badge numbers on the last page. I showed it to Martin Ryan."

"The sneaky sons-of-bitches. What did he say?"

"He said it was illegal to ask us to put our names to an informal internal poll, and that question thirty-six was a form of union-busting and that we should ignore the whole thing. Or at least, not answer that question."

She turned to him in the seat, which hurt, but she needed to see his face. "Who's 'we,' Kraut? You mean all the PCs got this letter?"

"And the sergeants." He looked away from her, uncomfortable. "Anyway, Ryan says the whole thing's illegal and we don't have to respond, but the thing is, illegal or not, it may be the only chance any of us get to have a say. If we want one. I mean, if OPSC does decide to move any of us around, and a bunch of us ignored this letter, then maybe they can say they took an informal survey and got an idea of who wanted to go where and the rest of us are going to be sent to Bumfuck. And, Skip, I want to stay in Port Dundas, but if there is no Port Dundas, I don't want to be in Bumfuck."

"Oh, for *god's* sake. So you're going on the record?"

"I'm thinking I have to. If I want to have any say in my future, you know? And as the detachment's union rep, I think I have to tell the rest what I'm going to do. It wouldn't be right otherwise."

"Even though your regional rep tells you the letter is illegal."

Fraser looked down at the steering wheel. "I think this Chip Willan guy is even more of a hard-on than Mason was."

"How hard can he be with a name like 'Chip'?"

"Listen, he's not staring down retirement any time soon, and I think he's going to bring it, if you know what I mean."

"You let OPSC control you like this, Kraut, it won't matter where they send you. And they won't bother asking you your opinion next time."

He turned the car on and began to back out onto the road. "I'm sorry, Skipper," he said. "But I'm fifty next year, I got two kids in high school, and I have to speak up."

"I'm sixty-two in less than a week. Where does all this leave me?"

Fraser stretched his neck. That wasn't a question he could answer. "Like I say, I'm sorry. I hope you understand."

"I do," she said, not looking at him. "Damn it. I guess it's time I met Chip Willan."

] 10 [

She woke to the sound of a tray being put down close to her ear. The smell of bacon wafted over her. *I must have died and gone to heaven*, she thought. She opened her eyes and saw her mother standing by the bed, drinking from a mug of coffee. "You here to taunt me with your breakfast?" Hazel asked her.

"You need your strength now that you're getting better."

Hazel pushed herself up to sitting. It was a little easier than it had been yesterday. Not bad, in fact. She reached over to pluck a piece of bacon off the tray, watching her mother the whole time, but Emily didn't interfere at all. "Glorious," she said as she ate it. She reached for the steaming mug of coffee. "You don't come round here much anymore, do you?"

"Gotta get in line if you want to be of use."

"You're just worried you're going to have to see me naked."

Emily smiled in a pained fashion. She sat down on the edge

of the bed, in exactly the same place Andrew had been sitting. "What the hell were you thinking?"

"I know," she said. "But it's hard. Him up there and me down here, and he seems so reluctant to see me."

"Well, wouldn't you be?"

"I don't think so."

"Come on," said Emily.

"You're right." She stuck her chin out so as not to appear to be capitulating completely. "But to be *this* close, you know? And stuck down here, aware of where they are at night?"

"You've known where they are at night for three years. Four, really. What difference can it make?"

"It wasn't above my head before now." She sipped the coffee. "When he was sitting in the bathroom, it could have been any time in my life but now. It felt that natural." Emily let her talk, although Hazel could tell her mother was going to run out of patience for this line of conversation quickly. "The way he smells . . . that's . . . it's impossible. When's *that* going to go away?"

"I can't say," said Emily, brushing crumbs off the blanket. "I couldn't smell your father after he passed."

"I'm not joking."

Her mother looked up at her, and her eyes were impossible to read. "There's always something, Hazel, but I'm not telling you anything you don't know. It never goes. And why would it? You just have to live with it, that's what it costs you to have had someone. You remember that fringed leather bag your father carried books in? I use it sometimes for shopping and when I put it over my arm, that stiff old strap is still curved to fit his shoulder. I have to brace myself when I pick it up."

She covered her mother's hand with her own. That was the most grief she'd ever admitted to after the day of her father's death. It moved her. "Did I wreck the weekend?"

Emily withdrew her hand and stroked the corner of her mouth with her index finger. "No. Glynnis mentioned it to me, but she didn't seem to want to talk about it."

"Did they fight?"

"No," said her mother. "Not at all. Glynnis didn't seem angry, to be honest."

Hazel took the plate down from the table and laid it on her lap. She didn't usually eat before brushing her teeth, but she was famished this morning. There was a single fried egg sitting on a piece of seedy toast on the plate with the bacon. She picked up the toast and took a large bite of it. Salty and hot: perfect. "She didn't really seem angry on Friday night, either."

"She's not that kind of person, I guess. You've got an appetite, I can see."

"I think I'm making progress," Hazel said, and washed down the egg and toast with another glug of coffee. "I told Wingate I was going to take the day off, but I might go in."

"Good for you." She borrowed the teaspoon off Hazel's tray and stirred the dregs of her coffee with it. "They have the idea that you could behave yourself if they threw you a birthday dinner Thursday night."

"Really."

"You can decide later." Emily put her coffee cup down on the tray. "Well, that's enough bonding for one morning, I think."

She removed the tray and pulled back the covers. Hazel got out of the bed and walked slowly to the bathroom. She did her morning ablutions and brushed her teeth. In the cabinet was a small pile of pills and she pushed her finger through them, selecting a Percocet. On her way out of the bathroom, it rolled over her palm and onto the floor. She leaned over and picked it up. "Hey," said Emily, standing at the door to upstairs with the tray in her hands.

"What?"

"You bent over."

Hazel nodded approvingly. "So I did."

"Maybe you should leave that thing on the floor then."

When her mother was gone, she popped the pill into the back of her throat and washed it down with the rest of the coffee. She dressed, fully this time, right to the cap. Her mother had left one of the city papers behind and she flipped through it as she finished her coffee. The long weekend in Toronto had met statistical expectations: a car crash on Lakeshore Boulevard in the middle of the night had claimed the lives of two young idiots who'd been using one of the straightaways to race. A few shootings: two downtown at clubs, one in the city's northeast corridor. A large number of people ticketed or arrested for DUIs.

She turned to the amusements page whose puzzles were even more impenetrable than human nature. The regular crosswords, which she attempted from time to time, were hard enough, but the cryptics seemed designed for a different kind of person altogether. Was Andrew a different kind of person? Altogether? She suddenly wanted to be able to solve this one, to build a secret bridge to him. One of the clues was "direct a bull." Five letters. She knew the answer wasn't the name for a cattle driver; it was too simple, even if she could think of the word. (A "drover"? – six letters, though.) She stared at the clue, willing the answer to appear, but it wouldn't. If, in her heart, she wanted to feel closer to Andrew, she wasn't sure her head was going to cooperate.

Insoluble puzzles put her in mind of OPS Central, and she put the paper away and picked up the phone. She dialled headquarters in Barrie and asked for Chip Willan. There was a long pause on the line, and then the secretary, a man, came back on the line and said the commander was not available. "I'd like to make an appointment to see him," she said. "Can I come down this afternoon?"

"Oh god, no," said the man. "Commander Willan is booked solid today." *Golf*, thought Hazel. "The earliest he can see you is Thursday. Can you make it down for seven-thirty?"

"The commander works late, does he?"

"In the morning, Inspector. He starts early and ends late. He's got a lot of work."

"I bet he does," she said. "I'll be there. Tell him it's my birthday so he'll be extra nice to me."

Gilmore was the town every other town in Westmuir was hoping it wouldn't turn into. Everyone had watched it happen, but no one had done anything about it and now it was too late and the town, about ninety kilometres northeast of Port Dundas, was a sort of kitsch midway. At one end of Lake Munroe, it had once been a pretty lumber town; now it was hemmed in on one side by garish summer homes (for here were the so-called cottages of the media elite, both Canadian and American, and at least one steroidal movie star had bought an entire island in Munroe and used Gilmore as his home base), and on the other side, in summer, the highway go-kart tracks, the waterslides, the paintball fiefdoms, and in winter, the manmade giant-innertube snowruns, the maple-syrup tours, the winter carnival site. There seemed no licence the munici- pal government wouldn't sell, and during fifteen bad years ending in the nineties, when "cooler heads" finally prevailed, Gilmore had been boxed up and made available to all comers.

Bellocque lived on one of the lakeshore roads, where the log- gers' shacks used to be, and Hazel expected to find him living in one. And indeed, 41 Alder Road was a beat-up wooden house with its shutters hanging off the windows like broken wings on a big, cluttered lot full of broken farm machinery – tractors, tillers, threshers – held in place by years of growth. The col- lection extended up the hill into the forest behind the house, like an outdoor museum of metal dinosaurs vanishing into the wild. She got out of the car in his weed-choked driveway and went up to the door.

After knocking, she heard the movement of a body coming toward the door and then it opened and she was looking at a kind face behind a woodsman's salt-and-pepper beard. He was wearing half-lens reading glasses partway down his nose, and his small, grey eyes regarded her with curiosity. He was huge, she thought, more a bear than a man, but a bear in a flannel shirt. He was holding what looked like a small magnifying glass in his hand.

"Mr. Bellocque?" she said.

He looked her uniform up and down. "Oh-oh. What have I done now?"

"I don't know," she said. "Is there something you should tell me?"

His mouth broadened into a smile. The whiskers of his moustache (which she saw now had a tinge of red in it) had not been cut in some time. "This sounds like it's going to take a pot of coffee." He left the door open and retreated to the kitchen.

She shut the door behind her. The inside of the house echoed the state of the lawn. It was a mass of clutter; the room was packed with every imaginable kind of detritus: old newspaper, broken furniture, piles of hardware catalogues, and everywhere objects in half-repair — birdhouses, motors, little machines or parts of machines, broken crockery half-mended, and on a table in the middle of the room, a reel-to-reel tape recorder taken down to its springs, motors, and belts. The walls were festooned with stuffed fish, exactly as Gil Paritas had said. They were a little creepy. "Have a seat if you can find one," he called from the narrow galley kitchen.

"I'm afraid to touch anything."

"I wouldn't worry about breaking stuff. Take a look at that little fellow in the uniform." She scanned the table and saw what he was talking about: a little jointed wood and tin soldier in a red uniform and a strange conical hat. Bellocque entered the room with two mugs and put them down.

"He's an acrobat," he said. "I made him out of birch and paperclips. Look at what he does." Bellocque put the little soldier at the top of a set of stairs he'd made out of matchstick boxes and bent him backwards over the top edge. The soldier did backflips down all the steps, until he got to the tabletop, stood upright, and his head popped off on a spring.

"Does he always lose his head?"

"It's a warning to the kiddies not to try it themselves. I've also made a crocodile bank that eats quarters, but you can never get them out."

"What's the use of that?"

"Don't feed crocodiles," he said, looking at her like it should have been obvious.

"Might be hard to market." She stared at the soldier's bobbing head. Bellocque nodded to a chair at the end of the table and Hazel sat. It was hard to tell what all the bits and pieces of things were for and she wondered if he was in the business of building sinister moralistic toys for children. She noticed a rotary phone on a table near the front door that had been broken down into parts. He was cannibalizing working things to make his little oddities. He passed her a cup of coffee, which he'd already milked and sugared, and retreated to sit beside one of his bookshelves in a rocking chair. "Now," he said, "let's discuss the trouble I must be in."

"You're rather jovial for a man being visited by a high-ranking police officer."

"Oh, I'm just relieved."

"Relieved?"

"Gil called me from the road and told me what you showed her. I knew it wasn't a body, but it was still a relief to have it confirmed. Is that hot enough?"

She looked down into her mug. "It's fine. How did she call you, Mr. Bellocque?"

"On the phone?"

She cast a look at the dismantled rotary phone on the table near the door. "Really."

"Really," he said, and when she turned around, he was holding a cellphone like a tiny biscuit between thumb and forefinger. His hand was enormous. Bigger, much bigger, than the hand in the video.

"And here I thought you were a Luddite."

"Is that the word she used?"

"Among others," she said, and he laughed heartily, throwing his head back. "I'm curious about something," she continued. "If that phone there doesn't work, why would you have given it as a contact number to Pat Barlow?"

"I didn't," he said, then he squinted one eye at her. "Did I? *Crud*, I might have. The grey matter isn't what it used to be."

She lifted the mug to her face and looked over the rim at the room, searching it for a door. The coffee was excellent. "Ms. Paritas is reluctant to call you her boyfriend. Did you know that?"

"It sounds silly to her. That's what she says. A woman her age having a boyfriend. I just let her struggle with the proper word on her own and let things be what they are. I suppose it matters what things are called." He crossed one leg over the other, a strangely dainty thing for a man like Bellocque to do.

"What's that thing for?" she asked, looking at a strange metal object on the table. It seemed to have a lens in it – she wondered if it was something that could be used on a video camera.

He looked a bit perplexed for a moment, then, following her sightline, reached for a small black square that opened into a box with three sides. "This? It's a loupe, you know? So many of the things I build have little parts." He passed it to her, then gestured her to look behind where she sat, at the reel-to-reel. "For instance, do you think you could get these screws in or out without aid?"

The screws on the magnetic head assembly were almost as small as the tip of a ballpoint pen. She took the loupe from him and looked down into the machine. The screwheads seemed almost manageable through the magnifier. "I guess not."

"Try it." He passed her a screwdriver with the screw already magnetized to it. She held the loupe to her glasses and man-oeuvred the screwdriver over the head assembly and put it in.

"It is easier."

"Even *with* that thing, I feel like my eyeballs are going to start bleeding."

Hazel nodded. It was hard to tell where things were going here. Bellocque was too friendly for it not to mean something, unless, of course, it meant nothing. What if he was just a nice guy? Policework inclined you to think about what people might be capable of, rather than what they're actually doing. It was a good habit for work, but it failed you everywhere else. She couldn't help but think of what happened in just about every cop flick she'd ever seen: there was always some nice-seeming guy with a hobby who turned out to be a lunatic. If Bellocque was a lunatic, she didn't want it coming as a surprise. She laid the small screwdriver down on its side. "So," she said, noncha-lantly, "how did you manage to get Ms. Paritas to fish exactly where you wanted her to?"

"*Ms.* Paritas doesn't do anything Ms. Paritas doesn't want to do, trust me. Not only that, but she's skilled at making it appear as if you've chosen to do something she *wants* you to do. But I like that about her." He smiled at Hazel. "I like anyone who can think for herself."

"I don't think you heard my question."

He leaned forward a little, his massive forearms on his thighs. "I'm sorry. I thought we were talking about relationships."

"How is it that Ms. Paritas found that mannequin in ten metres of water, Mr. Bellocque? Someone must have known it was there."

"Ah," he said, and he leaned back. "Gil warned me you might ask some pointed questions. So, you want to know how, after hiding it there, I directed my girlfriend – or whatever you want to call her – to the exact spot and got her to fish it up, seemingly at random?"

"Sure. I'd be curious to know that."

He tilted his head toward the ceiling, searching it with half-lidded eyes. Finally he looked at her again. "Psychokinesis?" When she didn't respond to that, he said, "It might have been post-hypnotic suggestion. I lose track of all my nefarious plots."

"Do you have a basement in this place?"

"You mean where I keep the bodies of my victims?"

"Mr. Bellocque –"

"Look," he said, "if there's something you *really* want to know, why don't you just come out and ask it? I'll answer anything you put to me honestly. Just stop trying to catch me out. I've nothing to hide."

So this was it, she thought. Her last chance to establish a link between the people connected to this mannequin and the video of the captive man. But Bellocque wasn't the man in those images, neither the man in the chair nor the man with the knife. But that might mean nothing. "Is there anyone else in this house?" she asked.

"Apart from us?"

"Apart from us."

"No."

"So, you're not holding a man captive in your basement?"

He threw his head back and roared with laughter, but when he looked at her again, he could see she was serious. "Honestly?" he said.

"You told me to be direct."

"All right then," he said, and he stood. "Will you come with me, Detective?" He rummaged through the mess on his dining room table and found a flashlight, then gestured with it to the back of the room. There was an open doorway she hadn't seen behind the bookcase; it led to a set of stairs that went down to a door. So there *was* a basement. He led the way, shaking the flashlight as he went to get it to function properly. Only a feeble beam came from it, and when he opened the door to the basement, it cast a small orangey glow. "Watch your step here," he said, "it goes down again."

"Can you turn on a light?" she asked. Normally she would have carried her Pelican, but she hadn't worked a night shift in almost a year and it seemed pointless to carry the extra weight on her belt. Now she wished she had it. "I can't see a thing."

"The switch at the door doesn't work. You have to pull the string," he said. "It's just a few steps this way. Careful, though."

She went through the door, her hand on her metal baton. He went to the right, and she couldn't see him, although she heard what she thought was the flashlight rattling again, and suddenly she felt scared. Then she felt him beside her, his hand brushing near her, and then she knew something was wrong, he wasn't standing where he should have been, he was getting himself into position. She braced herself for the blow and tried to step away, but then he was behind her, reaching around her head, and she instinctively tucked her chin down. The light from his flashlight slid along the floor at her feet. "Bellocque —" she began to say, and there was a blinding flash; she covered her eyes with a forearm, stumbling away and falling backwards over something. She cried out as she struck the ground, a flare of pain shooting down into her leg.

He was standing over her, blocking the light now, his huge face in darkness, his eyes shining darkly as marble, and she pushed back along the floor, striking objects with her elbows and legs. In her mind's eye, she saw the little backflipping man and his head popping off. He loomed down and said, "You find what you're looking for?" and the light played over the surface of his teeth like sparks were coming from inside his mouth. She flicked the baton out in the air beside her to extend it, but before she could swing it, he had that arm tightly in his grip and he was pulling her up.

"Hey —" she shouted.

He brushed the dust off her arm. "You okay?" he said. "I told you to watch your step."

She had the baton cocked, but she held it still. The bare bulb hanging from the ceiling was almost as bright as a headlight. She could see his face now, as friendly as it had been at his front door. "I'm fine," she said, "I landed on something soft."

"It has its benefits, doesn't it?"

She blinked at him, breathing heavily, still unable to chase the feeling that she was in danger. But she wasn't: her imagination had run away with her, and Bellocque was just standing there, his hands in his pockets. They were in the midst of the rich vein of garbage from which Bellocque had mined the main floor's disorder. Bike wheels, boxes of equipment, reels of wire, flattened cardboard boxes, and many piles of vaguely related things, such as a pile of metal pipe and ductwork arranged into something like a tower. Her lower back was throbbing, but there was no pain in her leg. She'd been lucky.

"If you can find a man down here, I suppose he'll be grateful to be freed from this chaos. I could probably build you a robot if you're desperate, but maybe you'd better conduct your search first."

"That's fine," she said, pushing the end of the baton against her knee to collapse it.

"I'm guessing now there's more on your mind than a drowned mannequin."

"You could say that."

"Well, you have my attention. If there's anything I can do to help, any other details from our afternoon on the lake that might help . . ."

"Like what?"

"I don't know."

"Do you think Pat Barlow wanted one of you to find that mannequin?"

"I suppose it's possible," he said, and he pushed his glasses up his nose. "But if she did, that means she's mixed up in what-ever else this is, right? And what the hell would one thing have to do with the other?"

"It all has to do with something the *Westmuir Record* is running right now. A story."

"About what?"

"A short story."

"That Pat wrote?"

"No. A man named Colin Eldwin."

He breathed out dramatically. "Look, you've really got my head spinning now," he said. "I'm going to leave you down here and you can open any box or drawer you want to, okay? Move things around. And when you're satisfied that there's nothing of interest down here, I'll have a fresh pot of coffee done. There's even pie if you want it."

"I don't need to look around, Mr. Bellocque."

He held his palms out to her. "Nope, you stay here and do whatever it is you folks do when you're hot on the trail of something. I want you to be able to say, when you leave here, that the most remarkable thing about my house was the pie."

She watched his face for a moment. Not a twitch. "What kind of pie?"

"Blueberry."

"I'll be up in five minutes."

She did as she was invited to do. Rickety shelves against the back wall were piled high with boxes of miscellanies: index cards in one, bits of screen rolled up in another. Taxonomies of innards: rubber washers, small motors with the wires hanging off forlornly, discarded bits of leather. Some mysterious machine with an as yet undiscovered purpose could be made from all of this, some huge, marauding, clanking thing of metal, polished to a shine and puffing smoke. A mechanical Dean Bellocque. She grimaced at the thought.

She cleared one of the shelves to look at the bare wall behind. It was concrete, as in the video sequence, but a thick coat of anti-mould paint had been applied over its surface. She touched a fingertip to it: it was dry and even cracking in places. It had been applied years ago.

The floor itself was bare, which means, strictly speaking, a carpet could have been laid down here and removed, but the state of the wall argued against such a masking and unmasking, and anyway, the shape of the room was wrong: the room in the video sequence had been long enough to permit an uninterrupted pan from one extreme to the other; this basement was made of discontinuous shapes, one small square space opening into another. There was no wall long enough, without a passage into another room, for this basement to have been used for the purposes they'd witnessed.

She stood alone under the single bright light and noted, as well, that the light in the video had been dimmer. In all, she was satisfied that this was not the site of the captivity and attack they'd seen. She was grateful for Bellocque's suggestion that she take her time. She'd made progress, the kind that limits possibilities, but progress just the same.

Upstairs, Bellocque was bent over the reel-to-reel, pulling a belt over a couple of rollers. He'd slipped the wing of the loupe with the magnifying glass in it behind his reading glasses, and closed one eye as he used a thick finger to thread the belt into place. He looked up at her and pulled the loupe out. "Pie is ready," he said.

"Actually, I'll pass. I've got some work I'd better get back to in Port Dundas."

"Oh, that's a pity," he said, and he got up from his tabletop, wiping his hands. "Do you know, you never actually told me your name."

"Ah, yes. I'm supposed to do that, aren't I? Hazel Micallef. Detective Inspector Hazel Micallef."

He held out his hand and she shook it. "What did you find down there?"

"Not much, I'm afraid."

"Well, isn't that a good outcome for us both?"

"It is for you, Mr. Bellocque," she said, and she offered him a smile. "Look, thanks for the coffee, but I should be on my way."

He held a finger up in the air, his eyebrows raised. "Hold on, hold on," he said. He rushed behind the table and snapped a couple of levers on the old tape machine.

"I should be on my way," she heard herself say. Clear as a bell, as good as any digital recorder. She was impressed.

"Saved from obsolescence," she said. "That's a good trick. I don't suppose you can do it for people?"

Dean Bellocque smiled. "There's a difference between skill and magic."

] 11 [

It had been four days since the mannequin had been found in
Gannon Lake, and so far, the meaning of what they'd learned
was still far from clear. Hazel disliked the sense that someone
else was in control here, was doling out the information at a
pace that suited them. The case was like a dark wave forming
in the distance and they couldn't be sure when it would crash
at their feet. She had to consider that there was no proof that
the man in the internet sequence was actually being attacked,
or that the images they had seen were anything more than a
bad short film concocted by someone to make them look. But
the connection of the mannequin to the internet address; the
black photographs and the dirty shadowy wall in the film;
Eldwin unreachable in Toronto, and Bellocque and Paritas at
large for the whole weekend . . . it was a strain to think nothing
was going on. But it was also a kind of law in policework that
the most innocent things often turned out to have malevolent
cores, and complex sets of interlocking clues just as often blew
apart to vapour. What you learned was to pay attention to

everything, presume nothing, and never be surprised. Her vigilance would not wane, but it felt like an impotent readiness, like she had her gun drawn on fog.

It was midday Tuesday and all was quiet in the detachment. Apart from the ongoing intrigue concerning the trapped man, there was nothing of interest to report. A couple of traffic tickets was all. The cityfolk had returned to their city, and the locals were sweeping up. Summer, with all its danger and amusement, was soon to be upon them. It was time for a coat of paint and a restocking of shelves.

PC Bail had been keeping an eye on the internet film. It was running in a window on her desktop, like an unimportant conference call. "Nothing," she said when Hazel asked. "Just the same two minutes of depravity over and over."

Hazel thanked her and went into her office. She opened the laptop there and confirmed what Bail had said: the film sequence had not changed. It made almost twenty-four hours of the same loop playing over and over. She would have to keep herself occupied with about three weeks of daily reports piled on her desk for her perusal. Most of these she'd seen already – Wingate had brought them to the house in dribs and drabs, but evidently, he wasn't confident enough to have them filed with only his initials on them. There was still nothing more interesting than a stolen iPod in week one, and week two had a complaint from a Mr. Stoneham about a scratch on his car. The current week's files, which she hadn't seen, were three strong: a domestic, a stolen bicycle, a beef in a café that escalated into someone throwing a teacup. That might be the quintessential Port Dundas crime, she thought. A fight that ends with someone getting scalded by Darjeeling.

Wingate knocked. "Come," she said.

"Are you busy?"

She screwed her mouth up at him. "Are you for real?"

"How'd your visit to Bellocque go?"

"It was fine. Better than fine. Too bad he's not single."

Wingate gave her a crooked smile. "I gather nothing has changed onscreen."

"No. Every hour that passes though, I feel more and more the victim of a prank. What's the deal with Eldwin?"

"Nothing yet."

"Jesus."

"Claire Eldwin promised she'd call the second he turned up."

"She sure didn't sound like she was baking him a Welcome Home cake. You kind of got the feeling she'd be happy if he stayed away as long as he liked."

"You starting to think he's tied to a chair in his own basement?"

"Can't rule it out," said Hazel. "He doesn't sound like the kind of guy a lot of people would miss."

"Well, the mannequin came up on Friday," said Wingate, "which means whoever put that video on the net had it ready to go from that point, and that's the day Eldwin went to Toronto."

"Hmm," said Hazel. "Where's the loose thread here, Wingate? What about Jellinek? Do we know where he is?"

"We can find out." He opened his notebook and flipped a couple of pages, then picked up the phone on her desk and dialled. "Is this Cal Jellinek?" He listened for a moment, then cupped the phone. "Do you want me to ask him if he's currently being held in a basement and/or being threatened with a knife?"

"Ask him if Pat Barlow is there."

Wingate did, and then passed Hazel the phone when she gestured for it. "Ms. Barlow?"

"Yes."

"How did you know where that mannequin was?"

Wingate creased his eyes at her. "What?" said Barlow.

"You must have known exactly where it was if you drove your customers right to it."

"Jesus Christ! Are you kidding me?"

"Well?"

"It's bad enough the lake is full of fry this year, Detective Inspector. You really think I make up for bad fishing with jokes?"

"So you just happened upon that thing."

There was a pause. "I had *no* idea what was down there," Barlow said slowly. "I'm not lying."

"If you were, that's what you'd say anyway."

"If you want to arrest me for something, do it," said Barlow angrily. "But if you just want to blow smoke up my ass, leave a message next time." She slammed the phone down and Hazel pulled her head back smartly. Wingate was looking at her with an unimpressed look on his face.

"It was worth a try," she said.

"Was it?"

"Look, *something* has to give here! *Someone* is waving their hand in front of our face: *hey! look here, look here!* But what are we supposed to be doing?"

"What can we do?" he asked. "We can't inspect every basement in the county."

"It would be better than sitting on our rear ends."

"I'm frustrated too," he said.

She held up the last folder she'd been reading. "I'm starting to think I've got a better chance of clearing the Darjeeling Caper than making heads or tails of what turned up in Gannon Lake. Maybe there's a next move, but I don't know what it is. All I can think of is Eldwin now. You keep on his wife and try to nail down where her husband is."

"Will do," said Wingate.

She closed the files that were in front of her and pushed them to him across the desk. "I'm done with these."

Wingate was about to leave the paperwork when there was a knock at the door, and Cartwright pushed it open partway. "Busy?"

"I was just leaving," said Wingate, and he slipped past her in the doorway. Cartwright came in with a coffee and a giant chocolate muffin, both of which she put down on Hazel's desk.

"Early birthday present," she said.

Wingate bent back into the doorway. "Your birthday?"

"Thursday," said Hazel. "I'm going to be thirty-nine again." He looked blankly at her. No one had got her Jack Benny joke in ten years. It was sad how things kept changing.

She was aware of the shadows of her personnel sliding by in the frosted window in the door, but for almost an hour, no one had disturbed her. She watched numbly the endless attack on the unknown victim unspooling on her laptop. It was like a song she couldn't get out of her head, a song without lyrics, although the more she watched the sequence, the more she became aware of the dreadful music in it. The Percocet she'd taken before leaving the house had peaked and was wearing off: it made the footage seem more raw to her, it hurt more to watch it, and she thought of the other pill, the one wrapped in tinfoil, in her pants pocket, which she wasn't going to touch unless she really needed it. She'd taken the morning pill as a precaution, although if she were being entirely honest with herself she'd admit she'd taken it because she wanted to. In general, she could feel various aches reasserting themselves at various times, but the truth was she was beginning to feel certain that she could get through the day on her own. She could keep the bottle of pills – and the one in her pocket – as a promise of comfort if she needed it. *Needed* it, she told herself.

She got out a scrap of paper from a drawer and wrote down in point form some of the things she thought she should bring up with Willan tomorrow morning. She'd try at first to focus on what they were actually *doing* in Port Dundas before he trotted out his ratios and his per-capitas. She wanted him to hear what they were dealing with, especially now, and how important the police department was in the community. Willan was going to use the word *catchment* and talk about efficiencies. He was going to tell her Port Dundas would take on the mantle of county HQ, and she'd be in charge of *more* people than she was now: it was going to be a *challenge* and he knew she could *rise* to it. And when she told him it would mean lost jobs and fewer services and maybe not being able to solve crimes like the one they were working on *right now*, he was going to shrug and tell her redistribution of employees would amount to a couple of lucrative early retirements, a couple of redeployments, no one was getting fired, and all they'd have to do after the re-arranging would be to stay on top of their game . . . *just like they are now!* She'd never met this man – apart from the letter that had been sent around to her beat cops, she didn't know a thing about him – and already she didn't like him.

She let Melanie bring her a late lunch of a club sandwich and a Diet Coke, and stayed at her desk writing out facts and figures as they pertained to Port Dundas. While she wrote, she kept the laptop screen tilted discreetly away so as not to be distracted by it. But she saw the loop repeat and repeat in the corner of her eye.

She saw their detachment's case clearly, but she knew he'd only hear her trying to save their own bacon. What did OPSC know about Westmuir? When did those clowns ever leave their desks and come and see the policing realities up here? Anything north of Central was a pin on one of their maps, a line on a graph. She hoped she wouldn't be reduced to shouting.

Melanie knocked again about half an hour later, and Hazel didn't look up from her notes, just told her she was done lunch and thanks, but Melanie was standing in the doorway. "What is it?"

"Surprise!" she said.

Hazel put down her pen. Cartwright was holding up a large box wrapped in bright paper. It seemed half the detachment was standing in the hallway behind her. "Come on, now," said Hazel. "You guys are too much."

Cartwright pushed the door fully open and came in to put the box down on her desk. Windemere, Bail, Wilton, Wingate, and Forbes followed her in with big grins on their faces. It was one of those department-store wrapping jobs: hospital corners, ribbon, and a rosette. "This better not be another cellphone," she said, and they all laughed. She turned it around. "You all tossed five bucks into a hat, but you couldn't manage a card?"

Cartwright turned on the officers and gave them an exasperated look. "You guys raised by wolves, or what?"

"Hey, don't look at me," said Forbes.

"Never mind," said Hazel, and she began to tear at the paper. Within was a child's toy, a game called Mouse Trap. Everyone laughed and clapped, and someone said it was a very clever gift. Hazel remembered the game from Martha's childhood: you won by building a Rube Goldberg machine that dropped a plastic net on top of a mouse. She looked up grinning at the officers. "Absolutely fitting," she said. "Whose idea was this?"

They looked back and forth between them, but no one was taking credit.

"What? I have a secret admirer?"

"Well, I just followed the bright paper," admitted Windemere. "I actually, uh, didn't contribute." She turned to her colleagues. "Yet!"

Hazel put her hands on top of the box. "So . . . this is from all of you?" No one said anything. She picked up the gift. "What's going on?" she said, but then all at once she dropped the box on the table and stood, alarmed.

"What?" said Wingate, stepping forward into the room.

"That doesn't smell right," she said. "There's something in there, that isn't a . . . isn't a —"

"Okay," he said, "let's everyone get out of this room —" but he didn't finish what he was saying, because the box was moving. There was a sound from within it, like a mechanical whine, and then something was tearing frantically at the end of the box, moving it in short jabs toward the end of the table until it upended and went crashing to the floor.

"Jesus," said Hazel, instinctively stepping away, but as she did something blew out of the top of the half-opened box, a red, screeching blur like a child's firecracker, and she dove for the ground, batting at the air over her head. There was general disorder in the room, strange half-uttered cries, and a crush for the door, but then Forbes called out, "Hold on! Hold on —"

"Fuck!" yelled Hazel, now standing again. She stared at what Forbes was staring at. "What the fuck?"

It was a mouse. It was standing in the corner, its eyes shuttling back and forth between the two sides of the room. She supposed it was a regular white mouse, but this one was red, or at least it had been painted red, although she could see a darker line of what had to be blood dripping from its mouth.

"Why is that thing red?" said Hazel. "What the hell is going on here?" Forbes and Wingate stepped deeper into the room, walking carefully to the side of her desk where the game had fallen. Wingate toed the lids apart and then recoiled.

"Good god," he said.

12

Down in Mayfair, on Jack Deacon's mortuary table, it looked unreal, a movie prop. But it *was* real, and as Deacon turned it over with his living hand and Howard Spere took notes with a pen held in his gloved hands, the whole scene took on an even more surreal aspect.

Deacon was talking into a tape recorder as Spere wrote. "Left hand of a caucasian male, age between forty and fifty, no distinguishing characteristics —"

"Apart from its being separated from its owner," said Spere.

"Apart from that. The cut has been made under the carpals, a rough cut to judge by its raggedness and the bits of shattered bone we find here. I can only hope the victim was knocked out or dead when it was done."

"I don't think he was," said Hazel quietly. She was standing away from the brightly lit table, not wanting to look too closely on the thing that had been sent to her wrapped in colourful paper. She was sweating in the cold room. Wingate stood beside her, leaning forward to get a better look. "We have the attack on film."

"We don't actually have the attack," said Wingate. "Just the moments leading up to it. There's no proof that this hand and that . . . that person in the chair . . ."

"Is there a way to tell if the victim was alive when his hand was . . . removed?" asked Hazel.

"It's not really possible to say with any certainty," said Deacon. "Not with this body part, at least. I'd want to see more necrotized blood to be certain it was a post-mortem amputation. This thing is very pale indeed, so there's been blood loss, and that's consistent with an extremity disambiguated while blood was still circulating." He held the hand palm up and studied it for a moment. "The wrist tendons have retreated into the cut a little – that windowshade effect you see when living tendon has been cut . . . and I guess that tends to argue for the hand being cut from a living body. But you'd *still* see some of this pre-rigor spring-back immediately post-mortem. So what we have in front of us doesn't *rule out* that the victim was alive at the moment of amputation. Or that he was dead, mind you."

"Jesus," said Hazel. "Do you *want* us to throw up?"

"Look," said Spere, "what about the puncture wounds, where the note was pinned? Is there any bruising?"

Deacon looked again at the top of the hand. A note written on a square white piece of paper had been attached there with a fishhook. A "nice touch" was how Spere had put it when he saw it. Deacon pulled the skin tight with latex-gloved thumb and forefinger and shone a pinlight onto it. "Good instinct, Howard. Hazel?"

She stepped forward reluctantly. "Do I really need to see this?"

"Slight purpling at the wound sites," he said. "Dead bodies don't bruise."

Spere held his palms up to the heavens. "Ah, an *answer*."

"That only means he was alive when the note was pinned to him," said Wingate.

"That's correct."

"So this fuck pinned the note to the victim's hand and *then* sawed it off?" said Hazel.

"*That* strikes you as particularly barbaric?" said Spere, wiggling a finger around in his auditory canal.

Wingate was holding the note, in its zip-lock bag, up to the light. "'Just wanted to give you a hand with your investigation,'" he read.

Spere shook his head. "*And* he's funny."

Hazel had retreated again and was leaning against one of the autopsy tables on the other side of the room. If she had to look at that severed hand again, she really was going to be sick. "This brings things to another level," she said. "We have to think through our options."

"What if this person just wants us to watch?" said Wingate. "What if this is a demonstration of some kind?"

"Of what kind?"

"Of power."

"And for what purpose?"

"I don't know," he said.

She pushed off the table. "The first thing we're going to do is we're going to visit the *Record* and see what they can tell us about Eldwin. Why is he writing about this stuff? The body in the lake, the fishhook, the note . . ." She fell silent a moment. "I'll tell you one thing: he's not getting any more ink, not until we understand what this is all about. We'll flush him out: if he wants to keep telling this macabre story, he's going to have to show his face."

Wingate was looking right through her. He was lost in his thoughts. After a moment, he approached her and spoke quietly. "What if he *can't?*"

"Will we know the difference between *can't* and *won't?*" Wingate didn't have a response. "Fingerprint that thing and put it on ice," Hazel said to Spere. He nodded to her, holding a finger up. His cell had buzzed.

"Just a second." He held the phone to his chest. "I've got Allen Barry on the phone. He's my imaging guy in Toronto. He wants to know if we can receive a file down here."

"You mean couriered?" said Deacon.

"No, a singing telegram, Jack. He means over the net."

"We can go up to my office."

Spere put the phone to his ear. "I'll call you back in five."

Jack Deacon wrapped the hand and put it back on dry ice, in a red cooler like the kind you'd use to store beer for a picnic. It was going to put Hazel off her beer for months.

She realized she'd never been in Jack Deacon's personal office. She only ever saw him under those harsh blue lights in the basement, surrounded by the stench of preserving fluids and human flesh arrested in its decay by science. He took off his white coat, under which he wore a proper suit, also the first time she'd seen him look like anything other than a nice ghoul with a scalpel. He looked presentable.

"You can put him on speakerphone," he said to Spere, pulling out his black leather chair so Spere could sit.

Barry's voice came through the tinny speaker. "Who am I talking to?"

"Me, DC Wingate, DI Micallef, and Dr. Frankenstein."

"Hi Jack," said Barry. Deacon waved at the phone. "Okay, so listen. Those little black photos aren't what you think they are. They *are* pictures, but not twelve individual pictures, like you thought. They're one image."

"One big black image?" said Hazel. "Is that more helpful?"

"I scanned them and got them into Photoshop. Once they were all laid out on one template, I moved them around fitting edges together. There's enough texture in the images to see where one edge goes against another. Jack, what's your email there?" Deacon gave it to him. "Okay, I'm sending the first image through."

They waited, listening to Barry tapping his keyboard in Toronto.

"Don't expect too much from this one. But you need to see the 'before' picture if you know what I mean." They checked Deacon's email and there was nothing. "That's fine, I'll keep talking. I brightened the image I had and then worked the contrast. Then brightened it again, recontrasted it, and so on; I had to do this four times. There's information there."

"And what is it?" asked Wingate.

"Hold on, it's through," said Deacon, and he clicked on the tiff file Barry had sent. It loaded: it looked like a picture of an oil spill, shot through with faint lines, like reflections off its surface.

"Okay, I'm sending the reworked image through. It's not

going to look like a real picture, but you have to believe me, this is what was in that black mess."

They waited as Deacon repeatedly clicked his "receive" button. They could hear Barry breathing over the line.

"You got it?"

"Just tell us what it is, Allen," said Hazel impatiently.

"Naw, you should see it."

The email arrived. Deacon clicked it open, and over the pitch, swirling black image appeared something like a ghost emerging from dark smoke.

"What is it?" said Spere.

"I think it's a dead animal of some kind," said Barry over the speakerphone.

Deacon put on his glasses and leaned forward on the palms of his hands to look closely at the image. It looked like a pile of fur, but there was no face, no limbs. "Is it a pelt?"

"Maybe," said Barry.

They all studied it. It seemed to have a shape; something about it seemed to infold on itself.

"Hold on," said Hazel, putting her finger against Deacon's screen. "Is that the end of a sleeve?"

With her eye, she traced up from the crushed edge of what had appeared to her to be the armhole. She moved her finger up. "This is a hem. Look . . ."

She waited for the others to see it. "So it is," said Deacon. "It's a black sweater."

"Jesus Christ," said Spere. "All this trouble for a fucking sweater?"

"Well, glad to be of service," came Barry's voice. "Now you folks get to figure out what it means."

13

Wednesday, May 25

She'd successfully avoided visiting the offices of the *Westmuir Record* for almost twenty years. The last time she'd been through those doors had been to check the proof of her father's obituary in person. She hadn't wanted such a thing faxed, and her mother was so sick with grief she couldn't do the job herself. Back then, at the end of the eighties, the editor had been an inoffensive old man named Harvey Checker. His *Record* had been the classic country newspaper, with jam recipes and pictures of kids dressed up in period costumes for the Sunny Days Parade. None of this "real" reporting that Sunderland liked to dream up. When Sunderland had taken over in 1997, he'd changed the paper's motto from "Eggs, Coffee, and *The Record*: a Perfect Westmuir Morning" to "On *The Record* for All of Westmuir."

The paper was housed in an old tool and die factory at the top of Main Street; it was one of the first businesses you saw after crossing the bridge over the Kilmartin River. Hazel and Wingate went in and asked for Sunderland, but after a five-minute wait, a young woman with short black hair came out and offered her hand. "I'm Becca Portman," she said. "Mr. Sunderland isn't available." She looked back and forth between the two officers, smiling mildly.

"Did he see me standing in his lobby?" asked Hazel.

"Actually, no. He's in Atlanta this week for a conference." Hazel mentally added Sunderland to her list of the unaccounted-for. After all, it was in his newspaper that the short story was appearing. And he was no fan of hers. Although it was hard to credit how what was happening had anything to do with her. Portman leaned toward her and said, with a hint of embarrassment, "'Reupping Small Market Ads: Supersize Your Customers, Supersize Your Revenues.' It's sorta gay, I know, but this is a business."

"And what are you?"

"I'm the managing editor. And for three issues, I'm the interim publisher, which is, honestly, *so* . . ."

"Awesome," said Hazel.

"Yeah."

Wingate took her hand and shook it. "It's good to meet you. Do you have an office?"

She did; it was Sunderland's office. She led them to it and closed the door. There were pictures of Sunderland on the walls with celebrities who wouldn't be recognized twenty kilometres south of Port Dundas. Wingate put a picture of the severed hand on her desk. Portman covered her mouth with her hand. "Wow," she said. "That's kinda gross, isn't it?"

"Does Gord Sunderland know it's my birthday tomorrow?"

Becca Portman narrowed her eyes. "I don't think so. But happy birthday?"

"Someone sent that to me in a wrapped box." She took her notebook out of her hip pocket and removed a Polaroid picture. She held it out to Portman. "And this was found in Gannon Lake on Friday. You're running a story that features a body in a lake." Portman was looking at the picture. "Can you get your boss on the phone?"

"I'm sorry, but what does that nasty hand have to do with this mannequin? Or the story?"

"There are aspects of our investigation we can't discuss right now, Miss Portman," said Wingate. "But you can trust me: it's connected."

"So," said Hazel, "your boss?"

"All I have is a hotel number, I'm afraid." She handed back the picture. "Mr. Sunderland told me to hold down the ship."

"The *ship*?"

"What?"

"Never mind."

"Miss Portman," said Wingate, "can you show us the next chapter of the story you're running?"

"No," she said, blithely. "I can't."

"We're not rabid fans," said Hazel, "who can't wait until tomorrow morning. We're police officers."

"The problem is, we don't have it yet," said Portman.

"Don't you have to go to press?" asked Wingate.

"Tonight." She looked at her watch, as if the evening could creep up on her without her noticing. "Mr. Eldwin's giving us the chapters one at a time now."

"So when are you expecting him?"

"Expecting him?"

"You have a poor grip of English for a woman who works at a newspaper," said Hazel. "Expecting, anticipating, looking forward to *his presence*."

She looked at Hazel queerly. "I'm not *expecting* him," she said. "He sends the chapters in by email."

"Fucking technology is going to be the death of policework, I tell you."

Wingate brought her attention around to him again. "From where, Miss Portman? Where is he emailing from?"

"Um? His computer?"

Wingate looked at Hazel. Hazel said, "Can we see the last email he sent?"

Now she was happy to help. "Sure," she said, and she leaned over Sunderland's desk and brought up her email, turning the screen to them. Hazel went behind the desk, gently pushing Portman out of the way, and sat in Sunderland's chair, turning the screen back to herself. There were dozens of emails still in the inbox. Two were from Colin Eldwin, and she opened the one that was from this past Saturday afternoon. It said, simply, "Hi Becca, I've had a couple of new ideas for the story, so toss what I sent on Thursday, okay? Here's chapter three for Monday – I'll get this Thursday's to you asap. Thanks! CE."

She opened the first email. It was dated Thursday, May 12. "First two chapters," it read. "More in a week. CE." Both emails were sent from Eldwin's email address, *eldwincolin@ontcom.ca*.

"Where are the original third and fourth chapters Eldwin sent?"

"I trashed them. Always respect the writer's wishes." Hazel thought, *Editorial Relationships, second year*.

"Did you read them?"

"Yeah."

"And why do you think he wanted to rewrite them?"

Portman shrugged, an all-encompassing shrug of total incompetence. "I guess he wasn't happy."

"What were they about? What happened in them?"

"Oh gosh," she said, searching the ceiling. "Let's see, they drag that poor girl into the boat and Gus throws up some more, and then they take it to the police and it turns out it's some girl that's been missing for months and the police, like, they hold Dale and Gus, but they're innocent and they let them go. But Dale has a bad *feeling*."

"A bad feeling. What kind of bad feeling?"

"I think that's where the fourth chapter ended. I can understand why Mr. Eldwin wanted to revise. It was a little too *on-the-nose* for a mystery story. I like what he's doing with it now."

"Do you?"

"Oh yeah, it's goosebump stuff, don't you think?"

Hazel stared at the girl for a moment, lost for anything to say, and then she returned her attention to the computer screen and scrolled down the inbox. There were emails from Sunderland, from other columnists and writers, from advertisers. Nothing looked out of the ordinary. She went back to the Eldwin emails. "I want copies of these," she said. "You have a computer person here?"

"I'm a computer person," said Portman. "What do you need?"

"I just told you what I need."

Wingate stepped forward. "If you could just make us printouts of the emails, with full headers, that'd probably do for now."

"Hey, no problem," said Portman, and she flounced behind the desk. Hazel got up and stood in the window, trying to control the urge to smack the girl. Portman disconnected the computer from a scanner, then unplugged the scanner and plugged in a printer, connected the USB cable from the printer to the computer and tried to print the two emails. "Whoops," she said, "wrong cable. Hold on." She fiddled for a couple of minutes, failed to find the problem, smiled emptily at Wingate, and called in an associate, a gangly guy with a mass of uncombed hair and a worried expression on his face. He fiddled with the cables for a couple of minutes before plugging the printer into the right sockets.

"Okay Mizz Portman, that should, that should do 'er." He almost hit the doorframe on the way out.

"He has a crush on me," said Portman.

"Well, you're adorable, aren't you?" said Hazel.

"Thank you," she said.

"And you run a tight fort," she added.

"Well, there you go," said Portman, handing Wingate the printouts. "Let me know if I can be of any more help."

She hop-skipped to the office door and opened it for them, relieved to have the visit over and done with. Hazel stopped halfway out. "One more thing, Mizz Portman." The young woman waited behind the officers, a benign smile on her face. "Regardless of when the next chapter comes in, don't print it."

"Sorry?"

"You heard me. I don't want you to publish another word of this story unless you have permission, personally, from me."

She looked to Wingate, hoping for a sign that Detective Inspector Micallef was joking. But she found no assurance in his eyes. "Well, I can't do *that*," she said. "I mean, I can send you the story as soon as we get it, but our readers are expecting —"

Hazel took a step back into the office, and Portman quickly retreated. "What your readers are expecting is seven interesting things to do with celery and cream cheese. But if you run any more of this story without my permission, you'll be directly interfering with an open police investigation. Do you want to do that?"

"I, I'd have to ask Mr. Sunderland for permission to —" She stopped talking, staring at Hazel's eyes. "If it's that serious . . ."

"If I even see a *mention* of 'The Mystery of Bass Lake' in tomorrow's paper, I'm coming back here, alone. And your office crush won't be any use to you if things go wrong in here again. You understand?"

"I understand," she said, making violent little metronomic nods with her whole face. "No story Thursday."

Hazel offered her hand, and the girl took it immediately. "Nice talking to you," she said.

Wingate walked with his hands in his pockets, his face pointed straight up the sidewalk. "What?" she said.

"You ever heard the saying that you catch more flies with honey?"

"Are you going to turn into my mother now, James?"

"No."

"Because one is too many."

"It's not Rebecca Portman's fault she works for a man you hate. That's all I'm saying."

"You're the one who called her a fly."

"It's your call."

"You're right," she said. "It is my call." She looked at her watch. "I don't think we can wait any longer to get news from Claire Eldwin. We better go up and see her. You call and make sure she's there, but don't tell her why we're coming."

He got out his cell and dialled. There was no answer. "I'll keep trying her," he said.

They turned down Porter Street and headed for the front doors of the station house. She walked into the detachment with her head down and went straight to PC Eileen Bail. "Tell me the web sequence now shows a map to where that guy is being held."

"Not quite."

"Not quite?"

"It just happened," said Bail. She turned the screen to Hazel and Wingate. It was a solid dark frame now. But something was shuddering. The camera was pulling back slowly.

"What is it?"

"Blood," said Bail. "It's blood, I think."

The zoom out took a full two minutes, revealing a number of shapes as it went. When the image was revealed, it was seven letters about fifteen inches high, and they spelled out the words SAVE HER. The letters were slowly flowing down the wall. They watched the image repeat a number of times. Hazel felt sick to her stomach. "Are you sure it's blood?"

"I don't want it to be," said Bail. She waved Sergeant Renald over. He was a trained SOCO officer. "What do you think?"

He stared at the display. "'Save' who?" he asked.

"Tell us if you think it's blood," said Wingate.

Renald put his face close up to the screen. "The top edges are hardening as the fluid is washing down," he said. "See the darkening line at the top of that round shape?"

"Paint would do that," said Hazel.

"Paint dries," said Renald. "Blood clots. Look at the lumps forming."

She wanted to puke. "Jesus Christ." There was a whirring, tinny noise coming from somewhere, and she turned her head to listen to the speakers built into the computer, but the sound wasn't coming from the video.

"So, 'save' who?" Renald repeated.

She pulled her head away from the computer but she still saw the letters bleeding down the wall in a basement somewhere. "That's *it*," she said, talking to the room. "I'm getting heartily sick of being the dog wagged by the tail. I want *control*, people – let's everyone get working on what's happening here. This town can go without parking tickets for a while until we figure this out."

Bail said, "I don't think any of us know where to start."

"Begin by thinking it through. By the end of the day, I want one good idea from each of you . . . does everyone . . . what the hell is that sound?"

The irregular, metallic noise was coming from somewhere behind her. Without another word, she pushed into the back of the pen and went in the direction of the sound. It wasn't a fan, it was too loose, too rattly. No one stopped her as she made her way to the coffee station behind Windemere's desk. There, beside the creamers sitting in their little plastic tub of ice, in a cage, and spinning a tiny exercise wheel at top speed, was the mouse that had popped out of the box. There was a small black scab on its lower lip. Its fur had faded to pale pink. Windemere was standing beside her. "We named him Mason," she said. "We gave him a bath, which he didn't much like. But he's a lot better now."

Wingate was standing beside her. "Do you think someone is asking us to raise the dead?" he asked.

She put her hand into her pants pocket and pushed past the little pill-shaped ball of tinfoil between her thumb and finger to her car keys. She passed them to Wingate. "Go see Claire Eldwin. Right now."

"On my own?"

"On your own. And come back with some answers."

] 14 [

Claire Eldwin lived thirty kilometres away in a town he'd never heard of, Mulhouse Springs. There were so many small towns in this part of Ontario that he figured you could live here for thirty years and not find them all. He was driving along Highway 79, to the west, below Gannon. There was a road every five hundred metres leading to cottages. If you owned a cottage up along here, then you were from away. It was like having another country nestled inside this one and he could see how the summers changed what home felt like for those who actually lived here.

The disconnect between this landscape and what sometimes went on in it was still hard for Wingate to accommodate. In Toronto, it didn't take a great effort to sense the seething chaos that moved beneath the surface of civilized life in the city. There was always something on the verge of happening: as an experienced police officer, you could scent it under the patina of order. You could almost move yourself to its contrapuntal beat, be in the right place just as something was about to happen.

Only in the neighbourhoods where there was enough money and white skin to presume a kind of harmony did crime ever surprise you. Although not enough: there was always someone breaking down, a domestic that went ugly, someone craving silverware. Even so, his life at Twenty-one Division was truly clockwork: a drug bust at ten, a stolen bike at noon, a gunshot at two, high-school students threatening more than mere unrest at the Eaton Centre at exactly three-fifteen.

But here, here in Westmuir County, everything had a fugitive nature. You couldn't read those closest to you, and this was because everyone's guard was down. (Well, except for Hazel. He felt naturally closer to Hazel than anyone, precisely because she was slightly paranoid.) And because it seemed no one had anything to hide, and not even the police lived in a state of alert suspicion, it was possible to run the kind of plot they were caught in now: someone using a lake, a newspaper, the internet, and colourfully wrapped packages to tie a leash around an entire police force and tug it in the direction they wanted it to go in. It made him wonder if someone had *specifically* chosen Westmuir to bring all this stuff to life. It was worth a thought.

He'd called Eldwin's house again on the way up and found the wife at home. She didn't seem particularly surprised that he wanted to see her in person, just gave him proper directions and rang off. That only confirmed his theory. In Toronto, the police don't call ahead, and what's more, if they did, both sides of the conversation would hang up and immediately begin forming dire anticipations. Claire Eldwin, he found when he arrived, had put on the kettle.

She came to the door in a shiny gold housecoat with pale blue jeans underneath, and she was smoking a handrolled. Out of habit, he sniffed the smoke and checked off the *tobacco* box mentally. She blinked at him in her doorway, looking him over with interest and gripping the doorframe like she was going to twist it out of the wall.

It was a big house for two people, he thought, but it looked small because it was stuffed with furniture and knick-knacks. Either Eldwin or his wife collected obsessively. Cloth flowers, paperweights, small busts of famous composers, colourful replicas of birds in tiny gold cages. It all crowded in, making the rooms seem darker. She led him to an oval dining room table in wood that looked out onto a big garden full of larger, but equally extraneous, baubles. Cement arches, birdbaths, four little doghouses scattered along the serpentine flagstone paths that wound toward a stone fountain in the middle of the yard from its edges, looking as stranded as a ship run aground. There wasn't a dog to be seen anywhere. He stood at the window as Mrs. Eldwin made tea. "It's a quiet week," she said. He looked at her quizzically. "You're wondering why I have so many empty doghouses, aren't you?"

"It occurred to me." There was something strange about that yard, he thought. It wasn't just its busy emptiness, it was something else . . .

"I sit dogs," she said. "It was crazy busy over the long weekend, but there's no one now. I had a St. Bernard, a Brittany spaniel, and a chihuahua for three days."

"Sounds like a Disney film."

"It wasn't."

He turned away from the window. She was pouring hot water

into a teapot. "How long have you lived in Mulhouse Springs, Mrs. Eldwin?"

"You don't look like your phone voice," she said. "You sound like a small man on the phone, but you're not."

"Thank you," he said. "I think."

"It's a compliment."

He sat, accepting tea from her. "Well, thank you. You didn't answer my question."

"We moved a year after the wedding."

She was at the very least extremely drunk. He could tell she'd been drinking when he spoke to her on the phone. A drunk interview could be good, but if you needed any of it later in court, someone might argue that the statements were unreliable. Still, he needed to know the basics. "And the wedding was when?"

"What?"

"When did you get married, Mrs. Eldwin?"

"September . . . two thousand and one. It'll be four years this fall."

"And before Mulhouse Springs, where did you live?"

"Toronto," she said.

"And why did you folks move up here? Mulhouse Springs isn't exactly Yonge and Bloor."

"It was Colin's decision," she said, coming to the table. "He wanted more *space*."

"For what?"

"To 'think,' he said." She gave a nasty little laugh. "Writers, huh?"

"What does he need to think about that he couldn't think about in Toronto?"

Her face suddenly became serious. "I've stopped asking."

Wingate put a cube of sugar into his tea and stirred it. "Tell me more about Colin."

"Like what?"

"Who do you think he went to see in Toronto?"

"Someone probably wanted to hire him to ghostwrite a computer manual. Or a biography of their cat."

"Is that how he makes a living?"

She laughed that knowing, exasperated laugh again. "Make a living? Colin's been working on the Great Canadian Novel for fifteen years. From long before I met him. He's never published anything that actually had his name on it. You know, before the *Westmuir Record*."

Wingate nodded. An unpublished writer and a dog-sitter had bought this house? "How did the two of you meet?"

Claire Eldwin reached behind her and took a pouch of Drum off the countertop and began to roll herself a cigarette. "In a class. Nine years ago. He sometimes fooled one of the colleges into hiring him to teach a continuing studies class."

"I don't know what that is."

"You know, adult education. Most institutions of *higher* learning have a cash cow on the side called 'continuing studies.' It's evening classes taught by alcoholics and sexual deviants to anyone with a pulse and a chequebook. His class was called Get Published Now. You know the saying *those who can't, teach*, right?"

"I've heard it said."

"There's a corollary: *those who can't teach, fuck their students on the side*. That's how we met. Romantic, huh?"

"Well, you married him."

She lit the cigarette. "Guilty."

"And now you think he's having an affair."

"Colin is *always* having an affair."

"He sounds like a super guy. What's his novel about?"

"Damned if I know. It's the Great Canadian Novel. It's probably about the snows of yesteryear. I can hardly wait. Do you want a drink?"

"No, thank you. Do you know where your husband's staying in Toronto?"

"All I know is that it's warm and wet."

"Mrs. Eldwin."

She stood and went into the kitchen and took a bottle of Grand Marnier out of the fridge. "This stuff gives you a wicked hangover and then you have to drink *more* of it to get *rid* of the hangover. It's the perfect consumer product. Imagine making yourself necessary."

"I just want to get this straight," he said. "The people who called your husband on Friday offered him a job, is that right?"

"That's what I understood." She leaned on the counter. "Why are you so interested in my husband, Officer? Just lay it on me: what's he done?"

"He hasn't done anything as far as we know. It's just that . . . we think he might be in some trouble."

"What kind of trouble?"

"We're not sure." She looked at him, seemingly lost in thought. "Did you ever hire that PI?" he asked.

"Your boss offered to be of use, so I didn't. Should I have?"

"No," he said.

"You don't think my husband is fucking some bimbo, do you?"

He hesitated a moment. "No, Ma'am. I don't."

"Well, you don't know him, trust me."

"It doesn't sound like I'd want to."

"No . . ." she said, rubbing an invisible mark off the counter-top. "You'd like him. Everyone *likes* him. He tries to be good."

"Is that why you tolerate his behaviour?"

"I don't tolerate it. I live with it."

"You've got plenty of choices, Mrs. Eldwin. You could leave him. You could kick him out. Hell, you could kill him."

She gave him a weird look. "You know, he tells me I should. Sometimes I think he's just trying to preempt my anger, but I know he thinks he doesn't deserve me."

"Do you think that?"

"Everyone deserves their fate. You know that story about the rattlesnake that asks the horse to carry him across a flooded river?"

"I haven't heard that one."

"Snake says, Take me to safety, and the horse tells him to forget it, he'll bite her if she lets him near. The snake says, If I bite you, we both die, and the horse sees his point and lets him get on her back. Halfway across, he bites her. You've killed us both, she says, why did you do that?"

"Because it's my nature," said Wingate.

"Right. How can I hate him for his nature?"

"You don't have to love his nature, but you don't have to live with it, either."

She finally poured herself a drink. "You talk like a man who's never been in love." He watched her drain the Grand Marnier in one long draught. "You get used to being bitten when you're in love. You find yourself getting used to the poison. You even start to crave it."

She was pitiful. He couldn't rule out that she was crazy enough to tie her own husband to a chair in their basement and chop off his hand. Maybe Claire Eldwin was the "her" that needed saving. "Do you mind if I take a look around?"

"Hey, *mi casa*, etcetera."

He thanked her and got up from the table, went down the hallway behind the living room. It was a nicely appointed house with some decent paintings on the walls and shelves of books and CDs. The house spoke of people who spent money easily. So where did it come from? There were bookshelves in the hallway full of paperbacks and piles of magazines with their spines hanging over the edge of the shelves. He picked one off the top: a copy of *People* from a couple of years ago. He pushed the door open that led into the master bedroom, with its neatly made bed. He was out of Mrs. Eldwin's view now, and he pulled on a pair of black gloves and opened the closet doors. Four seasons' worth of slacks and pants and dresses and dress shirts hung from a bar. He ran his hand along the shelf above and then quietly clapped the dust off his gloved fingertips.

There was nothing of interest in the drawers, nor in the bathroom. On one of the bedside tables, he found a pile of paper with one of the drafts of Eldwin's story on it. It was written over with small cuts and corrections. Eldwin had crossed out the word *gaspingly* and replaced it with *mind-manglingly*. Wingate looked more closely at the sentence. He thought the word Eldwin had probably wanted was *horrorstruck*. He made sure the papers looked the way he'd found them.

He retreated to the hallway. A guestroom with a convertible couch was across from the bedroom. Some books lay piled on the couch, leaning against one of the arms. The room next to it appeared to be Eldwin's office, and Wingate spent a little more time in it, shuffling through papers on the desk. These appeared to be pages from the Great Canadian Novel. From what he could tell at a quick glance, Eldwin had been working on a section that took place in a mining town in northern Ontario. It looked as if Eldwin did most of his composing on his desktop computer, a bulky PC model at least six years old. Listening for Mrs. Eldwin, he leaned down under the desk and turned the computer on from the hard drive. It bonged softly and took two minutes to boot up, and then Wingate quickly searched the root directory for text files. He found the first four chapters of "The Mystery of Bass Lake," but there was no evidence of the replacement chapters he'd told Portman he was going to send. He stared at the screen and then tried to open Outlook to go through Eldwin's email, but the program was password-protected. Wingate blinked at the empty box and then typed in Verity and Verityforms, knowing he was just shooting in the dark, and neither worked. He couldn't remember the DNS number from the back of the mannequin, but he was pretty sure that wouldn't have worked either. He shut the computer down and then stood in the office a moment or two longer, looking at the shelves. The books here were mostly hardcovers, recent fiction in English, as well as some of the classics in old paperbacks. Tolstoy and Joyce. Chesterton, Gogol, and Graham Greene. On a higher shelf, Trollope and Flaubert and the essays of Michel de Montaigne. He realized these books were in the original French. He breathed in deeply and sighed an arrow of air out of his mouth. He wasn't sure what any of this meant, apart from the fact that this guy was obviously hoping to punch above his weight.

Back in the hallway, he saw a closed door and, checking behind himself to be sure Mrs. Eldwin was keeping busy with her bottle, he went to open it. Behind it were stairs leading to the basement. He unsnapped the strap on his holster and switched on the light.

As he descended, he could see the basement wasn't anything like the one in the video. It was upholstered and furnished: almost a separate apartment. There was an expensive-looking bar with four stools behind it and it was fully stocked with good whiskies and other liquors. A couch faced a fireplace and there was an end table stocked with interior design magazines. At the far end of the room stood a stationary bike and a rowing machine. He walked over to the bar and stood beside it. It was difficult to imagine the Eldwins as big entertainers, and he concluded that all of this, all this good living, was for them alone. There was a pair of birthday cards standing on the bar. He picked one of them up. It was one of those cards with an earnest, rhyming message on the inside on the subject of the inverse relationship between the recipient's age and her beauty. The handwritten note said, *You're a flower that blooms more beautifully every year. I'm grateful for everything you've given me, my love, even if I'm the toadstool in your garden. Lots of love, Colin.* Wingate stared at the card. Every relationship was a mystery.

He returned upstairs and put his cap back on. "Find what you were looking for?" she asked him.

"I wasn't looking for anything," he said. "Just seeing if anything jumped out at me."

She swayed a little. He imagined she'd been able to get a couple more stiff drinks into her while he'd been snooping. "Did anything *jump* out at you?"

"No."

"Well, then you can have that drink."

He sat down at the table and let her pour him one. She put it down in front of him, but he didn't touch it. "Do you mind if I ask you a personal question?"

"Before wasn't personal?"

"I was just wondering how the two of you afford all of this. I mean, Colin isn't a successful writer —"

"*Yet*," she said.

"Right, yet. And you take in dogs. Does that pay well?"

"It pays okay. But not enough for all *this*," she said, sweeping her arm out. "That's what you're asking?"

"Yes."

"My parents died in a car accident six years ago and I got everything, including a large settlement. It was our chance to start over. I put everything into this house I thought he'd like to have. But I guess it's not enough."

"I'm sorry. About your parents."

"You lose everyone eventually, or they lose you. There's nothing to be done about it."

He stood out on the sidewalk, looking back at the house. From the front, a nondescript, one-storey bungalow on a country sidestreet. There was no hint that a crazy, heartbroken woman lived behind that door, nor a man who could inspire the kinds of passionate feelings he'd seemed to inspire in his wife and, by her report, others. The world of the case had fully opened up now; so many parts of it were in motion. In his mind, he saw the elements moving over each other, emerging out of the fog of hints, beginning to jockey for position in the play of cause and effect, relationships and connections . . .

Suddenly, he realized why the view of the back garden had rattled him. In the most recent chapter of the Bass Lake story, the father had brought the body to a house with a flagstone path and a fountain. And – he turned and looked behind himself – a willow tree. There was one across the street, a huge, healthy willow with a wide trunk, its long green leaves cascading over the lawn it stood on. It was as if Eldwin had rearranged the elements of his own house for his story. There was nothing strange about that – writers had to draw on something. What was strange was that he'd had a fictional character bringing a dead body here, to *his* house.

He looked back toward the bungalow. He was imagining Mrs. Eldwin ranging madly through that huge backyard, waving a half-empty bottle of Grand Marnier at the heavens. They needed something else to fall into place now, something that would bridge the unknowns. He reached into his pocket with a gloved hand and removed the computer mouse he'd stolen from Eldwin's office. He felt he already knew what Fraser would tell him when he ran the prints. He got back into his cruiser and pointed it east.

] 15 [

Thursday, May 26

Her alarm went off at 5 a.m. Someone had reprogrammed the
LED clock beside the bed to flash HAPPY BIRTHDAY OLD GIRL.
She was sixty-two.

She brushed and washed up and in the time between getting
out of bed and coming out of the bathroom, a glint of red dawn
had appeared in the corner of the window. For the rest of
Wednesday, she'd waited by her phone in her office like some
disappointed prom queen, but no one of interest had called.
She'd spent part of the afternoon obsessing over how much
blood, exactly, it would take to paint the message they'd seen.
Surely, it was too much blood? For the rest of the day, the site
had shown the vile sequence over and over. By the time the
night shift came in, Bail and Renald and Wilton had figured
that the quantity of blood required to make such an image was
at least two pints. That was a fifth of a normal person's blood.
They were killing him. And she was waiting for news that wasn't

coming. She felt that she was being played for a fool and for the first time on this case, it began to feel personal.

She'd taken her cruiser home and planned to make a drive-through breakfast at the Timmie's on 41, a birthday breakfast, perhaps, a double-double and an actual donut. Yes, a Boston Cream for her birthday, even if it *was* going to be 6 a.m.

You catch more flies with honey. She'd sugar herself up and go to meet Chip Willan and be super-sweet. That never worked with Ian Mason, but Mason had been spiritually diabetic: niceness never worked with the man. Maybe the new commander could be charmed.

Just the same, a pill to pave the way, she thought. She dressed – full uniform – and opened the sidetable drawer, but she realized she'd left them in a jacket pocket. Or she thought she had: they weren't in the jacket either. Strange. She got down on all fours (not so bad, she thought, an impossible pose even a week earlier) and searched under the bed, but it was dark, and even with all the lights on, she couldn't see into the middle of the space. She checked the other side. Nothing. Well, there was still the loose stash of Percs and Ativans and sleeping pills piled in a little pyramid inside the bathroom medicine cabinet. But when she opened the mirror, instead of the jumble of welcoming blue and white and yellow pills, there was a little bottle of extra-strength Tylenol and a note taped to it. "Fuck," she said, snatching it down.

The note, in her mother's hand, said, "Happy birthday old girl. It's a brand new day. See you at dinner."

She gripped the red-and-white Tylenol bottle in her hands, squeezing it to keep from shouting, and then she threw it against the wall behind her. She pulled a muscle in her middle back doing it, and found herself on one knee on the bathroom floor. "Goddamnit, Mother." The top of the bottle had burst off and a spray of white, useless pills was rolling around on the cold tiles. "Goddamnit." She reached forward carefully, grabbed a small handful of them, and stood. The space between her shoulderblades was cramping and uncramping. She popped three of the pills and washed them down with a handful of water. Just for that, she was going to have a greasy breakfast sandwich, too.

The sun was fully up as she pulled onto Highway 41 and headed south. She had to drive with her arms locked out straight in front of her to keep her back pressed against the seat. She was seething. What right did anyone have to take away her comforts? By acting on her own, her mother had ruined Hazel's plans to wean herself off, and she was ready to wean herself off, she'd even thought she'd begin on her birthday. But Emily had taken the choice out of her hands. She'd be getting a mouthful at dinner, that was for sure.

She pulled into the Timmie's below Kehoe Glenn, but she no longer had a taste for anything solid, all she wanted was a coffee. She'd have to manufacture her own sweetness with Willan. She was out of practice talking to others, she knew this, she didn't even need yesterday's experience at the *Record* as proof. Or her shortness with Wingate afterwards.

She wasn't entirely sure why she'd behaved the way she did. Threatening that girl. Partly because she was on Gord Sunderland's turf and that naturally made her lip curl, and of course there was the building stress associated with the case. But if she was being honest with herself, it was Becca Portman

alone who'd triggered her anger. She was Martha's age, and
shiftless and stupid. Martha hadn't found her way in the world
yet, and girls of Martha's age, perceiving diminishing returns,
are as likely to cut their hair badly and go work for idiots as they
are to dig in and try harder. She saw the possibility, in Martha,
of a future of accepting second best just to have *something* and it
terrified her. Emilia, the elder, was fully formed, even if she
didn't realize it, even if, like all first children, she felt like she'd
been sent out into the world without a complete set of tools.
But Emilia always landed on her feet; she was like her namesake,
unflappable, possessed of solid common sense, and skeptical
enough to avoid being taken in by dreamers and fools. Not so
Martha, whose life had, thus far, been stocked by a rotating cast
of lightweights, druggies, actors, depressives, and charlatans.
She'd taken one look at Becca Portman and wanted to pound
some sense into her. At least she hadn't done that.

She paid for the coffee and pulled around the corner to buy
a *Record* from one of the boxes. Maybe Portman had disobeyed
her, or Sunderland had overruled her, and Wingate would get
his chance to see things unfold in a more measured fashion. But
she opened the paper and the story wasn't there. There was no
mention of its returning, nor a reason given why it hadn't
appeared. So, whether Hazel liked it or not, the next phase of
the game was afoot.

She pulled back into traffic, the paper tossed into the back
seat. There was no traffic at 5:45 in the morning, and she could
have bombed down to Barrie in an hour, but she decided to
drive at the limit and give herself some time to think, to go
over her points. She found her mind too busy with the details
of the mannequin and the man in the chair to focus. But she

would have to put all of it aside if she wanted to get her message across to Willan.

She pulled into OPSC headquarters at ten after seven. Twenty minutes early might look desperate, she thought, and she sat in the car for another ten minutes before going in through the front doors. The middle of her back had relaxed, finally, and she was grateful she wouldn't have to look like a hunched old woman in front of her new boss. She had to be buzzed in by Willan's assistant: the building didn't open until eight. "Chip's been here since six," said the assistant, whose name was Jeremy. *He calls his boss Chip?* thought Hazel.

At seven-thirty on the button, Commander Willan came to get her from the waiting area. He offered her a hearty hand-shake, and she took his hand and shook it distractedly, taking in the man who had come down the hallway to meet her. Willan was no older than thirty-five, tall and lean, with a glossy head of long black hair tied back into a ponytail. He wore a dark blue powersuit instead of a uniform, and he had brilliant white dress sneakers on his feet. He looked like the head of an animation studio, not a police commander. He put a light hand on her back and led her into his office. She'd only seen Mason's office twice in all his reign, and it had been cluttered with official regalia, including the force's colours on a staff behind the desk. All of his awards and medals had been framed on the walls to the left and right. Nothing about Mason's office let you forget that he had it over you in rank, experience, and decoration. It had been an office to cow all opposition.

Willan's office, on the other hand, was almost bare. Gone was the dark furniture, the leather chairs, replaced by a thick glass desktop supported by heavy silver legs. The only decoration in the room was a marble pillar with a sleek black ball on top of it, turning endlessly on a jet of water. A cord from the back of it ran discreetly along the side wall to a plug.

The commander's chair was a strange, ergonomic device that he kneeled on, tucking his feet beneath him, the seat itself tilted forward at about sixty degrees. When he sat in it, it gave the impression that he might spring out of it, over the glass table, and into your lap.

Willan gestured to her to sit down and then he opened a wooden coffer on the desktop, taking a silver object from it, and pushed it over toward her. Were they going to smoke bloody cigars at seven-thirty in the morning? "Chocolate sardine?" he asked. She waved them off. "I'm an avid fisherman. And I have a sweet-tooth," he said. "So I can't resist them." He unwrapped the fish and snapped it in half between his perfect teeth. "So, what a pleasure."

"Is it?" she said.

"Absolutely. To meet the famous DI Micallef. I'm honoured."

"Well, thank you," she said. There hadn't been a trace of irony in his voice. "I'm glad we're getting a chance to talk."

"Terrific," he said. "So tell me what I can do for you."

Maybe she wouldn't have to charm this Chip Willan; he had enough charm for both of them. "Well, Commander Willan —"

"Good Lord," he said, "it's Chip, or you're outta here."

"Okay, then. Chip."

"Hazel."

"I've come to talk about the future of policing in Westmuir County."

"Sweet."

She rubbed her palms against the tops of her legs. "*Chip* . . . I know that there are fiscal issues the OPS needs to tackle, and of course, every detachment in this province needs to find efficiencies" – she cringed inwardly to use the word – "but I'm here today to say that I hope Central understands that it can use its voice within the provincial federation to protect its communities. Places like Westmuir, with its rural and small-town populations, can't be policed the same way a big city is policed, and I'm a little anxious about the things I hear, about some of the changes being discussed."

"Give me some specifics, Hazel. Specifics will help me see your issues more clearly."

"Well, one specific is the questionnaire you – your office – sent my personnel recently. Asking them for, among other things, their redeployment choices. As in, *should* there come a time when they might be redeployed, what would their prefer-ences be and so on. Before any kind of mission statement has even been issued by the OPS, to ask people where they want to go *in case* of clawbacks . . . well, I find that, with all due respect, to be a little underhanded."

"It was, wasn't it?" said Chip Willan. "I apologize for that. You have to understand, Hazel, I'm still cutting my teeth here."

She felt herself relaxing into the chair. Thank God for new blood. Was this generation one that would actually allow itself to *reason*? "Okay, I'm glad you said that. Because I really feel we really need to sit down, all levels, and talk about what *we* need, and of course, keeping all of the fiscal issues in focus. But I think it would be *educational*, it would open your eyes, to see what we do with our resources, Chip. How well Westmuir's detachments and community policing offices work and who they serve. And how, even though our police-to-population ratios seem high, they're *right* for the places we work in. Hell, you know, we're working on a case right now that couldn't possibly be handled correctly if our detachments were centralized, or if there were fewer people to work on it. People's lives *depend* on us being able to do the work we were trained to do, with the resources we need to do it with. It could be very bad for *people* if budget formulas invented for cities were applied willy-nilly to places like Westmuir County."

He was holding his hand up, warding her off comically, as if she'd overwhelmed him. "You *really* need a chocolate sardine, Hazel!" He held the box to her, and now she gratefully took one and unwrapped it. It was excellent, toothsome chocolate. He watched her eat it. After a moment, he said, "Do you ever think about the dinosaurs?"

"The dinosaurs?"

"Yeah," he said, and he leaned forward, that position that made it look like he might sail over the desk. "I mean, they were *so* successful. They had flying dinosaurs and dinosaurs that could eat the little leaves at the tops of ancient redwoods and dinosaurs the size of your pinkie. I just think about them sometimes, wonder who they were. Because they were *everywhere* and they, like, ruled the earth. But success has its costs, right? Too many dinosaur mouths, not enough trees or meat. Now, if only they'd had some smart dinosaur to tell them they had to change their ways before they screwed up all the good stuff, maybe this would still be a dinosaur planet instead of a people planet. But they didn't have that smart dinosaur so instead the universe sent a meteorite to blow all their scaly behinds to kingdom come so the planet could start over." Hazel chewed more slowly. He was smiling at her. "Dinosaur days are over. All the dinosaurs are gone. But we're not going to wait for a meteor to sort *us* out, are we? Hell, no. We're going to sort *ourselves* out. And – this is the thing, this is the *hard* thing – even though we want it to be about people, it isn't. It's about money. It's always about money. You know that and I know that. So first we show the dinosaurs in charge that we can handle the money side of things. We take the meteor hit, you know? And after that, we make it work."

She felt about as heavy as a brontosaurus. "Jesus," she said. "You had me for a minute back there. I thought everything might be okay."

"It's all good," he said.

"You'll still be paid *your* salary, is what you mean."

His eyes sparkled, as if he'd just fallen in love. "We need people like you, Hazel, people with a strong connection to the way we do things, so there's *continuity*, you know?" He put both his palms down on his desk. His body language said they'd just solved all the world's problems. "Change goes badly when systems fail to negotiate the transitions sensitively. We're not going to make that mistake here. No meteorites, you know what I mean? It's going to be more like a fine sandpaper, moving slowly over the rough patches." He was practically beaming. "I have to say, I'm so glad we had a chance to meet, Hazel. I want you to know my door is open to you, any time, for any reason."

She stood. "When's it going to happen? Can you tell me that?"

"When's what going to happen?"

"Amalgamation. Redeployments. Clawbacks." She gripped the back of the seat she'd been sitting in, where she presumed she'd looked like a complete fool. "When are you going to start fucking us?"

"That's salty," he said. He stood up behind his desk, and his ergonomic little chair rolled back silently. "The needs and views of all our partners in policing will be solicited before anything happens."

She went to the door and turned around. "I wonder how soon after policing standards go to hell up here you'll be telling your bosses in Toronto that we're not 'managing our resources' well. Because the blame for a fucked-up system always lands on the ones who have to live in it, not the ones who invent it."

"Don't fall for that kind of thinking," said Willan. "You invent your own reality, Detective Inspector Micallef. And if you want it to be one in which your higher-ups are trying to suffocate you, you *will* wither away."

"God, you sound like someone I know. She doesn't live in the real world, either."

"Happy birthday, by the way."

"Yeah, thanks," she said.

] 16 [

They'd put together a nice evening for her, something to mark her birthday and the beginning of a new chapter in her life, but none of it went the way they were planning. When Emily heard the door to the downstairs apartment slam shut, she knew Hazel wasn't going to be the most receptive guest at the evening's celebrations, and she put her hand on her granddaughter's wrist and prevented her from opening the door to the basement. "Judging from the sound of your mother's boots on the parquet, Martha, I'd give her a couple more minutes."

"I can handle my own mother."

"Just handle her in a few minutes. She's going to be feeling a little under the weather tonight."

Martha released the doorknob and stood back a couple of feet, as if expecting the door to dissolve and admit her on its own terms. She and her grandmother listened to the sounds emanating from below, a combination of heavy footfalls and hoarse mutterings that seemed liberally sprinkled with language one didn't usually use in front of a child, even a thirty-three-year-old one.

"Son of a fucking bitch," they heard, and then the sound of a drawer being thrown.

"She *does* sound a little under the weather," said Martha, grinning nervously at Emily. "Was she sick when she left for work this morning?"

"Something like that," said Emily.

"MOTHER!!" came Hazel's voice from below, volcanic.

"You want to go down there?"

"Maybe I'll wait another few minutes," said Martha.

"Hand me that bottle."

Martha passed her a full two-sixer of J&B.

The basement apartment was littered with thrown things: two full drawers, towels, shoes, sections from various newspapers. She was puffing in a corner of the room like a bull. The door to the upstairs had opened, and she heard her mother descending. "Are you armed?" said Emily from behind the basement door.

"You better not be coming down here without something for my back."

Her mother opened the door six inches and held out the bottle of J&B. "This is the best I can do."

Hazel strode to the door and snatched the bottle out of her mother's hand. She was beginning to feel the heebie-jeebies: it had been almost twenty-four hours since her last pill. Waves of nausea accompanied the anxiety. There was a tumbler in the bathroom meant for drinking water out of; she filled it to the rim. When she came out, Emily was standing in the middle of the room, looking around at the mess, her arms behind her back. "You want a straw?"

"You had no right."

"I had no right."

"I had surgery seventeen days ago. I have *pain* and I have a prescription for pain *killers*. What the hell were you thinking?"

Her mother was dressed nicely, in a grey wool dress with a thin, shiny black belt around her waist. Elegant. She hadn't put her shoes on and she was tilting back and forth on her heels in her black hose. "First off," she said, "keep your voice down. There are people upstairs planning a nice evening for you and they don't need to hear you swearing like a fusilier."

"Fuck 'em," said Hazel. "Where are my pills?"

"You really want to know?"

"Yes."

Emily pushed past her in the bathroom doorway, grabbing Hazel's arm on the way in. Whiskey sloshed onto the cold tiles. She tugged her toward the toilet bowl. "There they are," Emily said, lifting the lid. "They're down there somewhere. If you can't find one, maybe you should just lap the water. You might as well, with the mess you're making of yourself."

Hazel saw something on the floor behind the toilet, and shook herself loose of her mother's grip and leaned forward to close the toilet lid. She sat down on it, straddling the toilet tank, and put the glass of whiskey down on the floor as she felt around behind. She was sure she'd seen an escapee, a pill that had bounced off the toilet rim and rolled onto the floor. Her finger grazed it, pushing it farther along the floor, but then she had it. She closed her hand around it and stood. Her mother was shaking her head ruefully.

"Look at you," she said. "Look how small you are now."

"Get out."

"Give me the pill."

"You're not supposed to go cold turkey. Did you know that?"

"Your daughter's here," Emily said. "You want her to see you like this? I can call her down right now."

"You're lying."

Emily turned her head toward the door. "Martha!" There was nothing for a second, but then they heard footsteps coming down.

"Jesus Christ," said Hazel, hanging her head. "It's my *birthday*. This is what you do to me on my birthday?"

"*For* you," said Emily. "Not *to* you. Now give me that pill."

"Can I come in?" Martha was standing just inside the apartment. "Mum?"

Emily took a step toward Hazel, a careful step, like she was approaching a mad dog, and she put her hand out. "You're an addict, Hazel. Now give me that pill."

She turned her fist over into her mother's hand and opened it. The pill fell out silently into Emily's palm. Emily looked at it and then, to Hazel's surprise, her mother popped it into her mouth. "What the hell are you doing?"

"It's a Tylenol," said Emily. "After all this nonsense, I need one. Now go say hello to your daughter."

But Martha had crept slowly into the room and she was already standing in the doorway. "Mum?"

"Sweetie," said Hazel, going to take her child in her arms. She tried to ignore the nausea roiling inside her. "What a wonderful surprise."

————

She did her best to behave. Glynnis had made duck breast with a tart raspberry sauce that made Hazel's stomach flip when she smelled it, but once she started eating, her gut settled down. It was, frankly, one of the most delicious things she'd ever eaten. And Andrew made a serious toast, one without a single euphemism in it, wishing her a year of renewal and happiness, a year of closeness with those she loved, and success in her work, and the entire time, Glynnis had sat beside her new husband with her glass raised, beaming at Hazel. Was she happy because she knew with Hazel back to work she'd be out of her house soon, the devil in her basement? Or was she – this strange, strange woman – genuinely happy to see Hazel up and about, despite the fact that only six days ago, she'd caught her husband feeding her spare ribs in the bath? Nothing had ever come of that, Emily had been right, no angry words, no delayed consequences. It really had been, in Glynnis's eyes, an instance of her husband "caring for another human being." It wasn't right. It should have blown up in all their faces. Is that what Hazel had wanted? Maybe. But in that, she had failed as well.

Martha sent her mother shy looks of love and sadness from the other side of the table. They hadn't seen each other since February, when Hazel had felt well enough to go down to Toronto for an afternoon and they'd had coffee. Their meetings didn't always end well. The undercurrent of Hazel's worries about the girl infected a lot of what she said, and Martha heard her mother's criticisms of her life in everything. Hazel could not offer to pay for Martha's lattes anymore when they met because such a gesture – no matter how natural it might have been for a mother to buy her daughter a cup of coffee – Martha saw as a judgment on her joblessness, her failure to choose a path and stay on it, her eternal singleness, her at-least-once-yearly need to be bailed out of some mess. All of this in a three-dollar cup of coffee. When Martha had been in her late twenties, Hazel and Andrew had talked about it all as a phase – she was young; she would find her way; this generation started everything later; she'd be sorted out by the time she was thirty. Then, after the breakup, Hazel excused her daughter's rootlessness as a reaction to what was happening to her parents. But now she was thirty-three, and there was no sign of her waking up. What was going to happen? Would she find someone to share her life with, who would shoulder part of the burden that loving this girl entailed? What if she or Andrew died? What if Martha became dependent on her sister? Would she ever be able to stop worrying about this child?

And yet, here she was, her thin white skin shimmering in front of the candles (although not the *special* candles), and that wan, loving smile on her face. How could she not want to save her, this gorgeous, lost child? Hazel reached across the tabletop and took one of Martha's hands in hers. "This is the best birthday present I've gotten so far." She was, perhaps, now a little drunk on wine and whiskey, but Martha still smiled broadly at her and accepted the compliment. "Thank you for coming."

"Happy birthday, Mum."

"Another toast," said Andrew, standing. They all raised their glasses again. "To family," he said, and again, Glynnis was beaming that bright, terrifying gaze of pure joy at her. But she drank and the clocks struck ten and she was drunk.

They shooed her out of the kitchen with a cup of camomile tea, and Martha beckoned her into the sitting room, near the door.

"Your birthday's not over yet," she said. They went down the hallway together and Hazel saw the glass table in the front room was mounded with a small pile of gifts. They sat down together on the couch. "Mine first," said Martha, passing Hazel a limp, wrapped package. She hefted it in her hands; it was a blouse or a blanket or something like that. "It's a hat," said Hazel.

"So close."

She unwrapped it. It was a handmade case for a throw pillow, a needlepoint that was a painstaking copy of a photograph from Martha's childhood, of herself at the age of three on her mother's shoulders. It amazed Hazel and she held it in her lap, staring at it. "My god, Martha. This is beautiful, just beautiful." She leaned across the couch and held her tightly. "You *made* this?"

"You didn't know I could needlepoint, did you?" Her face was bright with joy. "Well, I just learned. And it's not easy. I pulled that apart three times before I got it done."

"It must have taken you months."

"I calculated it took about two hundred hours," said Martha. "I figure if I wanted to sell that thing and make minimum wage I'd have to charge, like, twenty-three hundred for it."

Hazel laughed, but she was already cancelling the things she wanted to say that she knew would be translated in Martha's head into something dark. It was hard to think straight, with the J&B in her and the wine, and the withdrawal symptoms, which had begun to make her sweat, like she was running a fever. But she had to be careful. Any comments on how much free time her daughter had, the fact that the gift had been made, not bought, anything around the idea that maybe this newfound talent was a "calling," reference to the fact that Hazel would have to buy the pillow to put in the case herself, anything, to be sure, that wasn't unalloyed gratitude. "Amazing," she said. "You're amazing."

"Am I?"

"Yes. You surprise me."

"In a good way?"

There it was, thought Hazel, she'd already gone through the bad door without realizing it. But she was drunk enough to shimmy back over the threshold. "If you hadn't shown up here tonight, sweetie, this day would have had no saving graces. You're a miracle."

Martha hesitated, and then she allowed the compliment with a warm smile. "And you're drunk."

"Let's open the rest of these impersonal, pointless gifts, shall we?"

"Absolutely."

Martha lined them up, the smaller gifts in front, the larger ones behind. Hazel was touched to see her mother's handwriting on one of the envelopes as well as Andrew's. There were five more gifts in total. She reached for one of them, but then pulled her hand back, feeling a chill run up her spine. "Maybe we should wait for the others?"

"Sure," said her daughter. They sat silently for a minute, Hazel staring at the wrapped boxes. "What was all the shouting about earlier?" said Martha quietly.

"Huh?" said Hazel.

"I heard some shouting."

"Oh . . . it was just a rough day."

"It's hard being in this situation, huh? Living here. With Dad and Glynnis."

"It's temporary, honey." She recognized the handwriting on all of the cards, she thought.

"Is that what you were upset about?"

"It's okay," said Hazel.

"Are you listening to me?"

She turned sharply to Martha. "Sorry, sweetie. Honestly, you don't have to worry. Today had nothing to do with you."

"Why do you think I'd be concerned only if it had some-thing to do with me?"

"I don't . . ." She got up from the couch, with difficulty, and wiped her hands on her slacks. "Are all these gifts from you and Nanna and the, um, Pedersens?"

"Mum, why don't you want to talk to me?"

Hazel looked down at her daughter. It was getting hard to think straight. It felt like her brain was bumping around inside her head. Pay attention, she told herself. "I do. You know . . . recovering from surgery has been hard. Going back to work has been hard. And it was a rough sixty-second birthday. But it's better now."

"Nanna is worried about you."

"I know, but I promise you," Hazel said, looking Martha in the eye, "that everything is okay and that everything is *going* to be okay."

"Good," said Martha.

Emily emerged from the kitchen and started down the hall. "You ready for us?"

"Actually . . . Mum, if you wouldn't mind, could you pass me the phone?"

Emily gave her a look and then retreated to the kitchen and came back with the portable. "You want to invite someone else over?"

"Sort of," she said, and she dialled the number of the station house. Wilton answered. "Spencer? Who's on shift tonight?" She listened. "Will you ask MacDonald to put down what he's doing and come over here, please?"

"What?" said Emily.

Hazel cupped the phone. "I'll explain in a second." She put the phone back to her ear. "Yeah, as soon as he can."

She passed the phone back to her mother. Andrew and Glynnis were standing in the hallway behind her now. Andrew was drying a wineglass. "What's going on?"

"We had a bit of a scare at the detachment on Tuesday. A gift that we weren't expecting."

"Like what?"

"I don't think you want to know," she said.

Martha had stepped away from the sitting room and was standing in the hallway behind her mother. She quietly took Hazel's hand. "There's nothing to worry about," Hazel said. "Sean MacDonald is a trained scene-of-crime officer and he'll know what to do."

"Scene of *crime*?" Emily said, rather incredulously.

"It's nothing to worry about."

"Is he going to blow up your presents or something?" Martha asked.

Hazel squeezed her hand. "No. But he'll tell us if I can open them."

Glynnis made some more camomile tea while they waited, and they sat in the kitchen together, stiffly. "Most of that stuff in there is from us," Andrew said. "And the rest is from people you know. The Chandlers came by with something. Your deputy dropped a couple of things off."

"You saw him? Wingate?"

"*I* did," said Glynnis.

"And he said the gifts were from *him*?"

"He said they were from your staff. Nothing was ticking, as far as I can tell," she said.

"Well, I still think we should wait for MacDonald."

"Never a dull moment," said Andrew.

The sergeant arrived ten minutes later, and she took him aside and explained her concerns. He nodded seriously. He held his kit bag up. "I got a chemical swiper thing in here," he said. "And some litmus strips."

"You're going to test whether my gifts are too acidic, Sean?"

"Maybe."

"Just get to it. Don't blow up the house."

He vanished into the sitting room, and she stood apart from the others, waiting. She couldn't untense her hands. After a few minutes, she took a couple more steps backward down the hall. Glynnis poked her head out of the kitchen. "You want us to wait outside?"

"Or in Fort Leonard, maybe?" called Andrew.

"I'm sorry, okay? Just better safe than . . ."

"Than what?" asked Glynnis.

"Never mind."

MacDonald whistled while he went over the packages. Five

minutes turned into ten. Finally, he was done and he emerged into the hallway.

"No strange lumps, no wires sticking out, no oilstains, nothing stinky or rattly. No animals or bodily fluids. I'd say you're all clear. Unless you don't like fifteen-year-old Glenfarclas."

"What?"

"Ray Greene sent you a nice bottle."

She frowned at him. "How do you know that?"

"I had to open the packages. But I resealed them. Nice to get something from your old deputy, huh? No hard feelings."

"All right, thank you, Sean. You can go now."

He smiled at her – he loved doing SOCO stuff and the opportunity so rarely came up – and she told him to wait a minute. She went back into the kitchen and sliced him a thick piece of the vanilla cake Glynnis had made, and put it on a plate and brought it back to him. "Just leave the plate with Melanie when you're done."

"Should I frisk it first?"

"Sure, you do that."

She asked Martha to help her bring the gifts downstairs. Knowing that there was something from Ray had put her off opening the presents more than the possibility of finding a body part or a bomb had. Some nerve: not a word for months, and then a birthday present. It pissed her off.

Martha put the gifts on the table downstairs and helped her mother arrange the room. It was still a mess from earlier. When she was done, she said she'd leave her alone and maybe see her in the morning. Then she stood at the door to the stairs, looking forlorn and lost.

"What is it, honey? Why the faraway look?"

Martha shook her head instead of speaking, a worrisome prelude to tears. But she settled herself down and said, "That was weird, huh?"

"Yeah. A little. That why you're upset?"

"Well, yeah. I don't like to think of you being in danger."

"Aw, sweetie, that's so nice of you. But don't you get all —"

"And . . . well, also . . . it's just . . . look at all the people who care about you. Who love you. Those guys upstairs, and that guy coming from the police station to make sure you're safe. All these people sending you gifts."

"Maybe they're just all afraid of me. They're *appeasing* me."

"I know," Martha said distractedly. "It's just . . ."

"It's just what, sweetie?"

Martha leaned against the wall beside the door. The whole room was between them. "You have so many people in your life. So does Dad. You're both just . . . naturally likeable. I wish I had that talent."

"No one sees themselves the way others see them," Hazel said. "You could never see yourself the way I do. And for your information, I don't feel that loveable myself."

"Well, obviously, other people disagree."

"Maybe you just need to get out and be around people more, hon. You can't have people in your life if you're hiding from them."

Martha nodded, her tongue stiff against the inside of her upper lip. Hazel had known it was the wrong thing to say the instant it was out of her mouth. Her daughter stood up straight against the wall. "So I'm living under a rock? What do you know about how I spend my time?"

"I'm sorry, I didn't mean to accuse you –"

"I go to the gym, I go out with friends, I go to the library. You think Toronto is the kind of place you strike up conversations with people on the street? And then they come home for a cup of Lemon Zinger and you're BFFs?"

"You're what?"

"Never mind." She turned and opened the door sharply. Hazel crossed the room quickly and put her hand on her daughter's.

"*Hey* – wait . . . I'm sorry, Martha. Honestly. I hate saying the wrong thing. I only want you to be happy and feel loved."

"I know," said Martha, quietly. She was already embarrassed that she'd shown her vulnerability to her mother. She was always see-sawing back and forth between appearing strong and being helpless. She hated it. "I should let you get some rest." She still hadn't looked her mother in the eye.

"Do you accept my apology?"

"I do," said Martha.

"Will I see you in the morning?"

"Yeah."

She let her go.

When the door closed, Hazel went over to the couch and sat down. She pulled the gift that had to be the bottle over toward herself and opened the card attached to it. The card said *We can still raise a glass, right? Hope this is still your brand. Ray.* She felt less pissed off after reading the card, but the discomfort remained.

Her mother had bought her a beautiful blouse; Glynnis and Andrew a matching pair of slacks. The gift from Wingate was a copy of *Great Expectations*. Sweet man. She'd never read

Dickens. Nor had she ever had great expectations – it was nice that he thought it still possible.

The final gift was from Robert and Gail Chandler, a long, purple silk scarf. It was gorgeous. She wrapped it around her neck and then pulled Greene's bottle toward herself and stared at it a long time.

It had been more than thirty-six hours since her last Percocet and her nerves had been crying out for solace ever since. But the adrenaline that had been roaring through her since the visit to Willan had done some of the work she'd counted on the pill to do. To painkill, yes, but also to numb, to reduce the noise in her head. After her birthday evening, though, she could feel the noise returning. The burn in her guts, the dizziness, the shakes. She recalled the small object wrapped in tinfoil that she'd had in her pants pocket yesterday. She went to the closet and found it still in the pocket of the black slacks she'd worn yesterday. She unwrapped the pill and held it in her fingers. How could something that small take such a hold of a person? She lifted it to her mouth and touched her tongue to it. It was bitter, like aspirin, and she thought she could feel it sizzling. In a day or two, it would begin to get easier: she believed this now. She was on the dividing line between one life and another and she need do nothing to cross it; the line was coming toward her. On the other side of it was a manageable pain, a clearer head, maybe even her own pillow and sheets. And, more importantly, she was going to need a clear head from here on in. There was a chance to save the man in the video; a chance to save "her," whoever she was.

She went into the bathroom and flushed the pill down the toilet. It turned in smaller and smaller circles, arrowing in on something like it was supposed to do in the body, and then it was gone into the grey tube in the middle of the bowl as if down a throat and she pictured it streaming end over end into the sewer. From one bottomless place to another. It was progress.

Friday, May 27

She was in early on Friday morning and called a meeting with Wingate, Sergeant Geraldine Costamides, and Kraut Fraser. These were her most senior people now and she was going to need them. After confirming that nothing had changed on the website, she ushered them all into the office and closed the door behind them.

"Where are we with the prints from Eldwin's house?" she began.

"I had to send the mouse down to Spere," said Fraser. "It's going to take more than powder to get a print off that thing."

"Why?" She noticed Wingate was looking down at the ground.

"Well, your cubscout there was standing in a room full of things Eldwin's touched, including a keyboard —"

"— how'm I supposed to smuggle a *keyboard* out of Eldwin's house?"

"Anyway," Fraser continued, "there are about two hundred imprints of the guy's index finger all on the same spot – *click click click!* – a giant smudge where his thumb spends half its life, and a latent of half a pinky. Then there's a partial print of the palm, from the base of the thumb. So Spere's going to have to collect and collate digitally. He told me he'd have an answer by the end of the day."

"Fine," said Hazel, and she shot Wingate a look. "Don't worry about it. Let's focus on our next move."

"Which is?"

"Geraldine, I have a job for you if you're up for it." Costamides turned her attention to her. Hazel didn't get much chance to work with this sergeant, as Costamides preferred to work nights, but she liked her. "How'd you like to eat crow on behalf of your commanding officer?"

"I'm listening."

"I browbeat Gordon Sunderland's young deputy into can-celling yesterday's instalment of 'The Mystery of Bass Lake.' I'd like you to go back over there and employ your charm in shaking loose the chapter that didn't appear. And any others they've received since we visited their offices on Wednesday."

"I think I can do that."

Hazel knew she could. It was Gerry on whom the job of wrangling difficult favours often fell. She had a certain way of holding herself – solid and sad all at once – that made it hard for people to say no to her. The irony was that, unlike most people, Costamides did not have the face she deserved. She was one of the most joyful, vital people on the force. Hazel thanked her, and Costamides left right away for the newspaper's offices.

"I'll check up on Spere," said Fraser, and he left too.

When the door was closed, Wingate said, "Sorry about the mouse. I didn't know it would be that hard to get fingerprints off —"

"I told you not to worry about it," she said, and she sat behind her desk.

"I'm sure Gerry will get you what you need from the *Record*."

"Yeah. She will." She pulled the cellphone off the table and pocketed it. "In the good old days, I would have had Ray handle it. He could be subtle." She shook her head sadly. "You know he sent me a bottle for my birthday."

"That was nice of him."

"I guess that means I should call."

"Maybe you should," said Wingate. "Maybe if . . ."

"Don't finish that thought."

He didn't. "You know," he said quietly, "back in Toronto, people didn't get as close as you guys do up here. We didn't live on top of each other."

"It's probably better that way."

"I'm not so sure," he said. "I like the sense that everything matters here. I like people taking things personally."

"Well, you'll have plenty of opportunity to take things personally in Port Dundas, James. Be careful what you wish for." She was looking at the computer screen. The dripping SAVE HER was revealing itself anew. An awful lot of planning had gone into what they'd seen over the last seven days, almost as if the people who had uploaded this material knew their audience better than it knew itself. Hazel entertained, for just a moment, an inside element, someone within these walls who was communicating, either on purpose or unwittingly, with the perpetrators. But what made better sense was that the people who were driving this macabre charade had a strong grasp of investigative process. They knew it would not take long after the mannequin was found for the police to make their way to the website. And at that point, they'd have the attention of the OPS for as long as they wanted it. It made her feel like there was a ghost sitting on her shoulder. That made her think of what was sitting on her other shoulder. "I don't think I told you I met with Commander Willan. You know, Mason's replacement?"

"You didn't mention it. What's he like?"

"Stalin with a surfboard." She sighed. "He sees me as the rope bridge all you young folks are going to walk over to get to the promised land of efficient policing. He basically called me a dinosaur."

"All the dinosaurs I've known were the best police, Hazel."

"The dinosaurs may be good police, James, but they can never solve their own extinctions."

Wingate found himself riven by the image of his superior officer looking crestfallen behind her desk. She seemed more defeated now than all the times he'd visited her at home, when she'd been in nearly unbearable pain, looking tiny on her couch in a terrycloth robe. "Skip? Are you okay?"

"I'm okay," she said.

"Because you seem —"

"I know," she said. "Apart from having a man trapped in my computer, live animals and body parts appearing on my desk, a CO who thinks I've outlived my usefulness, and expensive gifts coming from missing friends, I also happen to have a pill problem. And it appears I'm to quit in the midst of all this nonsense. So, I'm slightly less than okay."

"Is there anything I can do?"

"No," she said firmly. "Just do your job and don't think about me. We need to get in front of this."

"I should have thought through what I was doing at Eldwin's."

"You did. You're not a dinosaur, remember that. Now go back to your desk and have a good think. At the rate things are going for that man in the chair, we all need to get on our game."

] 18 [

Sergeant Geraldine Costamides had been successful, as Hazel knew she would. She returned to the station house looking slightly shame-faced, which meant that she'd spun a particularly good story for the benefit of Becca Portman and managed to shake loose everything they needed. There were two unpublished chapters now. Costamides made copies of them and passed them out to Hazel, Wingate, and Fraser. Then she stood at the lectern, her glasses hanging around her neck. She cleared her throat. "Are we ready? Everyone tucked in with their hot milk?"

"Go ahead, Gerry," said Hazel.

Costamides lifted her glasses clear of her long chin and settled them on the bridge of her nose. She curled the pages she held in her hands and clacked the bottom of them against the lectern before laying them flat. "The Mystery of Bass Lake," she began, "chapters four and five."

Nick Wise had been sitting at his kitchen table, the newspaper open in front of him, his pen hovering over the page, when his

doorbell rang. Ah, he thought, "damaged," but then there was
the sound of a car driving off and he laid his pen down and
went to the door.

What he saw on his front stoop froze his blood. Wise looked
hurriedly up and down the street, but there was no one and he
quickly stepped around the form and got his arms under the
greasy tarp. There was a note pinned to it with a fishhook, but
it would have to wait until he got inside. He struggled with
the weight and finally got it into his living room, rivulets of
sweat running off his chin. Then he went back to the door and
shut it hard, turning the lock and putting on the chain.

He stood in the hallway looking at the grey thing staining
his fireplace rug. He'd moved away to make sure she'd never
find him again, but here she was. The bitch. He leaned over the
tarp and unpinned the note. It said, "If you love somebody, let
them go, for if they return, they were always yours." He put
the note aside and slipped his finger under the edge of the
wet tarp and slid it back. It fell away from its contents with a
wet slap against the floor and there she was, at least, there
was most of her. She lay headless on his floor, immutable as an
eternal verity. He reached behind himself and pulled a chair
toward him. "What am I going to do with you?" he said.
Brackish water was damaging his floor. She stank. He sighed
heavily. "Fine. Wait here."

He went out the back, across the big lawn to the garage, and
got into his car. The old house was almost two hundred kilometres away, but obviously, whatever plans he had for a quiet
afternoon were shot, so he might as well drive. Two hours later,
entering the city, he felt like the past two years had never happened: he was still in that city, still living that life. He drove in

along the lakeside highway, up past the no-longer-new baseball stadium, through the bustle of Chinatown, and up into the university district. There, he turned onto Cherry Tree Lane, drove under the chestnut trees, and parked. Perhaps there had once been cherry trees here. Maybe the street was misnamed. He stood on his old front porch under one of the hundred-year-old chestnut trees and turned to take in the view he'd had for so many years: the two little parks, the old church. But there was no time for nostalgia: he had a mouldering body lying in his front room.

A path in the alleyway between houses led to a gate. He pulled the little string that opened the latch and went into the little laneway separating them. There was a second gate leading into his old backyard; the same old string that lifted the latch hung out from between the slats. In the tiny yard behind – there had only ever been enough space there for a couple of tomato plants in tubs and maybe a little pot of basil – he went directly to the corner farthest away from the gate and got on his knees. Luckily, nobody walked back here and the soil was pretty loose, so he could dig at it with his hands. How he hated to get his nails all dirty, but this had to be done, and so he dug concertedly until his nails scraped against the top of something made of wood. He worked around the object until he'd revealed a little damaged casket big enough to hold a bowling ball.

No one had seen him. He knew people barely paid attention in cities. You could get away with anything in cities if you were just a bit careful. You could get away with murder.

He drove at a good clip back to the house, made it in ninety minutes, and parked in the rear. Before he went in, he grabbed a little round tin from the shed in the garden, of the type that once held pastilles. Her body was exactly where he'd left it (he'd had, perhaps, an ounce of doubt about that, considering the fact that it had found its way to his house), and he kneeled beside it and opened the little wooden box. Her head – green, shrivelled, hollow – was inside. He laid it on the floor, face-up, pressing the two halves of her cut throat together. Dirt trickled out of her dry eye sockets. The little pastille tin was full of fishhooks and he used them to pin her head to her neck, a neat little row of black, gleaming stitches. When the last one was on, she sat bolt upright in her place and swivelled her face to him. Her bright, brown eyes came through the dark of her sockets like headlights coming out of a tunnel. "Hello, Nick," she said. "Long time."

"Not long enough," he said.

Sergeant Costamides laid the pages down flat and slipped her glasses off. "Well, that was interesting."

Her audience appeared riveted. "Keep going," said Hazel.

"I just want to get this straight. Someone has dropped off a two-year-old corpse at this gentleman's house, and he's not in the least surprised to see it, so he goes back to his old house –"

"– in Toronto," said Wingate.

"Yes, and digs up the victim's head so he can have a chat with her."

Fraser studied his copy of the story. He said, "That seems to be it."

"Okay," said Costamides, and she smiled brightly at them. "Just checking. Chapter five."

"What am I going to do with you?" said Nick Wise, leaning against his bathroom door. The dead girl was standing at his sink, gazing at herself in the mirror.

"I look like shit," she said.

"You look like death warmed over." She smiled at him in the reflection, one of those playful, sexy smiles that used to do wonders for him. It made him a little sad to see it, but he put the feeling aside. "I'm serious, sweetheart. You can't be seen wandering around. People'll talk."

"I bet they will." She opened his medicine cabinet and pushed aside a can of shaving cream and a bottle of Tylenol and lifted out a comb. She closed the mirror, and her face came back into view and she began to pull the comb through her twisted, ratty hair. It came out in clumps. "Goddamnit," she said, "I had awesome hair."

"I told you it was over between us, doll, but that wasn't good enough for you. You could never take no for an answer."

"You never said it was over, Nick."

"Well, it was."

"You never said it." Her eyes rested on his in the mirror, knowing.

"Well, showing you didn't fucking work either, did it? Because here you are."

She turned away from the mirror now, and he saw her eyes were gleaming with tears. One rolled down a cracked, brown cheek, washing the dirt clean and revealing pink skin beneath. "But you called me back, Nick. Why did you do that? If you really didn't want me anymore?"

"Just because I remember you doesn't mean I want you."

She was crying now, crying for real, and as the tears swept down her dirty cheeks, they wiped away the dry, encrusted dirt, and she was under there, her true face. Those round cheeks, the full, gentle mouth. Why would anyone have ever hurt her? When all she knew was how to love?

"Maybe you called me back for another reason? Maybe you had second thoughts?" She was walking backwards through the bathroom door, back into the house, her hands supplicating in front of her. "Maybe you really did want everyone to know about us?"

He was following her back into the living room, as if magnetized to her. He could not tell a lie: he remembered now how much he'd loved her, how, in the beginning, when they lived in that house together, he would have done anything for her. Why the heart runs out of fuel for loving was a mystery that had evaded him over and over in his life. He'd always been one to lose heart, to see his passions fade, and he'd never known why.

"Because you've never really made anything of yourself," she said. She was standing over the tarp, and she was whole and unclothed, the way she was that night, that last night. She tilted her head at him and her luxuriant bronze hair fell over one breast. "But you had your chance, didn't you?"

"I should have burned you up, so there was nothing left of you. I should have chopped you into little pieces —"

"Why didn't you, Nick? Why didn't you just have done with me and no one would ever have found me?"

"I won't make that mistake again," he said and he wheeled and strode into the kitchen to find his weapon. It was lying on its side on the counter beside the stove, and he snatched it up and then went down the hall to his office. A sheaf of paper lay on his desk, months' worth of work, and he strode back down the hall, brandishing it in front of him. In his other hand, he held the lighter.

She saw him and laughed. "It's a bit late for that, isn't it, Nick? I mean, it's like you conjured me out of thin air and now you want to make me vanish again? Again? You're just not that good, honey."

He lit the paper and it flared in his hands like a magician's trick. And then, just as quickly, it was ash at his feet and he was alone. The room was empty. The walls were blank. He was standing in a room with no windows and just a single closed door in one wall. The light flooded in and he looked up and she was standing above him now, towering over him, a giant, and she leaned her face down into the light, her angry, tearful face, and she almost blotted out the light. "You better hope they learn the truth about me before it's too late, Nick."

"Where am I?" he said, a note of fear finally creeping into his voice.

"Why, honey, you're caught in a lie," she said, and then she closed the lid of the box. In the deep, awful dark, he heard the door in the wall open.

A voice said, "You're inside it now, aren't you, Wise?"

Nick looked around. "Who . . . me?"

"Draw closer."

He waited to hear more, but there was only silence and darkness.

Costamides flipped the last page of the story, in case there was more, but she looked up at them shrugging, and laid the papers aside. "Well, if you were wondering how your friend on the internet ended up in that basement —"

"We know as little now as we did twenty minutes ago," Hazel said.

Fraser was staring down at the pages. "And we're thinking of letting the *Record* run this shit?"

"Is that our prime concern right now?" asked Wingate. "Whether they run it or not, we have to decide what it means to us and what our next move is going to be." He held up his sheaf of papers. Hazel had noticed he'd been underlining words on it. "If I understand this correctly, we're being alerted to a murder, as well as a suspect."

"Or someone wants to watch us dance like marionettes," said Fraser.

"If we're marionettes," said Hazel, "I think we better learn our parts. Whoever this is, they want people to see everything. Which is why they want this in the paper."

"I don't care what the fuck they want," said Fraser. "Who's in charge here?"

"You're forgetting about their collateral," she said to him. "We have to at least give the appearance of cooperation. Or we're going to find a body on our doorstep, and I'm not sure it would stop there." She jutted her chin at Wingate's copy of the story. "What were you writing?"

He flipped back to the first page. "I don't know what you're all thinking, but I read chapters one and two, like, ten times, and I don't think three through five were written by the same person. The beginning was, well, it was *bad*. This isn't exactly . . ."

"Dickens?" said Hazel.

He smiled at her, a little shyly. "Yeah. But it's better than what preceded it."

"Practice makes perfect," said Costamides.

"No," said Hazel, "the agenda has changed since those first chapters. It's not a story anymore. It's . . . it's a map of some kind."

"If we choose to believe it," said Fraser, harshly. "And mind you, even if we *do*, how the hell do we know exactly what we're believing in?"

"We're being asked to figure that out," said Wingate. He spread his fingertips on top of the pages, making a bridge over them. "The story is our guide. The stuff on the internet is for us to keep track of how we're doing."

"And how are we doing?" asked Costamides.

"We fall any further behind," said Fraser, "they might start to run out of body parts to send us."

Wingate ignored him. "Well, I noticed that he uses the word *damage* a lot. He says it when he's sitting at the table, and then he talks about the water *damaging* the floor. And he does it somewhere else too, but I can't find it."

"The box he digs up in the backyard is 'damaged,'" said Hazel. "It might mean something."

"He's doing the crossword at the beginning, isn't he?" said Costamides. They all flipped back to the first page of chapter four. "'Damaged' is in the clue." She looked up. "What's a word that means 'damaged'?"

"Broken," said Wingate. "Smashed."

"Something that's 'damaged' isn't necessarily completely ruined."

"Damn it," said Hazel. "I know what it is." They all looked at her. "It's a cryptic clue, like for a crossword. *Damaged* or *broken* or *messy* – words like that – they signal anagrams."

They all turned their eyes back on the page. "Surely we're not thinking this whole thing is, like, a palindrome?" said Fraser.

"No," she said. "But something has to be rearranged before it makes sense. A detail or a word."

"Fine. What, though?"

"I don't know," said Hazel.

The four of them stared at the pages. To Hazel's eyes, the longer she looked, the more the letters and words seemed like meaningless marks against a vast, empty field.

Her phone rang and she picked it up. It was Melanie. "I'm putting him on speakerphone," she said.

It was Spere. "It's official, people. The hand in Deacon's freezer once held that computer mouse." There was silence from the room. "We had to digitize the layers of prints, but we were able to separate and collate. We have a match."

"Well, I guess that means I don't have to play the rabid fan up at the missus's house to shake loose a drinking glass," said Fraser. "Good work, Howard."

"Yeah, good work," said Hazel. She reached forward and punched the disconnect. For the first time in this case, something was as it seemed. Her eyes were drawn to the computer screen, which continued to show its plea in blood. "What did you do?" she said quietly to it and then she slowly turned her gaze on the others. "What did Colin Eldwin do?"

She gave Melanie a couple of tasks. The first was to connect her with the *Westmuir Record*. A panicked Rebecca Portman came on the line. "Mr. Sunderland is on the warpath," she said. "He just called from Atlanta and I had to tell him about our Thursday edition. I, um, have a message he made me write down. He told me to read it to you."

"I didn't call you, Miss Portman, to pick up messages from your boss."

"I'm sorry, but, just the way he sounded . . ."

"I have a couple of needs you can take care of for me. Do I still have your attention?" Portman murmured that she did. "The first thing is, I've decided you can run Colin Eldwin's story again. In fact, I want you to run both chapters four and five in Monday's edition."

"*Both?*"

"Yes. Is that going to get you in trouble again?"

"I'm afraid it will. Maybe I should read you Mr. Sunderland's message, Ma'am? He asked me to read it to you."

"Does it have the word *feckless* in it?"

"Um . . ." She was scanning the note. "Not exactly."

"Is your boyfriend in today?"

"Who?"

"Beaker, Miss Portman, your nervous little friend in IT. I want him in my station house in fifteen minutes. Tell him to put all the emails Colin Eldwin has sent you – all of them – on a CD and have them bring it over to me. I have some questions for him."

She thought she could hear Portman's heart pounding over the phone. "He's uh, not in today, Detective. Friday is usually pretty quiet."

Hazel wanted to reach through the phone and wring the little dope's neck. "Do you know where he lives?"

"Um –"

"Tell him I won't keep him long. And I'm 'Detective Inspector' to you."

"Sorry, Ma'am." Hazel closed her eyes and held her tongue. "He really wants me to read this note to you."

Cartwright appeared in the doorway. Hazel covered the mouthpiece. "What?"

"Mr. Pedersen says he's having brunch with his wife. Is it urgent?"

"Tell him to come in when he's done. And if he's at Ladyman's have him bring me a peameal bacon sandwich."

She put the phone back to her ear. Portman was evidently reciting Sunderland's message. "'. . . and don't think I won't.' I'm sorry for the strong language, Ma'am. But he insisted."

"My ears are burning. Tell him you could hear me swallowing nervously. Hey, do you want to know what we called your boss in high school?"

"No."

"We called him 'Pokey' because he was always in other people's business. Probably the boys called him that too because he had a small penis. He might still answer to it." There was silence on the other end. "Send me your little friend, Miss Portman. Burn him his CD if you know how, and get him over here. He has thirteen minutes now."

Hubert Mackie – that was the kid's name – showed up fourteen minutes later, out of breath and looking panicked. Cartwright offered him a cup of coffee, but he told her coffee made him sweat and she gave him a glass of water instead. He was wearing a black cloth jacket with a broken zipper and his wispy hair kept falling over his forehead. "I guess we're going to need a computer," he said, and Hazel led him out to Wingate's work station. The kid walked through the pen with his head down, muttering "hello" left and right and pushing his hair away from his eyes.

Hazel pulled the chair out for him, and Mackie sat, apologizing as he did, and Hazel asked him if he wanted a sedative.

"Oh no, Ma'am, that'd just make me sleepy."

"Then let's get to work."

"What is it you were wanting to know, Ma'am?"

"That story the paper is running – did the chapters all come from the same email address?"

He'd popped the CD into Wingate's drive and was waiting for it to show up on his desktop. "I had Rebecca turn the emails you wanted to see into rtfs to make things easier."

"Meaning?"

"Just text files, Ma'am. They'll open in any word processor."

His fingers flew over the keyboard. He used the first two fingers of each hand to type and he seemed to be faster than Cartwright with all ten. The windows started opening on the screen, blooming and expanding until there were more than a dozen. "Thirteen in total, Ma'am."

"Where are they coming from?"

"There's his email address right there," the kid said, putting his finger against the screen. The address read *eldwincolin @ontcom.ca.*

"Is it always the same? Like, is it coming from the same email address every time?"

"Yeah," said Mackie.

"So that means it's him writing to you guys."

"Well, it's his email address."

"Is that a 'yes'?" she said, getting impatient.

"It's just that, you know, when you write an email, there's an IP address attached to the ISP both sending and receiving the email –"

"English, Beaker!"

"I'm trying!" He hunched over the keyboard for a second, making an effort to become invisible. He spoke faster now. "IP: Internet Protocol. Every machine, you know, a computer or a device of any kind, that's connected to a network – like the internet – has an IP address. It's a unique identifier, it tells you where the device is located. *Most* of the time. ISP: Internet Service Provider. Simply said, your email originates at one IP address, that of your ISP, and arrives at another, the IP of your recipient's ISP."

"Fine. Where were these emails sent from?"

The kid started cycling through the text files. He ran his

finger down a long string of gobbledegook that preceded the first bunch of the email messages. "Well, these all both originate and terminate at a Mayfair hub." He quickly put his hands in the air to keep Hazel from yelling at him again. "A hub is the physical location where the ISP has its computers, and where all information is received, processed, and/or sent along. Eldwin's provider is Ontcom, which has a hub in Mayfair, and ours is Caneast, which does too. So he sent these from his computer to the Ontcom servers, they sent them along to the Caneast servers, and we uploaded them to our hard drives from the Caneast servers."

"So, broken telephone."

"Sort of," he said. "Except in the internet version, you can trace every step of the journey."

"What about the rest of the emails? I want to know where chapters three, four, and five came from."

He brought those up. She could see for herself that they still came from *eldwincolin@ontcom.ca*. "These were sent from the internet, but still from his account."

"*Meaning*."

His shoulders slumped a little. "How come you don't know this stuff? Ma'am."

"You want me to slap your cranium?"

"You can send email from your desktop, you know, at home, off a program, or you can send it from the internet itself, from your ISP's webmail program – it's called a 'shell' and they all have one – which means you're logging on to your account from some homepage – and this could be anywhere in the world – and you can send and receive mail from there."

"Does the IP address change?"

"Yes," he said. "Different servers." He quickly added: "Servers are machines connected to the internet."

"Can you find the location of these servers?"

"Yes," he said, and he opened the browser on Wingate's computer. He was copying and pasting strings of numbers onto a webpage. He clicked something and waited. Then he said, "Or no."

"What do you mean *no*?"

"I mean these later chapters were sent from Colin Eldwin's email address through the shell, but he was anonymized."

"For Christ's sake!"

Mackie turned in the chair, panicked anew. "Please, Ma'am, don't slap my cranium. There's all kinds of ways to be anonymous on the internet these days. You can send email, surf, chat, all anonymously. You can be untraceable. Anyone can do it."

"So we can't know it's Eldwin physically sending the emails?"

"That's right," he said, and he sounded proud of her. "Someone could have his password and is using his account. That's all they'd need. Then they could cloak, log on, and send email and no one would be the wiser unless they ran the IPs, like we just did."

Hazel stared at the screen. The string of numbers Mackie had input was now superimposed over an image of planet Earth with a big yellow question mark beside them. "So what you're saying is these last three chapters could have come from anywhere."

"Well, they *came* from Ontcom's shell, but the person who logged on to the shell could have been in Mozambique for all we know. This person used a site called Anonymice to cloak themselves. It says it here in the expanded headers."

"What if we serve Anonymice with a warrant?"

"Good luck," said Mackie. "These sites don't keep any records at all. They don't know who's accessing their service. Theoretically, you could identify a user if you somehow got legal control of the site and you found him *while* he was online, because the Anonymice servers know, at some level, who's logging on and generally where they are before they cloak them and send them forward into the internet. But once your guy's logged out of the site, he's a ghost." She leaned over him and brought up the window with the video in it. She let him watch it. "Omigod. Is that blood, Ma'am?"

"What can you tell me about that url?"

He copied it from the address window and pasted it into trace search. "It's the same thing. The path begins and ends on the internet."

"Is there any way to link the url with the company that anonymized the emails? Is it the same company?"

He did some typing. "Yes. This is being processed through Anonymice as well." He pointed to a string of numbers. "That's their IP address."

"Right now?" she asked. "The connection is live right now?"

"Yes."

She patted him on the head, and he shrunk a little under her touch. "You can go."

She went out the back of the pen toward her office. "Cartwright?" Melanie Cartwright appeared in the hallway. "Where's my bacon sandwich?"

"Do you mean Mr. Pedersen?"

"Him, too."

"I'm expecting him any minute," she said.

Hazel went into her office. The missing link to Eldwin was some internet service that existed solely to allow people to work untraceably on the internet. But she knew what the average person didn't: even a buried footprint still exists.

Something landed on her desk. The homey scent of peameal bacon wafted up from it. "I serve two masters," said Andrew Pedersen.

"Thanks for coming in," she said. "Have a seat. There's something I want to show you."

He sat in the chair opposite her, looking around the office. Another phantasm of the past settled on them both, him in that chair, having brought her lunch. The comfortable silence of ritual. Would there come a time when she wouldn't be stumbling into these hollows, shaped like her, that belonged to another time?

She opened the wax paper that wrapped the sandwich and passed him a small sheaf of papers. "I'm wondering if you can look at this for me. We think it's written in a kind of code you might be familiar with."

"Really."

"It's the fourth and fifth chapters of the short story in the *Record*. We're not sure it's still the same writer, and we think he might be leading us to something. Only we're not sure what and we're not sure where he's telling us to look."

His eyebrows went up. "Interesting." He accepted the papers as she took her first bite of the thick, fatty sandwich. It was gorgeous. She let him read the papers in silence. When he'd finished them, he went back to the first page and read them through again. By the time she was done her sandwich, he'd finished as well. "Pretty sick stuff."

"It's not the plot that's got us confused. It's the sense that there's something buried in it. Did you notice how many times he used the word *damage*?"

"I did."

"So?"

"Well, he *is* better than the first writer —"

"So you agree it's not the same person."

"Absolutely."

For some reason, his confirmation of what they believed weighed on her. "That's what we thought, too."

"The guy who wrote the first two chapters is incapable of something like . . ." He shuffled the pages. "'Her bright, brown eyes came through the dark of her sockets like headlights coming out of a tunnel.' That's almost good."

"Fine. So someone's taken over the story."

"That doesn't bode too well for the first writer."

"No. It doesn't," she said, and she decided not to say anything else. "Go back to 'damage.' Does it point to anything for you?"

Andrew looked down at the pages in his lap. "Well, there's some pretty graphic 'damage' in the story, don't you think? Maybe the writer's just pointing you to its importance. Telling you it's meaningful."

"And nothing else? I'm of the mind that these two chapters are telling us what to do. The Wise character talks to this dead woman. Tries to destroy her again by burning something he's written. *This* story. Then he finds himself trapped. I shouldn't tell you this, but the man who wrote the first two chapters of this story seems to be missing. This isn't a yarn anymore."

He flipped through the story again. On the last page, he began to nod.

"What is it?"

"You might be on to something." He got up and came behind the desk. "Look at these three lines at the end."

"Someone's speaking to him."

"No. Someone's speaking to *you*." He reached for a pen. "A good cryptic clue gives you a definition, an action, and something to perform the action on. Listen again . . ." He read the lines:

> A voice said, "You're inside it now, aren't you, Wise?"
> Nick looked around. "Who . . . me?"
> "Draw closer."

"Repunctuate that first line – *You're inside it now. Aren't you wise?* Maybe that's a challenge. 'Aren't you wise?'"

"Wise to what?"

"The first part is the action." He nodded at the paper. "This is actually kind of smart. *You're inside it* – that's a container clue. It means that what you're looking for here is hidden inside other words. The next two lines are 'Who . . . me?' and 'Draw closer.' Do you see it now?"

"Andrew, I don't! That's why you're here."

"What does 'draw closer' mean?"

"Um, to approach . . . to look into . . ."

"To home in on?"

"Okay."

"The container is 'Who . . . me?' The word is *home*. It's inside in the line. Wise ends up in a box, something he's *inside*, but the writer wants you to *draw closer*. To what?"

She became very still and touched the lines on the page as if they were embossed there and she could feel their contours. "Home. He wants us to go to the house."

"Cherry Tree Lane."

She pressed the intercom. "Melanie, get me Wingate."

Her Detective Constable was in the office within seconds. Andrew showed him what he'd found. "Are you sure that's what it means?"

"Once it's unravelled, it doesn't seem at all accidental," said Andrew.

Hazel pointed to the words *Cherry Tree Lane* in the story. "Where is this?" she asked.

"Umm . . . There's a Cherry *Street*, but I've never heard of a Cherry Tree Lane. At least not downtown." He thought for a second. "Yeah, I don't know what street he's referring to. Maybe something out of downtown."

"But he describes a drive to the city centre, doesn't he?"

"Yeah," he agreed.

She looked at her watch. "It's too late to go now." She looked up at him. "I need you to start on something else, James."

"You don't want me downtown?"

"No. I want you to get some legal advice for me concerning a company that operates on the internet."

He squinted at her, a bit confused, but he could wait for the details.

She continued, now talking to Andrew. "Anyway, I think I need someone who knows downtown and cryptic crosswords about equally." He was looking at her suspiciously. "What? Were you planning on having a quiet Saturday?"

"No. But I wasn't planning on being seconded by my ex either."

"Would a decent sushi lunch make it worth your while?"

"Define 'decent,'" he said.

"Set your alarm for eight."

] 20 [

Saturday, May 28

It was a drive like any they'd taken to visit one or the other daughter at school in Toronto, drives to campuses, the back seat loaded with Chelsea buns from the bakery, a box of Tide, a crate of apples, perhaps a couple new shirts or a case of local beer, and a suitcase packed for one night. Often these trips down to the city were precipitated by some crisis, usually minor, in one of the girls' lives, and yes, if Hazel were honest with herself, it was usually Martha who spurred them to action. So often these drives were punctuated by feelings of anxiety and anticipation: what untoward shock had the girl prepared for them this time? And they'd arrive at her downtown sorority and try to ignore the accusing or worried looks of the sisters as they went up the stairs to Martha's room to see what needed putting back together again.

They drove out of town and stopped at Tim's, him ordering her what she'd always order: a large double-double and a raisin tea biscuit. He got himself a steeped tea and a maple dip. These first twenty or so kilometres were the most familiar to them: they paced them out of everything that meant home to them, or told them that they were returning to it. But even here, things were changing; the suburban imperative was spreading farther north. Just before the town of Dublin, cornfields were being converted to "Modern Country Living," which was to say, a grid of streets surrounding a shopping centre were going to be plunked down in the middle of what was still good land. The sign along the highway announced excitedly that the ground-breaking would take place in the fall. She noticed Andrew shaking his head.

An hour later, they passed Barrie and the highway angled into its final, long approach to the city. This length of road always soured her stomach and made her heart race – in anticipation of the difficulties to come or just because she was truly out of her element – and this time it was no different. The urban lichen was well established at this latitude (a preview of what awaited them at Dublin), and the new suburbs, each one built around an unwieldy palace of worship – a giant mosque, a towering white church, an outlet mall – had much the same architectural weight as the plastic buildings on a Monopoly board: a tidy arrangement of buildings that hid the fact that the environment was built for money, not for people. It was intended to capture and keep captive some segment of the population, upend them in the crush of prettiness, and empty their pockets. It occurred to her that, at least, the city itself could not hide its agendas. What it wanted from you it asked for once you passed through its gates.

They were driving eastward beside Lake Ontario. Its bright blue-black expanse shone in the sun, with the green gem of the Toronto Islands just a kilometre offshore. Ahead of them the towers of the city rose over the downtown like crystal, the needle of the CN Tower at its centre; from this vantage point the buildings looked like massive toys ajumble in a box. It seemed impossible that this much steel and glass and concrete could be in the same place, but as they approached it, the buildings stepped apart and the streets appeared between them, and then the cars and the bicycles and the people themselves and they were within it and part of it. There was always a strange thrill here, for Hazel, to be in this bustle, no matter how it scared her. "I think this is the first time since the girls moved out that we've been here for some reason other than to put out some fire in their lives."

"Well, Emmie lives in Vancouver now. Harder to drive to."

"It just seems like a different city without some small problem to attend to. Like anything could happen here."

"And it usually does," said Andrew.

"Let's get the street guide out and let's try to follow this guy's directions."

Andrew took the Perly's out of the glove compartment and flipped it open to the page they were driving over. The world outside the car windows flattened out to red and yellow lines. "Spadina goes up past the *no longer new* stadium," he said. "And into Chinatown." They drove north past the theatre district and into bustling Chinatown. At a stoplight, a vegetable seller hacked the tops off coconuts with a heavy machete. North of Chinatown, the crazy quilt of restaurants and grocery stores gave way to more institutional buildings. This was the western boundary of the University of Toronto. They tracked up to Russell Street and pulled over.

"Okay," said Hazel. "This is where you get to shine. Find me a tree-street. Or a fruit-street. With a church on it or somewhere near."

He held the mapbook open in his lap and clutched the page from the story with the directions to the house in his right hand. His eyes shuttled back and forth between his hand and the Perly's. She leaned over toward him and scanned the pages along with him. There was a Hazelton Avenue, but not a Hazelnut, and a Concord, as in grape, but no Apple Street, no Banana Avenue. Leaning this close to his shoulder, she was reminded of what her mother had said about her father's book bag and she pulled back a little.

"There's a Chestnut Street pretty close to here. Beside City Hall," he said.

"Church?"

"Not close by. Holy Trinity tucked in behind the Eaton Centre."

"What else?"

"Birch Avenue, up at Summerhill. Oh, there's Elm Street too. That's close. And there's a church on St. Patrick Street, right around the corner."

"Well, let's go take a look at it," she said.

He directed her into a U-turn and sent her east along College Street as he continued to study the mapbook.

"I just wanted to thank you again, Andrew."

"For what?"

"For coming to our aid."

"Your aid, you mean," he said.

"Yes."

"Well, I'm getting a sushi lunch out of it, don't forget. Turn right here."

She drove south down Beverly, cut across Baldwin to McCaul. Elm Street was a short jog south, and they parked illegally and got out. There were no houses on the street, just big apartment buildings and offices. They were behind the hospital strip of University Avenue. Midtown rose up at the end of the street. "Doesn't feel right," she said.

They walked down the street. From the top of St. Patrick, they could see the spire of Our Lady of Mount Carmel. But the topography was all wrong. There wasn't a front porch for miles around. Nor chestnut trees. "Maybe we *should* go down to City Hall and look around," she said.

Andrew had the Perly's open with the story held against one of the pages. He'd narrowed his eyes to slits. "No," he said. "Listen to this."

"What?"

"'He was following her back into the living room,'" Andrew read, "'as if magnetized to her. He could not tell a lie: he remembered now how much he'd loved her, how, in the beginning, when they lived in that house together, he would have done anything for her.'" Andrew looked up into Hazel's questioning eyes. "*He could not tell a lie.* When they lived in that house together? On Cherry Tree Lane?"

"You really have always thought I'm much smarter than I actually am. Spell it out, Andrew."

"Who cannot tell a lie?"

"Pinocchio?"

"George Washington, dummy." He shifted the story over to the right-hand page. "There's a Washington Avenue back off Spadina."

"Why doesn't he just *say* this, if it's so fucking important to him."

"I think he wants it to be important to you too."

"Let's go."

Washington Avenue was lined with chestnut trees, and at the end of it there were two small green spaces and, where it made a "T" with Huron Street, a church. They parked and stepped out and a horripilating thrill went up Hazel's back. It felt now that she had stepped into someone else's territory and she wasn't entirely sure that they were safe. "Would you be offended if I suggested you wait in the cruiser?" she asked him and he said he would be, so the two of them set out along the sidewalks to find the house under a chestnut, with a verandah and a view of both parks and the church. The houses on the south side of the street didn't afford these views, so they focussed on the northern side of the street. Those houses closer to Spadina lacked the necessary vantage, and they ruled out the first half of the street. Four big Victorian duplexes took up the second half of the street, two with verandahs and two without. But only one stood directly in the shade of a chestnut tree, number thirty-two. Like all of these houses, many of which were owned by the university, number thirty-two was divided into apartments. There were five of them and five buzzers under different names. They buzzed P. Billows, J. Cameron, G. Caro, and D. Payne before they got a response. It was a woman's voice. "Hello?"

"Police, Ma'am, sorry to disturb you. Who am I speaking to?"

"How do I know you're the police?"

"I'm in a police uniform and I have police ID. Those will be your first two clues."

There was a pause, and they heard a window open above their heads. A young woman in jeans and a white T-shirt leaned out to the side of the verandah with her portable phone to her ear. Hazel held her ID up over her head. "What do you want?" said the woman.

"You're Miss Caro? Or Miss Payne?"

"I'm Gail Caro. What do you want?"

"I wanted to ask you if there have been any recent disturbances in this house. Anything out of the ordinary, anything that required the attention of the police?"

"Like what?"

"I'm asking you. Anything."

"No."

"Do you know everyone who lives in this house?"

Her attention had tracked over to Andrew, who was standing with his back to the house, looking down the street. "Who's that? He's not in uniform."

"Plainclothes," she said, and she could see Andrew stifling a grin.

"How'd you get here? Where's your car?"

Jeez, thought Hazel. She'd forgotten how paranoid city life could be. She pointed toward Huron Street, to the cruiser, and the woman leaned farther out the window and looked at it.

"So," said Hazel. "Who do you know in the house?"

"No one. I see them on the stairs, but I live alone. People come and go from places like this."

"Is there a basement in the house?"

"There's storage."

"Could we come in and look at it?"

Caro paused. "Just hold on a second," she said, and she closed the window.

"Are you sure you want to go in there?" asked Andrew.

She laid her hand on her Glock. "That's why I asked you to stay in the car."

"Don't you need a warrant?"

"I thought you were the lawyer here, Andrew."

"I don't need to know about warrants to settle property disputes."

"We have cause to enter the premises. And anyway, if she consents, we don't need a warrant."

They waited on the porch. After a couple of minutes, Hazel buzzed Caro's apartment. There was no answer. "I don't like the feel of this."

"Let's go."

She stood back from the door and called up to the now-closed window. "Miss Caro?" There was no reply.

"Hazel?"

"What the hell is going on?"

"Hazel," said Andrew, his hand on her forearm. She turned to the street and saw a police car driving up. "The local cavalry have arrived."

The black-and-white cruiser pulled up in front of number thirty-two, and Hazel saw a man and a woman in the car; the female cop was talking into her radio. "Shit," she said.

The officers got out of the car. They were both tall and well built, a pair of stars. "Good morning," said the male officer, coming up the walk. He was inventorying them both quickly, deciding whether this was going to be routine or not. "What seems to be the problem?" The casual opener, thought Hazel. "Can I see some ID, Ma'am?"

"I'm OPS, Officer. I presume you've seen the uniform before."

"Nature of the call, Ma'am. I just have to be sure."

She got her ID out, and he took it from her, flipped it open. He studied it briefly and handed it back to her, saying, "Detective Inspector." He looked at Andrew. "You're not OPS, Sir?"

"No."

"She said he was plainclothes," called a voice from above. It was Gail Caro. "They don't look like cops. You can get a policeman's costume from a hundred stores in this town."

"It's okay," called the officer. His nametag said K. Hutchins. "They're provincial, Ma'am." He had his arm on Andrew's elbow and turned to his partner. "Constable Childress will keep you busy for a couple of minutes, Sir. I'm going to talk to your, um, partner."

She watched Childress lead her ex-husband away helplessly. Hutchins stepped away from the house and onto the lawn and she followed him. The window on the second floor had closed again. "What brings you to Toronto, Detective Inspector Micallef?"

He'd pronounced her name the way anyone who'd only ever seen it written pronounced it. *Mickel-eff*. It made her skin crawl to hear it that way.

"It's *mih-CAY-liff*, Officer, and we've got reason to believe someone living in this house could be involved in an abduction we're investigating."

"Do you have a name?"

"Not exactly," she said. She was pleased to note she was getting what seemed like cooperation. The OPS, of course, had province-wide jurisdiction; she could investigate anything she cared to anywhere she cared to. But the Toronto Police Services weren't always the biggest fans of what they sometimes called the "Kountry Kops" and you couldn't always count on friendly support.

"What brings you to this house, then? If you don't mind my asking."

"I don't. Let me show you something," she said. He had to make way for her when he realized she needed to go to her car. She walked down the lawn to the street. She saw Childress had spared Andrew the humiliation of having to sit in the back seat of the black-and-white, but she wondered exactly how long it would take before he had real regrets about agreeing to help her. But as she walked past him, her eyes lowered, he whispered her name urgently.

"I have to get something," she said.

"It *is* 'damaged.' The street name. It's an anagram."

"*What?*"

"Detective Inspector," said Hutchins from the front of the house. "We have other calls . . . sorry to rush you."

Hazel carried on to the car and got the photocopied pages of chapters four and five of the story, as well as a copy of the *Westmuir Record* in which the first chapter had appeared. She returned to Constable Hutchins and handed him all the paper. "I better set this up."

She went over it with him. When she got to the part about the hand in her basement, Hutchins called his partner over and asked Hazel to start again. As she spoke, Andrew crept up and finally stood with them, and the two Toronto officers passed the pages back and forth. When she got to their reason for being in the city, Constable Childress had the *Record* from May 16 open to page five and looked at the picture of Eldwin beside his name, the picture of him standing in a parking lot. "This your missing guy?"

"We think so."

"He looks like a used car salesman."

"I think he might have that kind of character," Hazel said.

"And has anything happened since the 'save her' message?" Childress asked.

"Nothing," Hazel said. "I think we're supposed to work through what we've been given first —"

"Given?" said Childress.

"Yes. We're going on hints here."

"A severed hand is a hint?"

"The hints are backed up. Just in case we didn't think there was anything urgent about this."

"Sounds like you have your work cut out for you. So to speak."

Hutchins backed away from them and went up onto the verandah of number thirty-two. He cupped his hands over the glass in a window on the main floor and tried to look in. Then he buzzed Gail Caro again.

"What?" came her tinny voice.

"Miss Caro, Constable Hutchins of the Toronto Police Services. Come open this door, please."

"I'm not the landlord," said Caro, "I can't just let you in."

"If I ask you to, you can. It's just that easy."

"Hold on a second for god's sake."

"You better hope she isn't calling the RCMP now," Hazel said, coming up on the porch.

They heard Caro clomping angrily down the stairs.

"Eternal cry here," said Andrew quietly in Hazel's ear.

"What?"

"Cherry Tree Lane points you to the street, but it *is* 'damaged' as well. 'Cherry Tree Lane' is an anagram for 'eternal cry here.' I think this is a murder scene, Hazel."

21

Caro opened the door and stood aside, looking on the small collection of law enforcement on her front porch with an expression verging on disgust. Hazel had to wonder what her face looked like when she needed help from the same professionals she obviously held in such contempt. "I'm not being quoted in any report, I'm just telling you that now," she said.

"Hold on," said Childress, getting out her PNB. "Let me just write that down . . . *not being quoted*. Okay, great. You can go back to your apartment now."

Caro made haste up the stairs. Hutchins had his flashlight out. "Okay, we're going to take it from here," he said. "You two can wait upstairs or on the verandah."

"All due respect, Officer –"

"Yes," he said. "All due. We'll make full disclosure afterwards."

"Please," said Hazel.

Hutchins and Childress traded a silent communication. "You have a gun?" asked Childress.

"They do arm us in the OPS." She turned her hip to them.

"He has to stay," Childress said.

"Oh, I don't want to go," said Andrew, and she narrowed her eyes at him and then threw a glance to her partner. He shrugged.

The entry to the basement was beside the door that led to the upper apartments. Hutchins took the lead, but he kept his gun holstered. She wanted to say something about that, but decided to stay silently grateful that she was invited along on her own ambush. And that Hutchins was in front of her.

The basement door wasn't locked, and Hutchins opened it on a set of dark stairs. He tried the light on the wall, but it didn't work. Hazel felt her insides go a little liquid as she recalled her terror at Bellocque's house. Her breath came in short bursts. Hutchins turned to his partner and whispered, "This is where one of us breaks through a cracked step and lands in a pile of bodies."

"I saw that one, too," said Childress. She passed him her flashlight off her belt. It directed a powerful white beam of light into the space in front of them. The stairs were concrete. "So much for that theory."

"Anyone down here?" called Constable Hutchins. There was no answer. Not much of an ambush, thought Hazel, but she realized as well that the space below them was completely silent. They went down the stairs, the beam of light juddering around in the dark, catching dust and webbing here and there. The basement was cool. Hutchins flipped the switch in the wall at the bottom, and they were standing in a large, single room that ran the length and width of the house. On one wall, standing nakedly against the grey concrete, were the house's washer and dryer. A fragile drying tree was to one side with three bras hanging from it. There were five badly constructed wooden storage lockers at one end of the space and they went over to inspect them. Behind the flimsy wood-and-chicken-wire doors, four were empty, and one had a bike in it. Hutchins half-heartedly tried the doors of three that were padlocked. He turned to Hazel. "Nothing here, Detective Inspector. Not much reason here to do anything but turn around and go home. Or take in a show."

She smiled, a little defeated. Hutchins got out his card and handed it to her. It gave his first name as Kevin and his division as Twenty-one. She snapped it against her hand. "I don't suppose you know James Wingate?"

"Who?" said Hutchins.

"He came to us from Twenty-one. Last fall."

"We're, like, two hundred and fifty men and women at Twenty-one," he said. "It's the largest division in the city. Two guys could earn their pensions ten feet from each other at Twenty-one and never meet."

The hair on the back of her neck was prickling, and she turned around to look behind her. The bare wall at the back of the basement was a smooth concrete surface. She turned back to Hutchins. "He's a detective. Wingate."

"Oh, well that's the other side of the building, Ma'am."

He shone the light toward the stairs. She kept waiting for something to catch her eye, but all the smooth grey surfaces were blurring together. She held her finger up and walked over to the concrete wall and stood close to it. It was a bare wall, no sign of human fluids on it at all. She smelled the wall, knowing how ridiculous she must look. "Are you a building inspector in your spare time?" Hutchins asked her.

"Not quite. There was blood on the wall in the video. I just wanted to see."

The officers joined her at the wall, and they all inspected it together. It was a fairly smooth surface, but not so smooth that a recent bloodstain wouldn't be worked into the small pocks. There was nothing. "If this had been recently cleaned," said Childress, "we'd smell it. You need bleach to get that much blood out."

"Why are we here?" said Hazel quietly. "I'm sure he wanted us to come *here*."

"Maybe he wanted you here so you wouldn't be *there*."

She snapped around to the female officer, and her heart started pounding again. "Shit."

"What could be happening back in Port Dundas with you occupied in Toronto?"

"I don't know," she replied.

The officers shared a look, and then Hutchins held his hand out to show the way back to the stair.

When they got back to the main floor, Hazel could see Andrew through the door sitting on the top step on the verandah. "Do you mind if I harass this Miss Caro one more second?"

"Be my guest," said Hutchins. "She seems to delight in the company of the police."

Hazel knocked, and after a moment, the door opened again. "Haven't I done my duty for the day?" said Gail Caro.

"There are two empty lockers downstairs. Does that mean there are two empty apartments?"

"People come and go, Officer. And it's the end of the school year."

"You're still here."

"The university doesn't only rent to students."

Childress stepped forward. If Hazel had met her on the street, she would have assumed this strapping woman was a volleyball pro. "You didn't answer her question."

"The ground floor just turned over," said Caro, rolling her eyes. "And the apartment beside me is empty. I don't have the *dope* on anyone else in this sad shitbox, okay?"

"Who moved in down here?"

"I forgot to bring a cake over, so I didn't meet him."

"Him?"

"Or her," she said. "*I didn't meet them.*"

"What number is the empty one upstairs?"

"Three," she said.

They thanked Caro again and she huffed back up the stairs. Andrew stood when they emerged from the house.

"You find the temple of doom down there?"

"Just *actual* dirty laundry," she said.

"I guess that's preferable to the alternative."

Hutchins had squared to them, his hands on his hips. "The alternative was no bras on the line. I don't think your guy wants to give up his hideout yet."

"But he wanted us to see this house."

"That's what you say," said Hutchins. "But you might want to entertain the possibility that you followed what you thought was a trail to something that doesn't mean anything."

"You read those chapters, Officer. *Something's* going on." She went down the steps behind him and stood on the lawn. There was an alleyway between thirty-two and thirty-four leading to the two backyards. "Just wait here for a second," she said. She walked down the paving stones that forked to two gates and tripped the latch on the right-side one with the string that hung between the slats, as Nick Wise had done in the story. There was a small patch of garden behind the house with a couple of tomato plants doing poorly in the chestnut's shade. A beaten-up plastic chaise lay to the side of the door that led from the house to the yard, and behind it was a stack of empty clay flower-pots. Their contents had not been transplanted to the garden: someone had long ago given up on growing flowers back here. She walked the perimeter of the garden looking for disturbed or sunken earth, anything that looked like it might be worth digging. She kicked at dry clods and pushed the toe of her shoe into patches, moving the earth around, but she realized if she was going to be serious about it, she'd need a reason, and so far, she didn't have one. A *feeling* wasn't going to win her a warrant to dig this place up.

She went back out front. Hutchins was standing on the lawn now, looking faintly amused. "See . . . the difference between us beat cops and you dicks is we're led by our feet and you're led by your nose. We just keep walking, you know, to see what's what, but you 'know' there's something at the end of the trail because you're *sure* you smelled smoke."

"I'm not sure I get you," said Hazel.

"If I *see* smoke, I know I'm not imagining it," he said. "But my taste for the here-and-now is what makes me what I am, right?"

"Does that mean you don't look for what you can't see, Officer?"

"It means we beat cops have enough on our hands with what's right in front of us."

"Well, that's the difference, isn't it?" she said, ignoring the little voice reminding her she'd gone into the backyard on a hunch. "We need both of us if we're going to get the job done, though, don't we?"

"Sure," he said, and he sounded friendly, but she knew there were those police out there who saw the art of investigation as only one step above voodoo and she thought Hutchins was probably one of them.

"Anyway, speaking of the here-and-now, I better call in, see what's going on back home." She turned away from the other officers and made contact with the station house. Her nerves had been jangling ever since Childress had made the suggestion that she was here in Toronto in order not to be *there*, in Port Dundas. She got Wingate on the line. "Tell me it's business as usual, James."

"More or less."

"Meaning?"

"The video changed again."

"Shit." Childress shot her a look. "What is it now?"

"Nothing. It's nothing."

"What do you mean?"

"I mean it's basically black. There's a sound though."

"A sound?"

"A scratching sound."

"So you can *hear* now?"

"Yeah."

"What do you mean by 'basically black'?"

"It's black, but there's a small green triangle in the bottom left corner of the screen now. Like a 'play' button on a VCR."

She wondered what that might mean and couldn't come up with anything that calmed her guts. "Mute the mic, James."

"Already done."

"Now, what about Anonymice?"

"They're in Grand Cayman."

"Great."

"I've made contact with the Royal Cayman Police Force. I'm waiting for a call-back."

"You make sure they understand this isn't about money laundering. We've got a crime in progress. A man's life depends on their assistance."

"Got it," he said.

Childress was looking at her watch. "Detective Inspector, I can get in touch with the housing office on campus this afternoon. See if there's a list of past tenants. Maybe something will crop up."

"I'd appreciate that," said Hazel. There was a strange hesitation, and then Hazel realized that Childress was waiting for her to pass her her card. She hoped she had one on her, but she didn't. "Uh," she said. "I'll just tell you my number."

"Okay," said Childress, and she flipped her notebook open. "Shoot." She wrote down the number and closed her pad. "Well . . . if we find anything . . ."

"Thanks," said Hazel, and with that, another signal passed between the two cops, and they headed down the stairs. She and Andrew watched them drive off.

"I can't tell if that guy was high-hatting me or just passing the time of day," she said to Andrew.

"What do you care what he thinks?" he replied. "You're in the right place and you know it."

"Do I?"

"You're just nervous because you're off your turf, Hazel. But that doesn't make them any less clueless."

"I feel like I should try to get back in there. Look around without those beat cops' eyes on me."

"If there *is* a reason for you to snoop around again here, don't you want to have the right paperwork? I get the feeling they could have given you trouble on a technicality if they wanted to, Hazel."

"Fine. Then what do I do with this feeling?"

"Feed it sushi," he said.

They sat at one of the tables in the back of the green-and-black restaurant on Bloor Street. The whole interior looked like the lacquered boxes they served the food in. Hazel had never been partial to Japanese food: she didn't like its prettiness, its attention to the little detail. She preferred her food to take up the whole plate. Still, she had to admit it tasted good and they said it was good for you. She couldn't think if she'd ever seen a fat Japanese person. It was just past one and the place was full of young people expertly wielding their little wooden sticks over plates full of bright squares of food.

The last time she'd shared a meal with Andrew, just the two of them, she'd been reduced more or less to begging. Here, too, he'd come to her aid, but at least it wasn't as personal as before. She tried to think of the last time she'd ever done anything for *him*. That was something to store away.

"Five Japanese restaurants on a single stretch of road and the whole of Westmuir County can't manage even one," he said. He was holding a piece of salmon sashimi in the air on the end of a fork. In all his years of proclaiming himself a sushi aficionado, he'd never learned how to use chopsticks. It was this shameless confidence in himself that had long ago attracted her to him. He popped it into his mouth. "Fire was the worst thing that ever happened to fish," he said.

She toyed with her avocado maki. "Maybe we call Martha and take her out for a coffee?"

"And let her call me Watson all afternoon? No thanks. Plus, I told Glynnis I'd be back in time to marinate some flank steak." It was the first time her name had come up all day. Four hours and counting, Hazel thought. Progress, if she were foolish enough to think of it that way.

"I was expecting you to say you didn't want to give her false hope. Seeing us together."

His fork stilled, mid-air. "Is that how you see this, Hazel? A relationship-building exercise? I came because you asked me to help. Don't make me think you had ulterior motives."

"*Moi*?" she said, splaying a hand against her chest. "Never."

He eyed her carefully, admitting the ghost of a smile. "I thought you did very well today."

"Nothing happened."

"I mean with your back. You drove almost two hours this morning and it's going to be two hours back and you're in tip-top shape. That's an excellent sign."

"You mean I'll be moving out soon."

"There's that as well."

"Maybe I'll stub a toe and try to prolong my visit."

He forked up a mound of white rice and dropped it into his mouth. "You are always welcome to stop by, Hazel."

She felt the withdrawal symptoms still nibbling away at the edges: a faint sizzle behind the eyes, of worry, or dread. And then she realized it wasn't the lack of Percs she was feeling: it was grief. And she permitted herself, at last, the thought in full that she'd only let flit on the periphery: that she wished the last three years had never happened. And not just because she missed him and still loved him, but because they were not done; they had not finished telling the great story of their lives. It was true that it had not always been *great*, but it was their story, and it was going to be the only story they had. Well, the only story she had. Of who she was with him, of who they'd been together and what they'd done. What she had of him and he of her made it impossible that anyone else could know them as they'd once been. Letting herself think this, a too-big space opened in her chest and she realized how much grief she had over losing this most important friendship of her life. And at the same time, she realized that he was happy and that there was nothing she could do, or should do, to change things between them.

"Hazel?"

"You have rice on your chin," she said.

"Well, you don't have to cry about it."

"Wasabi," she said. "It's two o'clock. We should get ourselves home."

Back in Port Dundas, she sat in her office with Wingate. The screen showed a black as solid as a moonless night with the little green arrow at the bottom. The scratching sound was repetitive, like it was on a loop. They let it run with the mic off. "They serve a thousand warrants a year on the anonymizing services registered in the Caymans," Wingate said. "There's like eight of them down there and another five or six in the

Seychelles. All the addresses are post office boxes and *when* they pick up the mail down there, they systematically challenge the warrants. The detective I spoke to said they're still trying to get records from 1998."

"Why don't they just walk in and bust these people?"

"They have no idea where they are."

"What about the ISPs? Don't the providers know who's using their service and where they're located?"

Wingate had raised his eyebrows at her, like she'd grown a third head. "I guess Mr. Mackie gave you a crash course?"

"Well?"

"I asked the detective," he said, a little defensively. "About the ISP. These companies are their own ISPs. They're totally untraceable."

She slapped the desk. "Then get in touch with the company directly. Do they have an email address? Tell them what their service is being used for."

"Okay," he said.

She turned the laptop screen back toward them. "So what is this now? Why is there sound? What is it?"

"It sounds like someone scratching a tabletop."

"And this triangle. Is it possible there's a link open now? Why would they want us to connect?"

"Tell them what we know."

"Forget it. I want to get one step ahead of these people if I'm being asked to make contact. I want to have something they don't think I have."

"You know who the captive is."

"They sent us his hand, James. They know we know. They *wanted* us to know."

He was lost in thought, tracing the top of her desk with a finger. "What about we let slip we're onto them through Anonymice? See if they react. Maybe we can catch them changing directions."

"They might just go to ground, James. Turn off the feed and hit the road. Where are we then?"

"But they want us to *see* them," he said. "To *hear* them too. Whatever we're being asked to do by proxy can't be done if they break off contact."

"If they're smart enough to cover *all* their tracks, aren't they going to know their friends in the Caymans won't give them up?"

"It's worth a try."

"Man," she said. "I'm starting to understand what Hutchins was talking about."

"Who?"

"Toronto cop. He made a comment about the difference between beat cops and dicks. I didn't much like it, but I see now why he thinks that way. Because we're both sitting here throwing bones. Street cops see it differently."

"Yeah," he said, "they call in investigators when they get stuck and then stand around on the other side of the squad room mumbling about voodoo. Don't listen to the beat cops, Hazel."

But she was thinking that the searchers and prognosticators were too much like what bothered her about Glynnis. Never before had she worried that her work entailed any kind of blind faith, and yet it did. To her mind, spiritual investigation drew on the loosest of the goosiest presuppositions, beliefs that were, in fact, wishes. She'd always thought policework was not like that. And yet, this case was becoming more and more like an act of fortune-telling, an extended tea-reading. The risk, as it was in interpreting the unseen world, was that you'd pay attention to the wrong things.

"What about the backyard?" she said.

"At the house?"

"Doesn't it make sense we should be digging back there? Why don't we ask them if we should dig? See what they say."

"I see where you're going. Nick Wise has buried her in his backyard." They both fell silent, working it through. "We need to know if Eldwin ever lived in that house, Hazel."

"I agree." She looked across the top of the keyboard for the button that would unmute the microphone. The laptop made a popping sound to indicate the connection had been reopened. Hazel leaned down toward it. "How do we *save her* if she's already dead?" she asked, and although it was difficult to make out at first, they could both see the camera already pulling away from its black field.

22

The darkness resolved into a texture and then a field of cloth appeared and they recognized the weft of a black peacoat seen from the back. The scratching sound continued as the picture widened and shoulders appeared at the top of the screen. A chairback swam into the frame at the bottom. The figure was seated at a table, its head lowered. One of the shoulders juddered in time to the scratching sound: an arm moving like a mechanical toy. The figure was writing.

The surface of the table broadened and when its farthest edge drifted down they saw beyond it, into the gloom of the basement, to the wall with its dark message scrawled. When the camera had completed its zoom-out, Eldwin appeared in his chair, at the distant right edge of the screen, his back to the camera as well, his head also lowered. He was motionless. The image of the compulsively writing arm in the foreground and the still, slumped figure in the background made for a contrast that gave Hazel a cold feeling on the back of her neck.

The figure continued to work and paused to lift a scribbled sheet off the table, holding it up to read it, and then placing it face down to the right. "I'm wondering how this story is going to end," said a woman's voice. They waited silently. "I know you can hear me."

"It's going to end with you in handcuffs."

The voice laughed softly. "Oh, I have no doubt about that. But we're getting ahead of ourselves, aren't we, Hazel?"

"Show us your face."

"Soon," said the voice. "But for now, let's talk."

"You talk," said Hazel. "I'll listen."

The figure lifted its head slightly. "Who's there with you right now?"

"I'm alone," she said.

"That's not true."

"You going to cut off my hand?"

"Let's deal plainly with each other, DI Micallef. We'll get along better. Who is with you?"

Wingate spoke into the microphone. "This is DC James Wingate."

"Hello, Detective Constable," said the voice.

"Ma'am," he said.

"Tell me, DC Wingate. Were you a part of the decision to cancel my appearance in the *Record* on Thursday? I was rather upset to see I'd been bumped from the paper."

He gave Hazel a searching look, not sure how to answer. She said, "We don't discuss procedure with the target of an investigation."

"I think what you mean is you can't discuss an investigation you're not leading."

"Oh I'm –"

"– just a second," said the voice. She leaned down to write. "Had another idea. They come so fast and furious. Everything connecting."

"Why don't you tell us your ideas?" said Hazel.

The head rose again and seemed to be searching in the middle distance. There was a sharp inhalation of breath. "In every pause in a story, something enters. Like a radiowave full of invisible news. Most people can't hear those pauses. Can you, Hazel?"

"I'm reading between your lines."

"Yes, yes you are," said the voice. "I've been very pleased. I think we're doing very well together. Maybe the story will have a different ending than the one I've been planning."

Wingate spoke. "What ending have you planned?"

"Now, now, Detective Constable. Do you read the end of a book before its beginning?" She began to write again. "I knew someone who used to do that. Couldn't stand the suspense of not-knowing. Let's just say the *trajectory* of a story has a natural end-point. We're wired for it, did you know that? The shape of our lives imposes itself on the way we tell stories: a welter of possibilities at the beginning narrows and narrows and inevitabilities appear that obligate us to take certain turns. And then the end is a foregone conclusion. However, twists are possible in such stories as the one we're telling. Unexpected outcomes. In my experience, it happens only rarely. But we can see."

"We've read chapters four and five –" he began.

"I know," the voice said.

"How do you know?"

"You were at the house, weren't you? How would you have known to go if not for those chapters? Excellent reading, by the way."

Hazel felt her cheeks heat up. Where had this woman been this morning? Had she been in the house? "Is this Gail Caro?" she asked.

The figure put the pen down with a clack. "Oh, don't be stupid now," she said. "I'm counting on you to know a red herring when you see one." She shook her head and muttered *Gail Caro* under her voice. "If I can find you through a computer screen, don't you think I can see you out in the open?"

"Fine," said Hazel. "How do we find *you*?"

"I'm not hiding," she said. "Not exactly. You'll have me when it's time. But for now, forget about Anonymice, forget about tracing signals, forget about driving up and down the highways and byways of this great province looking for electronic signatures . . . you'll just be wasting your time, and you know it."

"Then why are we talking right now? What is it you have to say to us? Because I don't feel like wasting any more of my time gabbing with a sick fuck like you. And I *will* find you, on my own time, not yours."

The figure sighed and came to stillness. Then she turned in the chair and faced the camera. "You already found me," said Gil Paritas, "and you let me go. What makes you think you can find me again, or keep me if you do?"

"Goddamnit," said Hazel.

Paritas stared into the camera. "*Great Scott*, she thinks, *I had her in my clutches. And I let her go.* But of course you did. I'm presiding over more than one story at a time, Hazel. The one in the paper, the one you're starring in, and the one that's already been written."

"I don't understand."

"Why didn't you ask me for ID? That would have been a fine twist. Those two nice constables this morning thought to ask for yours. In fact, it was the first thing they settled: that you were who you claimed to be."

"What would your ID have said?"

"Something that told you I was Gil Paritas. Fake ID's easy to get, DI Micallef. But the point is, you didn't question what you were being told. You took what you saw in front of you at face value, and that's not going to work. Not for what we're doing."

"And what are we doing?"

Paritas turned and tilted her head at the camera, quizzically. "We're solving a murder. I thought you knew that. Didn't you ask me how to save her if she's already dead?"

"I did."

"Well then, don't you want to know how?"

Hazel felt crestfallen. She imagined Chip Willan on one shoulder and her old mentor, Gord Drury, on the other. Willan's legs dangled down, his arms were crossed over his chest. *Tsk, tsk*, he muttered, *stegosaur trouble*. Drury leaned into her ear. *You can never give them too much rope*, he said.

"Yes," said Hazel. "I want to know how."

Paritas nodded approvingly. "Then let's carry on."

"First . . . I want to know if that man in the chair over there is still alive."

"You mean Colin?"

"Yes."

Paritas half turned away from the camera. "Colin? Dear? You still breathing over there?" Eldwin remained motionless in the chair. "He must be sleeping."

"I've got no motivation to listen to you if I think that man is dead."

"Oh, he's not dead, just a little hard of hearing."

"Colin Eldwin!" Hazel called out suddenly. "We can see you! We know where you are and we're coming to get you! Give me a sign that you can hear my voice!"

Paritas appeared to be watching as intently as Hazel was, her eyes switching back and forth between Eldwin and the camera. She shrugged theatrically. "Maybe he doesn't respond to bluffs. Or maybe he's just lost in his own world."

"We're turning you off," said Hazel.

"I'll say   "

"Give us proof Eldwin is alive."

"Hold on," said Paritas. "Let me whisper in his ear." She turned back toward the table and leaned down. Her face appeared to be close to the table's surface. Hazel felt ice forming in the pit of her stomach. "Colin?" Paritas whispered quietly. "You awake? There are some nice people here who want to talk to you." She sat up and looked over her shoulder at them. "I don't know, guys," she said. "Maybe you should talk to him." She slowly raised a hand into view: she was pinching two small pieces of discoloured purple meat between her thumb and forefinger. It took them a moment to recognize them as a pair of human ears. Wingate staggered back from the desk with his hand over his mouth. "But I should warn you," said Paritas, "he's never been much of a listener."

"Oh *fuck*," said Hazel, and she felt the damp heat rising in her throat —

"Hold on," said Paritas, and she got up now, and carried the dripping parts over toward Eldwin, who, feeling her footfalls on the floor, sat up stiffly in the chair and turned his face, his eyes gleaming wide in terror. They saw the dark red chasm in the side of his head, and when Paritas pressed the severed ear back into place, Eldwin began to scream. She turned back toward the camera. "I think he's alive," she called. "What do you two think?"

Hazel and Wingate were standing behind the desk, unable to speak or move as Colin Eldwin continued to struggle, crying out incoherently, the chair bumping sideways, its feet shrieking against the floor like fingernails on a chalkboard. Paritas pulled the ear off the side of Eldwin's head and looked at it, a string of thick liquid still connecting it to him. "They make excellent paintbrushes," she said, coming back toward them. She walked past the table, dropping Eldwin's ears on top of what she was writing, and continued directly toward the camera. "Now let me ask you: do I have your attention?"

Hazel's breath was coming in short bursts. "Yes."

"Good," said Paritas. "You've already heard what you have to do next. Figure it out and we'll talk again. Make yourselves worthy of *my* attention." Her gaze went beyond the lens now, to behind it, as if she were staring through the wall they now stood against. "Dean?" she said, and the screen went black again and the green transmission icon vanished.

They dispatched a car to Gilmore anyway, but Bellocque's house was dark and locked up tight. She knew a warrant to force entry would get them nowhere, but she put it in motion and left it with Sean MacDonald. He'd go in and check every meaningless inch of that cluttered mess of a house and she knew he'd find nothing. They discussed keeping a car on the site, but Hazel remembered Paritas's words: if they could find them through the internet and in the streets of downtown Toronto, they were probably smart enough not to go back to Bellocque's.

She put Forbes on the Paritas name and told him to spend the rest of the afternoon unravelling it whatever way he could. A simple search of the telephone book and then county records confirmed, as they presumed, that there was no Gil Paritas anywhere in Westmuir, and Hazel kept her own rueful counsel on that fact, recalling the toss of Paritas's head when she asked her what the name meant. *Greek for woman-stuck-in-traffic.* And Hazel had watched her flounce down the steps to her car. Not for one instant had Paritas worried that Hazel would not do exactly what was expected of her: she played good-cop/bad-cop all by herself, she laid a bluff, got called, and then showed Paritas her whole hand. And the woman had practically walked out of the station house whistling. *Idiot,* thought Hazel. *You've been made to order.*

Forbes was waiting at her office door with some handwritten notes. He reported that web searches on the word had finally brought him to a Latin translation page that gave "paritas" to mean "equal." But one site offered a more tantalizing translation: *we are the same.*

"As what?" Hazel wondered aloud. "Who's 'we'?"

"Her and Bellocque? Her and Eldwin?" said Forbes.

"Maybe."

She went to find Wingate. "We have to tie Eldwin to that house. That's our next move."

"I'll call Childress back. See if she has anything for us yet. And I think it's time we should get back in contact with Claire Eldwin. She has a right to know."

"Don't tell her about the hand," Hazel said. "Or the ears." She thought for a second. "Don't give her any details at all."

"I'll handle it." She seemed to be studying his face. "Skip?"

"Three stories, Paritas said. We know two of them. The third is 'already written.' What is that third story, James?"

"I don't know."

"And what can you save the dead from?"

There was a long silence, as if they were watching something take shape in the air between them, and then Wingate said, "A lie."

"A lie."

He'd already picked up the phone. "If I call and Childress has something we can use, we're going to have to get into bed with Twenty-one. Are we sure we want that?"

"Will they help? They're your people."

"They'll help, but no one likes to be wrong. If something went south in their own backyard . . ."

She thought about that for a moment. Then she said, "I don't care. Make the call."

23

Sunday, May 29

Childress got back to Wingate at the beginning of her next shift, Sunday morning. It came through as a handwritten fax, a dated list on Childress's notebook paper. The fact that it was off her PNB and not on a piece of scrap paper meant the matter had entered Twenty-one's caseload on some level and they were already on the division's radar, whether they wanted to be or not.

There were twenty names covering all five apartments from 2000 to the present. Most of the tenants were long-term and their start and end dates were in full-year increments. Three rental terms ended prematurely, but there was no Colin Eldwin or Nick Wise or any other name that could resolve to Eldwin. But one of them was a "Clarence Earles," and it seemed as good a place to start as any. Wingate called Mrs. Eldwin to give her an update and to take the opportunity to ask if her husband ever used pseudonyms.

"*That's* why you're calling?"

"We need to tick off all the boxes, Mrs. Eldwin. I'm sorry."

"Shouldn't you be out there trying to *find* him?"

"This is part of it."

"Why would he use a pseudonym?" she asked. "He's never published anything anyway."

"What about when he gets hired to write something?"

"You mean *How to Use Your New Garage Door Opener*? I don't think those 'texts' get signed, Officer."

"Okay," he said, trying to calm her down. "Can I ask you if the name Clarence Earles means anything to you?"

"Clarence Earles," she repeated, flatly. "Does it mean anything to *you*?"

"They're his initials, Mrs. Eldwin."

"*That's* your lead, Detective? You found his *fucking* initials? Did you find them carved on a fucking *tree*?"

"Mrs. Eldwin, please –"

"Why don't you put out an APB for Clint Eastwood, then? Or Carmen fucking Electra? Surely a girl with tits that big must be hiding something."

He forced himself to continue over the sound of her furiously sucking on a cigarette. "Ma'am, did you ever live on Washington Avenue in Toronto?"

"Yeah, I did. For ten years with Chris Evert. You know, the gay tennis player? Did you know I led a whole secret life with a lesbian tennis star who shares her initials with my husband? Hey, with me as well. Isn't that something?"

"Mrs. Eldwin," he said firmly, but she interrupted him.

"FIND MY HUSBAND!" she shouted. "Don't call me with code words, addresses, trails of breadcrumbs, or smoke signals until you know where he is, do you hear me? That's *your* job. You fucking . . . useless . . . piece of –"

He hung up.

He found Hazel feeding Mason a sunflower seed through the bars of his cage. "Um, I don't think she knows anything. Claire Eldwin."

"Okay," she said, watching the mouse eat.

"She might be crazy, that one."

"You think so?"

"She thinks Chris Evert was gay, for one."

Hazel squinted at him. "She wasn't?"

"No. It was Martina Navratilova. Evert was straight."

"They weren't lovers?"

He sighed. "No, they weren't. Evert married another tennis player. I think."

"Why do you know this?"

"Tennis fan," he said. "Anyway, she never had a place on Washington."

"When was this Earles person in that apartment?"

Wingate unfolded the fax from his pocket. "January to August 2002."

She took the sheet from his hand and studied it. "The rental was for eight months."

"So?"

"So Earles moved out the beginning of September 2002."

She waited for him to cotton on, but she'd lost him.

"That's when the Eldwins moved to Mulhouse Springs. He rented that place for eight months and then got out of town."

"How can you be sure it's him?"

"Paritas sent us there for a reason. And the initials, the time frame . . . it all fits. That, or we're being shined on for no reason at all."

"That's a possibility," he said.

"Even so, between the choice of acting on what we think we know and doing nothing, what choice do we actually have?" She cracked a sunflower seed between her teeth and took the kernel out to feed the mouse. He took it from her between the bars with his tiny, pink paws. When he sat back on his haunches, he looked like a little old man eating a sandwich.

"So," he said. "January to August 2002. That's our starting time frame."

"Right. We have a house, a picture of a sweater, and an eight-month window."

"There must have been thirty homicides in Toronto in the first half of 2002."

"No," she said, and she came away from the cage. "It's not a murder, James. That's why we've been deputized. *We're* investigating a murder, but whatever it was in 2002, that's not how it was ruled. You get it? It was something else."

"But some of this is pretty contingent, Hazel."

"Something you can see right in front of your eyes doesn't require a leap of faith."

Wingate pulled a chair out from the desk behind him and sat. He stared at the mouse cage. "So it looked like a natural death," he said. "Or an apparent suicide. Or maybe it was an accident that wasn't an accident – someone messing around with the brake cables, you know? It's not hard to set it up. Someone falls out a window, leaves the gas on, tips over a candle." He disappeared into himself for a moment. "We're not talking about a missing person here though, because that suggests foul play and there'd still be an open file. If I kill someone and then want to get married and move away, I don't want anyone asking questions. I want to be sure the body is in the ground and the file is closed."

"That's right. So we have to find that file and reopen it."

"That's a needle in a haystack, Skip."

"At least we have it narrowed down to a haystack." She pushed herself off from the coffee table. "Let's get back down to Toronto. Make an appointment to see them first thing tomorrow and sit down with them, show them some respect, get them onside."

"We're the ones who're going to have to get onside," Wingate said. "If there's a case, it's theirs."

"Maybe I'll let you do the talking." He smiled uncomfortably at her. "Being the prodigal son's got to be worth something," she said.

Cartwright was waiting in the hallway by Hazel's office door. The door was closed. As Hazel approached, her secretary seemed to move to block her. "Skip?"

"Melanie?"

"I just want to say I asked him to wait somewhere else, but he insisted on going into your office."

"Who?"

"I didn't think it was right to insist."

Hazel leaned in and lowered her voice. "Is it that goddamned Willan with his fucking surfboard?"

"Who?"

"It's *your* job to keep people *away* from me, Melanie."

"I did what I could," she said.

Hazel put her hand on the doorknob, straightening and pushing her shoulders back. She opened the door and the man sitting in the chair on the guest's side of her desk turned and it was Ray Greene. She jerked to stillness and stood paralyzed in the doorway. "I'm sorry," he said. "I didn't want to start people talking by waiting around somewhere they could see me." He stood up and turned to face her. He was in a dark blue suit, civilian uniform, and she saw he'd lost a good fifteen pounds. She couldn't speak. "Did you get my bottle?"

"I did," she said. "That was thoughtful of you."

"I hear not all your gifts were as welcome."

"No," she said, and she finally entered the room, closing the door behind them. "Where'd you hear that?"

"I'm not totally out of the loop."

"The fact that you're sitting in my office speaks volumes to that. You didn't pour yourself a drink, though."

He smoothed down the front of his jacket. "I didn't want to take liberties. But if you're offering –"

She took her seat behind the desk and reached down into a drawer to her left. It had been almost six months since she'd spoken to Ray Greene, and apart from his gift, she'd had no proof he was still in Westmuir. She had just the one glass and she poured and pushed it over to him before shaking her coffee cup over the garbage can and putting a shot in it. He held his glass up to her in an awkward, incomplete gesture and then drank it back. She put her mug down untasted. "You're not here to ask for your job back."

"No," he said.

"You're not the kind of person to butter someone up with a twenty-sixer and then show up hat in hand, are you?"

"You know me that well."

"I guess I do. Then what is it?"

"I wanted you to hear it from me."

"Shit," she said.

"Willan's going to put me in as the CO of the amalgamated Westmuir force. Port Dundas is going to be headquarters."

"When?"

"January one."

"Fucking hell."

He looked down into his empty glass. "I don't like amalgamation any more than you do, Hazel, but standing on principle is just another way of doing nothing and being nothing. And I need to work."

"You couldn't work under me, Ray, you think it's going to be easier with the reins?" He hadn't made eye contact again, not since he'd tried to toast her. "Jesus," she said. "Are they just going to pasture me or are they hoping I'll resign in a snit?"

"They're hoping for a resignation."

"And if I don't?"

Now he looked up. "Then you'll have me backing you. I don't want you to quit."

She pushed the meat of her palm into her forehead. "I can't handle this right now. There's too much going on —"

"I can come back —"

"Why'd you say yes? There'd have been a brand new desk anywhere you wanted in the OPS. You could have gone to the big smoke if you wanted to. Why come back here?"

"Because this is what I know." She waited for him to deliver the rest of the speech. How he could be put to best use here, how they'd be able to work out their differences and be effective together. But that was all there was, and she had to admit, she understood. He wasn't just police, he was Westmuir police and probably six long months hung up drawing early pension was enough to convince him that taking over Westmuir was a good portion even if it meant coping with her resentment, her anger, perhaps her insubordination. Willan had calculated it would be her dinosaur moment, but she was already pretty sure she wouldn't let him have the satisfaction.

She was silent, not allowing him the release of a reply to his astonishing news. His shoulders were halfway to his ears, as if he might disappear into his suit jacket. Finally, she said, "Are you ready?"

"No," he said plainly. "I want it to be two years from now, when all the growing pains are over."

"Suddenly you're an optimist, huh? Two years?"

He appeared to find something in his glass and lifted it to his lips. A thin rill of Scotch ran down the side into his mouth. "Hazel, I know this is not the way you imagined the future, not at all. But there were a lot of ways this could have shaken down and this is one of the not impossible ones. I want you to consider the upside."

"I already see it, Ray."

"Good."

"I'm going to shove this in Chip Willan's face and I'm going to give you a stomach ulcer. And then, when I do retire, on my own clock, you can throw me a giant party."

"If you'll stay, Hazel, you can even choose the flavour of the cake."

"Mine will be chocolate and yours'll be crow." She looked to the clock on the wall. "I presume you can find your way out?"

He seemed surprised that their conversation was already over and he stood awkwardly, as if a person of importance had just entered the room. He'd come ready to battle with her and she'd denied him that – he looked confused, as if he'd bought something he'd not meant to buy. But, after a moment, he got up and took his overcoat off the back of the chair. "I know you're busy, so I won't keep you any longer."

"I guess we'll be talking," she said.

"I guess so," he said. "Thanks for seeing me."

She let him get to the door, and then she said, "Did I have a choice, Ray?" She saw him stiffen with his hand on the knob and she braced herself. But then he took his hand off the door and turned square to her.

"Do you mean, why weren't you consulted?"

"Sure, start there."

"Would *you* have consulted you?"

He had her there. "But why punish me? I've done so much here. I've been an asset. I don't deserve to be squeezed like this."

He came back to the chair he'd been sitting in and leaned against the back of it. "You've never deserved anything but to be on the case. That's who you are. You're a brilliant detective, but you should never have been put in charge of anything. You became so-called 'interim' out of loyalty to the force, to ex-Inspector Drury, to the people the OPS has left waiting for another shoe to drop. But would you ever have chosen to be CO? Is it what you really wanted?"

"No," she said, unable to look at him now.

"I left because when I was underneath you I couldn't do anything about your . . . *lesser* instincts. There were cases here that almost got away from you entirely with no one to balance you out. You can't be a maverick and a leader at the same time, Hazel – no one can. But without the pressure to wonder what a more sensible version of yourself would do in a given situation, you might actually feel *free* for the first time in years. It's not a bad situation if you look at it more closely."

"I'm sure almost anyone would be honoured to work under you, Ray. But think of how it looks for me."

"It looks like survival, Hazel. Those who work for you can keep *coming* to work. Direct your pride toward them and you might see it differently."

"Watch it. You're not my boss yet."

He stood his ground, wondering if he'd detected a softening, even a tiny one. He couldn't be sure. He let go of the chair. "How's your case coming?" he asked.

"Slowly. We're up the creek with a paddle."

"At least you have a paddle." He smiled warmly, glad to be ending on a slightly better note than it appeared they would. But she was frozen, as if she'd seen a ghost. "Hazel?"

"We'll be talking, Ray. Thank you for coming in."

He looked confused, but then decided he wasn't going to push his luck. He murmured *okay then* under his breath and saw himself out. She noticed her hand was shaking. Cartwright was standing in the doorway. "You have calls."

"Anything pressing?"

"Maybe one." She handed Hazel a pink sheet. The message said: *Stop at A & R Electronics on your way out of town. GP.*

She crumpled the note. "Jesus. She knows when I'm going to take a piss, for Christ's sake."

"I'm sorry?"

"Never mind. Get me Wingate."

He appeared in her office a moment later. "Was that Ray Greene?"

"Don't suffer future pain," she said. "I want you to call your people again."

"My people?" He watched her, noting how upset she seemed. "What did Ray tell you?"

"He congratulated me for being up the creek with a paddle."

"That doesn't sound like Ray."

"That's not exactly what he said. But it did trigger a thought for me. I think we've been squinting our eyes a little too much. We should have seen this clearly a long time ago."

"I'm not following you."

"The mannequin in Gannon Lake? The story in the paper . . . the body in the tarp? We're looking for a drowning, James."

He thought about it for a moment. "We might be, yeah."

"Twenty-one has most of the waterfront, doesn't it?"

"Yeah. And the harbour as well as the Islands."

"It could fit. I want to be there first thing in the morning." She looked at the laptop on her desk, and the site was still dark. For the first time in a week, she closed the computer. "Call your people and set it up," she said.

] 24 [

The huge stone and glass building that was Twenty-one Division occupied half a city block between John and Simcoe streets on Richmond Street West. Its jurisdiction was tiny: only six square kilometres of downtown, plus the waterfront and the Toronto Islands, and yet it served a population of over three hundred thousand residents and another two thousand transients. A baseball or hockey game could increase its catchment by ten percent. It went out on over fifteen thousand calls in an average year, fielded two hundred and thirty officers and twenty detectives, and was justifiably proud of its clearance rate.

Detective Constable James Wingate hadn't passed through Twenty-one's glass doors in almost a year. Since his leave, he'd been in and out of the building in his dreams, but not in the real world. The prospect of entering it again was not one he'd entertained since moving to Port Dundas (a rare out-of-force transfer), and as he and Hazel pulled in behind the building, he felt a fist clenching in his guts. He pulled his OPS cap down hard over his eyes and walked behind her as she went around the front of the building, but keeping his head down and staying in her shadow could not lessen the pull the place had on him. He felt, all of a moment, as if the last six months of his life – months in which he thought he might even heal – had never happened and someone had snapped their fingers to bring him out of his trance.

"James?" She was standing now a few paces in front of him, looking at him. He hadn't realized he'd stopped in his traces. "What's going on?"

"Smog," he said. "Makes me dizzy."

"Well, get out of it, then," she said. She strode up to the doors and held them open for him. "The air'll be better in here."

"I guess."

"Think anyone will remember you?"

"I doubt it," he said.

They were inside a bright atrium. "These are your old stomping grounds," she said. "Lead on."

They crossed the floor toward the intake desk, where a sergeant was talking to a young woman. The sergeant offered Hazel his flat, all-purpose gaze and then returned to the woman in front of him. "He's got a permit for the street, Ma'am?" he said, and she agreed that "he" did.

"But he's my *ex*," she said. "He doesn't even *live* in this part of town. What does it sound like to you?"

"It sounds like he enjoys parking on your street."

"Doesn't he have to live on the street to get a permit?"

The sergeant stared dully at the sheet. "You have a point."

"*Thank* you."

"But unfortunately, unless he tries to enter your property, this is a job for City Hall."

"What?"

"Parking office. If his permit isn't valid, they're going to have to deal with it."

"But —"

"Next," he said, and he turned his face to the OPS officers. He offered them an expression that said he'd heard everything, many times, and that all of it bored him, bored him to *death*, and here was your chance to change all that, to tell him something new. He looked back and forth between them, staring dully at their uniforms as if he were looking right through them. "You two selling cookies?" he asked.

"Yeah," Hazel said, trying to start off on the right foot, "you want chocolate or vanilla?"

"I like funny people," he said, his mouth making a line as straight as a knifeblade.

Wingate stepped forward. "Hi, Carl. We're here for DC Toles."

"Oh, hey there, Jimmy." It was as if Wingate had just stepped out for a coffee, not left the force a year ago. "He expecting you?"

"Yeah."

"All right then," said the sergeant named Carl. He picked up his phone. It had at least fifty buttons on it. "Detective? I've got a couple OPS here at the front desk." He listened for a moment and then laughed. "Okay then." He hung up and his face reverted to its deadened expression. "The newbie's coming out to get you."

Hazel nodded. Wingate was slowly trolling the posters on the wall opposite. What was it with him? Was it this hard to be back in his old division? She'd have to ask him about it later.

"You want to know why I laughed?"

It was Carl talking to her. "Sure," she said.

"Detective Toles asked me if you were dropping bread-crumbs behind you."

"That's funny."

"That's why I laughed," he said. "Toles's going to fit in here just fine."

"How new is he?"

"He's still wearing the coat hanger his jacket came on."

A door behind the sergeant's desk opened and they got a glimpse of the busy squad room behind: men and women walking around half in a hurry, cops leaning over computers, cops talking on phones. The man who came through was tall and held himself so he extended to his full height. He wore square black-framed glasses over brown eyes and looked more like an art director than a detective. Then the door closed behind him and it was strangely quiet again. He came over and shook hands. "Danny Toles," he said. He chucked his chin in the sergeant's direction. "Carl tell you any good ones?"

"A couple," said Hazel.

Toles led them through a door at the end of the foyer and down a hallway to a set of stairs. Twenty-one seemed bigger inside than it did from outside. Every person she passed, sitting in either an office or a cubicle, seemed busier than any one of her people. The interior of the building was a din of human voices, a multitude of doors opening and closing, phones ringing, laughter.

The sound of the phones reminded Hazel of what was in her pocket. They'd stopped, as the message had told them to, at A & R Electronics, one of the newer stores in the chain of big box stores that continued to spring up behind the town. She gave her name and the man behind the counter passed her a box in a bag. It was a "Mike," he explained: a closed-circuit radio-phone. Not much call for them, he said, what with all the new-fangled cellphones. She took it reluctantly and turned it on: it was the second handheld talking device she'd been bought in less than a year, and the first one was rotting in a landfill some-where now. The little window glowed dully in her hand and she'd left it on ever since, but no one had called.

Toles led them up a flight of stairs to the second floor, which was given over to meeting rooms and evidence rooms, various offices and lounges. Hazel presumed the cells were in the base-ment. "Thank you for setting this up," said Hazel. "I know you folks must be busy."

"Usually with this kind of request, we just fax the particu-lars, but since you're not sure what you're looking for, you're going to have to let your fingers do the walking." He unlocked a door with a small window in it and let them go in in front of him. The plaque on the door said *Room 32*. There was a table already stacked with files.

"Wow," said Hazel.

Toles said, "I pulled everything we had for January to August 2002. Accidents, suicides, unusual circumstances."

"How many?" asked Wingate, looking at the table.

"Our division, forty-one for the period. Citywide, just over a hundred."

"Good lord," said Hazel. "That many?"

"Those are just the sure unnaturals. Three hundred times that number of people died in the period in the GTA alone, and surely you could set aside another twenty as 'maybes.' Someone helping Granny over the last obstacle, you know?"

They'd decided not to tell Toles that they were looking for a drowning. But with a hundred bodies to go through, there were surely more than just a handful of floaters. Hazel was beginning to see the size of their task. They moved to the table to take the two chairs that had been provided. "Here they are," Toles said, which seemed an odd thing to say when he'd already shown them the files, but she realized he wasn't talking to them. A shadow had appeared in the door. A whip-thin black man with intelligent eyes and long hands stood there with his fingers laced in front of him. Wingate stiffened.

"DC Wingate," the man said.

"Superintendent Ilunga."

"Change of heart?"

"No, Sir."

"Too bad." The man stared at Wingate, then lifted a hand and stroked the tip of his nose with his forefinger. "You just going to stand behind that chair like you're about to train a lion?"

"No, no," said Wingate, starting forward. He offered his hand, but instead of taking it, the superintendent gripped Wingate on the shoulder and pulled him into a hug. Hazel saw the look on the man's face and it surprised her: his officious bluster hid a heavy heart.

"Welcome back whatever the reason," he said. He released Wingate and offered Hazel his hand. "Peter Ilunga," he said.

"Superintendent."

He held her hand a beat too long; the gesture silently asserted his control. "I gather you two are here to find something we missed."

"It's not like that," said Hazel.

"Yes it is." He smiled easily. "Just be careful and remember we live and die here by our clearance rate. If you're going to move something from one side of the ledger to the other, you better be sure."

"I understand."

He turned to Wingate. "Does she?"

"We do, Sir."

"Detective Constable Toles is *eager* to be out on the streets detectiving," he said, shooting the new dick a friendly look, "but he's here to be of *service* to you. However, at the first sign that you're throwing spaghetti at the wall, we turn back into a fortress and the two of you can return to fining people who have too many trout in their coolers."

"Understood," said Hazel.

At last, Superintendent Ilunga stood aside and gestured to Toles to leave. "Then the room is yours." Toles left and Ilunga, leaning in to close the door, said to Wingate, "Come and see me when you're done here, will you? You know the way."

"I do."

"Good luck," he called over his shoulder.

Toles had left a handwritten key to the files on the table. It said, "Blue=suicide; Brown=death by misadventure; Purple =anything that doesn't fit anywhere else. Purple usually=bad smell. ½ get reactivated w/in a year, get solved, other half are black holes. Good luck."

"Okay," said Hazel to Wingate. "Maybe we should begin with the blues?"

"Sounds about right," said Wingate.

Hazel separated out the blue files and placed the pile between them. "What was that with Superintendent Ilunga?" she asked him.

"What?"

"Come on, James. He held you like a long-lost son. You should have seen his face."

Wingate took the top folder off the pile and opened it in front of him. It told the story of a subway suicide. "Yeah, that," he said.

"You don't want to talk about it?"

"I don't know, Skip. It's a long story."

"Maybe later, then."

"Yeah," he said, "later." He closed the file and pushed it to one side. "Subway. Don't look at the pictures."

"I won't." She opened the next one. "Jumped from a window."

They started rifling the piles faster. "Sleeping pills."

"Same here."

"Hanged himself." He turned one of the scene-of-crime pictures on its side. "That's disgusting. How could anyone do this to themselves?"

"I hear it goes wrong most of the time," Hazel said.

"Well, not this one. He about tore his own head off."

"Thanks, James."

They continued through the files, shaking their heads and muttering causes: razors, guns, overdoses, bridges. Carbon monoxide, suicide by car, by cop. Even within the litany of despairing deaths, there were those that stood out: one man had beaten himself to death with a hammer (his fingerprints were all over the handle and forensics determined the blows to his forehead had come from waist-height), and in another case, a girl of ten had stabbed herself in the stomach with a kitchen knife. The autopsy report in that file revealed a twenty-week fetus inside the girl. There had been three drownings as well: these they set aside.

They moved on to the "death-by-misadventure" pile: there were stories here as horrifying as those in the blue pile, reports on people who'd bumbled their way off the planet. At least half of the files involved cars: people in them, people under them. It never stopped amazing Hazel the different ways people could screw up their relationship to a machine weighing a ton and a half. In these files they found the boating accidents as well: crashes and drownings. They added five more files to the watery-grave pile.

In the undefineds they found the electrocutions, the accidental falls, the unwitnessed deaths that forensics failed to solve. Here there were no drownings at all, drownings, by definition, being less mysterious than a man who turns up behind an after-hours gambling den, face up, eyes open, and dead as a nail, as one of the files reported. The SOC pictures in that folder were particularly surreal: a man lying on his back staring up at the stars.

So they had eight drownings between January 1 and August 31, 2002. They laid them out in a row and stared at them. Three men, five women. They set the men aside. Hazel held up one of the women; she'd come out of the "misadventure" pile. "Janis died in her bathtub," she said, spreading two photographs on the table between them. They were colour pictures that showed clearly the gradations of colour on the woman's swollen face. "That strikes me as a real challenge, don't you think?"

"To make it look like a suicide, you mean?"

"Yeah."

He took the file from her. No signs of a struggle, the woman had been found alone. Blood alcohol of .17. Coroner ruled it accidental. "Someone could have gotten her drunk and stuck her in the tub," he said.

Hazel thought about it and nodded. She put Janis on the *maybe* pile.

Georgia Marten had died going through the ice on Grenadier Pond. Her husband, who'd been taking a walk with her, had been ruled out as a suspect. Misadventure.

The next two had both drowned in Lake Ontario in the summer months. The first, they'd concluded, had jumped from one of the island ferries. There'd been a receipt for a ticket in one of her pockets. Lana Baichwell, thirty-two, single, no criminal record, no history of depression or drugs, lived with her mother. "I like her," said Hazel. "She fits. She doesn't look like a candidate for suicide. Someone could easily have pushed her over the side of the ferry."

"Those ferries are full in the summer," said Wingate. "No witnesses to some guy forcing a woman over the railings?"

"But what about no witnesses to a suicide?"

"If she wanted to do it, there are ways to slip over quietly. But you'd think someone would have heard the screaming if someone was pushing her."

Hazel looked more closely at the file. "It happened on the last ferry of the night. Eleven-fifteen from the city. How many people could have been on the boat?"

He nodded. "Okay. Well, put her with the bathtub then."

The next one had stolen a rowboat from one of the docks on the island side, out of her skull on Ativan and alcohol, a bad combination at the best of times. They'd found the boat bumping up against the south shore of Centre Island and her body in two feet of water at the edge of one of the island channels. Brenda Cameron, age twenty-nine, been brought in many times on drug charges in the four years before her death; she'd been a regular in the part of town known as the Corridor. Fined a bunch of times for drug misdemeanours – most for crack, but a few pot busts too – and, as the file said, "known to police." History of depression.

"What do you think?" said Wingate.

"Possible," said Hazel, "but she sounds like a suicide waiting to happen." She flipped through the folder. The coroner had found a mark in the middle of her forehead where he figured she struck it on the edge of the boat, but the skin hadn't even been split. Hazel could picture the girl, completely blotto, trying to get one leg over the rim of the tilting boat and then the other and barking her head on the gunwale.

"What's the tox report like?"

"A recipe for disaster." She turned to the last page. "Marijuana, blood alcohol of .19 –"

"– Jesus, and she could row a boat?"

"Evidently not . . . pot, lorazepam too, good level of that. I guess she didn't want to feel it."

"I guess not." He considered the victim for a moment. "How do they know there was a boat involved? It sounds like she could have been dumped."

Hazel scanned the rest of the report. "They found a rowboat drifting in the harbour with one of her earrings in it."

They put her with Mrs. Marten and turned to the last file.

"But not least," said Hazel. "Let's hope this one has *suspicious* written all over it." However, the last file was a clear misadventure: a sailboat mishap. Two drownings, in fact, one of which was one of the two men they'd set aside. Theresa Dowling. The boyfriend went down with her. Two amateurs out on a gorgeous August day. "How about Eldwin hired the boyfriend to knock her overboard and the guy screwed up and got himself killed too?"

Wingate just looked at her.

"That's what I thought," she said, laying the file aside. She swept the three possibles back down toward the edge of the table. "Janis Culpepper, Lana Baichwell, and Brenda Cameron. Well, ladies? Were any of you murdered?"

The three faces stared up from the front pages of the files. Cameron had been a slim-faced woman with bright, happy eyes set far apart and a wide nose. She might have had some East Indian blood in her, but it was a black-and-white photo, and sometimes that changed a person's skin colour subtly. The morgue photo showed a tragically bloated face—they'd estimated she'd been in the water for more than thirty hours—but Hazel could still make out the impression on the woman's head from her pre-drowning tumble from the boat. Culpepper had been fifty-five at the time of her death and she looked well acquainted with the bottle. Her skin was edemic, mottled, her eyes unhappy. Suicide seemed a realistic diagnosis, if not an expectation. The other woman's face was rounder, blanker. The expression suggested she didn't want to be photographed. Lana Baichwell. What had happened on that ferry? There was no morgue photo of the face: they'd found Baichwell hidden, pinned between freighters at the Redpath sugar factory just east of the ferry docks and the boats rising and falling at the water's edge had worn most of the skin off her face. Unless that kind of damage had been done premortem? Hazel put her hand on Baichwell's file, and at the very same moment, Wingate put his on Cameron's.

"Cameron," he said. "The name was on Constable Childress's list."

Hazel released Baichwell's file. "You mean Brenda was one of the renters?"

"No . . ." He fell silent a moment and then got out his cell. "It was another name."

"Hold on—did it start with a J?"

"Joanne," said Wingate, remembering immediately. "You saw it on Childress's fax, right?"

"No . . . I saw it . . ." She got out her PNB and opened it to the most recent page. Her hand was tingling. She turned the notebook to him where she'd written down the names on the tenant list at 32 Washington Avenue. He marked the J. Cameron she'd written there, and then lifted his eyes to meet hers.

"Joanne Cameron."

"*We are the same*," she said.

"Paritas is Brenda Cameron's mother."

"Oh my God, James. She's renting the same apartment Eldwin was in for those eight months under the name Clarence Earles. She's living at the scene of the crime."

"What she thinks is a crime scene," Wingate said.

"'Eternal cry here,'" said Hazel, and he looked at her strangely. "Cherry Tree Lane was an anagram. Andrew worked it out. This is it, James. Brenda Cameron is the one we're looking for."

"Okay . . . okay, I buy that. So we know who Paritas is then."

"Yes."

"But who is Belloque?"

"He's the boyfriend."

"Are we sure?"

"I don't know. But the man I met in Gilmore seemed to care a lot for her. Maybe he wants to prove his worth?"

"Kidnapping and torture is a pretty extreme way to show you're boyfriend material. Whatever happened to chocolate and roses?"

"Shows what you know about modern courtship."

He scanned Cameron's postmortem report again. "Well, I think our next step is to have a discreet conversation with this investigating detective." He ran his finger across the names at the top of the file. "Detective Dana Goodman caught the case. You want me to see if Toles can track her down for us?"

Hazel put her hand over the cell he was getting ready to dial. "Hold on a second. Did you know this Goodman?"

"Never heard of her, actually. I didn't make detective until the spring of 2003. That's when I got my placement at Twenty-one. But there was no Goodman here then."

"What if she wasn't here because she blew this very investigation? Paritas—I mean Cameron—and Bellocque obviously feel it was a cock-up. I think we keep this Goodman out of the loop unless we absolutely need her. In fact, I don't think we should talk to anyone yet."

"This isn't our house, Hazel."

"We're *so* close, James. But there's still something missing, something we need before we can be sure we're safe talking to the people here."

"You think there was a cover-up?"

"I don't know."

"Ilunga's a hard-ass, but I don't think he's —"

"Do you feel strongly enough about him that you'd go to him right now with what we have? You're *that* sure he wouldn't show you the wrong side of his door?"

He thought about that for a moment. "Well, you're not sure, and you're my commanding officer. But what are we doing then?"

She was staring at the Cameron report, flipping pages. "Maybe now that we have a name, we expand the canvass. Start talking to other Camerons. Where's the father, for instance?"

"If he's not totally in the dark, then I doubt contacting him will do anything but blow our cover."

"Fine. Maybe we can get Toles to dig some more for us."

"For what, though?"

"Find out what happened to Goodman. How the investigation went. Maybe there's something internal, something that got hushed up —"

"If that's where this is all leading, we've got more on our hands than a misfiled suicide."

"Do you have the stomach for it if we do?"

"We've come this far," he said.

"That's what I . . ." She frowned. "That's . . ."

"Skip?"

She spun the file back toward Wingate. She'd idly flipped up two pages while she was thinking aloud, but now she creased them down and held her finger against a name on the third page. "What the hell is that?"

"Cameron's arrest record."

"No . . . *that*."

He leaned in. "Oh shit."

Her finger was on the name *Constable D. Goodman*. "What's the likelihood that there was a *Constable* D. Goodman and a *Detective* D. Goodman working here pretty much at the same time?"

"Pretty low."

"So constable in 2001, detective in 2002?"

"There's nothing strange about making detective, Hazel."

"But she's a beat cop with a link to a future suicide and then she makes detective and catches the case? A case that—later— at least two people think was botched?"

He started reading the file again. Cameron had been arrested too many times to count between 1998 and 2002, all misde-meanour drug busts. The ones made in '98 and '99 and a couple final arrests in 2002 were by a series of different officers, but almost all of the many dozens that were made in 2000 and 2001 were by Goodman. James locked eyes with Hazel. "So what's the connection, then? Are we looking for Goodman? You think Goodman *murdered* Cameron?"

"No, James. This Goodman arrested Brenda Cameron —" she craned her neck to look at the rap sheet "— like eighty times in a two-year period. Never charged her. Just kept her two hours, three hours, overnight once in a while. Why?"

"I don't know!" He sounded exasperated.

"You can't stop a dumb kid like this from destroying herself. But you can slow her down. Goodman was getting Cameron off the street. Giving her a cup of coffee and telling her there was help if she wanted it."

"She was protecting her."

Hazel could see it in his eyes. He was getting to the place she'd already got to.

"Oh Jesus . . ."

"Go on . . ."

"Dana's a man's name too, isn't it?"

"There you go," she said.

"Bellocque."

She smiled at him tightly. "It's not chocolate and roses, is it? Goodman's working the Corridor and there's a few of them out there that break his heart. Then he makes detective and next thing he knows, he finds one of them in the drink. Comes up a suicide, he's not happy, and he's *still* working the case. He must have pissed your boss off pretty bad to get turfed, too."

"Why'd he try for detective if he had his hands full in the Corridor? If he was some kind of Mother Goose down there, why would he opt to leave the beat?"

"Maybe he wanted to go after the cause? Maybe he got kicked upstairs. I don't know."

Wingate had a far-off look. "And does he think it's a murder because he can't accept that someone he was protecting slipped past him? Or does he really have a case?"

"He's convinced Joanne Cameron that he has a case."

"Has he convinced you?"

She stared at him without blinking for a few moments. "No," she said at last. "Not yet. And I don't see the connection to Eldwin either. But I have to admit . . ."

"What?"

"He has my attention now." She stood up. "I have to get back to that house."

"But wait —"

"No. We're there. We've got to the place they want us to get to. A man's life depends on convincing them we're working this."

"But are we?" asked Wingate.

"Goodman doesn't have to know our angle. Right now, I want to know if this really is a cold case, or if we're just dealing with an obsessed cop. But either way, I have to get to them. I have to hear the rest of it from them."

He was looking at all the paper on the table, his hands on either side of it like he was going to gather it into a ball. "What if you're still doing exactly what they want you to do? What if it's a trap?"

"What if it's a trap? Of course it's a trap, James. But I can't get out of it until I'm in it."

"Skip —"

"They've known our next move before we have ever since they sunk that mannequin in Gannon Lake. The rules aren't going to change now simply because we've figured them out. You just keep a line open and be ready to move."

Toles noticed her on her way out. "That's it?" he asked.

"Not quite," she said. "I need a break. The files are . . ."

"Hard to read," he said. "I get you. You must not see a lot of that kind of stuff where you're at."

"Not much," she said. "Listen, there a Tim's anywhere near here?"

"Go out that door and turn right, left, or go straight. You'll hit one in less than a block."

"Thanks," she said. She had her hand on the door when she turned back to him. "Detective Toles?"

"Yep?"

"You ever work the Corridor?"

"Oh yeah. Rite of passage for anyone in Nineteen or Twenty-one."

"So you must have known a Constable Goodman at one point?"

"I knew him a little, more by reputation. I was over at Nineteen when he was working the Corridor down near Mercer and Peter streets. Why're you interested in him?"

"Just his name was on a couple of arrest reports is all."

"His name would be on a lot of arrest reports. He was an occupational hazard down there if you were dealing or buying."

"Yeah," she said, keeping her tone even, "I gather he had his favourites."

"You do a lot of repeat business working a patch like that. A lot of sad, hard cases you just want to send home to their mothers, but they keep coming back. You learn to keep an eye out for the really hopeless ones."

"So it's not unusual to, like, adopt one or two of them?"

"You're lucky if your heart bleeds for only two. Goodman made something of an art of it. I still see kids down there wearing his necklaces." She was careful not to react. "Yeah," said Toles, laughing lightly, "he gave them keepsakes, thought if he marked them in some way, it would send a message to the bad-asses to leave them alone."

"Did it work?"

"Well, we weren't *bad-asses* in Nineteen, but if we picked one of his stray lambs up we'd know to call him. But you learn no matter what you do, most of them end up where they end up, right?"

"Right," said Hazel.

She went out the door and walked right to the Tim's on the corner, trying to keep her pace slow and even, just in case someone was watching, but inside, she was bursting. She got herself a coffee with two creams and two sugars, then went to the corner of Richmond and John and flagged a cab. "Number thirty-two, Washington Avenue," she said.

She changed her mind on the way and had the driver drop her on Huron Street and she walked in, the nearly empty coffee cup catching the wind in her hand. It was lunchtime and the street was quiet, the great chestnut trees making a cool, dark canopy to walk under. She kept to the even-numbered side of the street and drifted down to where she could stand across from number thirty-two. It stood on its patch of earth, looking very much like the houses on either side of it, pretty and unremarkable little Victorians, typical downtown Toronto houses, once grand, now rundown, chopped into "units" and inhabited by a rotating cast of characters of every description. But was number thirty-two different? Had it seen a murder? Did it have a truth to impart if the right person asked the right question? And was she the right person?

She crossed the street and walked up the path to the steps that led to number thirty-two's door. There was no hint that anyone knew she was there. Caro's window remained closed; there was no sound from inside the house. She checked the name list beside the door and confirmed that a J. Cameron did, in fact, live in that main-floor apartment to her right. She pressed her face to the window, as Hutchins had on Saturday morning. Yellowing venetians with no more than two millimetres of opening between them covered the windows. She pushed her right eye against the glass and tried to see into the space beyond, but all she could make out was an opening in the far wall, a passage into the room beyond. This could mean the front room of the apartment was empty or that she simply couldn't see what was in that room. It seemed important right now to determine whether someone lived in that space beyond the venetians or not. If Cameron lived there, in a kind of ongoing memorial to her daughter, or if it was a staging point of some kind. The former made her feel safer, but she felt certain it was the latter. The place had been reserved for a form of theatre and she'd been invited to see the show.

She returned to the front door and tried it gently, somewhat relieved to find it locked. Then stepped back onto the path and took the whole house in again. There was no one at the windows, no sense of movement from within. In fact, the house seemed as still as a dead heart. She wasn't sure what she'd been expecting, but as she crossed the street and began to walk in the opposite direction out toward Spadina Avenue, she felt disappointed.

She wasn't surprised to feel the radiophone in her pocket begin to vibrate. She took it out and put it to her ear without saying anything.

"I didn't think you gave up that easily."

"You want me to commit a B & E, Joanne?"

"Ah," she said. "It's nice to hear you say that name."

She'd stopped before reaching the avenue. Red and black streetcars swam past on their rails. "You can see me," she said. "Where are you?"

"*Someone* can see you," she said. Hazel turned around and looked behind her, but the street was empty.

"Have you rented a room in every house on Washington?"

"If you didn't want us to find each other, then why did you come back here?"

"I came back because I have questions." Cameron said nothing. "We found her," Hazel said. "Your girl. She drowned in Lake Ontario on August 4, 2002. She was not, at the time, someone who should have been operating a boat."

"Tell me how long we're going to stick to the official story."

"Marijuana, alcohol, and Ativan. That's what she had in her. That's what I know." She'd decided to play her cards close to her chest for the time being. "There was water in her lungs, so she was alive when she went in. It's going to be hard to convince any examiner that she did anything but end her own life."

"There's a key between two empty flowerpots at the back of the house."

Cameron hung up. Hazel was facing the direction she'd come in. She took a deep breath and began walking back to the house. It seemed to her that all the windows in the houses on either side of the street had sprouted eyes and every move she made now was being marked. The skin over her spine was tingling. She slid her hand down to her belt and flicked the snap on her holster open.

She walked up from the sidewalk at number thirty-two again and followed the path to the right gate, tripping the latch. Her heart was beating fast in her chest as she stepped into the garden, keeping to the wall as she moved slowly to the pots. There was a keychain lying in the second one down, as Joanne Cameron had told her, with two keys on it.

The fact that she would need a key to get in meant she would be alone in the apartment. But how would she know what to look for? Cameron would tell her. She knew this now. Cameron was leading her, completely. She realized she had accepted this, no matter the danger it posed her, or the rules it broke. Her hunger to know the rest of the story was greater than her sense of self-preservation.

She walked back down the pathway to the front of the house and went up the steps. With the key in the front door (she'd had to try both keys) she was joining herself to Cameron now, she was complicit.

She held the phone, waiting for a sign that Cameron was with her. She gripped the silent device in her hand. It felt hot.

The door opened silently on the dark hallway. The door to the main apartment was to her right. She stood in the hallway and listened to the house. Apart from the sound her entering had made and her weight on the floorboards, there was silence. The other key opened the apartment door.

It was empty. From the window outside, she'd viewed a denuded space. Inside, it was a generous, open set of rooms with blond wood floors burnished to a warm glow. The apartment was an empty shrine. A fireplace was bricked up in the wall across from her. She crossed into the room carefully, her hand on her hip holster. She took small, shallow breaths. Behind this living room, through the opening she'd seen, was the dining room, perhaps the main dining room in the house of old, from the time when it contained a single family and servants as well. The most gracious room in the house. A window in the back wall looked out on the half of the garden she hadn't walked through. She passed into the room, taking small steps. And then she was alone there as well. Her watchfulness intensified as the space she'd moved through diminished.

To the side of the dining room was the kitchen, and behind the kitchen, a small hallway leading to a bathroom and a bed-room. Her footsteps followed her through the apartment. From a vantage in the doorway leading into the kitchen hallway, she could see all four rooms of the apartment. It seemed a good place to establish as her blind, and she stopped there and listened again.

She thought she saw movement through the open bedroom door and pressed her back against the end of the hallway, beside the kitchen, and then smartly transferred herself to the other wall and slid down it, giving herself a vantage on the bedroom. It was empty. She felt comically grateful the closet had two doors on it, both of which swung open outwards. The closet was empty as well.

A shock went through the palm of her hand and she dropped the phone. It buzzed against the floor like a mad insect. She snatched it up and marched back to her post with the handset against her ear.

"Detective Inspector."

"I'm here," she said.

"Thank you."

She stayed completely still to listen for the voice under the voice, but if Cameron was anywhere near her, she wasn't within earshot. "There's nothing in this place," Hazel said. "Am I supposed to tear up the floorboards?"

"You could, but I can do it for you. Look around at the space you're standing in. I can fill it with tables and chairs and hang paintings on the walls. I can put my daughter here on the night of August 4, 2002, with Colin Eldwin."

"What's putting me in an empty room going to show me, Ms. Cameron?"

"It might look empty, but there's a heart under these floors."

Hazel couldn't help looking down at her shoes and, as she thought of the box buried in Nick Wise's garden, the back of her neck went cold. "I'm listening," she said quietly. She slid down the doorframe until she was sitting half in the hallway, half in the dining room. The action had pulled at her lower back, but the pain was bearable. From this vantage, she'd be able to see anyone coming from any direction.

"He'd placed an ad in one of the university papers," Cameron began. "That was where he threw his nets. 'Creative writing tutor,' it said. He auditioned them in a student pub up on Bloor Street, looked them up and down to see if they had any *talent*, and if he liked them, he told them he could help them improve. Get them published. Brenda was in a good place then – she'd signed up as a 'mature' student in the night-class programs at U of T. She wrote poetry. Did you know she wrote poetry?"

"They tend not to include that kind of detail in a police report."

"Just the bodies, not who lived in them. She wasn't a good writer, yet, but she was trying to grow. That was my daughter, always looking around for another chance at life. She'd had a lot of them. Almost as many lives as a cat, I always told her. She'd been messed up with drugs, in trouble with the police; she hooked up with the wrong men, took stupid jobs in rotten parts of town, but she always got up and dusted herself off. She made me proud of her."

Hazel shivered, thinking of Martha, and felt herself shift a spiritual inch closer to Cameron, a fellow watcher in a world where people like them suffered for others. "Anyway," she continued, "she answered his ad and went and had a beer with him. Brenda was a beautiful girl. And for all her familiarity with the street, she was unworldly. That kind of thing can help you in life if it keeps you open to the right kinds of things. They had a couple of meetings and he went over some of her poems. Then he suggested they meet here. In this apartment." Cameron lowered her voice and continued. "Maybe the first time, he served her coffee, there in the front room. Then he suggested she come for dinner. What do you call that, Detective Inspector? The *modus operandus*? That's how it worked. Like there was a conveyor belt from the front door to the bedroom and it took a few weeks to get there. Where are you right now?"

It took Hazel a moment to realize Cameron was talking to her. "I'm in the hallway beside the kitchen."

"Go into the living room."

Her heart jolted and she pushed herself up the doorframe. "Why?"

"I want you to see it as it was. I want you to be there with her."

She walked cautiously into the living room, but it was still empty. She strode to the apartment door and locked it, then stood with her forehead against it.

"There was a couch with its back to the window," Cameron said, "and a round, low coffee table in front of it. In the corner, beside the opening to the dining room, a comfortable chair with a lamp beside it."

"How do you know this?"

"She described it to me."

She turned around to look at the room. "There's nothing here, Joanne."

"All of this happened here, in this place. You don't see it yet, but you will if you let yourself." Hazel wondered if Cameron was repeating lines Dana Goodman had once said to her, when he'd turned her grief to his own purposes. "Put me on speakerphone." There was a button on the side of the device and Hazel pushed it, then leaned down and stood the phone upright in the middle of the floor. Joanne Cameron's voice radiated out of

it. "All Brenda wanted was someone to show her some kindness. I knew what Colin Eldwin was the moment she told me
about him. A carnivore. I warned her. But the heart is a puzzle,
isn't it?"

"It doesn't mean he killed her, Joanne."

"No, of course it doesn't." Hazel heard a car drive past outside the house and for a moment her attention wandered, but
she brought it back. "Brenda fell in love," the voice from the
floor said. "And that was an inconvenience to him, you know,
but he dealt with it. He used it, when he wanted her; he shot
Cupid's arrows at her, full of promises. But he tired of her. He
was too busy to see her this time or that time, but he still told
her he loved her. She couldn't read between the lines."

"She told you all this?" she asked.

"She never hid anything from me," said Joanne Cameron.
"Whether she was in love or despair, troubled or happy. I was
always there for her."

"It must be hard feeling it wasn't enough," said Hazel.

"People like Brenda . . . they're beautiful in so many ways.
They believe in others, but they can be taken in. Their love
goes out into the world and finds its kind, even if it's really
only a shadow or a show. They're blind to things like that. I told
her all the stuff you tell someone when they're on a bad drug.
That it's going to let you down. That the world doesn't look
that way when you get the juice out of your system. But she
was an addictive personality. She started turning up at his
place, unannounced. And she saw how many students he had.
She found out he had a lot of Brendas. She wasn't special."

"She must have been crushed."

Cameron ignored her. "It got bad enough that he broke up with her, finally. I guess even Colin Eldwin had his standards."

Hazel had picked up the radiophone and moved into the dining room. She imagined candles on a table set for two. "Get to the night in question," she said. "How do you know she was here?"

"He broke up with her in July, but she wouldn't stay away. She had other troubles and they were clouding her judgment."

"Drugs?"

"She'd been clean since the previous fall, but she started back on crack and she was unravelling. She showed up at my place a few times talking about how they were going to get back together, how she had a plan. He just needed her to show him the way back, she said. The night of August second, she was with me before she went to him."

"And?"

"She said she was pregnant."

Unbidden, the dead girl with the knifed fetus swam into Hazel's mind. But she knew Brenda Cameron had not been pregnant.

"Said it was the sign she was waiting for. She was going over to tell him the good news."

"She wasn't pregnant, Joanne. I saw the report this morning, remember?"

"I know she wasn't pregnant."

"The members of your family stop at nothing to get what they want, do they?"

"She's at the door," she said quietly. "It's about ten o'clock at night on August second. She knocks, calls his name."

Hazel's heart was thrashing now. She heard nothing, but when she turned to look back into the living room, she saw them in her mind's eye, Brenda Cameron walking into the apartment, Eldwin standing there, his arms crossed. She asks him if he's alone. He tells her she has to stop this, it's over, he doesn't want to have anything to do with her. She puts a hand on his arm, slides it down to his wrist, and puts his palm against her belly.

"We can't know any of this," Hazel said. "There were no witnesses to what they said to each other. To what happened here, *if* anything happened here. Just because you saw her and she told you she was coming to this house, it doesn't mean she did. She might have gone straight to the ferry docks."

"But she didn't. She came here."

"Fine. And then she killed herself. Whatever happened here that night drove her to it."

"He drugged her. He knocked her out and dragged her across the floor. He took her out to his car —"

"No, Joanne," Hazel said. "I know you want that to be true, but all of this is a figment of your grief. You and Dean Bellocque have abducted and wronged a man you *want* to be guilty of murdering your daughter. Have you thought about what it means if you're wrong? Have you thought about what you've done?"

"I know what I've done."

"I want to know where Colin Eld —" She stopped midsentence. She realized the last thing she'd heard had not come from the device she held in her hand. She looked down at it and saw the call had been disconnected.

From behind her, Cameron said, "There was a witness."

] 26 [

Hazel dropped the phone and, in one motion, freed her gun from its holster and spun, weapon extended. Joanne Cameron was standing in the living room, the light from the closed venetians spreading in a bright fan around her body. She hadn't flinched. Standing before her now, Cameron only faintly resembled that confident woman who'd shown up at her office one week ago. She looked smaller, her clothes hung off her, and her smart bead necklace looked cheap. She was holding a large white plastic bag with something inside weighing it down. Hazel's eyes flicked between Cameron's face and the bag. "Step back, Joanne," she said. "Back away."

Cameron ignored her and reached into the bag. Hazel decided if she brought out Eldwin's head she was going to shoot her on the spot. But she removed an official evidence bag and Hazel knew right away what was in it and who had given it to her.

"She was wearing this the night she was killed," Cameron said, holding out the bag with the black sweater in it. "There are bits of wood in it, and varnish. It was all in the lab report, but they ignored it."

"I told you to back away."

"Why would they ignore evidence?"

"There was no lab report on the sweater, Joanne. No report and no mention of it in the inventory of documents. I saw it all just an hour ago. It showed, definitively, that your daughter drowned herself. There was no struggle, no witnesses on the island who heard any cries for help, nothing that points to anything apart from a girl who wanted to end it all. You said it yourself: she went up and down, she hoped and she despaired. It doesn't always end well for people like Brenda, Joanne. You have to accept that."

Cameron was smiling sadly. "There's a lab report. It was done afterwards. But they wouldn't reopen the case."

Hazel hesitated a moment and then lowered the gun and put it back in the holster. She took a step toward Cameron and gently slipped out a necklace tucked into her shirt. It was a lamb dangling from a leather cord. "He couldn't save Brenda with this," Hazel said, looking at the talisman with a heavy heart. "What makes you think it can save you?"

"Do you have children, Detective Inspector?"

"Joanne, that has nothing –"

"He dragged *my* child across the floor. *This* floor. The varnish, the wood fragments are embedded in the sweater, not just on the surface. What really happened to Brenda is written on what she wore. I still believe you want to see it for yourself."

Hazel took the evidence bag from Cameron, who stood in front of her with her hands at her sides, empty. Her eyes had gone flat, like someone had turned the lights off in a room, and

Hazel realized that this was it, this was as far as Cameron could come on her own and it had cost her everything.

"I'm going to call my partner now, Joanne, and he's going to come and get us." She held the evidence bag up between them. "And I'll take care of this. I'll bring it to the police lab, I'm willing to do that for you. But it's all over now, you understand that, right?"

"Yes," said Cameron quietly. "I do."

"You're going to come in and help us put an end to all of this, Joanne."

She held her radiophone up. "I'm supposed to call at one."

Hazel looked at her watch: it was five past. "Well, let's not keep him waiting then. Dial his number. But I'll do the talking."

Cameron dialled a number and passed the device to Hazel. She held it to her ear and heard it ringing. "Joanne?" came the voice on the other end.

"Hello, Detective," Hazel said. "Although I'm ashamed to call you that."

"Ah," said Dana Goodman. "How nice to hear from you."

"Where are you?"

"That's not important right now. I want to tell you, Detective Inspector, how pleased I am. You've done a good job. Now I hope you'll finish what you've started."

"I'm not doing anything while you still have Colin Eldwin. You tell us where he is, give yourself up, and I'll do whatever I think is warranted. But right now, I have your evidence in my hands as well as your accomplice – who's a wreck, thanks to your hard work – so how about you do what I ask before you make things worse for everyone?"

"How about," he said, and he hemmed like he was trying to work things out, ". . . yes . . . how about you dust our friend off and send her on her way and then do what you're told? How about that?"

"How about Joanne Cameron gives us what we need and you go fuck yourself?" She sidearmed the phone across the room. It hit the dining room wall and shattered.

"He's not going to like that."

"Turn around and give me your hands," Hazel said. Cameron did as she was told, and Hazel had one cuff on when the radio-phone she'd dropped when drawing her gun began to ring.

"I think that's for you," said Cameron.

Hazel snapped the second cuff closed and picked up the phone. Goodman said, "Please hold while I connect you to your caller." There was an electronic buzz in the background. It repeated. Then she heard her daughter's voice.

"Hello?" said Martha.

Hazel's stomach flipped.

"Who is it?" repeated Martha, and then Hazel heard her own voice, replying:

"Hazel Micallef."

"Never heard of 'er," Martha laughed. "What are you doing in town, Hazel Micallef?"

Hazel, her limbs tingling with horror, began moving toward the door as the voice said, "I've got some work." She froze in the middle of the living room.

"Well, this is a nice surprise. You going to come up?"

"Yes."

Hazel began to shout into the radiophone: "MARTHA! DON'T OPEN THE DOOR!"

"Come in then, you weirdo."

"MARTHA!!!"

But she heard the buzz and clack of the door to Martha's building opening. Goodman came back on the line. "Let Joanne go. She'll call me when she's sure she's not being followed. I'll wait in the lobby for two minutes, and then I'm getting into the elevator." He disconnected and Hazel stared at the phone in her hand in disbelief.

"You don't have long," said Cameron. She held out her wrists.

Numb, her mind racing, Hazel got the keys and unlocked Joanne Cameron.

"I'll call him – it'll be okay, I promise," said Cameron. "I don't want any harm to come to anyone's child, you can believe that. Just . . . keep going, okay? He's serious."

"I swear to god, I'll kill you both." There was a high shrill sound like the engine of a small plane swimming around the inside of her head and her heart was pounding like a fist.

"He's getting in the elevator. I'm sorry –"

"We're going to meet again, Joanne . . ."

"I know."

Hazel watched her walk out the front door, her fists curling and uncurling as the sweat poured down the back of her collar. And then as soon as she saw her turn left toward Huron Street, Hazel burst from the house and ran as hard as she could out to Spadina Avenue without looking back. It felt like someone was clubbing her on the base of her spine. When she got to the avenue, a light rain had begun to fall and the air smelled like dust. There were no cabs, but she stepped into traffic and flashed her badge, stopping a kid in a white RAV-4. "Whaddi do?" he squeaked when she tore the passenger-side door open.

"Nothing," she said, getting in. "You're going to drive me to Broadview and Danforth as fast as you can."

"What?"

"You heard me, let's go —"

"Are you a cop?"

"Jesus Christ, has anyone in this town ever seen an OPS?"

"A what?"

"Just floor it, kid, okay? I'll take full responsibility."

The kid murmured *okay* and hit the accelerator. Martha's apartment building was on the other side of town. She saw the elevator climbing in its shaft like a bullet leaving a gun.

He couldn't have been older than seventeen and he drove like he was trying to outrun a missile. She instructed him to pause at red lights and then run them and after a couple of kilometres, the kid seemed to get into it, shooting her wry looks of excitement. "Are we tailing someone?"

"Yeah. Go faster."

"Am I gonna get on the news?" He shot a red, swerving around a left-turning truck, which honked furiously at them.

"Only if you kill us. You know any shortcuts?"

"Um — I don't really —"

"You don't have your licence, do you?"

"I have my G2."

"Aren't you supposed to have someone in the car with you when you drive?"

"Um, I have you."

"Right. Excellent." They were barrelling along Bloor Street, crossing Sherbourne. She raised Wingate on the radio.

"I was wondering when I was going to hear from you. What happened at the house?"

"I can't talk right now. You need to get to 1840 Broadview."

"What?"

"Just get in the car!" She disconnected. The kid didn't wait for her signal to run the light at Parliament and the rear of the RAV-4 fishtailed a little. She gripped the handle above the door.

"Too fast?"

"No, but watch the traffic coming off the Don Valley Parkway."

"Man, are we going on the parkway? That's awesome!"

"We're not."

"Oh, so, like you're drawing the line at the frikking parkway?"

"Watch your mouth. Stay straight." He honked going through the light at Castle Frank and a gaggle of teenagers crossing the road from Rosedale Heights Secondary School flew apart.

"I hope one of them filmed that," the kid said.

"Keep your eyes forward," she said as they crossed the Bloor Street Viaduct. She'd flagged this car seven minutes ago. The kid could drive. "Turn right at Broadview."

He did and she directed him to Martha's apartment building, shouting to him to stop when he got there. When she threw the door open, he said, "Hey, you want me to wait?"

"No, I want you to go home. Slowly. And don't break the law again."

"Don't forget your damn sweater," the kid said, holding the evidence bag out to her. She took it and slammed the door and ran toward the building. The drops of May rain still held a hint of shivery cold in them, or maybe it was the anxiety driving all the blood to her extremities as she traced her finger on the call-board down to the Ps. She buzzed Martha's apartment and then waited with her heart slamming itself against her ribs. There was no answer and she buzzed again, her breath shallow in her chest, the knuckle of her index finger turning bright yellow against the button, and she unsnapped her holster. She was going to have to blow the electro-maglock open. "Damn it, answer your door, Baby, just answer it!"

She stepped back, levelled the gun at the door, and took the safety off. "Christ," she muttered as she began to squeeze the trigger. Behind the door, in the dim light of the lobby, she saw one of the elevators open and she raised the muzzle to the widening space. Then she saw it was Martha. Alone. Hazel hurriedly put the weapon back and tried to put a smile on her face. Martha opened the door with a bemused expression, an expression that told Hazel nothing untoward had happened. "Where the hell did you go?" she asked.

"I'm an idiot," her mother said breathlessly. "I forgot which apartment was yours."

"I've been up and down twice. God, you're white as a sheet."

"I ran down the stairs."

"What? Why?"

"The elevator —" she said, but she couldn't complete the sentence and had to lean forward and grip the steel frame of the door.

"Well, don't stand there in the drizzle, then, come in. I'll put on some coffee."

Hazel caught her breath and straightened up. "No," she said.

"*No*? After all this?"

"I want you to wait here."

Martha jerked her head back, her mouth creased in perfect confusion. "What?"

"No, you're right. Come up with me."

She led her daughter to the elevators, Martha behind her saying, "What the hell is going on?" but she didn't answer her, just waited for the doors to open again, ready to tear the gun out of its holster. The elevator was empty and she ushered Martha in.

"I'm sorry," she said. "But I think someone might be stalking you."

"What? Nobody is remotely that interested in me."

The doors opened on the fourth floor and Hazel stepped out. "Wait in the hallway," she said, but Martha strode around her mother, huffing, and unlocked her apartment door before Hazel could stop her. She had no choice: she rushed forward with the gun drawn and shoved past Martha in the doorway into the living room, spinning with her head tilted and the gun in front of her. She tossed the bag onto the coffee table and stood still, facing the hallway that connected the bedroom and the bathroom. The drawn gun had silenced Martha, and Hazel gestured her into the apartment and down onto the couch. She crept into the hallway and tried to sense movement in her periphery, but both ends of the hall seemed to be empty. She held a palm out behind her to warn Martha to stay where she was and then she moved silently toward the bedroom. It was a mess – anyone casing the apartment would think it had already been tossed – and Hazel could see there was no one in view in the room. She knew Martha's closet was so packed with crap that no one could hide in it, but she went to check it anyway. She could hear banker's boxes groaning against the door and she only opened it halfway before closing it again. The bedroom was clear. She retreated down the hallway and heard "There's no one in the bathroom either," and she spun, her breath catching, and Martha was walking toward her. She put her index finger lightly on the gun barrel and pushed it down. "Do you want to tell me what's going on here?"

"I got a call."

"Uh-huh."

"It was from downstairs. That wasn't me in the speakerphone before. Someone recorded my voice."

"Are you kidding me?"

"No."

"Someone was *here*?"

"They're not here now, though," said Hazel. "It's okay now."

Martha shook her head angrily and walked back into the living room. She sat heavily back onto the sofa. "Do you mean to say you keep track of my every move, imagining all kinds of harm coming to me, *living* in worry for me, but you didn't know some creep with a recording of your voice might be paying me a visit?"

Hazel holstered the gun and sat across from Martha, unsure what to tell her. "It's a live investigation, Martha. I had no idea it was even a possibility. Your dad's name is on the lease, your number is unlisted. We did all that for a reason."

"What was that reason again, Mum? Do you think all cops' kids live in witness protection or something?"

"It was just a thought for your safety."

"You would never have felt the need to do the same thing for Emilia."

She'd come here worried for her daughter's life and now, without so much as the wind changing, they were in familiar territory where Hazel couldn't save Martha from anything. "I'm sorry," she said now. "I didn't mean to worry you."

"So now what?"

"I think maybe you should come back home until all this is wrapped up."

"No fucking way."

"Martha —"

"I'm thirty-three," her daughter said. "This is my home. How about I stay here and if it sounds like you're downstairs, I'll just pretend I'm not home."

"Please, Martha."

Her daughter said nothing. After a moment, the intercom buzzed and Martha blinked twice without moving. "You want to answer that or just shoot it?"

Hazel spiked the call button on the intercom. "Who is it?"

"I'm here," said Wingate.

"We'll be down in a minute," she said. She disconnected and took Martha's coat off the hook by the door. "I know how pissed off you are at me right now, but I have to insist. I don't know if you're safe here."

After a moment, Martha pushed herself up from the couch, exactly the same gesture Hazel could see in her mind's eye when, as a teenager, Martha had finally acquiesced to a higher power and reluctantly taken direction. She came to her mother and took the coat from her, lifted it into the air, and put it back on its hook.

"Don't worry about me," she said.

"Do you want to know who was here, Martha?" she said, finally furious. "He was a cop once, and right now he's got a man tied to a chair in a basement somewhere. Although not all of the man. He cut his hand off and sent it to me in a box and then he sliced the man's ears from the sides of his head and painted a wall with them." Martha was blanching. "So it's your choice: put on that fucking coat and come downstairs with me now, or keep your apartment locked up tight and hope he doesn't know how to kick in a door."

She told Wingate to take his time going down Broadview, she'd had enough fast living for one day. Martha sat in the back seat, looking out the window in silence.

Wingate spoke quietly. "What the hell happened back there?"

"Goodman happened. But I had her . . ."

"Who?"

"Joanne Cameron. She was at the house. She gave me this." She held up the sweater in the evidence bag. "Then Goodman called from the bottom of Martha's building."

"Jesus."

"We have to move quickly now. With the both of them down here – I don't know what he might do next."

"That's the sweater from the picture?"

"Supposedly it proves that Colin Eldwin killed Brenda Cameron."

"How?"

"I don't know. But I'll tell you something: we lucked out with Toles. He's not the sharpest biscuit in the tin and he's probably the only guy at Twenty-one who doesn't know that

Goodman made detective and then went berserk. We have to keep it quiet, but if we can get him to handle the sweater for us, we might have some new evidence we can go to the superintendent with."

"You sound like you're onside now, Hazel."

"I'm getting close. Joanne Cameron is consumed by grief, but Goodman hasn't put a foot wrong since he sank that mannequin in Gannon. Everything he's done has been considered and carefully executed. I don't like him, but he's too smart to be a loose cannon and if he's spent three years looking for someone to bring this to Twenty-one's doorstep again . . . ."

"What? We owe it to him to carry it over the goal line?"

"No," said Hazel. "We owe it to Joanne Cameron. This woman has lost everything. She deserves an answer."

"She got her answer, Hazel. If you're right, he convinced her to disregard it and if she did, that was her decision. Why is it our problem?"

"Because we caught the case, James. And we should see it through."

"If this is as you say, we're not going to be welcome at Twenty-one much longer."

"That's why we need Toles onside and Ilunga in the dark."

They drove to the bus terminal on Bay Street and Hazel bought Martha a one-way ticket to Port Dundas. Her daughter didn't argue at all. "I'll call your father to pick you up," she said. "He'll be happy to see you."

"What makes you think this guy won't show up in Port Dundas?"

"He's not leaving Toronto while I'm still here."

"How does he know you're still here?"

"He just does," she said.

They waited until the bus moved out onto Edward Street and made its turn south toward the expressway. "Let's see if Toles feels like having a coffee," she said.

Toles met them in the Tim's. He'd brought Lana Baichwell's file, like she asked him to. "You been here the whole time?" he asked. "I didn't realize you guys were from Quebec," he said, smiling.

"Uhh?" said Hazel.

"A two-hour lunch? I just figure you must be French."

"Well, actually," said Hazel, "something interesting came up." She lowered her voice. "I think we found our girl."

Toles reached carefully into a small black portfolio and drew out the file. "This one, eh?"

Hazel took the file and opened it. "She went over the side of the *Ongiara* on July 10, 2002. We've come across some evidence that she might have been pushed."

"Really. Like what?"

She nodded to Wingate, who produced the sweater. She took it from him and handed it over to Toles. "We can't talk about our source yet, but if you can get that down to your lab and there's the wood or varnish we expect to find on it, then I think we're going to want to establish some kind of joint force to carry forward. And you're already attached, Detective."

"I hear you."

"It might be a way of getting in good."

Toles looked thoughtful, running his tongue around the inside of his bottom lip. "I went to school with one of the girls in the hair and fibres department at CFS. I could talk to her this afternoon."

"How well do you know her, Danny?" asked Hazel.

"What do you mean?"

"Would she rush a job just for you?"

He smiled, happy to have his other charms noted. "It wouldn't hurt to ask." He held up the evidence bag. "Why don't you two keep having your lunch. I'll see what my girl can do for us."

———

They hadn't actually had a first lunch, and they were both starving. Wingate knew a decent sandwich shop over on Adelaide Street, and they ordered and sat in the window looking over the sidewalk.

Hazel tore off a piece of her club sandwich. If she lived in Toronto, she could have bacon every day and her mother would never know. "You have a good talk with Superintendent Ilunga?"

"Yeah," he said. "It was good to catch up."

"I get the feeling they really care for you down here."

"Yeah," he said. That wall of his was going up again. She decided to plow through it.

"I didn't realize you'd been down here for less than two years. I thought it had been longer."

"I did the exam in January 2003. I'd been in Etobicoke since the academy; they thought I had promise for CIB."

"You do."

"I guess so."

The sandwich shop was almost empty: people ate and worked on a strict schedule in this part of town. He wasn't taking on the unasked question and she was going to have to ask it. "So, James. You left. Why did you leave? Why did you get as far away from here as you could?"

He kept his eye on the world beyond the window. "The superintendent wanted to know if I'd consider coming back."

"That's what he wanted to talk to you about?"

"He was wondering if I thought enough time has passed." She put her hand on his forearm to bring him back into the room with her and he looked down at her hand. "I lost my partner," he said. "Just over a year ago, in fact. April 12 last year."

"God . . . I didn't know. I'm sorry."

"Yeah."

"Did it happen on the job?"

"No," he said, and he glanced at her. His eyes were shining. "He wasn't a police, Hazel. That's not the kind of partner I'm talking about."

The blood left her face. "Oh shit," she said. "Oh god, James, I didn't know —"

He nodded. "His name was David. They beat the hell out of him on the boardwalk in front of Queen's Quay at one in the morning. A Wednesday night. He was walking our dog. We lived in one of the condos across from Harbourfront. There were witnesses, but they didn't do anything. They were too scared, I guess. Six guys swarmed him, they hit him with everything they could get their hands on: bottles, a couple of chairs from one of the patios, they kicked his ear into his skull. Then they toed him over the walkway and into the lake. They killed Grace — the dog — too, as if she could have identified them." He slid his eyes over hers and then looked back out the window, toward the lake. "When I learned this whole case was going to focus on the lake here, I just wanted to get in my car and drive. As far away as I could. Again."

"James."

He coughed into his hand. "This detail about the Cameron case, the water in her lungs, it, you know . . ."

"What?"

"It just makes me want to die."

She could feel the heat radiating off him, as if finally telling her his secret had set him on fire.

"Did they catch them?"

"One of them." He was far away now, and strangely calm. "Brought him in, put him in one of the holding cells downstairs after they booked him. They told me where he was. There was no one at intake, but there was a key on the desk. I took off my gun and my stick and left them on the table."

"What happened?"

"He lived. Then he went to prison. Second degree. He'll be paroled in four more years, the rest of them are out there somewhere."

He hadn't taken his eyes off the passing show, but that was all he was going to say. She was trying to get more experience showing the people she cared for that she really did love them, but even at Martha's apartment, despite her fear for the girl's life, it had taken an effort. That was who she was: her love stayed inside her too much. She was nothing like Brenda Cameron, nothing like that dead girl's mother. The hot core of another person had always frightened her. She preferred relationships that didn't have to be plumbed, that could be resolved in guilt or innocence. This was neither, these crimes James Wingate had just described to her, a murder and an assault, and she didn't know what to say.

So she said, "You wanted to know what Ray Greene was doing at the station house."

"Sure," he said, as if he was going to sleep.

"He's coming back."

"That's good, isn't it?"

"Probably it will be. He's going to be CO."

"And you?"

"They want to give me the gold watch."

"Will you take it?"

What she'd told Greene had been calculated to cause maximum discomfort. But now she told Wingate the truth: "I don't know."

He pushed his plate away. He'd taken two bites of his tuna sandwich. She wasn't hungry anymore, either. "I hope you won't," he said.

They paid and left. When they were outside on the sidewalk, turning back toward the police station, she put her hand on Wingate's shoulder and turned him to face her again. "James, look, I'm no good with the comforting word, but honestly, I feel sick right now. I just wish I could –"

"It's okay," he said. "I'm glad I told you. But I can't talk about it anymore. If you're worried I'm tempted to come back here, I'm not. I'm never coming back."

She had been worried, and she was glad she didn't have to ask.

As soon as they entered Twenty-one, the desk sergeant stood and waved them over. He looked at his watch. "Nice lunch?" he asked.

"It was fine," said Hazel.

"I'm happy for you. The two of you have another date, this one with Superintendent Ilunga. He'd like to see you right away."

Hazel hadn't noticed a slender woman holding a clipboard standing at the end of the countertop. The desk sergeant gestured to her and they realized this was Ilunga's administrative assistant: she was going to take them to him. Hazel's sandwich gurgled in her gut. Something was wrong.

The assistant didn't say a word as she led them up the stairs to Ilunga's office, which was past the room they'd been given to examine records in. There was a heavy wooden door at the end of the hallway with the single word SUPERINTENDENT on it. The assistant knocked and then stepped away and vanished into her cubbyhole.

After a delay of ten or so seconds, Superintendent Ilunga opened the door and gave them both a smile, his eyes lingering on them each individually. "Come in, come in," he said, moving back toward his desk. "Close the door."

They entered and stood in front of the man's desk, waiting for the customary invitation to sit, but when he sat, he appeared to forget the etiquette, and they remained there, slightly uncomfortable and standing vaguely at attention.

"Do you mind if I eat?" he asked them, his hand hovering over a brown paper bag.

"Oh, not at all," said Hazel, gesturing stupidly. She tucked her hand behind her back.

Ilunga took a tuna sandwich on whole wheat out of the bag and took an enormous bite out of it. He worked the corners of his lips around the bits that stuck out, manoeuvring a lettuce leaf into his mouth. His thin, muscular features distended powerfully as he chewed. After working the sandwich for a full minute, he swallowed and immediately took another bite as large as the first one. This too he chewed for a full minute, watching them both as calmly as if he was looking out a window. Hazel slid her eyes sideways toward Wingate without moving her head, but she couldn't tell what his expression was.

When Ilunga finished his second mouthful, he held the sandwich out to them at arm's length. They stared at his half-eaten lunch as if they were being hypnotized by a cobra. At last, Ilunga spoke. "Neither of you wants a bite?"

"We just ate, Sir," said Wingate.

"So *neither* of you wants to eat my lunch?"

"No, Sir."

"Strange." He drew the sandwich back and bit the remainder in half. He seemed to be nodding thoughtfully to himself as he masticated the giant chunk of food. "See," he said, with his mouth still partly full, "I went to Room 32 to check how the two of you were doing, and there were all your files – well, *our* files – but you were gone."

"We did go out for an hour or so," said Hazel. "Should we have notified you?"

"No, no," Ilunga said, with an expansive gesture. "You're free to come and go as you please."

"Well, that's good to know."

"Of course, it's also good to know if you're coming or going." He examined the edge of the remaining quarter of his sandwich. "Because some people get confused."

Hazel shifted on her feet. "May we sit, Superintendent?"

"Oh," he said, pleasantly. "I'd rather if you didn't. I don't want any of your slime to come off on the fabric." He finished his sandwich in the stunned silence and then clapped the crumbs off his hands. He laid them flat on the desk and looked at them both with his head slightly lowered. "I thought we treated you rather well, James."

"You did, Sir."

"And is that what inspired you to hook up with the Hayseed Squad and come back down to cast aspersions on us? I'm curious."

Wingate drew the side of his forefinger down the corner of his mouth. "Sir?"

"We have our own internals to keep us in check. We don't need any smalltown cops keeping an eye on us."

"As you're not my commanding officer anymore, Sir, I hope you'll forgive me for speaking frankly," said Wingate. Ilunga remained silent and still, as threatening a stillness as either of them had ever witnessed. "I'm an OPS now, and Toronto is in our jurisdiction. Your division is in our jurisdiction. If a crime we're investigating brings us to your doorstep, you're obligated to assist us. We appreciate that assistance, and we thank you for it. And if there is nothing else, we'll get back to what we were doing."

Ilunga laughed. "Oh, I don't believe you will, son. If you're investigating the conduct of my officers or calling into question our results, then you can get yourself a subpoena and then we'll talk. Maybe."

"We're not investigating your officers or your division. We're investigating an abduction. The facts have brought us here."

"Dana Goodman brought you here. You're a pair of country suits doing triage for a disgraced officer and a certifiable lunatic. You're just the Angels to his Charlie, yes? I hope he's sent you your divining rods, because you'll need them to find your way out of the pile of shit you've got yourselves into. Now, my advice is that you scouts pack up your knapsacks and your canteens, say your dib dib dibs, and proceed to get scarce."

Hazel had felt an electric shiver when Wingate spoke. She wanted him to finish this arrogant prick off, but instead, Wingate appeared thoughtful. "Why was he disgraced, Sir?" he asked. "Detective Goodman."

"Oh, he didn't tell you, did he?"

"We haven't spoken all that much."

"First he appointed himself judge, jury, and almost execu-
tioner when he was a beat cop. We don't mind turning a blind
eye to some dealer who ends up with the stuffing beat out of
him in some alley – hell, some junkie could have done that. But
you can trace a bullet."

"He killed dealers?" Hazel asked.

"No, but there are a few of them out there with some of
Goodman's metal still in them. We took him out of there, but
of course one of his favourite crack feebs has to top herself on
his new watch and he goes off the reservation. After it was
ruled a suicide – and let me tell you, the evidence was conclusive, in case he's got you both trying on your merit badges – he
took it on himself to keep investigating the case. And a month
after it was put to bed, he committed a home invasion on one
of the victim's associates and threatened to kill him unless we
reopened the case. It took blind bombs and tear gas to get him
out of that house."

"Colin Eldwin's house."

"Well, he told you that much at least."

"That's who he's abducted."

Ilunga's upper lip quivered a little. "Well, I guess he got his
man then. Good for him. You want something on q.t.? Colin
Eldwin is a piece of garbage – we looked into him long and hard
at Goodman's insistence. That man would have fucked a snake
if he could have got it to hold still, but he had an alibi the night
of Cameron's death and it was watertight, if you'll excuse the
choice of words. If Goodman's managed to snatch him a second
time, you two should just stay out of his way and let the law of
the jungle run its course."

Now Hazel finally had something to say. "He doesn't just have Eldwin. He has Cameron's mother as well."

"He's *abducted* the victim's mother?"

"Not physically. But emotionally, yes. He's co-opted her. She's the other suspect in the abduction."

"You see? You see what a clusterfuck Goodman is? He worked under me for *fifteen* years and he was a great cop." Ilunga pushed his forefinger against his head. "But if *this* goes rogue, because you think too much and you don't have any discipline, then you start thinking the walls are passing on their secrets to you and only you. Goodman lost it, and you will too if you follow him into his rabbit hole."

She took in what he was saying. "Superintendent . . . we owe you an apology. We didn't know any of this."

"You should have asked."

"We didn't know to ask. We didn't know any of this until we got here."

Ilunga laid his electric gaze on both of them, one at a time. "So what are you going to do?"

"We're going to find some way to let him know we've gotten ourselves off his hook. And hopefully we'll find Eldwin before Goodman kills him."

"Don't sweat it if you can't," said Ilunga. "One less piece of shit on the planet won't make a difference. And frankly, if Goodman gets satisfaction, maybe I'll never see him in my rearview mirror again."

She turned to Wingate. "Well?"

"Well, what?" he said angrily.

"Let's go."

"You're kidding me."

She didn't answer him and he left the office without another word. Hazel extended her hand to Superintendent Ilunga. "We were just trying to do our jobs, Sir," she said.

"Do them elsewhere," he said, smiling again. "And call ahead if you need anything next time."

She laughed good-naturedly and closed the door behind her.

She had to speedwalk down the hall to catch Wingate. "Slow up," she whispered hoarsely to him.

"For what? You got other asses to kiss?"

"James." Her tone made him stop. "You don't fight little Napoleons like Ilunga. You go along. They're deaf to any subtlety if you flatter them a little."

"Is that what you were doing?"

"He doesn't know how far we've gotten. He thinks we're trying to read tea leaves. Let him sit and stew in there – in the meantime Toles is working for us and if he gives us half a reason to reopen the case, Ilunga can shout all he wants, but we'll have carte blanche."

"And if the lab comes back a bust? That thing's been in a bag for three years."

"Then we're done down here."

"And Colin Eldwin is a dead man."

She waited for two constables to pass behind them. "The results don't matter, James. If Goodman wants to know what we find out from CFS, he's going to have to show himself. And we'll be back on our own turf when he does."

"It doesn't sound like a plan, yet."

"Have some faith, James. We've gotten this far." She looked at her watch. "In the meantime, I've got to track down Toles and make sure he's as green as he looks. We're not going to get this all done in one day." She looked back toward Ilunga's door and then quickly stole forward to Room 32. She went in and out quickly. "I hope you weren't planning on sleeping in your own bed tonight."

"Skip?"

"I mean get us a couple of rooms somewhere, Detective." She grinned at him. "I like you, James, but I just don't think it would –"

"– I knew what you meant."

"I know you did." She started off down the hallway and then spun on her heel and walked backwards a couple of paces. "You should have seen the look on your face, though."

] 28 [

Hazel called in first thing in the morning and got Monday's report from Costamides. As she'd expected, nothing had appeared on the website, in fact, the feed was dead. She salted this away: with both Goodman and Cameron in Toronto, that suggested the basement they were looking for wasn't in the city. That bird was going to have to be killed with another stone. Costamides told her the *Record* had done as instructed: both of the missing chapters of "The Mystery of Bass Lake" had appeared in the Monday edition. Hazel wasn't sure what value appearing to follow instructions would have now, but the abductors had threatened more bodily damage to their victim if the chapters didn't run, and Hazel hoped they would keep their word, at least for the time being. The least powerful impression she'd formed over the last twenty-four hours was the one concerning Eldwin's guilt. Whether he'd committed a murder or not, she was intent on bringing him out of that basement alive. If he was a killer, then he could stand trial; she would not let Goodman or Cameron mete out their own brand of justice. That would constitute the ultimate failure on her part.

She thanked Costamides and got Toles at his desk. He'd been able to work his charms: the results of the examination of the sweater would be ready sometime before lunch. Hazel thanked him copiously and then suggested that since he'd messed with CFS protocol, it might be a good idea for them to get his friend to fax her results somewhere unofficial. "Cover your tracks in case someone thinks ill of a new DC jumping the queue on his own say-so." Toles saw merit in the suggestion. He called back half an hour later to say that his contact was faxing the results to the Kinko's on University, above Dundas. He'd told her to use a cover sheet addressing the pages to "D. Hammett."

"Good one," said Hazel.

"The whole escapade is costing me dinner at Lucy Than's new restaurant. Not that I'm complaining," he added.

"Dinner's on Westmuir County, Detective. With our thanks for a job well done."

She waited until noon and then, under dark skies, she walked from the hotel to the Kinko's Toles had told her the fax would be waiting at. The geniuses behind the desk searched through a pile of papers and insisted there was nothing for a Mrs. Hammett. Hazel went around the corner for a coffee, thinking perhaps Toles's connection at CFS had a later lunch than most people. Wandering down Dundas toward Yonge Street with her hot coffee, she found herself thinking of Hammett and his

heavily alcoholized detective Nick Charles: she knew why she
felt the kinship. She'd always loved the elegance of *The Thin
Man*, despite the sheer level of stupefaction in it. She hadn't
read it in years and wondered if Wingate had ever read it: she
could repay his Dickens with something she loved. There was
a used bookstore just down the street she'd seen wandering the
day before and she went in and perused the crime section. No
Hammett. But she browsed a bit longer, thinking if she was
going to have to stay over another night in Toronto, she might
want a book to read. A paperback with the title *Utter Death*
caught her eye and she brought it to the counter to pay. "Is he
very popular?" she asked.

"People like him," said the guy at the cash. "We can't keep
him in stock."

She put the book in an inside pocket of her jacket and returned
to Kinko's. This time there was something for D. Hammett.
The document, with its cover sheet, was three pages long. She
studied it, standing in the open doorway of the copyshop, and
then folded it in three and returned to the hotel.

Wingate sat in his cramped hotel room with a plate of fries and
a half-eaten burger in front of him and read the pages. "Wood
and varnish on both the inside and outside of the sweater and
within the fibres as well," he said. He put the papers down and
spread them across the desk. "Being in the water for any length
of time could explain the varnish migrating through the
sweater," he said to her, "but not the wood fibre trapped inside
it. It *has* to have been ground in."

"Now, look at this." She put her finger on one of the lines
in the report. "'The debris field comprises two strips – wood

and varnish mixed together – transverse across the back of
the sweater, each about four inches wide.' What do you think
of that?"

"I have no idea."

Polarized light microscopy had separated the wool fibres
from the varnish and the wood. There were at least two hundred tiny wooden shards, ninety percent of which were facing
the same direction, like iron filings drawn by a magnet, or
grass laid down in a footprint. "I'm drawing a blank. Maybe
this all happened post-mortem."

"They had to drag her out of the water, maybe they pulled
her up on a dock in the channel?"

That made sense to her. In fact, the more she thought about
it, the more she felt the door finally closing on their specula-
tions. "That's it, isn't it?" she said. "A body sodden with water,
she weighs double. They hook her out and pull her over the
side of a dock, drag her over two planks. Four inches wide."

"Combine that with the hemorrhaging in the lungs, calcium
and potassium levels through the roof, massive heart failure,
you name it. No scrapes, bruises, defensive wounds . . . where
does it get you?"

"I know."

"She went into the water within a hundred metres of the
shoreline but nobody heard her cry for help. How can we not
come to the same conclusions the coroner did in 2002?"

"We have to keep thinking this through. If she *didn't* kill
herself, this is her last chance to be heard." She looked at the
floor, tilting back slightly on her heels. "She was wrecked, right?
We talked about this – what if someone knocked her out?"

"You want to make a case for someone injecting her with enough alcohol and Ativan to sedate her?"

"Can we?"

"Why would anyone have had to force her, though?" he said. "Cameron was perfectly capable of getting off her head all by herself, to judge by the collars in her report."

"Fine. So she gets herself high and hammered. Maybe after that, he talked her into it. Called her stupid, useless. Told her she was better off dead. Gave her enough drugs to addle her."

"It's still not murder. And what about the alibi Ilunga says is airtight?"

"He said watertight."

"I know."

"Fine – it's not murder, but maybe it's something else. Time-of-death, Eldwin is somewhere else, but he's put the suggestion into her head. Isn't telling someone to go kill herself a crime?"

"Look, I wanted as badly as you did for this sweater to turn up something conclusive. But it doesn't. If we try to stretch this any further, we'll be in Goodman's league and then it's the insane leading the blind."

She absently picked a fry off the plate on his desk. "Goddamnit," she said. "We've been wasting time we could have been canvassing, you know."

"We did our best."

"Your old boss will be laughing up his sleeve."

"Let him laugh. But let's put Plan B into action. It's time to figure out how to use this bait to get Goodman to show himself."

She looked forlornly at the useless fax on the desk in front of them, and then shook her head slowly. "I haven't had to outsmart him before now," she said. "I'm not looking forward to trying."

She went back to her room and tossed the lab report on the desk and sat in the chair, looking out the window at the blank wall of a building across the alley from her hotel. She wasn't sure now how they were going to communicate with Cameron or Goodman, but she felt certain the two of them were still watching her, somehow. Perhaps she would have to wait now until one of them made contact, but when they did, she had to be sure she could control the flow of information.

She hadn't wanted to risk speaking to Martha the day before, but now she felt she owed her a call, at least to smooth things over as much as she could before she returned home. She reached for the phone, but her hand froze in the air over it. A little uniformed man was bent over backwards on the receiver, his head lolling off his shoulders.

She wasn't half out of the chair when she heard a slamming noise and Goodman burst from the closet beside the desk and drove her sideways to the floor. She heard herself shout and the pain burst in an electric shower down both her legs as she struggled beneath him, trying to push backwards toward the wall where she'd have some leverage. But he was so much larger than she was and he pulled her back toward the centre of the room, the carpet scraping at her clothes and burning her flesh. She felt him slide his hand down her flank to her holster and she twisted and drove an elbow into his face. He grunted in pain and he fell away, but she saw a flash of black metal pass over her head and she knew he had the gun. He stood and spat a ribbon of blood out of the side of his mouth. "Get up," he said, gesturing with the barrel.

She stood with difficulty, the familiar feeling of numbness spreading down her backside. Her legs wouldn't take her weight – whether due to injury or fear, she didn't know – and she slumped on the floor against the foot of the bed.

"What did you say to her?" he asked.

"Who?"

"Joanne."

"We said a lot of things to each other." She leaned against the boxspring, trying to breathe. "I told her the truth about you. How you'd gone rogue well before she met you. It all made sense to her."

"Sure it did."

"Oh, and I complimented her on her necklace. You know, the one you give to all your victims?" His eyes were wild. The gun was shaking in his hand. Hazel said quietly, "She didn't like you paying a visit to Martha, did she? A little too close to home for her, eh? Now she wants out."

"Don't kid yourself," he said. "She knows there's no *out* except for you doing what we chose you to do. What should have been done in the first place."

She sneered a laugh. "There's no *should have*, Goodman. There's just what happened. There's just a broken woman, you, and all the people you failed to protect, all of them still out there shooting themselves full of garbage and filling their crack pipes, if they're not already dead." She shifted a little and felt the sensation in her legs returning. "So where is she? Joanne? Did she walk away?"

"She's exactly where she wants to be. Back with Eldwin, waiting to see how this all turns out."

"You talked her into it again, huh?"

He took a step toward her with the gun raised and she pressed herself against the edge of the bed, her breath catching in her chest. "How hard would they come for me if I blew your brains out right now? What's the chance you'd ever be a cold case, Detective Inspector?"

"I think they'd figure out pretty quick I hadn't killed myself," she said.

"They'd never rest. Never," he said. "But why? Why you and not her? Because you're inside the machine and she wasn't? You ever thought how lucky you are that your death would actually move people to action?"

"The right kind of action. Due process. A conclusion based on the facts. I wouldn't expect anything more."

"That's because you're not prepared to see past the surface. I was wrong about you."

"You've been wrong about everything. For one thing, Eldwin was at home the night she died." He was closer now and she wondered if she could get the upper hand. But she'd have to push herself up from the bed and be on top of him before he could shoot her and she was pretty sure he'd shoot her.

"Eldwin's alibi is bullshit," he said.

"So – what? He killed her and the wife covered for him?"

"There's a thought."

"Have you ever met Claire Eldwin? Take my word for it: she'd be thrilled to see him in an orange jumpsuit."

He ignored her. "Joanne gave you the sweater. Did you keep your word?"

"The lab report's on the desk. You can see for yourself." He drew back and, keeping one eye on her, retrieved Toles's fax and flipped through the three pages. Hazel carefully drew herself up against the end of the bed and sat on the edge. "I found the same thing you did. Except I can see it for what it is. It's from a dock, where she was pulled up."

"She was pulled out onto the grass."

"How can you be sure?"

He threw the pages back onto the desk and leapt forward, shoving his face in hers. She smelled the sour taint of his mouth. "Are you fucking stupid? I *caught* the case, I wrote the report – my name is on it – so what do you think? I saw it on the news? She washed up at the bottom of someone's garden. We pulled her onto the grass. No wood involved." He shook his head in disbelief. "Is that what you're hanging your case on?"

The hell with it, she thought, *if I'm dead, I'm dead*, and she pushed up from the bed and stepped quickly away from him. He trained the gun on her chest. She had pain, but the adrenaline was covering it. "You want to know what I'm *hanging* my case on?"

"You wanna get shot?"

"You're not going to shoot me. You need me."

"You still believe that?"

"Brenda Cameron was anaesthetized," she said, ranging in a semi-circle away from him. She knew there was no escape, but she had to keep moving. "Her blood alcohol was .19. That's more than twice the legal limit. You get to .26 and you might as well jam a swizzle stick in your brain and stir. And there were high levels of lorazepam in her blood, that's Ativan –"

"I know what the fuck it is –"

"Then you know it increases the effects of alcohol. She was knocked out. She did it to herself."

He said nothing.

She stood by the window, looking at him, the muscles in her thighs jumping. "Or, on the other hand, maybe someone did it to her. Maybe Colin Eldwin did it. Gave her so many drinks she didn't know what planet she was on. The problem is that you'll never know now. Nobody saw them together that night, no one saw anything happen on the lake, nobody heard anything at all. All we have is a stolen rowboat, a body, a grief-struck relative, and you. And that doesn't add up to anything but a tragedy. Whether you shoot me or not, Brenda Cameron's going to stay in her grave a suicide."

He was still sighting her straight down the length of the gun. "Well, if that's your conclusion, then tell me where you want Eldwin's body. I'll do you the courtesy of leaving a trail you can follow this time."

"You've got no reason to kill him."

"I told Joanne Cameron I'd get her justice. But it doesn't matter to me what size his cell is. I think you know I'd just as soon put him in a box."

"And then what? Are you going to bring Brenda Cameron back from the dead? Maybe she'll sell that necklace you gave her for some rock."

It was as if he hadn't heard her – he stood in the middle of the room, staring past her, out at the city. "Maybe," he said. "Maybe this time, she'll get out alive." He pulled his gaze back and he was looking at her, his expression stone cold. "You can't be everywhere at once," he said. "But you can tell them what happens to them matters to at least one person. You light the way a little, and maybe it saves a couple of them. Maybe they come in before it's too late."

"Or maybe it has nothing to do with you. Maybe you're one of them, except there's something else in your pipe."

His eyes travelled to the gun at the end of his arm and he raised it to his face and stared at it like he was trying to remember a name. Then he pressed the side of it hard against his temple, gritting his teeth, his eyes boring through her, his jaw shaking like he was going to blow up. It was a strange, desolate gesture, and she thought *this is it*, she'd reached him and flipped the switch. She didn't want to see him put the gun in his mouth and she closed her eyes, but then there was silence. She looked again and he'd turned the muzzle back toward her. He gestured her away from the window. She came toward the centre of the room and he grabbed her again, holding her at arm's length, the gun cocked beside his cheek, and pushed her toward the bed again. A space opened in her chest; it felt like a massive expanse, a pit she was going to fall into. He powered her down to the bed, her back against it this time, and held the barrel of the gun hard to her forehead. "Goodman," she said quietly, "Dana . . ."

His weight was concentrated on the Glock and it felt like he was driving a bolt into her skull. "I took what was in me and gave it to *you*. To help you *see*."

The pressure on her forehead made her eyes water. She felt her mind emptying out. She took his wrist in both her hands, as if she were holding the gun in place against her own head. "I don't need your demons to see clearly," she said. "I have my own."

She heard a click then and wondered if, in her last moment on earth, the world was breaking up into parts. First the trigger, then the firing pin, then contact and the flare and the sound of the bullet firing, all of it in discrete sequence, and she wondered if she'd be able to feel the nose of the bullet at the instant it touched her, right before it entered her: an atom of steel against an atom of flesh. But there was nothing, just the sound of something hitting the floor. She realized he'd released the clip and now he was leaning over and pocketing it as she rose to a sitting position, too weak to stand now, and he tossed the gun at her.

"If you open your door any time in the next twenty minutes, or if I see your partner in the hallway, I'll kill you both." And then he was gone and she spun to her right and vomited on the bedspread, hacking and choking, her head filling with spinning black lace. She sat there hunched over, her insides knotted, and then collected herself and lunged for the phone. "He's heading out to the street," she said when Wingate picked up in his room, her voice tight in her chest. "Get down there, get your safety off."

"What's wrong? Who's in the street?"

"Goodman. He was just here. He'll be on the sidewalk any second now."

"I don't un —"

"GO!" She hung up on him and went to the window, but she had a view of the wrong side of the building. She was pouring sweat and her legs felt weak. She pushed open the window and looked down to see if Goodman was running down the alley between buildings, but the alleyway was empty and all she could hear was the sounds of traffic out on the boulevard. She pushed her face out into the air as far as the window would allow and felt the wind against her, against her living flesh. She craned her head toward the front of the hotel, but if their man was out there, he wasn't making a scene. She imagined Wingate bursting out onto the sidewalk brandishing his sidearm and the people there suddenly flying apart in panic. And she knew he would find nothing: Goodman would have melted into the stream of people heading back to work after their lunches, he would already have transformed into Dean Bellocque, perfectly invisible because he didn't exist.

A minute later, Wingate knocked at her door and she let him in. "I couldn't . . ." He leaned over, winded. She let him catch his breath. "What was he doing here? What did he want?"

"He was in my room," she said. "He was waiting for me here, for *fuck's* sake."

"My God, Hazel. Are you okay?"

"He tackled me. He held a gun to my head."

Wingate sat on the end of the bed. He stayed motionless for many moments, and when he raised his eyes, they were blood-shot. He saw the vomit on the bedspread and looked at her searchingly. "What the hell did he want?"

"He wanted to give me one more chance to see things from his point of view."

"Did you?"

"What do you think?"

They fell to silence and she thought she could hear both of their hearts thudding. She blew a jet of air out from pursed lips. "We have to get out of here. I don't think Eldwin's got much time left."

"I'll get the car."

"I'm going to wash my face," she said. "I'll meet you outside in three minutes."

She turned on the too-bright light over the sink and shielded her eyes until the pounding it caused subsided. She felt dazed and overwhelmed. The thought of getting back into the car and making that long drive home, having to start the paper-work, initiating what was bound to be a long and difficult process of ending or suspending this sad affair – it made her want to go to sleep on the spot. When this was over, she realized, there was going to be no one to hand the finished thing to, no one to succour with the result. Because that was what an investigation was, it was a *work*, like a painting, and at the end of it, someone looked at it and saw what you'd done and knew you'd seen it through. But an unfinished work . . . who wanted that?

She ran cold water in the sink and cupped her hands under the flow. It sluiced over her mouth and cheeks and she pushed her hands up into her hair. Her eyes looked as if someone had pressed their thumbs into them and driven them into her skull. She was exhausted. She was spent. In the middle of her fore-head, she saw the perfectly round, fading pink imprint of her own gun-barrel, a target pointing to the part of her that had failed. The pale circle was like a hazy sun hanging over a body of water and she imagined gulls circling her eyes. That was where all this had begun: at water's edge. She'd been waiting in the cruiser while Wingate was in the boat. No idea what would be waiting for them down there, what it would mean to them. The boat had come back and the two wetsuits – what were their names, Tate and someone? – had hauled something off the boat wrapped in green netting. She'd hobbled down to the dock to take a closer look and Tate had peeled away the covering for her to see the plastic body within. "Someone was holding it down there, made sure it wasn't going anywhere," he'd said, and she looked at him, and the marks his scuba mask had made around his eyes made him look like a raccoon.

She looked at her own eyes again, the mark on her forehead. Her stomach fell two storeys.

She rushed downstairs, where Wingate was waiting in one of the chairs in the lobby. "What is it?"

"There's something I want to do."

"What is it?"

"Alone."

He hesitated a moment. "Do you want me to wait?"

"No. I want you to get back to town. Get every available car out looking for Goodman or Cameron. I'll be back tonight."

The Ward's Island ferry was loading when she got to the docks at three-fifteen, men and women and children weighed down with everything imaginable it could take to make a Tuesday afternoon on an overcast May day better. Bikes and rollerblades and kites with their strings wound tight, kids dabbed with hopeful sunblock, the granola locals with their organics, headed for home. She knew only a little bit about what was called the island "Community," but she understood it to be a tight-knit group of middle-class back-to-earthers and urban pioneers. They were living on city land, though, which in turn was also laid claim to by an aboriginal group, and every few years, the pot boiled over and you read of lawsuits and petitions and people saying things like "possession is nine-tenths": exactly the thing people said when they wanted to get away with straight-up theft. She wondered why the folks who were buying up the land around Goodman's place weren't these people, seeking peaceful enclaves, instead of the rich idiots who drove huge, disgusting cars and built cottages to impress others.

She'd rather a self-satisfied urban fool than the kinds of poison-
ous money that found its way north.

But just the same, she sort of knew these people. They were
the ones who made a fetish of sticking up for the community,
as if such a thing *shouldn't* be second nature; they were the
ones who helped their neighbours paint their houses and look
for lost cats. They were socially *conscious*, whatever that
meant, and she was going to have to use it to her benefit this
afternoon.

She sat on the upper deck, watching the docks and the high-
rises of downtown Toronto recede. They were calling for three
days of rain now and there were stormclouds in the east and
a telltale curtain of grey reached down somewhere over the
eastern suburbs. Someone in town who still swore by *The
Farmer's Almanac* had told her that the summer of 2005 was
going to be the wettest on record. Maybe the almanac would be
right for once.

The boat moved over the surface of the water like a huge
innertube, bobbing and tilting, and once they'd reached the
centre of the harbour, she thought of Lana Baichwell, waiting
for the right moment. She had to push the image of the dead
woman's swollen face out of her mind.

As the water passed under the boat, throwing up its white
foam, she took out the autopsy photos she'd stolen from Room
32. She looked closely at them again. Brenda Cameron's eyes
were half open, that expression of the mindlessly dead, one eye
hidden beneath its lid. The mark from hitting her forehead as
she went over the side of the boat was almost exactly centred
above her eyes, and symmetrical. The mark on her own forehead, the one Dana Goodman had imprinted on her, was just a

random thing, his choice of where to put the gun barrel, but as she looked in the hotel mirror, the question had come to her mind: what had actually made the mark on Brenda Cameron's forehead? Bumping one's head on the way out of a tilting boat would have been a *moving* injury; it would have broken the skin and left an abrasion. The marks on Cameron's head – and the closer she looked at them the more they looked like miniature griddle marks – were perfectly even, as if someone had carefully pressed something against her head. And the symmetry of the marks, like a Rorschach blot . . .

The boat arrived at the Ward's Island dock about three minutes later, and she watched the forward deck disgorge its eager band of locals and merrymakers. They flowed forward onto a road that soon forked off, and she slowly made her way to the stairs that led down and out. There was a building with a café in it straight ahead on an emerald patch of lawn. She recalled that the file had stated that the owner of the stolen boat was a man named Peace Swallowflight, a name not exactly hard to memorize, and that, in 2002, he lived on 6th Street. She hoped the slow turnover of houses on the island would work in her favour and that Swallowflight would still be a resident. She went to the café and ordered a coffee and the tall, pierced girl behind the counter passed the time of day with her. When she offered Hazel a refill, the girl said, "Come a long way for your coffee break, huh?"

It had been so long since she'd worn her uniform more than a few hours at a time that she'd forgotten what she looked like.

"Almost two hundred kilometres," Hazel said.

"I know the coffee is good, but . . ."

Hazel smiled. "You know a Peace Swallowflight?"

"Yeah. But he didn't do it."

That was strange. "Didn't do what?"

"Whatever it is you're investigating. He's the island sensei. He wouldn't steal a glance, if you know what I mean."

"I think I do. I'm not here to accuse him of anything. I just want to talk to him."

"Well, he's right there," the girl said, pointing through the window and over the porch. "That's the back of his house." She was indicating a wooden structure close to the shoreline, festooned with prayer wheels and colourful flags.

"Thanks," said Hazel.

"What's this about?"

"He's not in trouble," she said, putting down a toonie.

She crossed the grass again, cutting diagonally to the top of 6th Street. She walked down to the bottom of the street. The front of Swallowflight's house was somehow even more antic than the back, the porch busy with pinwheels and silk wind-socks and spinning colourful plates. It looked like the house couldn't sit still. She went up the steps and was about to knock on the frame of the screen door when a tall, muscular man in long pink pants and a tank top appeared in the hallway. His bare scalp gleamed. "Hello," he said, pushing the door open as if he expected her. "Come in."

"Did someone call you?" she asked.

"No, but I saw you make a beeline from the café. I was up-stairs sewing up a hole." He pinched his pant leg, a light linen weave that now had a line of yellow thread traversing the knee. "They're too comfortable to throw out, you know?"

"Okay," she said. His manner was calming and off-putting all at once. "What's a 'sensei'?"

"It just means 'teacher,'" he said. "I teach meditation." He stood away from the door. She realized she was apprehensive. Something smelled like burning grass. "Come on in."

He led her into the house and she sat on a futon couch in the large living room. It looked out along the shoreline toward where the ferry had docked. He stood in front of her, his head tilted just a little as if he was thinking of painting her, and then he left the room, holding a finger up. He returned with a tray holding two rubber-gripped glasses of tea.

"This will calm your nerves a little."

"My nerves?"

He sat across from her and held a glass out. "You're practically your own siren, Officer. There are brilliant flashes of red and green going off behind your head."

She took the tea and sipped it; it was pleasant if a little bitter. She put it down on the low table in front of her. "I hope I'm not disturbing anything."

"The stone is never disturbed by the river."

"I'm sorry?"

"An inner stillness can never be disturbed, is what I mean. I don't control the river. In other words, you're not disturbing me, Officer."

"Detective Inspector," she said.

He blinked twice in quick succession. "How can I help you?"

"I wanted to talk to you about a stolen rowboat."

"You think I stole a boat?"

"No. I'm talking about the one that was stolen from you."

"Oh," he said, sadly. "You're here about Brenda Cameron."

"I am."

"That poor girl."

"Mr., um, Swallowflight, I don't suppose you still have the boat, do you?"

He was swirling his tea lightly in his hand. "I still have it," he said. "I don't use it, though. I can feel her on it."

"What do you mean you can 'feel' her?"

"The room where a person dies . . . something lingers there. That's all I mean."

"Where is the boat?"

"They were here, you know. They did all this already. In 2002. For two weeks *I* was a suspect. How do you think that felt?"

She put the tea down with a neat *clack* on the tabletop. "It must have felt good when they ruled you out."

"I was out of the city when she died."

"I know all this, Mr. Swallowflight. You're not a suspect."

He sighed, blowing his cheeks out. He didn't look so peaceful anymore. "People respect me here," he said quietly.

"Where is it?"

"Under the back deck."

She stood up, her forearms tingling. "Let's go."

He led her out around the side of the house to the back. Hazel cast a look over the water. It would have been easy for Brenda to take the ferry from downtown and walk along the shoreline to the bottom of 6th Street. Swallowflight's backyard was open to the water, but the house itself blocked a view of the rest of the street. Stealing a rowboat from his yard under the cover of darkness would have been child's play. He leaned under his deck and was about to pull the boat out when she stopped him.

"Do you mind putting these on?" she said, passing him a pair of latex gloves she'd pocketed in the station house. "I'd drag it out myself, but I have a bad back."

He looked at the gloves uneasily, as if they implicated him in something, and then put them on. He went under the deck and she heard the sound of a metal hull scraping against the white pebbles that lined the dark space underneath. The simple rowboat emerged behind him. She watched the knobs of his spine shifting. The boat was a flat-bottomed number with a white fibreglass interior. There was no seat. "Where does a person sit in this thing?" she asked.

"Milk carton," he said. "You want that, too?"

"No," she said. "This'll be fine. How long have you had the boat?"

"I found it junked at the back of Hanlan's Point about six years ago. Bottom was rusted through in a couple of places and I put this insert in." He ran his latexed hand along the white interior. "I sealed up the rust and riveted this into place, but it still leaked."

She got down on her knees and looked closely at the insert. It followed the contours of the boat, including the three runnels in its bottom. But she could see he'd done a poor job of sealing it and the bottom of the insert was springy rather than tight against the hull. There was a slip-proof pattern on it which matched the mark on Brenda Cameron's forehead. "Do you still have the oars?"

He went back under the deck and brought out two standard wooden oars, their metal pins dangling from midshaft. She gestured that he should put them down on the grass and she kneeled over them, blinking to clear her eyes, and stared hard at one of the shafts. After three years of disuse, they were covered in a thin layer of dust and the varnish was cracked. Thin edges of it stood up where it was beginning to flake away. Examining these oars would be like trying to dust sand for fingerprints and she blew as lightly as she could at the surface to loosen the dust. The translucent layers of varnish rattled like dragonfly wings.

She stilled her attention to take in just a couple of square inches of the oar. Flecks of grit and thin filaments of fibre came in and out of focus among the yellowy parchment-like varnish. Some of the fibre was bits of old spider webbing, or dust strung up in some strange order. But there were also tiny strands of black fibre as well. She narrowed her eyes and tried to filter out everything but the black and as she did, more of it appeared, like a detail popping out of a landscape. She saw it accumulating – tiny black exclamation points – until it became a pattern and the pattern was heaviest in the middle of the oar, the thin part, and then its density diminished as she traced it down toward the blade. The marks stopped about six inches from the end of the blade. She turned to the other oar, but it was clean and she stared at it a moment until she realized she was looking at the wrong side. She used two sticks to turn it over: the same pattern – almost a mirror image – of black fibre ran down the shaft to within six inches of the end of the blade. A drop of rain hit the oar and instantly the fibres within the drop leapt to life.

"Mr. Swallowflight, did you lend this boat out to friends, or would you say you were the main person to use it?"

"A lot of people used it. Not these days, though. Back then." She stared at the oars. He leaned in closer behind her. "What is it?"

"A murder," she said, wiping her cheek. The rain was beginning to come down heavier. "Can I use your phone?"

Ilunga was standing far behind his desk, as if he wanted to vanish through the wall behind him. His right arm was crossed stiffly over his chest and he seemed to be choking the life out of his left bicep. He was furious. On the phone, he wouldn't even entertain dispatching any of his SOCO people. If she wanted to talk to him, she'd have to come in, and then he hung up. Now he was looking at her as if trying to decide what part of her to rip off first. "I told you to go home."

"And I think we told you we don't need your permission to investigate a crime in Ontario."

"This isn't Ontario, this is Toronto."

"Superintendent, are you hiding something?"

His mouth was half open, like he was going to reply, but then he sat and dragged Cameron's folder toward him. "Where are the pictures that go with this file?"

"I have no idea."

"We interviewed this Swallowflight faggot, we examined the boat – it's *all* in the file, Detective Inspector – we found the dead girl's earring *in the boat* and we made a ruling of suicide. We *found* the girl's fingerprints on the bloody oars, as well as Swallowflight's – *which* you would expect, it being his boat – however he was in New Orleans the entire month taking a course in . . ." He flipped angrily through the file. "In *self-hypnosis*. Which skill it would seem you have an advanced understanding of."

"She was drowned in the boat, not in the lake."

He stared at her.

"The marks on her forehead. They came off the bottom of the fibreglass insert Swallowflight used to seal the hull."

"She *hit* her head on the way out of the boat," said Ilunga.

"How does she hit her head on the bottom of the boat? Do *you* jump out of a boat backwards? Try to see what you're saying. And the marks are not abrasions." She took the victim's photo out of her pocket and slid it across the desk. He looked at it, then at her, and then back down at the picture. "This is an *impression*. Someone held her head down. One inch of water in the hull was all it would have taken."

"Then put someone else in the boat, Micallef. Give me a second person on that boat and we can talk."

"I think I can."

"How?"

"If your forensics people fingerprinted the oars, then I presume they noted the presence of black fibres? They were all over the oars."

"The presence of only one type of fibre is proof that Cameron was *alone* in the boat. The fibres are trace transfers. She rowed the boat out, the oars brushed up against her sweater. Then she stopped the boat, bumped her head on the bottom of it fumbling about while flying on alcohol and sedatives, and then she *jumped out*. And drowned." He shoved the picture back toward her. "You think I'll do anything to close a file, don't you?"

"I do."

"You should look at yourself. We *investigated* this death. You arrived here with a foregone conclusion."

"I'm not sure you're talking about me now."

"What I do here, what I'm doing, is standing my ground against the devil, who appears before us in the form of an intuition. Every time someone walks in here with a *feeling*, I want to reach for my gun. You know how much a hunch costs?"

"I know you're going to tell me."

"A SOCO team and a vehicle big enough to get that boat and its oars back to a clean room, the hours to *re*photograph the goddamned thing, the spectroscope, the *re*fingerprinting of latents now three years old . . . I'll start at thirty thousand, but I'm being optimistic."

"So it's the cost that bothers you? Or the revelation that you accepted a suicide rap because it's good for business? Are you going to ignore new evidence to keep your record?"

"I'm going to call OPS Central and tell them how you run an investigation. They might want to reopen *your* cases."

"Swallowflight told me he used to let people take the boat out. To borrow it if they wanted. He's that kind of *sharing* person, you know."

Ilunga was as still as a statue, his eyes glowing white. "So what," he said.

"So your dusters looked for the victim's fingerprints and noted significant repeats, meaning the owner of the boat. The rest were incidentals. They were leaning toward suicide anyway and there was no chance that there were a dozen people in the boat with Cameron that night. It was a sound conclusion, suicide."

"I see . . . and now you want me to fingerprint all of Ward's Island? Get alibis for twenty people between 7 p.m. and 3 a.m. on the evening of August 4, 2002?"

"No," she said. "You don't have to do that."

"Oh. You tell me what I have to do then."

She got up from her chair. "Nothing."

He looked at her suspiciously. "Nothing?"

"You'll know what to do next."

"Oh, really."

"I'd like you to get someone to drive me back to Port Dundas. Maybe Childress, since she's probably the only person left here who doesn't want to push me out a window."

"I doubt that. She still works for me."

She approached the desk and leaned on it, getting in his face. "You know what I'm going to do? I'm going to show you something that will allow you to draw your own conclusions. Because you're tired of listening to reason. Now: Childress?"

"Take the bus."

"I'm going to need her," Hazel said. "Jurisdictional issues, you know." She looked at her watch. "Have her meet me at the Day's Inn on Adelaide in half an hour."

"How do people work with you, Micallef?" he said, his pupils tiny black dots. "You're ungovernable."

"The stone is never disturbed by the river," she said, smiling sweetly.

] 30 [

Wednesday, June 1

Childress had driven Hazel back to Port Dundas in a frosty silence. Even when checking her blind spot on the right, Childress made an effort not to look at her. They put her up in Dianne MacDonald's B&B and asked Dianne to let them know if it looked like the officer was planning to leave. Martha was meanwhile fuming in Glynnis and Andrew's house, yet another storm on the horizon. But she was here, and that was all that mattered to Hazel now.

She woke up early and went into the station house. She called Jack Deacon and told him to pack Eldwin's hand in a *lot* of ice and courier it down, same-day, to Twenty-one addressed to Superintendent Peter Ilunga. She instructed him to label it "EVIDENCE" and "PERISHABLE." They had their own set of fingerprints from the hand, but she thought Ilunga deserved the chance to draw his own conclusions. It was too bad she couldn't be there when he opened the box.

It was a quiet midweek at the detachment. She'd instructed Wingate to pick up Claire Eldwin and bring her in. It was time she knew the whole story, and Hazel wanted her in the station house to hear it. She'd been of two minds whether to tell Eldwin the full extent of the kind of trouble her husband was in, but she'd never been totally sure of the seriousness of the danger. Now she was, and Claire Eldwin had a right to know. Wingate was spending the morning writing up a full report of what they'd done in Toronto, something she deemed essential considering how far under Ilunga's skin they were now. They might need to tell their side at some point, and having the official report was necessary. She knew Wingate's report would be measured, accurate, and sober. When he told her Mrs. Eldwin had elected to come in under her own steam, it looked like it was going to be at least a couple of hours before she arrived and Hazel took the opportunity to have some downtime. She decided to go home for lunch and wait until Wingate called to say Eldwin was at the detachment.

The rain was, if anything, heavier here than it had been in Toronto and she dashed to the front door of the house and let herself in. It was midday quiet and still; a kind of stillness that made her nervous, given what she'd found in her hotel room the day before. It would have been nice to have some company, but her mother and Martha had gone out in the morning and the house was as empty as it sounded.

She popped two pieces of whole-wheat bread into the toaster. To make up for the healthy amount of fibre, she took a half-eaten wheel of Camembert out of the fridge and left it on the counter to temper for a few minutes.

There was nothing of interest in the mail except for a forwarded property tax bill for her house in Pember Lake. Westmuir kept reassessing the house at higher and higher levels and this year had it at $325,000. A similar house less than a kilometre away had sold for $260,000 in January. She didn't mind paying her taxes – after all, it was tax money that paid her salary – but it made her sick that the county was helping itself to thirty percent extra with its upbeat evaluations. Too bad there wasn't a law that you could sell your house back to Westmuir for what they claimed it was worth.

The toaster dinged and she cut three big slabs of cheese onto each piece and sat at the kitchen table. She hadn't realized until now how tired she was. The buzziness of a week without Percocet had finally begun to die down – keeping busy had helped her ignore the jitters during the last few days – and she felt like the world around her was beginning to emit its real colours again. What a strange dream the last two months had been. Living in this house, half out of her mind in pain, depressed, hopeless at times. But now she was sitting at Glynnis Crombie's – all right, Pedersen's – kitchen table, in full uniform, thinking about the day ahead of her. She was escaping the immediate present, a state of mind that paid no heed to tomorrow, that hardly believed in it. She was shaking loose the bonds. It seemed to her now that days and weeks lay ahead of her, a topography of tasks and battles and puzzles and outcomes. She realized she felt calm and prepared for the first time since Christmas.

She worked her way through one melting, fragrant piece of toast and was picking up the second when she heard a sound from downstairs. She stilled her hand midway to her mouth and listened. There it was again. Something being pushed around on the floor. And now a voice. *Good Christ.* She put the toast back down on the plate, picked her chair up to move it silently back, and slipped her reloaded gun from its holster. No one would take it from her now, by god. At the door to the basement, she could hear more clearly now: faint bumps, gentle clattering, a murmur. A woman's voice, she was fairly certain. She breathed shallowly by the door, her hand wrapping the knob silently, opening it into the dark stairwell. She stepped down, once, twice, stepped over the creaky third step, and then down again, but the fifth step emitted its low groan and she stopped on it, her heart pounding. The sounds from below abruptly stopped. *Jesus,* she thought. *I should have gone around the back and come in through the door with the Glock out.* There were footsteps approaching the bottom door. *Fucking hell.* She brought the gun up to chest height. A high-pitched hum filled her head. Below her, the door opened.

"We have to stop meeting like this."

"Goddamnit," Hazel said, lowering the gun and leaning against the wall. "What are you doing down here?"

"You sure you don't want to shoot me first?" said Martha. She turned sideways to allow her mother to answer her own question. There were boxes opened and in various states of being filled around the room. "Nanna gave me a job."

Hazel descended the rest of the stairwell into the bedroom. Three finished boxes were closed up and taped shut against the wall by the back door. "I guess you're in the mood to stick me in a box, huh?"

"You put me out of my house, I put you out of yours."

"Ah," said Hazel. "Karma."

She crossed the room. It looked bigger with boxes of her stuff ranged around it. She didn't think she and her mother had brought much with them, but Martha was on six boxes and counting. Hazel sat on the bed. "Any chance we can start over?"

"At what point?" said Martha, her fist on her hip. "1971?"

"You really want to redo your whole childhood?"

"Maybe the parts where you somehow communicated to me that I was a screw-up and the world wanted to eat me alive?"

Hazel lowered her head and measured how much further lightheartedness was going to get her. She said, "Some things get lost in translation, Martha. I never thought you were a screw-up, but as for the world part, every mother thinks that. I never meant to make you feel that I was protecting you from yourself."

Martha tossed a pair of shoes into a box and leaned against the wall, her arms crossed. "So that's it? I just accept I've built my entire world-view on a miscommunication and move on?"

"It wasn't a miscommunication if it's what you heard. I should have done a better job of correcting the impression." She finally looked at her daughter. "But these kinds of things are hard to set straight, Martha. They go off true so gradually that by the time you realize you're wrong, the error starts to look like you. Do you know what I mean?"

"No."

"Belief is all we have," Hazel said. "What we believe doesn't weigh as much as a gram, but it's what we are. A wrong belief can ruin everything."

"You make it sound like you can just switch it off."

"I know you can't. It takes time, but you have to start." Her daughter sighed heavily. "Come sit with me." There was a pause, but then Martha pushed herself off the wall and came to sit beside Hazel on the bed. "There's still time, you know. We don't have to carry on thinking the same old wrong things about each other."

"What will we think about each other then?"

"Some new wrong things," Hazel said, and they both smiled. "I've only ever wanted you to feel loved. Everything else, no matter how misbegotten, was for that. I can't promise I'll be able to stop trying to protect you, Martha, but if you're able to convince yourself it's coming out of love and not fear, maybe it won't feel so toxic to you."

Martha shrugged. "Maybe." She looked slantways at her mother. "Where's this new Zen aspect coming from?" She closed one eye. "Is it the Percocets?"

"I beg your pardon?"

"Sorry, but I know about the pills. Nanna told me to keep an eye out for stashes when I packed up. She says you were developing a problem. Is that true?"

Who was protecting whom, Hazel wondered. "No," she said. "Anyway, I'm off them now. It's been six whole days."

"Is it hard?"

She wanted to say no, she wanted to say it was none of her business. But if it was time to change the beliefs, she was going to have to do her part. "Yeah," she said, at last. "It's hard. It's very hard. I still want them."

"Why?"

She realized she was crying. "I like the way they make me feel, Martha. But I'm not me on them. It's good that I stopped."

"So this is really you?"

"I think so."

Martha shifted a little closer and Hazel hesitantly lifted her arm off the bed and then settled it on the girl's shoulders and they touched the sides of their heads together, like birds. "We'll hardly recognize each other now," Martha said.

Martha said she'd handle the rest of the packing on her own – it was good to have something to do, she said. Upstairs, the Camembert on the second slice of toast had begun to go waxy and Hazel tossed it into the garbage can. She imagined herself rummaging in her own fridge again, and she felt a frisson of excitement that might have had an undercurrent of fear in it as well. To be on her own again. To start over. What would it feel like?

It was one. The phone had not rung and she felt no particular urgency to return to the station. She thought of going back downstairs to have a rest, but she didn't want to disturb the delicate peace she and Martha had begun to build, and she decided to use her mother's "room." The bed was neatly made, and rather than mussing the sheets, she just lay on top of them. Now the sounds from downstairs were even clearer, even under the noise of the rain rattling against the roof; had she listened more closely before unholstering her gun, she would have realized what was happening. She closed her eyes and then opened them and stared at the ceiling. Where was Eldwin? She'd instructed her officers to get their cars out and she had cruisers from Kehoe River, Fort Leonard, and Gilmore parked in various cul-de-sacs, side streets, and rural routes and no one had seen anything. Wherever they were, it had to be a place they knew, somewhere they felt safe, where they knew the lay of the land. But she'd been in Bellocque's basement and she

was sure it was not the site. Unless they were moving Eldwin
back and forth to different places. That was a dangerous strat-
egy and it was unlikely that Dana Goodman would ever go back
to that ramshackle cottage. No, the most likely thing was that
the ex-detective was trying to figure out a way to get rid of
Eldwin. They were in endgame and time was running out.

She closed her eyes and began to drift off. The bed felt warm
and she sank into it. She could smell the scent of her mother's
hair on the pillow. Her mother's scent hadn't changed in all her
life; from childhood on, it had always been this perfume of
warm flesh and washed hair, it rubbed off on anything her
mother touched. Old people were supposed to go sour; Hazel felt
that she, herself, was already like a pot of stale-dated yoghurt.
But her mother had stayed young in her body somehow.

She began to dream. She was on a beach, alone under the
sun. The water was blue and the sand was white. When was
the last time she'd felt relaxed? When she'd had time for herself? She picked up a coconut and shook it. It rang. She shook
it again and it rang a second time. She opened her eyes. "You
going to get that?" Martha called from downstairs and Hazel
picked up the extension beside the bed. It was Wingate. Claire
Eldwin had come in.

More than Claire Eldwin was waiting for Hazel when she
returned to the station house. Constable Childress had
appeared at the front desk in a state of considerable distress,
demanding to see Hazel. Wilton had kept her in the waiting
area, where she'd paced angrily, talking occasionally on her cellphone to someone who seemed as upset as she was. Childress
was containable, but when Gordon Sunderland had appeared

at one in the afternoon, he added to an already combustible atmosphere. He, too, insisted on seeing Hazel the moment she got back from lunch. And when, at one-thirty, Mrs. Eldwin arrived, Wilton began to think he should lock the front doors.

Melanie intercepted Hazel at the back entrance. "How do you want to handle all this?"

"Put Childress in my office, Sunderland in interview 1, and put Claire Eldwin in 2 with Wingate."

She stepped back in the corridor and waited to hear people moving about and doors shutting. No way she wanted to be in the middle of this bee swarm. If these people wanted each to tear her a new one, they were going to have to do it in an orderly fashion.

Childress's news was going to be the most important. She took a deep breath outside her office, and then opened the door confidently. Childress wasn't even sitting. She stood by the window, staring at the door, her eyes wild. She spoke in a whisper. "Are you crazy?"

"I gather your boss got my package."

"You don't send the chief of the biggest division in Toronto a human hand *to his desk*."

"Where does he like to take delivery of such things?"

"He threw up. Into the box."

"That sounds like he's taking it more seriously now."

"You better think twice before you ever go back to Toronto."

Hazel went around the desk and stood behind it, leaning on the blotter. "Look, I don't care if Ilunga shat his pants, Constable. I want to know what he's doing. Is he doing *anything*? Or is he still in denial?"

Childress sighed, as if it gave her pain to even speak. "He ordered the removal of the boat and its oars. He told me to tell you he's charging the whole thing to OPSC. All due respect, but he asked me to repeat this verbatim to you. He says after they get the bill, he hopes they string you up."

"That's nice. When do we hear back?"

"They're working on it now."

"Childress? When will I know?"

"Tomorrow morning. At the earliest."

"Go back to your B&B and wait for word," she said.

"He told me to come back to Toronto." She hadn't looked up at Hazel again, too afraid to see the look in her eyes. "I'm to leave right after speaking to you."

Hazel pressed her intercom. "Melanie? Send in Constable Jenner."

Jenner appeared within a minute.

"Jenner? Accompany Constable Childress to The River Nook and install yourself in the hallway to ensure she doesn't leave."

"You can't hold me," said Childress, angrily.

"You're seconded to me until this investigation is completed. That's how I've decided to interpret Superintendent Ilunga's agreeing to get you to drive me here. So you are under my command until further notice."

"You can't do that."

"I just did."

Childress stood up, passing a look behind her to Jenner. "He's going to make you a personal hobby," she said. "I'll stay. You don't need to send me a babysitter."

"Do I have your word?"

Her mouth was set in a straight line. "*My* word is worth something. You have it."

After she went out, Hazel said, "Call Dianne MacDonald and ask her to let us know if Childress tries to leave the building." Jenner nodded smartly and left.

Next was Sunderland. His hair was flat against his forehead where the weather had plastered it down. He'd prepared a presentation, laying out the last two weeks of the *Westmuir Record* on the tabletop. When she entered the room, he was standing behind the table and he made an expansive gesture at them. "Ah, here she is, Shiva the destroyer. And look, here is her handiwork. Five numbers of our proud paper of record, reduced to a high school 'zine." He came around the front of the table. "You are feckless, power-hungry, thoughtless, arrogant, and foolish, you know that?"

"How was Atlanta?"

"I'm going to make you front-page news, Hazel. I'm going to tell all our readers what you consider fair game. That you think strong-arming anyone you care to into doing your will is the way to run the Port Dundas P.D. I'm thinking of maybe doing a summer-length exposé. 'The Rot at the Heart of Westmuir.'"

"If you're thinking of ruining me, you'd better get in line. You have competitors."

"They can go on the record. I know I won't have any trouble finding them."

She peered down at the five newspapers arrayed on the table. She'd probably had more to do with their contents than Sunderland had. She pushed them apart with her hands. "You know what's wrong with your paper, Gord?"

He set his jaw. "That it's within a five-minute walk of the station house? And that members of this police force have, for years, been using it as their own personal bulletin board?"

"No," she said patiently, "it's that it's run as a cult of personality. Which would be fine if you had a personality, or if you had any competition. If the people had a choice of what to read."

His cheeks were shaking and she thought there was a very good chance he might sweep the papers off the table that separated them and crawl over it to wrap his fingers around her throat. She sort of relished the thought of it, calling for backup, someone being forced to use their truncheon to pull him off her. "I'm going to be here long after you, Hazel. But I'll promise you one thing: I'll keep your name alive."

He made to pick up the papers, but thought twice of it and walked around the table. "I'll close these doors so tight to you, Gord, that when you print news about Port Dundas, you'll have to put it beside the horoscope." He stopped. "Why don't you think for once? You've been running a short story that was probably penned, in part, by a murderer. The *Record* is actually *part* of the story this time. And if you want to find out how it ends, you'll change your tone."

"Oh yeah, and what is it, exactly, you can do for me? You going to write the editorial apologizing for the dog's breakfast we've been putting out the last two and a half weeks? *You* going to refund the people who actually *pay* to read this newspaper?"

"No," she said. "But if you can keep it in your pants, Sunderland, I may be able to help you save face."

He screwed up that round, fratboy's face at her and she thought maybe he'd spit. But instead, he was at a loss for words.

She had rarely seen him like that and it told her he needed her much more than she needed him.

"I know about Ray Greene," he said. "That's going into Monday's paper."

"You want a comment from me?"

"I'll do without."

"I'll make you a deal," she said. "You hold the Monday edition and I'll give you the end of this Eldwin story before the weekend is out. It'll be something special, unlike any other kind of story you've run before. It'll make you look like a genius. Haven't you always wanted to be confused for a genius?"

"I'm finished talking to you, Hazel."

He made for the door. "You know the *Toronto Star* is going to pick this up," she lied. "It has a Toronto angle. You're going to need a slam dunk if the *Record* isn't going to look like it's reprinting a wire story from the Big Smoke."

"I detest you," he said.

"I like your tan," she said.

She stood in the hallway outside of interview 2, hoping not to hear screams. She could see the back of Wingate's head. She prayed he was taking the initiative and starting without her. She dreaded this, but she straightened her cap and went in.

31

Claire Eldwin's face was streaked red and white, her hands wrapped tightly around a water glass. On the table between them was the cage with the mouse in it.

"What's that mouse doing here?" Hazel asked Wingate.

"I just . . . she was crying. I thought an animal might calm her down."

She sat at the end of the table. Mason was sniffing the air. "Did it?"

"No," said Claire Eldwin. "Is it true the man who kidnapped my husband sent this poor animal in a box to you?"

Hazel hesitated; she didn't know if Eldwin knew about her husband's hand. "Yes," she said. "He did. It wasn't . . . very nice. But he's okay now."

"Who?"

"The mouse. Mason."

Claire Eldwin put her hand out toward the cage and put a finger between the bars. Mason pushed himself up against an opposite corner. "This is my husband," she said. "In a cage somewhere." She looked up at Hazel and began to cry again. "I take back everything I ever said about him . . . I just want him home. Why haven't you found him?"

"We're close, Mrs. Eldwin. We are. We have . . . we know the man who abducted him."

"You know who he is, or you *have* him? Which is it?" She was quivering as if someone had run an electric current through her.

"We don't have him. Either of them, actually. Brenda Cameron's mother is involved as well. They believe Colin killed Brenda. Murdered her."

"Colin would never have laid a hand on anyone. Not that way."

"I'm sorry, Mrs. Eldwin, but I'm not sure now. In my line of work we see, time and again, that people don't really know those closest to them."

"I know Colin."

"I feel terrible about the situation he's in, but I still don't know what to think. Is there anything you haven't told us? About your life together in Toronto, about the night Brenda Cameron died? You told the police Colin was home with you, but did you notice anything strange? Was he behaving in a manner different than usual?"

Claire Eldwin's face had hardened. "These people abduct Colin, and your way of finding my husband is by investigating their claims?"

"It's been impossible to do it any other way."

"Colin's done nothing. You'll see. He's not necessarily a good person, but he's not a murderer. At heart, he's a coward and he looks for the easy way out. Killing a girl? He could never have done it."

"Did you know Brenda Cameron?"

"No."

"We're not sure she was alone in that boat."

"Colin was at home with me all that night. The police *questioned* him, you know. They *came* to the house and questioned him. You should know all this."

"I know it," said Hazel.

"Then what are you *doing* to get him home?"

"Everything we can."

Claire Eldwin searched Wingate's face, hoping to find reassurance there, but she came up empty. Quietly, she said, "What's 'everything'?"

She'd decided to spare Claire Eldwin the details for now. She already looked like she was going to faint. "Everything," repeated Hazel.

They led her down the back hall that passed behind the pen and Wingate showed her out of the station house. Hazel took him aside and asked him to follow her and make sure she got home. He went to his cruiser and followed Eldwin out of the parking lot. Hazel watched them pass through the rain down Porter Street on their way toward the highway, Claire Eldwin hunched over her steering wheel, her eyes blank. The woman had already seen too much, Hazel thought, and now there was this, an uncertainty more awful than any she'd experienced with her husband before now. She watched the two cars moving off toward the house in Mulhouse Springs.

She went back to her office and sat behind her desk. She checked the website one more time, but the camera had been turned off and the site returned a black square, a fitting monument to the entire case. It had been a case about faith, bad faith and broken hearts. She wondered silently to herself how often in the last ten days images of love destroyed had passed through her mind, her own hopeless love for Andrew, the broken marriage that was Colin and Claire Eldwin, Wingate's murdered partner, the unimaginable sadness that had driven Joanne Cameron to tie the last of her hopes to a rogue cop who probably loved nothing but his own convictions. She realized that she'd allowed herself to think of the relationship between Bellocque and Paritas as a sort of silver lining for Joanne Cameron: someone to love in the midst of her grief. But as soon as she had that thought, she recognized that it, too, was a lie: the affair between the two of them was strictly business. Cameron had been right all along insisting he wasn't her boyfriend.

For some reason, this thought ticked over into an image of Wingate following Claire Eldwin home, the both of them driving slowly, like a cortege without a body. She fixated on the image of the two cars, and in her mind's eye, she saw two other cars . . . She fumbled for her notebook and read through her notes from the Barlow and Paritas interviews. Barlow had mentioned her clients had arrived in separate cars and Paritas – Cameron – had confirmed it when she'd angrily denied that she and Bellocque lived together. She should have paid much more attention to that denial: they didn't live together, they had never been lovers, and now she realized it was important. She hurriedly got Wingate on the radio. "Come back," she said.

"I'm not in Mulhouse Springs yet."

"I know where Colin Eldwin is being held."

32

"It's the first thing we should have thought of when we figured out her name," Hazel said, signalling her turn onto Highway 121. "We slipped."

"We had other things on our plate."

They'd found nothing under Cameron's name in Gilmore, but the third real estate office they'd called told them a Joanne Cameron was paying the rent on a house let to a Nick Wise. Hazel had practically levitated out of her seat. "Too tidy for their own good," she said.

"Unless they want us to find them," said Wingate.

The clicking of the turn signal did time with the windshield wipers. They'd taken an unmarked vehicle, but in the increasing downpour she doubted anyone would have made them anyway. She turned east and took the car up to 140 kilometres per hour, holding the wheel tight.

"And meanwhile, another day has gone by and god knows what kind of shape Eldwin is in," she said.

They reached Highway 191 in fifteen minutes and turned north. It sounded like demons pounding the roof of the car. The address was 28 Whitcombe Street in Gilmore. They passed Goodman's falling-down rented shack on the way into town, slowing down to get a look. It was dark, as expected. She knew instinctively that he'd never return to that place. Three years waiting for a sign. That was how strong his conviction had been, how strong his obsession. Not even grief has that kind of staying power, Hazel thought. He'd divided his time between Toronto and Gilmore waiting for Eldwin to show his hand. It hadn't mattered to Goodman if the hand held something or not: he'd only wanted a reason to act.

And he'd gotten to Hazel. She was the perfect mark: a small-town cop with a willingness to go off the grid if the job demanded it. And she had daughters . . . it was as if she'd been made to order for them: just smart enough, just blind enough. She didn't want to admit it, that perhaps she was in this car, arrowing through the pouring rain on a hunch, for Martha's sake. Would justice for Brenda Cameron pay a tithe to the angels on her daughter's behalf? She had to tell herself she was motivated only by the desire to see justice done for its own sake, but then she heard Ray Greene saying *you can't be a maverick and a leader at the same time.* She wondered how often she'd have to push that voice away from now on.

She considered what it meant to have only her and Wingate's faith now driving the case. She'd made enemies of all her back-up: Ilunga with a severed hand and Danny Toles hung up like a dummy. She knew Willan was only a phone call away and was collecting news about dinosaurs from any and all comers. Any of her recent moves could spell a dishonourable discharge for her: this was the ever-present thought, the awareness that the end-of-days was near.

She blamed the weather for making her thoughts extra-oppressive. She had to focus on the task at hand and not think of the kinds of forces arrayed against her. The end of her career was supposed to be a source of pride for her and those she had worked with, those she had served. But she feared she was about to go out like her mother, hounded by innuendo and haunted by pride. But ex-mayor Micallef was immune to regrets. She was one hundred percent backbone. Hazel's back was made of lesser stuff.

They drove slowly down Whitcombe in the centre of town. It was just off the main drag, a quiet side street. They pulled over a few houses away and as soon as they stopped, the noise of the rain intensified. It bounced hard against the unmarked's window and hammered down through the newly green trees. The drops seemed to leap out of the asphalt, blown sideways by the wind. But however bad the weather was, the dusk-like light offered them the best cover they could have asked for.

There was an MX-5 Miata in the driveway at number 28. "That counts as sporty," Hazel said.

"The car and the house aren't a guarantee of anything, you know," said Wingate. "If they had the presence of mind to rent two houses up here, they could have rented a third. She knew we were going to find her name out eventually."

"Well, if I'm wrong about this, I've got nothing."

He wiped the fogged windshield. The humidity in the car was making them sweat. He stared up at the house across the street from them. It was a rickety-looking bungalow with a couple of sagging balconies. The house was dark and looked uninhabited. "So, what are we waiting for then?"

She was concentrating on the house, trying to fix it as a space in her mind. She presumed there was a door in the back as well. Probably the better one to get access to the basement. "Did you notice a van at the Bellocque house?" she asked. "Pat Barlow said he was driving a white van."

"I didn't see any vehicle at all."

"And it's not here."

"Does that mean *he's* not here?"

"I don't know," she said. "But I think we should wait awhile. See if he shows. I want to be sure they're both here when we make our move."

Ninety minutes passed. She had cars out trolling for sign of the van, but the infrequent reports she was getting suggested no one could make out the breed of a dog beyond twenty metres. Time and the weather were working against them.

Wingate shifted in his seat, uncomfortable and bored. "Well, I guess if I ever *wanted* to go back to Twenty-one, that bridge is pretty much burnt."

"Oh, it's ashes," she said. "I doubt there's even a tunnel now."

He laughed. "Do you really trust Ilunga to run those prints against the oars? What if he loses something on the way to the lab?"

"No," she said. "This is his chance to pin everything on Goodman. If he gets a match to the oars off Eldwin's hand, he saves face and buries his nemesis all at once. He's a hero. How's that inconsistent with his sleazy personality?"

"It isn't. I just hope he doesn't play you."

"I'm done being played."

They watched the street a while longer. "That was some good detectiving, by the way. I never said."

"Good for a has-been, huh?"

"You old folk have something to teach us after all." He gave her a warm smile.

"I like you, James. I'm glad you've chosen the slow lane."

"This is the slow lane, huh?"

She looked at the clock display on the dash. "Jesus," she said. "My stomach is turning acid."

"Maybe we shouldn't wait anymore," said Wingate. "If they've been one step ahead of us this long, maybe they've already dealt with this eventuality. What if they're both gone?"

"If we bust in there and Dana Goodman isn't there, we'll never see him again. Give it another half-hour."

"But what if they're moving him, Hazel? They're putting distance between us if that's the case."

She thought about it and his point was solid. "We should have patrols further af –"

"Wait," he said. "Look at that."

A light had gone on in a window at lawn-level. A basement light. Even in the dark of the rain, it looked like a beacon. "Okay," she said, "okay."

"Okay what?"

"One of us goes, the other stays and keeps an eye out for the van. We stay in contact on the walkies, low volume."

"I'll go," he said.

She put a hand on his wrist. "No. She knows me. If she's alone there, I might be able to talk her into giving up Goodman."

"What if she's not?"

"You'll hear shots, no doubt. Come flying."

He was shaking his head, nervous. "I don't know, Hazel. I don't like you alone in there."

"I don't think he's here, James. I think she's alone. He's come up empty . . ."

"Is that necessarily a good sign?"

"I don't know." She checked her gun. It had a full clip in it. "I'm going to go. Keep an eye out."

He didn't protest, but she could tell he wasn't happy. "Shoot first," he said.

"Stay on channel six."

She stepped out into the downpour and hunched her shoulders up. The wind drove the rain sideways and upwards into her face. She looked up and down the street for any sign of Goodman's van, but the street was empty. Only she and Wingate had lacked the sense to stay indoors today. She crouch-ran across the street to the even-numbered side and sheltered under a silver maple. She could see a side-window now from her vantage, also lit, but there was no movement she could make out from within, not even shadows.

She crept along the east side, throwing looks back up the street and toward the unmarked. Wingate's voice came in low from her belt. "Anything?"

"Another light, but I don't see anyone inside. The street is clear. I'm going."

Twenty-four, twenty-six . . . she was at the property line. There was a repetitive sound coming from the back of twenty-eight, like something being hammered, and her pulse rose. She could see the back corner of the house now, and she moved slowly along the wall of the neighbouring house to reveal the back of twenty-eight. There was a garden back there. No van, though. The hammering sound was louder. It was an irregular clacking noise. Wingate asked what it was and she told him it sounded like a shutter being swung back and forth in the wind.

She still wasn't sure if the missing van was a good sign or not. She had to presume that Cameron and Goodman were in constant touch if they weren't together: she'd have little time to roust Cameron before she made contact with her partner, and even less time if they were, in fact, together in there.

She knew the risk she was walking into a trap was high. She'd chosen not to share this with Wingate: she had to get into that house and see what was there for her own sake. She'd been led by the nose for this whole case, but this one time she felt fairly certain she'd caught the two of them out in a loose end. But not totally certain: Goodman had proven clairvoyant in these matters. The possibility that she'd go into that house and not come out alive had already occurred to her. He'd had one chance to kill her and she doubted he'd pass up a second. She crossed to the back of the neighbouring house and got a perspective on the rear of twenty-eight. As she'd thought, there was an entrance in back of the house, and a loose screen door was making the whacking noise. From this vantage, she also inspected the side of twenty-eight, but there didn't seem to be any live surveillance: no cameras, no electronic equipment at all. She began to feel a tiny wave of hope. "Okay," she murmured into the radio. "I'm going over."

"I'm calling for backup."

"*Don't*," she radioed back. "If Goodman's on his way here from somewhere, I don't want him encountering cruisers on his street. He's likely to see it as a not-very-good sign. We'll lose him."

She ran low to the cover of the corner of twenty-eight and flattened herself against the back of the house. Now she wouldn't be able to see the front or the street and Wingate would have to be her eyes. She knew he wouldn't let her down. She dialled the radio volume to one and pushed herself toward the door. The screen door might act as sound cover, she realized, glad to catch even a small break, although the closer she got to the door, the more it also felt like such a loud noise could blow her cover if anyone inside got sick of listening to it. Or if it suddenly stopped.

The wind was holding the door open and then crashing it shut. She waited until it was open and tried the handle on the inner door. It was locked. She got her truncheon out of her belt and held the thick side at the ready. The screen door slammed twice and then blew open again and she got in and put the base of the club where the knob was attached to the door and delivered a single blow to the top of it with the side of her gun. She twisted out of the way to let the door slam shut and then inserted herself again and pounded the knob. The screen door smashed her in the back, and she took one more swing with the flat of the gun and the cheap knob broke off, revealing the inner workings of the lock.

She stepped back again to catch her breath and stand at attention in case anyone was able to tell the two noises apart. The explosive clapping of the screen door was like thunder in her ears, competing with the sound of her blood roaring in her head. It felt like the rain was falling through her: she was drenched. She could hear Wingate's questioning voice trying to raise her, but she ignored him and held the screen door open with one leg as she worked an index finger into the hollow space behind the missing knob. She was able to move a metal bar within the workings of the lock and open the door. It swung in and she stepped into the dark at the top of a set of stairs. She quietly closed the door behind her and pushed the catch back into place with her finger. Dialling the walkie down to zero, she stood in the dark, waiting for her eyes to adjust. There was a faint line of light at the bottom of the stairs in front of her.

Hazel unbuttoned her jacket and took it off, leaving it on the landing as she began to descend. She leaned over and used the tail of her shirt to wipe her face, but the rainwater in her hair was sluicing down her face, carrying some residue of hairspray into her eyes. She blinked away the stinging and stood silently on the stairs, trying to hear past the door below. Someone was moving around in there, slowly shuffling. She heard a voice – Cameron's, she thought – but couldn't make out what she was saying. It was getting hard to breathe normally now, she was too worked up; it felt like her heart was going to burst out of her chest. Foolishly, she'd failed to check the gun when she had some light: it occurred to her now that hammering the truncheon with it might have damaged it. If the Glock didn't work, she'd have no protection at all, and no matter how fast Wingate could run, her nagging anxiety about her life ending in this basement might come true after all. She had a flash of herself lying on the concrete and Goodman advancing on her with his whetted knife and she considered remounting the stairs and checking the mechanism. But she'd come this far, and now she could hear faint sobbing, and she decided she could do nothing but trust the gun.

She was at the door. It was heavy-duty, something put there for a reason. She doubted they could have heard the screen door slamming or the sound of her breaking the lock. When, at the station house, they'd tried to listen past the sounds of the room on the webcam, they'd heard nothing telltale: no voices from elsewhere, no sounds from outside, and this was why. She presumed this door was locked as well and thought through her options. The only thing that made sense was to kick it in and rush the room with the gun out.

She steeled herself, pushing away the haze of anxiety, and retreated two steps to put her on level with the centre of the door's edge. She reared back, turning sideways, and as she lunged forward to kick, someone within opened the door and Hazel crashed forward, driving whoever was behind backwards and plunging into the open space. She twisted toward the wall and hit the door jamb with her face before she collapsed to the floor on her side. Joanne Cameron was screaming, *Don't! Don't!* from somewhere behind her and Hazel leapt to standing, the gun still miraculously in her hand, and lunged toward the sound of the woman's voice, only to find Cameron cowering against the wall in a crouch, her arms folded over the top of her head. Hazel swept the gun toward her and turned, keeping the weapon in front, rotating the muzzle in a semi-circle through the room behind her, stepping to Cameron's side to keep her in her peripheral vision. This was it, ground zero. She'd been watching this dark, evil space for ten days, wondering where on earth it could be, and now she was in it, as if she'd stepped through her computer. It felt eerie and wrong, like she was Nick Wise trapped in his box. Her back was to the bloody message, in dried, fifteen-inch letters, and the table Cameron had sat at was still in the middle of the room. The tripod with the camera was in its place, and Hazel noted the red light on the camera was blinking. It had been turned back on. A wire from the side of the camera ran down to the floor and to a hard drive in the corner.

Colin Eldwin was gone. As was Goodman.

Hazel turned to face Joanne Cameron, who had lowered her arms and was sitting, drained and docile, at the base of the wall. A fresh cut on her mouth where the door had hit her competed with a mass of welts, bruises, and gashes. Hazel looked at her sadly and brought the walkie to her mouth. "James?"

"Christ, why did you go silent?"

"I'm here. It's only Cameron. He's beaten the shit out of her."

Wingate appeared in a matter of moments with the first-aid kit, and they sat Joanne Cameron in the chair and attended to her. She hadn't said a word. Goodman had beaten her with his fists, and her mouth and cheeks were swollen. Her whole face was the colour of raw steak and a clear fluid leaked from her right temple.

Hazel looked toward the camera. "Can he see us?"

"He doesn't have to see us," said Cameron through her broken mouth. "He knows what we're doing. He knows what we're going to do."

"He sounds like Santa Claus." She went over to the set-up and tore the wire out of the back of the camera. "Well, that's one less window into our souls, then."

Wingate was daubing her eye. Cameron winced. "Why did he do this to you?" he asked.

"Does it matter?"

"Anything you can do to put the heat on him now can't hurt."

She laughed mirthlessly. "Is this the part where you tell me I can still save myself?"

Hazel kneeled in front of her. "That was your hand in the video," she said. "The one holding the knife."

"Yes."

"Do you want me to believe you severed Colin Eldwin's hand with that knife? That you sliced the ears off the sides of his head?"

"It doesn't matter to me what you believe. I'm done believing. I just wanted the truth about Brenda." She looked away from Hazel. "I don't care about anything else now."

"It matters to me. It matters to me if you let Goodman twist you into something you're not. Or if you did it because you wanted to."

Cameron speared her with a pitiless look. "You want me to say Dana cut him because you think in my place you'd never have done it yourself. But I'm here to tell you, you would. You'd have done anything."

"Then you'll be charged accordingly," said Hazel, rising. "But I look at you now, and I think you didn't do it. I just think you want to be punished."

Cameron took the gauze from Wingate's hand and held it to her cheek. It was stained yellow and red. One of her eyes was swollen and the lid was white and iridescent purple. Hazel's heart went out to her: no matter what this woman had done, she'd begun in a place of righteous grief. And now she was going to be charged with assault causing bodily harm and false imprisonment, among other things. And the man who masterminded it all had dumped her and taken their leverage with him. "I don't have to seek punishment," Cameron finally said. "My child was murdered and I've failed to avenge her. What else can be done to me?"

Hazel stepped away, turning her back. Cameron was living every mother's nightmare, and there was nothing anyone could say or do to bring her out of it. It was permanent. The only thing she could do now was try to bring Eldwin in alive.

"Where's Dana Goodman?"

"I don't know," Cameron said.

"If I told you I believed your daughter was murdered, would you help us?"

"Would you be lying?"

"Nothing I say will convince you I'm not, so I won't try. But if I do believe it, and you don't help us get Eldwin back alive, you'll have missed your last chance to see justice done in Brenda's name." She waited a moment for Cameron to decide what she was going to do, and then she asked, "How long ago did Eldwin leave?"

"Two hours," she said.

Hazel radioed dispatch. "Our 908's gone 908," she said.

"Come again?" said Wilton.

"We've got Joanne Cameron, but Goodman has abducted the abductee. We need an APB for this white van, anywhere within a two-hundred-kilometre radius of Gilmore." She held the walkie down. "What's his licence plate?"

Cameron's eyes shuttled between hers and Wingate's.

"She wasn't alone in the boat," Wingate said. "Brenda wasn't alone. We have proof now."

Cameron's mouth was moving, but no sound came out for a moment. "It started with AAZW," she said. "I don't know the rest of it."

"That's enough to start with," said Hazel. "You get that, Spence?"

"Word's already going out."

"Have someone clean out a cell. We've got a reservation for at least one. And send a SOCO team to 28 Whitcombe in Gilmore. They're going to need to block off the rest of today and tomorrow, I think."

Wingate helped Cameron out of her seat. "Do you have any idea where Dana took Eldwin?"

Cameron shook her head. "Not one. He beat me up in front of Colin. I saw the look in his eyes: he figured he was next. My guess is, he is."

"Why is that your guess?"

"Because Dean said he was going to give you people a crime you can solve."

"A trail I can follow . . ." Hazel murmured. "Did he say anything else?"

"He said *Thank God for the rain*."

] 33 [

Joanne Cameron was silent in the back seat as they returned to
Port Dundas. Hazel put a call in to the station house to find
out if there had been any news from Toronto, but neither
Ilunga nor any of his deputies had called. Wingate's warning
was still resonating in her mind, although she found it hard to
believe that Ilunga would destroy evidence in a case that had
its roots in his catchment. If Goodman was right about the rot
in the division, then maybe, but Hazel suspected he was only
right about this one case, a case that could have gone either
way, depending on how deeply the investigators were willing to
look into a death that looked like a suicide from every angle.

She had Wilton connect her with The River Nook, and
Dianne put Constable Childress on the line. She was frosty
with Hazel. "He's had the better part of the day to check the
prints," Hazel said.

"I told you it would be tomorrow. They've got to thaw the
goddamn thing out first, don't they?"

"They have microwaves in the morgue. Look, it's time your boss started taking this seriously. None of this is happening in an imaginary realm: we have to *work*. Now tell me how long until I hear back."

"I don't know," said Childress. "I'll try to push them for tomorrow morning. Everything's still at CFS."

"Well, you get yourself down to the station house where I can bug you to check in with your people every thirty minutes. If you can tear yourself away from Dianne's gingerbread cake."

Childress didn't answer, just hung up.

"I want to know," said Cameron from the back seat, "I want to know what you found on the island."

Hazel turned in the passenger seat. "I don't share information with potential murder suspects. Especially not about the cases they're suspects in."

The station house in Port Dundas was abuzz when they returned. Hazel handed Joanne Cameron off to Costamides, who led her down the back toward the cells. "Give her something to eat and clean her off. If you think anything's broken, get a doc in here. Make sure the cell is empty except for a table and chair. I don't want her to try to hurt herself." Costamides nodded smartly and took Cameron under the arm. She didn't resist.

Wilton reported there'd been no sightings of Goodman's van. "We need aerial surveillance," she said. "Can we get anyone up there to look in the trees or along the dirt roads? There's too much cover to see through, and the weather –"

"The weather's going to keep everything grounded," said Wilton.

"I know a guy." It was Fraser. "He's private, though. He'll cost."

"Call him," she said.

He started moving away, but then he doubled back and stuck a pile of paper in her hands.

"What's this?"

"When you have time," he said. "It's the questionnaires."

"I've got enough bad news as it is, Kraut."

"Is it true?"

"Is what true?"

"About Ray Greene?"

She was aware that the pen behind them had fallen silent. "What do you know about Ray Greene?"

"*Skip.*"

She looked down at the papers he'd handed her. She recognized the *Ontario Police Services Central Region Work Environment Survey.*

"Page five, question thirty-six," he said.

She unfurled the questionnaires in her hand. There were twelve of them. She opened each survey to the middle page. Question thirty-six read *If you were redeployed to another detachment within OPSC, which one would be your first choice?* The first respondent had answered "Port Dundas." So had the second.

"Keep going," said Fraser.

All twelve respondents had written in "Port Dundas" as their first choice in case of redeployment. "I think this is called shooting yourself in the foot," Hazel said.

She noted that six of the twelve respondents were in the pen this afternoon. Her constables and sergeants, many of whom had worked for Gord Drury loyally, and for her since then, and something had convinced them it was worth putting their necks on the line. "What about your kids?" she said to them. "What about having a say in what community you serve? I met Willan: he'll send you to the back of nowhere if he thinks you're going to be trouble." She looked at Fraser. "I thought you were half out of here already, Kraut."

"Is it true about Greene?"

She hesitated a moment. "Probably. Is that why you want to stay?"

"That's why we want to fight. We won't work under Ray Greene. He *left* – in the middle of a case. That was his choice. This week, we've all worked together, like we should. I don't agree with everything you do, but you do keep us together. We want it to stay that way. We're going to fight."

She was shaking her head. "The fight is over, Dietrich. The decisions have been made."

"They'll be unmade. Or there'll be chaos."

"Is this you or Martin Ryan talking?"

"It's the whole union. Province-wide."

She rerolled the papers and held them out to him. "Thank you," she said. The room was silent; she knew she was talking to all of them now. "It means more than you can know."

"Are you going to get behind us?" called Bail.

"I've always been behind you." She returned her attention to Fraser. "Listen," she said, "since you're still working for me, I have a little job for you . . ."

"What kind of crime does Dana Goodman think we can solve?" she said to Wingate. She'd taken him under the arm when she passed back through the pen and pulled him to her office. "He obviously doesn't think much of our investigative skills anymore."

"Maybe he'll light a flare beside Eldwin's body."

She held her door open for him. He entered and she crossed the room to her desk and punched the intercom. "Did Childress get here yet?"

"She's waiting by my desk," said Cartwright.

"Send her in."

"What is going on?" Wingate asked.

"We're going to light a flare of our own."

Childress entered, her cap still on her head, and stepped only as far into Hazel's office so as to officially be in the room without actually seeming to be in the room with them. "I just called down," she said.

"And?"

"And nothing."

"Maybe we should call again." She took the phone off the cradle. "Ask your superintendent about Goodman. Maybe he can help put us in his mindset."

"What makes you think the superintendent knows the first thing about Goodman's mindset? The man went off the deep end."

"You sound like a subscriber to the Ilunga theory of Goodman."

"You ask him if you're not."

"I'm not sure he and me are talking."

Childress seemed to weigh which of her options would get her out of the room the fastest, and she crossed to the side of Hazel's desk and dialled her boss's number. Hazel stabbed the speaker button, and the voice of the woman with the clipboard who'd taken them to Ilunga answered. "Constable Georgia Childress calling," she said. "Is the superintendent in?"

"Hold," said the officious voice.

"Childress?"

"Sir."

"I thought you were liaising with Sergeant Adiga."

"I, um . . ."

"Christ," said Ilunga. "What has she done now?"

Hazel stepped forward toward the mic. "Is he a killer? Does your Goodman have it in him to kill?"

"You're getting all the assistance you'll *be* getting from this office, Detective Inspector. Don't look to me to water your theories."

"Why wasn't he charged?"

"With what? Being an asshole?"

"He committed a B & E. He threatened a witness."

"We gave him a choice: dishonourable or quit. He chose to quit. We were happy to see him go. No lawsuits from the union, no paperwork. Just turn in your badge and off you go. You should be thinking along those lines about now, Micallef. Save everyone in the OPS brass some grief. Well, more grief."

"How crazy is he?"

"If I try to quantify his craziness, how are you going to understand it from the point of view of your own? That he's at least twice as crazy as you? Three times? Policework isn't supposed to be this relative."

Hazel reached forward and took the receiver off the desktop, and cancelled the speakerphone function. "Listen, Cap. You and I do things differently, but do you really want an ex-cop from your division to be guilty of murder?"

"Are you asking me if I care if one lunatic kills another? That's a hard one to answer."

"What if you people were right all along? It's not a murder?"

"Choose your conspiracy, Micallef."

"Fine. What if it isn't Colin Eldwin who committed it?"

"It better be after that goddamned package you sent me."

"Is he capable of killing? Just answer me."

There was a long pause on the other end. "Yes," Ilunga said finally. "I came to think he was."

"*Thank* you," she said.

"Do yourself a favour and shoot him the next time you see him."

Hazel repunched the speaker button. "What was that again?"

"Never mind."

She hung up and looked at Childress and Wingate.

"What?" said Childress.

"You have a cell?"

"Why?"

"Because there won't be any land lines for a while." She shifted her attention fully to Wingate. "Why did Goodman thank God for the rain?"

"Because he needed the cover."

"No. Because it lets him set up his last puzzle. And I think if we don't come up with the right answer this time, Eldwin dies."

"Why won't there be any land lines?" said Childress, unhappily.

"Because Goodman is going to let the rain do his work for him while he puts some space between himself and his mess. And he gets what he figures is a fitting punishment for Colin Eldwin's crime."

"He's going to drown him," said Wingate suddenly, catching up with her. "And *thank God for the rain* because it will fill whatever Eldwin's trapped in." He thought for a moment. "Which is a boat."

"Go tell Fraser he needs to reroute his friend with the helicopter."

They cleared the parking lot to make room for a landing pad, and she waited with Wingate and Childress in her cruiser. The constable, looking tired and irritated, sat in the back. Wingate's hands were knotted in his lap. They'd called Tate and Calberson and told them to suit up. "Can they even fit six people in a 'copter?" asked Wingate.

"You can ride on top if we run out of room." She caught Childress's eyes in the rearview. "It's time to call your liaison again."

"I told you, it's going to be morning before we know anything."

"Do they work through the night?"

"If they have to."

"Constable?"

"I don't know if they're there tonight. I don't know what's going on downtown, what the caseload is like, or *anything*. Remember, I've been seconded to Port Dundas." She looked out the window at the starless sky.

"You people would rather save face than break a sweat on this, wouldn't you? What are you going to do when you play a role in cracking a cold case? You going to deny it was worth it?"

Childress sprung forward in her seat, her eyes blazing. "No, I'm going to pin a fucking medal on myself!"

Hazel said nothing, just waited for the constable to settle back into her seat. "Just keep your phone on."

Tate and Calberson were speeding up from Mayfair; Wingate said Tate had received his urgent call and responded agreeably. They expected them by nine-thirty. Right now, Fraser's private pilot was coming back down from the area around Gilmore, where he'd been sweeping for the white van unsuccessfully.

At nine o'clock, they heard the sound of rotors in the dark coming from the north and the helicopter, throwing a hard beam of white light through the rain, hoved in and came down. Wingate shuddered to see it sheering sideways as it came in and the pilot had to reascend a few feet and level out before setting down. A man stepped out and lit a cigarette. Hazel flashed her beams at him and he crouch-ran through the rain to the car and took one last hard drag before flicking the cigarette away and getting into the car. He shook hands with everyone and introduced himself as Gary Quinn. He was a solidly built man of about forty-five with a full head of grey hair and wild salt-and-pepper eyebrows.

"We're dropping the search for the van. We think they're out on the water."

"Water? Where, though?" said Quinn.

"The suspect's been gone for more than three hours now, but my best guess is he hasn't been driving this whole time. So somewhere within a ninety-minute driving radius."

"That's a lot of lakes, Officer," said Quinn. "We can look here, though." He had a map, which he passed forward and they spread open on the dashboard. It showed all of Westmuir County. He leaned between the seats and pointed at the town of Gilmore. "If he started here, we're going to want to do a sweep of every major lake within reasonable reach of the town. That takes in Lake MacKenzie, Rye Lake, Pickamore Lake, Inlet Lake, and a whole hell of a lot of littler ones too."

"How long will that take?" Wingate asked.

"Even if it clears a little, maybe an hour per lake, but we've got to do a zed-pattern over everything and Pickamore and Inlet are huge. I wouldn't bank on being in bed before 3 a.m., folks."

"Hey, we never sleep anyway," said Hazel. "What have we got in the way of lighting?"

"Well, there's the directional on the front of the bird, but it's only got three positions. I've got a portable spot with a halogen parabolic in it, which would normally do the trick: it spreads a cone with a radius of ten feet from fifty feet up, but the problem tonight is that it has to pick through the rain. If we're low enough, we'll be able to see something, but it's going to look like ten thousand glow-worms are jumping in it. And with the wind, I don't think I can go lower than fifty feet or we might find ourselves climbing some trees."

"I need a Gravol," said Wingate.

Quinn clapped him on the shoulder. "You can always puke out the door."

"Great."

"There's also one pair of thermal infrared binoculars. So one of you can wear those and watch the colours go by, but the rain's going to put up a blue filter and everything in it is going to be pretty dim." He leaned in toward Hazel. "Couldn't wait until morning, huh? Anyone out in this weather is either half-sunk or capsized. Unless your guy's got a bailing bucket."

"I doubt he has anything."

"Then I suggest we go find him."

] 34 [

The divers arrived fifteen minutes later and they were six. Quinn led them to the helicopter and they clambered in, slipping on the slick rails. Wingate got as close to the pilot as he could. "Is the front better if it's a rough ride?"

Quinn was starting up the engines. "This ain't a 737, Detective, it's like flying a bathtub. Everyone gets the same ride."

Hazel smiled at him. "Good times!" she said.

"We better find him," said Wingate.

Quinn passed back headphones with wraparound microphones. "Everyone hear me?" He passed Hazel the thermal binoculars. "A warm, living body is going to be reddish-orange – 37 Celsius is calibrated to show up red, but anything alive in this weather isn't going to read that hot. A cold, living body is going to be closer to yellow. You start seeing purple or dark blue, then we're talking rocks, logs, fish, or something that's going to need putting in a pine box. Okay everyone? Ready for take-off . . ."

The blades whined into high speed and the tail of the helicopter rose off the ground, followed by its giant, insect-like
body. It took to the air with its head lowered, and Wingate
grabbed the arm of his seat with white knuckles. He mouthed
the words *I hate you* to Hazel, who nodded once to acknowledge
reception. The team of Tate and Calberson sat quietly in their
seats and Childress did her best to hide a terror that was clearly
at least as profound as Wingate's.

Quinn broke away toward the northeast; the helicopter
tilted to the right and pushed hard through the dark. In the
headlight, the rain seemed to be falling up, an endless flow of
jewel-like flashings. On the windows, it streaked sideways and
flew off in silvery ripples. It didn't feel like an airplane; there
was no impression of moving forward through a resisting
space; the helicopter felt like it was being lifted up and side-to-
side by means of ropes attached to it. It made Wingate feel like
a shoe in a dryer and he had to look down at his knees to keep
his stomach.

Quinn's voice came over the headsets, barely audible over
the roar of the machine. "We're heading to Inlet Lake first.
Fifteen miles long, up to two miles wide in places. There's an
inaccessible second and third lake, and I think we should
presume with your guy that if he's out in this that he got to
where he is from a shoreline accessible by a local road. We'll do
a quick flyby in any of these lakes with multiple bodies, but
lingering in them is going to be a waste of time."

Through the rain, they saw a black shape lying on the ground,
a greater darkness lying at the centre of the night. This was
Inlet, so named for the finger-like bays that poked off the main

body. Quinn descended to about fifty feet and flew back and forth in diagonals over the water as Hazel clicked on the binocs and pointed her face through the open door at the lake. The beam from the directional – pointed over Hazel's side – was like a moving pillar of marble in the rain. Its iris spread out over twenty feet from their height, riding choppily over Inlet's surface. Calberson had clipped her off to a heavy metal ring on the inside of the craft, and she could lean out into the weather and look down through the bright column of rain, which, stirred by the helicopter blades, whipped around her head and body cyclonically. "I see some green and blue, some faint yellow . . ."

"Where's the yellow?"

"Off your window. About eleven o'clock."

"I want a spot on it."

Wingate began to rise slowly, but the pallor of his face convinced Calberson to take over. He armed the spot and turned it in the direction Hazel had been looking. It was at the shoreline where it appeared as if a tributary of the lake ran off into a swampy background. Quinn, holding the helicopter in place, was leaning out his window, squinting. The helicopter seemed to lean over as well and Wingate and Childress both grabbed the edges of their seats. He looked over at her in what he hoped would be a moment of grand commiseration, but she wouldn't meet his eyes.

"What are you seeing, Detective Inspector?"

"Four shapes, two large, maybe the size of a cocker spaniel, and two small. All yellowy."

"Too warm to be body parts," Quinn said. "Any movement?"

"Yes," she said, hesitating. "One of the bigger ones actually seems to be moving. It is. Moving away from the shoreline."

Tate held his hand out for the glasses and looked through them, then passed them back. "Beavers," he said. "That's a dam down there."

She looked through the binoculars again and the shapes resolved into animals, two adults and two kits. The secret life of the lake. Quinn passed overtop and then turned steeply, aiming thirty degrees above his previous tack. Through the sights, Hazel saw a miasma of blue and black shapes; nothing that suggested life at all.

In this manner, with the six of them packed tightly inside, Quinn swept back and forth over Inlet Lake, suturing one shoreline to the other in lines of thrown light. The helicopter shook, jolted, slid sideways in the air, dropped suddenly, and generally shook them like a bartender making cocktails. For all this, they saw nothing. On his last pass, Quinn pulled the nose of the helicopter up and powered over the trees, pointing them in the direction of Lake MacKenzie. The sudden heave upwards made them feel like their stomachs had flattened out against their spines. It was well past eleven o'clock and the dark was full and thick with rain and they were all cold. Finally, at midnight, Wingate thrust his face out of the open door, gripping a cold steel reinforcing bar behind him, and vomited into the forest below. When he sat down, Constable Childress passed him a small white pill.

"What is it?" he asked.

Hazel leaned over and looked. She laughed. "Ativan. How fitting."

He chewed it, grimacing.

By two in the morning, they'd covered MacKenzie and Rye, and they were heading for Pickamore Lake. If anything, the rain had intensified; the sound of it in the dark made it seem a huge presence, an omniscient force conveying them through its violent mind. Even Calberson looked green, and he spent half his working life under water. When they'd criss-crossed Lake MacKenzie, Hazel had already begun to go blind to the thermal translation of the world beneath them, and she passed the glasses to Wingate, now becalmed by Childress's white pill. He pressed his face to the eyepiece and said *wow* quietly under his breath. Rye came up a blank under his inspection, and they doubled back to the southwest to get to Pickamore, the largest of the four lakes in the radius. Quinn had to refuel at a twenty-four-hour depot outside of Mandeville. When he put down, Hazel pinned Wingate with a look. "You're not getting out, you know."

"You're a horrible lady."

She grinned curiously at him. "You're stoned."

"Is this how she felt? Brenda Cameron?"

"She had at least three times the dosage you took. And her belly was full of alcohol, too. So, no. But can you imagine?"

"I couldn't kill myself in this state. I'd screw it up."

"You could do anything if you were desperate enough."

He wiped the back of his neck. "We're never going to find this guy. Alive."

"We'll see." She signalled to Childress. The shared horror of the evening had softened her somewhat. "Call your people again."

"It's three in the morning."

"See if anyone's there. Leave a message or page someone. I want your people on line in case we find Eldwin. If he's alive, he's going to be in rough-enough shape – I don't want to have to presume he's also a murderer. I'd like to *know*."

"Okay, okay," said Childress, and she started dialling.

Quinn detached the refuelling hose and clambered back up into the cockpit. "My guess is we see daylight in two and a half hours, and right about then, the rain stops too."

"Two and a half hours might be all this guy has left. Let's get back up there."

Childress was shouting into the phone, but Hazel couldn't make out what she was saying. She hoped there was someone on the other end. The constable hung up and pocketed the cell. She lifted the headset's mic to her mouth. "There's one guy there, not attached to our case. But he's going to nose around and see what might be ready. He's going to call me back."

"*Thank you*," said Hazel. Childress just nodded.

Quinn passed high over the town of Mandeville. The 'copter dipped down over the treelines and burst out over Pickamore Lake. Wingate pressed the binoculars to his face again as they began their sweep. At 4 a.m., at about four hundred metres off the northern shoreline, he saw a shape outlined in dark violet: unmistakably a canoe. There was a form in it. The middle of the form glowed pale orange and then began to fade to light purple at its extremities. He lowered the thermal binoculars to his lap and pulled the mic up over his mouth. "There he is," he called, pointing toward the rain-wreathed island. "That's him."

35

Thursday, June 2

There was a faint glow coming from the east, a pinkish light
that seemed to drive the rain away and limn the early morning
darkness with a phosphorescent edge. Quinn was descending
toward the lake surface, creating an undulating target of waves
beneath them. From within fifteen metres, they could see the
form of a man in the canoe, wound in white cloth like a
mummy, only his face exposed to the elements. The rainwater
had filled the boat to his chin. The bloody sides of his head and
the bloom of pink where the stump of his wrist was bound up
in cloth confirmed for them that they had found their man.
Eldwin's eyes were closed and he had not reacted to the sound
of the helicopter or their voices calling to him. Calberson
suited up and pulled on a mask, but went in without a tank: it
would be a simple-enough operation. He hit the water like an
arrow and surfaced right away, making strong strokes for the

canoe. At the same time, Tate was harnessing the rescue basket and lowering it down with the aid of an on-board winch.

Calberson reached the side of the canoe and put an arm in, feeling along Eldwin's torso with two fingers. He pressed his fingers in hard under the man's chin, then signalled the helicopter to slide the basket over. It drifted over the surface of Pickamore Lake toward him. The four other officers were crowded on one side looking over, no longer feeling any fear at all. Quinn had to bank back slightly to his right to keep the craft level. "Is he alive?" shouted Hazel, but Calberson couldn't hear her over the massive drone of the rotors. He dragged the basket toward him, gripping the hook and pulling it down. He detached it from the rope and affixed it to the metal loop at the front of the canoe and then swam to the stern and with his hands on either side of it, he lofted himself up and in. Ripples moved crossways through the concentric waves made by the blades. Eldwin had not reacted to the sudden weight of another body on top of him, and Hazel looked away. A dead guilty man was considerably better than a dead innocent one, but no call had arrived and she dreaded now knowing the outcome.

They watched Calberson sliding his way along the inside of the canoe, keeping his balance and straddling the wrapped man. The water in the boat sluiced over the sides as he made his progress. Hovering over Eldwin's midsection, the officer leaned forward and felt for a pulse again, but they still could not tell what he'd learned. "He's not going to be able to get him onto the stretcher from there," said Tate. "It's too dangerous."

"Stay in the bird," called Quinn in the headphones. "You don't have the gear."

"No, I'm going down," said Tate, and without another word, he yanked the headset off and jumped from the helicopter.

"He worries too much," said Wingate.

"Worries?" said Hazel.

"You weren't in that boat with them on Gannon. He was practically in tears."

"It's a stressful business," she said, watching Tate swimming over to the canoe. They could just barely hear him calling his partner's name.

"My guess is, there's more to it than that."

She turned slowly to him. He shrugged faintly. "Well, I suppose you'd know."

Tate was at the boat and Calberson was yelling at him, gesturing with his hands. Then he shook his head and unhooked the basket from the front of the canoe and Tate pushed it against the side of the canoe and held it steady. His partner unhooked his leg from around Eldwin and lay down in the water beside him. Then they saw Eldwin sit up, as if in a horror-movie coffin, and Calberson was behind him, levering him over the side of the canoe. Tate threw his arm out and grabbed the front of the white cloth and held the man steady as Calberson got the rest of Eldwin's body up on the stern of the canoe. Hazel watched, riven. This was one of the ways you threw a body out of a boat. But there were others.

Tate was reaching across the stretcher, Calberson a counterweight in the canoe, and between the two of them, they gentled Eldwin within his cocoon onto the basket. Quinn lowered the rope for the men to rehook the harness again, and, with a thumbs-up, he began to winch the apparatus off the lake surface.

"Let me bring him in," said Wingate, his arm on Hazel's shoulder. She stepped aside as, inch by inch, the white form ascended on the end of the rope. She smelled burning oil as the onboard motor strained to bring the weight up.

Quinn's voice buzzed in their ears. "Let's get you folks not involved in receiving the package on the other side of the cabin, please. Even things out and let's get this guy inside."

Wingate held tight to the inside of the door and leaned out, pushing against the rope to keep the stretcher clear of the skids. He wondered at his newfound ability to hang out of a hovering aircraft. David would have been proud of him. As Eldwin got closer to the helicopter, Wingate's heart fell – the man's face was white. He was surely dead. He held the rope at arm's length, getting ready to lean down and grab the basket once it cleared the skids, but then there was a flash against one of the skids and the sound of a metal ping and Wingate felt a searing pain in his cheek. He fell back into the cabin, his hand pressed against his face, and he heard the metallic sound again, louder this time, and Quinn's voice was in their ears, panicked: "Someone's shooting at us –"

The sentence was barely out of the pilot's mouth when the windshield exploded and the whole craft sheered sideways, giving them a view of the lake beneath them through the door. Eldwin's form in the basket swung wildly in the air between the helicopter and the water. Wingate felt himself sliding toward the open space as it fell away from them – Quinn was rapidly climbing to get out of gunfire range – and the sheer drop grew to fifty metres. He flung his arms around in a slow panic and felt a hand clasp him on the forearm and hold him tight. He looked behind him and it was Hazel, her teeth gritted, her other hand in Childress's, who was braced behind one of the bolted benches. He looked down and saw the rain falling in a cone past Eldwin's inert form and vanishing below them into the churning dark. "Hold on," cried Quinn as he tried to come level, and Eldwin swung up loosely at the end of the rope like the little toy Wingate remembered from childhood, the one where you tried to catch a little wooden ball in a cup. The man looked like he was floating, and the moment was frozen in Wingate's vision, it was something beautiful and strange . . . and then gravity took over again and all two hundred pounds of man and basket jerked down hard on the rope. The sudden yank fried the winch motor and it let out the spool with a high-pitched squeal. They watched helplessly as Eldwin plunged back toward the lake: five seconds of falling through space and then he hit the surface with a white explosion.

Over the straining rotors, they couldn't hear if the gunfire had stopped, but by now they were almost seventy metres high above the lake. "Jesus Christ," muttered Quinn. "I didn't know we were expecting visitors."

Hazel had scrambled to her feet and was radioing Port Dundas. "I need backup on the north shore road of Pickamore Lake, shots fired, we have three men in the water and a damaged aircraft –"

"I have to go back down," said Quinn in the earphones.

"Copy," said Hazel's radio, "cars dispatched. Injuries?"

Hazel looked at Wingate's bleeding cheek. "One . . . so far. Stand by."

Quinn was descending rapidly, trying to outpace any bead the shooter might have on them. "We're going to have to do this seagull-style, folks, hold on."

Childress caught Hazel's eye. "The gunshots came from the shoreline," she shouted. "You want me up front?"

"No," called Hazel, heading for the cockpit. "This is between him and me now." She came up beside Quinn and kneeled in the cold space behind the destroyed windshield, and brought her gun up in front of her face. "I want you to face the shoreline," she said to Quinn.

"You want to be a target?"

"No," she said, "I want to end this."

Quinn fell away on the diagonal, pointing the nose of the huge steel machine toward the forest while trying to get as close to the water as possible. Hazel kept her eyes on the shoreline and stole glances to the surface below to keep track of the rescue. Tate and Calberson were still swimming toward Eldwin with powerful strokes; from the helicopter, she could see now that the basket had righted itself in the water and Eldwin was still strapped in. Behind her, Childress had braced herself behind the bench and was leaning over, gripping Wingate's ankles. She was holding him tightly as he slid forward on his belly toward the open door.

Then there was a flash of white in the distance, from within tree-cover, and a half-second later, the empty seat behind Hazel's head spat a tuft of cloth and foam and Quinn bent the craft away from Goodman's sightline. "Hold her!" she shouted to him, and stood in the open space, firing as he ignored her and turned the side of the helicopter to the line of fire. Hazel gripped the edge of the broken window frame and twisted herself partway out into the lashing rain and kept firing at the flares from the treeline. The vast emptiness around them swallowed up the reports and it sounded to Hazel as if someone were setting off harmless fireworks all around them. Quinn was trying to make himself smaller as he leaned out his window to gauge the distance to the surface. More bullets tore at the body of the helicopter and Hazel returned fire for as long as she could and then yelled "Clip! Clip!" and Childress quickly freed her firearm from her holster, keeping hold of Wingate with one hand, and kicked it toward the cockpit.

Quinn was tilting dangerously now, the blades sending shockwaves over the surface in semi-circular surges; Hazel hoped all the soft, human forms below them were out of the way, but she knew, and dreaded, that Quinn had only a minimal amount of control over the bird. She took cover behind the passenger-side door and looked behind herself to see Tate pulling himself up along Wingate's arms and heaving himself into the cabin, drenched and breathless. He turned and braced his thigh against the open doorway and the two of them brought up Calberson and then the three men reached down out of the lurching craft and grabbed a hold of the slack rope, and pulled it and Eldwin in hand over hand. "ALL IN!" shouted Childress and Quinn pulled the helicopter up again, the whole body rising as if shaking itself free of a monstrous grip. The ding of bullets rang against the metal behind her and then she felt the passenger door shatter, and suddenly there was nothing holding her up. She sensed the space below her opening, and as she was falling into it, Quinn reached out and grabbed her by her belt and she spun around wildly and gripped the now-naked steel bar that separated the windshield from the door and fired wildly on the white reports bursting in the distance against the rain. She heard a voice shouting *FUCK YOU FUCK YOU* and didn't realize it was her own until she saw the white star of Goodman's muzzle flare suddenly rise against the wall of trunks and within it was a small bloom of red mist. She'd hit him. She'd hit him and he was down.

"Let's get out of here!" she called, and Quinn pulled away from the site in a wide turn, rising and twisting, until they were once again clear. Hazel looked around anxiously, but everyone was accounted for, and Wingate was standing in the middle of the helicopter, looking at Hazel with shining eyes.

"Turn around," he shouted, rotating his index finger in the air, and Hazel did and he ran his hand up the back of her jacket and under her shirt, feeling for the wound he was sure he'd find. But there was nothing. "He shot the glass in the door out – you were standing right there," he said, but Hazel shook her head at him.

"It was my turn," she said. "Not his. I hit him. Call dispatch, I want any way in or out of this side of the lake blocked and I want teams working on a grid in those woods until they find him or his body."

He called it in, and then Hazel leaned down to Eldwin's motionless form, and pulled the drenched layers of cloth away from his throat. She felt along below his chin for a pulse. "I want to know how hard we should be trying to save this man's life," she shouted to Childress. "Call your people now!" The constable backed away and turned to face the rear of the cabin. "I don't feel a pulse," Hazel said.

"He was alive in the water," yelled Calberson. He leapt to the back of the cabin and dragged his emergency kit out from under one of the benches. "Move aside." Someone finally closed the door and the howl of the wind moved to the front of the helicopter, where the windshield had been shot out. Calberson cut the soaked cloth off Eldwin. "There's a survival blanket in the kit —"

Childress shook the reflective blanket out and passed it to Calberson. Eldwin was naked beneath his windings; it was a pathetic sight, and Calberson put the thin survival blanket on top of him. He held one edge of it up. "You," he yelled to Childress, "get in."

"*What?*"

"You're the smallest one here, so you'll put the least strain on his chest. But we got to warm him up or he'll die for sure." She hesitated and he reached out and grabbed her wrist. "I'm not asking." Childress lay down on top of Eldwin, face to face with the unconscious man.

Hazel leaned down to her. "Did you get through?"

"I'm on hold."

"Jesus Christ," she said, "give me that phone."

She took off her helmet and put the phone to her ear. Calberson picked up the helmet and spoke into the mic. "Mr. Quinn? – where's the nearest hospital?"

"The only ER that can handle this is in Mayfair," Quinn said.

"Go." He had Eldwin's left wrist and was feeling the pulse. "He's twenty beats a minute. He's lucky it got cold or he'd be a corpse by now. As it is . . ."

"Hello?" said Hazel into the phone. "Who is this?" The man on the other end gave his name as Fredricks. She pressed the phone into her shoulder. "Childress? Fredricks is your guy?"

She nodded. She was looking ill – Hazel imagined Eldwin was somewhat ripe. Her radio buzzed and she passed it to Wingate.

She put the phone back to her ear. "Fredricks? I'm Detective Inspector Hazel Micallef, from the Port Dundas detachment of the OPS. I'm sorry, I'm in a helicopter – we're waiting on some forensic results." She listened for a moment. Wingate was saying *984, but we're going direct to Mayfair, call ahead 951* and Hazel put a finger in her other ear. "We know that already, but I sent the superintendent some . . . evidence yesterday afternoon. That's right. Okay," she said, squinting to hear better, "say that again."

She looked over at Wingate, but he couldn't tell what her look meant.

"You're sure? Okay, I understand. Now, we faxed a second set of prints up there . . . that's right. From the Port Dundas OPS, sender's name was Fraser . . ." She listened. "I need you to doublecheck that. You're certain? Thank you, Fredricks. Put all that stuff back where you found it now, and not a word to anyone. I appreciate this."

She turned back to face Wingate. "He didn't do it," she said. "He didn't kill Brenda Cameron."

Wingate looked down at the still form in the basket. Calberson had relieved Childress of her warming duties and was putting a tube in the back of Eldwin's hand, running fluids into him. "Poor bastard," he muttered.

"Let's get this man to hospital."

Quinn ascended, cutting wide back over the shore, heading southwest to Mayfair. Below them, the sunrise was spreading its pale, orange light. The rain had finally stopped. "Figures," said Childress. "Now that we're at the easy part it lets up."

Hazel was watching her, and gradually, feeling the woman's eyes on her, Childress brought her gaze around. "What?"

"You want to go home?"

"And face the ridicule of my colleagues? No thanks, I'm putting in for a transfer."

"You helped to save a man's life. That's not nothing."

Childress had retreated into herself, lost in thought. Finally, she said, "I've been on some wild goose chases . . . but this one . . ."

Hazel leaned across the cabin and patted Childress's knee. "I hope you have that medal you were going to pin on yourself." Childress smiled into her lap. "Quinn?" The captain acknowledged her. "We're going to be passing close by Kehoe River in a couple minutes, right?"

"Should do."

"How much of a crimp does it put in your flight time to put down for a minute? I've got cars down there and I can double back to Mulhouse Springs and get Eldwin's wife, bring her down to the hospital."

Quinn looked back over his shoulder. "I'm under the impression every minute counts."

Calberson said, "Probably a good idea to have next-of-kin present."

Quinn nodded and looked back out his missing windshield. Kehoe River was ten kilometres in front of him. Hazel radioed the community policing office that they needed a car. "Tell them to bring it to the parking lot of the Giant Tiger," said Quinn, and she relayed the information. They passed over the town and Quinn put down in the empty parking lot.

"I'll take Childress," Hazel said to Wingate. "Then I can drive her back to Toronto after stopping at Mayfair. You see Eldwin gets the attention he needs."

He looked back and forth between them, then offered Constable Childress his hand. "Thanks for your help."

"Yeah," she said, a little stunned. "Okay."

Hazel thanked Quinn, Tate, and Calberson and then the two women stepped down onto the parking lot surface. They moved back and Quinn took the rest of his passengers up again. He'd got down and off-loaded them in less than two minutes. They watched him angle down Main Street as one of the cars from the Kehoe River office pulled up. "You mind walking back?" Hazel asked the driver, as she slid into the passenger seat. "We have to get down to Mulhouse Springs in a hurry." The officer touched his cap and she watched him get smaller in the rearview mirror.

36

They were in Mulhouse Springs in twenty minutes and Hazel had to wake Officer Childress up. The lights were off in the Eldwin house, but all it took was a light knock to bring it to life and Claire Eldwin opened the door tying a housecoat around herself. The moment she saw Hazel on her doorstep, she began to cry. "Oh no, no . . ."

"He's alive," said Hazel. "But barely."

"Oh, thank God—" said Eldwin, stepping forward to embrace her. Hazel held her a moment, and then Eldwin stepped back and pushed her hair off her cheeks. "He's going to make it, right? Tell me he'll make it."

"He's at Mayfair General. They're going to do their best. But we'd better get you down there quickly just the same." She stepped into the house. "This is Constable Childress. She helped with the search."

"Thank you," said Eldwin, taking her hand. She looked disoriented and exhausted. Hazel guessed that the bottle had been her companion the night before. "You're soaked. Have you been out all night?"

"All night," confirmed Childress.

"You must be freezing. I'll put on some coffee and get dressed." She disappeared into the kitchen. They heard the beeps and grinding of the coffeemaker being started. "It'll take three minutes. Make yourself at home."

They went into the kitchen and Childress opened the fridge. It was nearly empty, but she found a carrot in the crisper and began to eat it. "Sorry, I'm starving."

"Go ahead," said Hazel. She watched the coffeemaker fill. Her eyes were drifting over the cupboards and countertops and she thought she might fall asleep in the chair. But her night was not over yet.

Eldwin returned in jeans and a black shirt and poured the coffees. She had a bag full of clothes for her husband. "Should we take the coffees with us?"

"No," said Hazel. "Maybe you should sit for a couple minutes with us. So we can prepare you."

"God," said Claire Eldwin, sitting. "It's bad, isn't it?"

"It's not good. He was set adrift in a canoe, wrapped in cloth, and it rained on him all night. He was barely alive when we found him, half drowned and freezing. He didn't have much of a pulse." She waited a moment as Eldwin took this in. "Mrs. Eldwin, he's missing a hand."

Claire set her coffee down with a jolt. "*Oh no —*"

"There'll be time to explain everything later. But I just want you to be prepared."

Eldwin stood. "We should go."

"Just another minute. There's more."

She sat.

"Your husband's innocent."

"I told you he couldn't have done it. He might be an un-repentant cheat, but he's not a killer."

"I guess you knew him better than we did."

"I *am* his wife," she said. Hazel turned to Childress, as if looking for confirmation of something, and when she brought her eyes back, Claire said, "What else?"

"There's this," said Hazel. She reached into her jacket and took out the book she'd bought in Toronto. She tossed it onto the table and watched Claire Eldwin's reaction. "Before we go, I'm wondering if you'd sign this?" It was a mystery novel called *Utter Death*, by Clarence Earles. Claire Eldwin extended her hand slowly and picked it up. She held it almost tenderly. "I thought the inheritance story I heard sounded like a load of bull."

"Clarence has been very good to us," she said. She turned it over. "This is an early one. I started it before Colin and I met. Taking his class helped me finish it."

"Did Colin even know he had a story in the *Westmuir Record*?"

Eldwin was still staring at the back of the book. "No," she said softly. "He got the *New York Times*. He thought the local papers were garbage. There was no risk he'd see it."

"But someone else did."

"Clearly," said Eldwin. She turned the novel idly in her hands and looked at the back cover.

"I'm betting Colin didn't even know it'd been published under his name until they showed it to him. Imagine what your husband's denials must have sounded like. Pretty far-fetched. I bet it made them bloody mad."

"I stopped writing it when Colin vanished. Then more chapters appeared."

"I've spent two weeks reading between the lines. Joanne Cameron was almost right, she just had the wrong Eldwin."

"I never meant —"

"Three years is a long time to live with the kind of secret you've been keeping, Claire. I guess you never imagined what it might cost to get it out of your system. He might die for your sins now, too."

"They're his sins as well." She looked at Hazel for the first time. "Putting two and two together is impressive, Detective Inspector. But it won't stand up in court. If you've ever read these books, you'll know deduction isn't the same as proof."

"I don't have to read books to know that, and you're wrong," said Hazel. "The glass you drank from yesterday when you came in? We took the prints off it and matched them to prints taken from the oars of the boat you and Brenda Cameron stole that night." Hazel waited for a response, a denial, but instead, a serene look stole across Claire Eldwin's face. "Tell me, Claire . . . how'd you convince her to take a boat ride with you?"

Eldwin exhaled deeply. "That girl would have done anything if she thought it meant she'd get something out of it."

"She got more out of it than she was planning, didn't she?"

"She came to me after Colin kicked her out. She told me that she was pregnant."

"You offered to help her confront him again."

Claire Eldwin pulled her coffee across the table toward herself. "There were so many girls. He had that place downtown for them, but he never really tried to hide them from me. They found me somehow. Complained about the way he treated them. Sometimes I thought he wanted me to know."

"How come you never left him?"

"Why does anyone put up with being treated badly? Because you think you deserve it. And because, despite yourself, you're still in love. And then this one shows up at the house." Her eyes were faraway, opening her door that August night three years earlier. "She's flying on something, her face all red and pale from crying. She apologizes for disturbing me, but there's something I should know." A tear splashed in her coffee. She looked up, her eyes distant. "She's pregnant! All this time, he'd been sharing something with these foolish women that at least he didn't deny me. But he'd never wanted kids. Always said he was too selfish to be a father, and I certainly believed him. Brenda said she wanted me to hear it from her: that he was leaving me, that they were starting a family. 'Why aren't you happy, then?' I ask her. 'You got what you wanted.' But she sits down . . . at this table, in fact – we had it in the old house – and puts her head in her hands. Then she tells me the 'truth' . . . that he's rejected her. He doesn't care that she's pregnant. But he loves her, she's sure of that. And she's come to tell me in person, out of a sense of honour, she says. Her story keeps changing, like a crazy person's. I feel pity for her. I pour her a brandy to calm her down. She drinks it like it's apple juice and I refill her glass. She must have been drunk when she arrived."

"She was full of sedatives."

"Glossy, staring eyes. I pour myself one. I tell her, we're going to sort this out tonight. He's got another place, one not even she knows about."

"On the island."

"She'd have believed anything I told her. She thought I wanted to *help* her." She laughed hoarsely. "We drove down to the lakeshore and took a ferry over . . . I kept telling her everything was going to be fine." Her eyes flashed up. "And everything was. I got Colin away from all that, we started over. I hid us better. I got us an unlisted number. None of them could find us. Find *me*. When he came home at night, it was just him and me. They didn't exist."

"Well, Brenda Cameron didn't."

"She was no longer a problem."

"Not at least until she started haunting you."

There was a glint of understanding in Claire Eldwin's eye. "Well, then there was that."

Hazel regarded the woman before them, a woman so sick with love that she'd considered anything she had to do to preserve it within bounds. Hazel had learned more about love this last week than she'd cared to, learned what it could do to those who are diseased with it. That it starts in longing and hope, but it can change, it can become something full of fear and anger, and she thought that Joanne Cameron and Claire Eldwin were linked in this. They had stripped the human patina off love, that social layer that makes people give of themselves, makes them put the loved one ahead of themselves. But under this human love was something more primitive; it stank of territory and possessions. It was something people would kill for, if they felt it threatened. She recalled times in her life when the thought had crossed her mind to go down to Toronto and give a quick pistol-whipping to one of the deadbeats who were making Martha's life a misery. What had held her back? Mere hope? Or simply the fact she knew it was wrong? Maybe people like Cameron and Eldwin were missing some kind of moral gene. Or did they have an extra one? Was their kind of love a higher love, that knew no bounds? She would never know.

Hazel gave Childress a faint nod, and the constable sprung forward and took her cuffs off her belt. Claire Eldwin heard the clink and stood. "She's your collar," said Hazel. "Still feel like it was a wasted night?"

"Mrs. Eldwin," said Constable Childress, "you are under arrest for the murder of Brenda Cameron, do you understand? You have the right to retain and instruct counsel without delay. We will provide you with a toll-free telephone lawyer referral service, if you do not have your own lawyer. Anything you say can be used in court as evidence. Do you understand? Would you like to speak to a lawyer?"

"I want to see my husband."

"Do you understand the charges against you?" Childress repeated.

"I do."

She turned Eldwin toward the kitchen door and began to walk her out of the house. Hazel refilled her coffee cup and followed. "Do you have a key to the house?" she asked.

"On the hook by the door."

Hazel locked up and followed Childress and Eldwin to the car. She could swear Childress was walking taller now. She folded herself into the driver's seat and waited for Childress to belt Claire Eldwin in. "One more thing, Claire," she said.

"What?"

"Brenda Cameron wasn't pregnant. She lied."

They turned back onto Highway 79 and headed for Mayfair, Claire Eldwin's last stop before the city of Toronto.

37

Monday, June 6

The girl lay utterly still in the boat, her hands laced together in her lap. She had closed her eyes and her head felt like it had doubled in weight on Claire's leg. Her jaw fell open. She's so drunk. Her face was peaceful, her eyes shuddering under her lids. What was she dreaming of?

They were going to the island to confront him together, to find him and make him choose. She'd believed Claire; she was a creature of faith. But when the ferry put in, the girl was too drunk to walk and she'd ranged up the little streets looking for a couple of bikes to borrow, still pulling on a bottle of red wine. Coming down behind 6th Street and looking into backyards, they'd seen the boat and Claire knew what they would do. It had been a challenge getting the little vessel out of the gate without making too much noise, and when the girl dropped her end on the sidewalk and collapsed laughing, Claire was sure they'd be caught. But no lights went on and they made it to a concrete launch at the bottom of the residential streets and slid the boat into the water. The girl lay on her back, cradling the bottle against her belly, and murmuring. "You're good . . . you're good to take care of me," she said, and she raised the bottle to her lips and emptied it. "Crap," she said. "Another dead soldier." She put the bottle down as Claire navigated the boat into the dark channel that ran into the centre of the Islands.

The moon slid along the curve of the bottle as she angled into the thin waterway with small sailboats and motorboats moored along its edge. She rinsed the bottle out in the water. When it was half full, it bobbed on the surface like a buoy, but if she filled it to the rim, it began to sink. She watched the bottle begin to vanish into the black water, but then she plunged her hand in and pulled it out. She put it down on its side in the hull. The water gurgled out of it, running into the lowest parts of the boat and filling the little channel in the middle. She filled the bottle and emptied it out eight more times. There was a long, two-inch-wide puddle running down the middle of the boat's hull, but nothing was going to wake the girl now.

She shifted her body and cradled the back of the girl's head in her hands. As she lowered her to the floor of the boat, she turned her face so her body would follow onto its side and the girl adjusted and turned into a fetal position, as if she were in bed. The boat bobbed with the shifting weight of the two women. The oars hung in their locks, the paddles dragging in the water as they drifted slowly up the channel between Ward's and Algonquin islands. Claire kneeled down and put her hand on the girl's shoulder and pulled it gently toward her. Slowly, receptive to the pressure, the girl turned on her belly, sighing. With one more nudge, her face was centred over the runnel that ran down the middle of the boat, and Claire could hear her blowing bubbles in the inch of water she'd emptied out into the bottom.

Leaning down, she could see her own face in the thin line of water, her long, sad face, full of knowledge. Because knowledge was the problem: if she had known nothing, if she had remained blissfully free of what he'd been careless enough to let her find out, she could have gone on. Welcomed him home in the evenings joyously igno-rant, shared her meals with him, his bed, his stories of his work, those stories she knew also to be lies, but she would believe them just the same. It was all she wanted: to remain in the dark. But he could not even do that for her, the women he destroyed found their way to her, full of sorrow and anger and spite, and she could do nothing for them. But this one, this one she could help.

The sky above was clear but empty: all the stars that hung above the city were devoured by its light and the only light in the sky came from the moon. It was a half-moon now, a drowsing moon, and it was as if nothing knew they were here, no mind, no heart knew her heart or mind. She was alone. In some ways, she'd always been alone, victim to a helpless love, but now she was more alone than she'd ever been, decided on an action that she knew would change nothing.

Where were the people who loved this girl, who could have pre-served her from herself? These people had failed her when she needed them most, and here she was, alone and insensate, in the dark, with the wrong kind of person. For a moment, Claire felt pro-tective of her, as if, for that moment, she was her mother, trying to show her the error of her ways. But such a love could smother. You could not make other people's choices for them, you could only suffer along with them and hope they would survive their mistakes.

Claire straddled the girl's lower back, letting her weight press down. Then she leaned forward, her fingers interlaced, and pressed the girl's face into the bottom of the boat, her nose and mouth in the water.

At first, nothing happened. Then Claire felt the girl go rigid and resist, her animal self alert to the threat even as her human self was already drowned in drugs and brandy. She bucked, lifting Claire off the bottom of the boat, but Claire kept her tenacious hold, pressing the girl's forehead hard against the boat's bottom, keeping her face in the channel, keeping her out of the saving air.

The girl began to thrash now, but even as her body struggled more and more desperately, Claire kept her in place, the tears rolling down her cheeks. Go, she urged the girl. And then the power of the girl's will and her bodily strength began to run down, and the sounds of choking diminished, the girl's force began to leak out, and the kicking of her legs became more and more involuntary, until, at last, she lay inert. Claire waited another minute, counting the seconds, and then gradually lifted her hands away from the girl's skull.

Nothing. No movement at all.

She would have to move quickly now. She lifted the girl off her belly by putting her arms under her shoulders, but as Claire tried to tip her into the water, the boat teetered perilously and she knew both of them would go in. Then someone would see a drenched woman crossing back to the mainland on the ferry. She laid the girl back down and thought for a moment, alert for sounds from the shoreline. Then it came to her. She pulled the oars from their locks and laid them crossways over the gunwales, as if she were going to sit on them.

With effort, she turned the girl over on her back. Her long black hair fell away from her face and the wet skin on her cheeks shuddered a little, as if she were fearful of what was about to happen to her. Her eyes were open, distant, a look of faint surprise on her face. Claire leaned to her left and gripped the heel of the girl's left foot, lifting it over one of the oars. Then she lifted the other as well, moving the oar into place under the girl's knees. The torso would be more difficult. She stood behind the girl's head, her knees braced against the other oar and, balancing herself as carefully as she could, she leaned over the oar and lifted the girl's head and then shoulders and, with her knees, nudged the oar forward beneath her. The little rowboat shook with the repeated jolts, but it quickly stilled, and then the girl was suspended there, the backs of her hands still resting against the bottom of the boat, as if she were levitating.

Claire rested a moment, but she would have to be done quickly now. She slipped crosswise under the girl, her knees bent up against the side of the boat, and pulled the thin ends of the oars together over her head in a V. The black canopy of the sweater hung down in front of her face.

Then there was a voice, a murmur in the distance, someone on the shore of one of the islands, calling out to her. She lay as still as possible, her heart pounding. And then she realized it wasn't a voice coming from the island: it was coming from above her.

It was the girl.

Quietly, she was moaning. Words, unintelligible, although she thought she heard her name. Claire reached up and covered the girl's mouth with her hand, the cold lips brushing against her skin, slowing down, and then stopping. Then Claire braced her feet hard against the side of the boat and, straining, began to push the oars into the air. They curved heavily with the weight on them, but slowly, the girl's body began to slide toward the opposite thwart. Claire could hear the sound of her sweater rubbing down the wood. She pushed the makeshift slip higher into the air and the girl began to slide faster and faster and now Claire had to hold the ends of the oars down to keep them from flipping into the water with the girl's mass sliding toward the paddles. Her body flipped once onto her face and then, with a sound like a boulder plunging from the sky, she disappeared beneath the surface.

The girl's name was Brenda Cameron. She was twenty-nine. She was someone's daughter, someone's friend, someone's lover. It was said of her that desperation and loss drove her to take her own life, but that was not true: Brenda Cameron wanted to live. But, more than that, she wanted to be loved. And for that human wish, she paid with her life.

Hazel hadn't been inside her house for over two months. It smelled close and felt anonymous, like a museum without its exhibits. They'd made two trips from the house on McConnell Street since early that morning – how had they amassed that much *stuff* in so relatively short a time? – and Glynnis had just appeared with her back seat packed full of their clothing. "Feel good to be home?" she asked, pushing open the door with her foot. "I got it, I got it," she said when Hazel rushed over to unburden her of the load. "You just drink it in."

It did feel good to be home. Or rather, it felt good to no longer be an invalid and a guest. Glynnis went up the stairs with the clothes, *like she owns the place*, Hazel thought, and she smiled at the thought. *But she doesn't.*

She went out to the car to see if there was anything else to bring in, but it was empty now. Glynnis returned and closed the hatchback. "That's it. If I find anything else, I'll send Andrew around with it."

"Make sure you put a tracking device on him."

Glynnis laughed. "Maybe *I'll* bring it around." She opened the door to the car, but Hazel put her hand on top of it and held it.

"Listen."

"It's okay, Hazel."

"No, I want to say this. You had no good reason to open your doors to me, but you did. I don't know what I would have done otherwise."

"You're not a mistake Andrew made, Hazel. You're a part of his life. That makes you part of mine."

"I'm not sure many people in your position would see it that way. I'm lucky that you did."

"I don't begrudge anyone the love they feel," Glynnis said. "Even if it hurts me a little to know of it."

The two women regarded each other. "It hurts?" said Hazel.

"I can't help feeling stuff I don't want to feel. The two of you have a lot of history. I admire that . . . and sometimes it makes me miserable."

She didn't think about it. She just stepped around the open car door and took Glynnis into her arms. They held each other silently for a moment and then Hazel, awkwardly, stepped back. "I'm sorry it makes you unhappy," Hazel said. "I want you to know how grateful I am for everything."

Glynnis pushed the bottom of her palm across a cheek. "Is this the beginning of a beautiful friendship?" she asked, and there was the briefest moment of hesitation before both women laughed nervously.

Hazel held out her hand. "Let's not push it."

In the dining room, Martha was pulling the drapes wide, opening the windows, and squirting Windex on the panes. Her mother was marvelling at the quantity of dead flies lying on their backs on the windowsill. "You'd think they'd see their buddies lying dead of exhaustion and go try another exit, but no."

"They're flies."

"Ex-flies. Go fetch a broom, would you?"

Hazel passed through the kitchen, where the groceries they'd bought were still only partially unpacked. She was sure she'd seen Andrew carry them in, and it was strange of him to stop partway through a job. There was a carton of milk sitting on the counter. She put it in the fridge and then stood over the sink and looked into the back garden. He was nowhere to be seen. "Andrew?" she called.

She heard him answer from the bathroom in the hall behind her. "Just a minute."

"Sorry," she called. She heard bubbling coming from the counter and turned to see the coffee finishing. The sight of a pot of coffee filling would, for some time now, link itself in her memory to the early morning encounter with Claire Eldwin in her kitchen, living the last few moments of her freedom. She'd wept in the car back to Mayfair, but neither Hazel nor Constable Childress had inquired whether she wept for herself, her husband, or Brenda Cameron. When they got to Mayfair, Eldwin was in surgery. They kept her cuffed in a curtained-off part of the ER for two hours, and when they had word he'd come out, they let her into the ICU to see him. He was still unconscious, but his pulse had risen and his colour had improved. The surgeon had had to amputate his right arm at the elbow: the cut wrist had become infected and gangrene was setting in — they'd had no choice. The sides of Eldwin's head were bandaged as well — they told her if he recovered he'd have to find a plastic surgeon to reconstruct his ears, but for now, all they could do was clean up the wounds and graft skin over the gaping holes to protect the structures within. She stood at his bedside, her hands behind her back, and called to him, but he'd given her no response. "He'll be asleep awhile yet," the nurse told her. She wanted to wait for him to wake, but the brief visit was all Constable Childress would allow her: they had a date to keep with Superintendent Ilunga.

Hazel had sent Wingate back to Port Dundas to start on the paperwork, but she lingered behind, hoping Eldwin would open his eyes. She had yet to actually *meet* this man, whose feck-lessness had set in motion the destruction of so many lives. She didn't know how she would tell him the news of what had changed in his world. She didn't even know how she felt about it. Would he grieve the knowledge that his wife had killed to preserve an illusion? Would he welcome the new freedom it gave him? She realized she didn't know the bounds of the man's depravity. The longer she sat with him – and he continued to sleep – the more she wished there was something she could charge him with. But there was nothing. For once in his life, Colin Eldwin was the victim.

Joanne Cameron was under observation. There would have to be charges – she was not innocent, she had chosen to accept Dana Goodman's methods – but Hazel thought an understand-ing judge would take the mitigating circumstances under con-sideration. Grief was not the same as insanity, but in some cases, it was close.

As for Goodman, the teams that had gone out to Pickamore to bring him in had found his body in the tall grass six metres back from the shoreline. She'd shot him cleanly through the throat: the autopsy showed he'd drowned in his own blood. It was the first time she'd discharged her gun in eight years, and it was the first time she'd ever killed a man. She looked into her heart and she saw that she could live with what she'd done.

Hazel poured coffee into four cups, two milks and two sugars for her, regular for Martha, and black for her mother. She was hovering over Andrew's mug when she heard him come out of the bathroom. "Are you still double-double, or has your wife reduced your sugar intake?"

He made a mocking "O" with his mouth. "My *wife*? Good god, you're really coming around, aren't you?"

"Don't push me, Andrew. Seeing you coming out of the bathroom with the newspaper in your hands is making me hallucinate."

"I'll go double-double for old times' sake," he said. She stirred and passed him his cup. He sat at the kitchen table, tossing the morning's *Westmuir Record* down in front of him with a faint slap. "Impressive ending to 'The Mystery of Bass Lake.'"

"You think so?"

"You're full of surprises."

"Still," she said.

He sipped his coffee, grimaced, and asked for more sugar. As he stirred it in, he said, "You and Gord Sunderland working together. I'm going to watch the sky for pigs."

"It was the only way to convince him not to print all the scurrilous rumours about Ray Greene coming back to town. Among other things."

Andrew raised an eyebrow at her. "Scurrilous rumours are usually true. *Is* Greene coming back?"

She hesitated. "Maybe."

"And how do you feel about that?"

"My feelings are mixed."

"Your feelings are always mixed."

"Then I guess it's business as usual."

It could have been five or ten years ago, the two of them bantering at the kitchen table. Any time but now. Except it *was* now, and her mother and daughter were airing out the house and another summer was beginning in which she would be, in all the ways that it mattered, alone. A great shudder of feeling went through her and the thought came into her mind that maybe this was how it would be, always, maybe she would be alone for the rest of her life. She reached over the table and covered Andrew's hand with hers. He smiled at her, at ease. "What harm would it do if you kissed me one last time over coffee?"

"None," he said, and he pushed himself out of his chair and leaned over the table. She met him in the middle, and their lips touched, lightly, chastely. He looked around. "The world still here?"

She laughed. "Thank you for everything, Andrew."

"You're welcome. *Mi casa es* . . . well, *mi casa*. Don't hurt your back again."

"Are you two arm-wrestling?" said Glynnis, entering the kitchen. She held up an alarm clock. "I forgot this. I put it in the glove compartment so I wouldn't, and I did."

"You should have kept it for your collection," Hazel said.

"Oh, no, it's yours. It's a different time zone out here anyway, isn't it?" She put it down on the table and gave Andrew a kiss on the cheek, but as she was leaving again, Hazel called her back.

"Stay for a coffee. You've earned at least that."

"At the *very* least," said Glynnis.

She sat and Hazel got another cup and grabbed the little box of sugar-coated donuts they'd bought. She called to her mother and Martha. Emily came into the kitchen with a fistful of wispy dead flies, which she dumped into the garbage can under the sink.

"Is my house arrest over?" asked Martha, sitting and taking her coffee.

"You're free to go under your own recognizance," said Hazel, "but you'll have to check in with your parole officer on a regular basis."

Martha nodded knowingly. "You think plastic surgery will help me?"

"Not a chance," said her mother. "I'd know you anywhere."

After washing her hands, Emily came to the table. Around it sat a collection of people who made up, in Emily's opinion, a very strange family indeed.

Andrew opened the newspaper to the conclusion of the summer short story and turned it to her. "Your daughter, the author," he said. Emily lifted her glasses off her chest and put them on and began to read. "Maybe you have another calling," he said to Hazel.

"I'm having a hard-enough time with this one."

"Another lifetime, then."

"Yes," she said, a little sadly, lifting her coffee cup to shield her eyes. "Another lifetime."